Jump

Jump

Terra Little

www.urbanbooks.net

Urban Books, LLC
78 East Industry Court
Deer Park, NY 11729

ISBN 13: 978-1-60162-438-3
ISBN 10: 1-60162-438-7

First Printing March 2011
Printed in the United States of America

10 9 8 7 6 5 4 3 2

This is a work of fiction. Any references or similarities to actual events, real people, living, or dead, or to real locales are intended to give the novel a sense of reality. Any similarity in other names, characters, places, and incidents is entirely coincidental.

Distributed by Kensington Publishing Corp.
Submit Wholesale Orders to:
Kensington Publishing Corp.
C/O Penguin Group (USA) Inc.
Attention: Order Processing
405 Murray Hill Parkway
East Rutherford, NJ 07073-2316
Phone: 1-800-526-0275
Fax: 1-800-227-9604

Acknowledgments

As always, I thank God for allowing the characters in this book to come to me, confide in me, and trust me with their lives. I'd also like to thank my family for their support and encouragement as I make my way along this literary journey; my friends (you know who you are) for always being just a phone call or IM away; and my muse for refusing to go away. A very special thank you goes to my agent, Pam Strickler, for always having my back and for "getting" me, and also to all of the literary venues who shine their lights on me and my work. I appreciate you more than you know.

Last but *never* least, I'd like to thank all the wonderful people who turn my pages. I read your emails and smile. I receive your posts to my websites and send you cyber hugs. I feel the impact of all that you have done to help bring me to this point and my heart sings a song of many thanks. I hope this one does you proud.

Dedication

This one is for Robert and Lavelma Little—my mommy and daddy—and for my daughter, Sierra G. Hughes. Love you guys to pieces.

This one is also for the women who have been or are incarcerated. Bars may keep you away from your families and loved ones . . . from your life, but they can never confine your mind. Be strong, be reflective and be blessed. Too, be prepared.

Two men look out through the same bars:
One sees the mud, and one the stars.
Frederick Langbridge,
"A Cluster of Quiet Thoughts"

Chapter One

I was standing over the body with the gun still smoking in the palm of my hand when the police finally arrived to secure the scene. I hadn't come to kill her and I didn't really mean to end her life the way I did, but that was the result. What should have been a rational discussion quickly turned into a shouting match and then a crime scene.

I don't really remember putting the gun in my purse before I left my apartment. I don't remember consciously digging it out in the heat of the moment, aiming it and pulling the trigger. All I know is that I did.

I do remember watching her body fall to the floor and take its last breath. I remember those eyes, focused on my face in a way they never had before, silently accusing me of losing my mind. And maybe I did lose it for a moment. At least that's what my public defender told the jury. That I had been temporarily unstable, incapable of making rational decisions at the time of the murder. He came up with that brilliant defense after I told him I had been tripping out on Ecstasy and tripping bad. It was ultimately what kept me from earning myself a murder one charge, and for that I guess I should consider myself grateful.

One after another, people who thought they knew me took the stand and testified that I had not been a drug user before—not to discredit me, though the prosecutor worked that angle, but to help me prove that I was a neophyte, ill-equipped to handle the side effects of a sneaky drug like Ecstasy. Supposedly, I didn't know what I was getting into when I took the pill and I didn't know what I was really doing when I pulled the trigger. It was my first time experimenting with drugs, and now I was a poster child for just saying no.

But the thing is this: I knew.

Is there a drug in existence, in the entire world, that can numb the mind and the heart so much that you don't realize you're aiming the barrel of a pistol at your grandmother's heart?

I don't think so, and the jury didn't either.

A female voice accepts the collect call that I tell the operator to put through to Vicky's residence. I wait as the phone rings and then I catch my breath when I hear a voice on the other end. It's not my sister's and I know whose it is, but I say nothing about who I am. I ask for my sister and wait for her to come on the line, listening to the sounds of her house in the background and wondering what it's like where she lives. I used to know, but I don't anymore.

There is a loud television blaring in the background as she puts the receiver to her ear. "Bey, turn that thing down, okay? I can hear it all the way in the basement," Vicky takes a moment to call out. Then, "Hello?"

"Vicky, it's me, " I say.

Her voice sounds strange to me, like I've forgotten the way she talks, the way she ends every sentence on a high note and sounds like she is asking a question instead of making a statement.

"Oh." She sucks in air through her mouth and I can almost see her bottom lip dragging the floor. She is surprised I'm calling. I know because the air she releases hits my eardrum like a hundred stomping feet in a hurry to reach their destination. "Lena. Hi."

"The parole office called you, right? You know I'm getting out tomorrow?" I'm curled around the pay phone, trying to talk low so my conversation is semi-private because completely private is out of the question. You hear everything, one way or another, in prison. Behind me, another inmate pushes up close to me and slips her arms around my waist, and I know semi-private is out of the question too. She presses a soft kiss to the side of my neck and then her lips drift behind my ear. She wants my attention, and I do my best to ignore her.

"She said to tell you that you have to report to her first thing. Soon as you get here," Vicky informs me, talking just as low. "She came by here a while ago and left her card."

I listed Vicky's address as the place where I will live after my release. I didn't think she'd actually agree to have me living in her house, but it was worth a shot. Now that I know that's where I'll be going, I don't know how I feel about actually living there. "You told the parole officer it was okay," I remind her because she isn't sounding too sure and now is not the time for her to pull some bullshit. If she changes her mind, I'm going to a halfway house, which is just like being in prison—which kind of defeats the purpose of getting out.

"Yes. I did tell her that."

I push at the arms gripping my waist, shoot an irritated look over my shoulder and feel them loosen slightly. I was curled around the phone like a parenthesis a few minutes ago, but now I'm looking more like an interrobang, a question mark and exclamation point combination. "Did you change your mind?"

"No, Lena, I didn't change my mind. What time will you be released?"

She wants to cry. I can hear it in her voice and I hate the sound of it. I haven't had much use for tears in a long, long time. "Ten o'clock," I tell her, harsher than I really mean to be, so she'll know to swallow the lump in her throat. "More like eleven by the time I get myself together. The bus doesn't get there until sometime after five though."

"They'll put you on a bus?"

"Roadway Bus Lines." I pause as an automated voice tells her that the call originates from the Dwyer Correctional Facility for Women. "Should be there by five-thirty. I can take a cab from the bus station."

"No!" Vicky damn near shouts in my ear.

"No, don't take a cab or no, don't come?"

"Don't take the bus. Don't let them put you on a bus, Lena. I . . . we . . . we want to come and get you. Do they allow that?"

"I'm three hours away." I haven't had a visitor, live and in the flesh, in over five years.

After the novelty wore off, they stopped coming. And I haven't seen my daughter, Beige, in over eight years. She is the *we* Vicky mentions, and the *we* knocks me in my face and sends me back a step.

"We can leave early in the morning and be there by ten."

"*We* can save some gas and pick me up at the bus station."

"You act like you don't want to see us."

I start to tell her that she has a lot of nerve saying that to me, but I don't. I catch myself just before I remind her that she hasn't visited me once in all the years I've been here. Not once. I guess she had her reasons for not coming, just like I have mine for not wanting her to come now. "I don't," I admit softly. "Not like this. Not . . . Look, if you have to come, don't bring her. She doesn't need to see this place and me in it. This is no place for a kid, so leave her, okay?"

"It's not like she doesn't know where you are. Plus, she's fourteen, Lena. Almost fifteen."

Like I don't know. "She's a kid and kids don't belong here." Vicky doesn't know what I know and she never will. If she brings my daughter to this place, the stink of it will seep into her skin and leak out of her pores for the rest of her life. No soap in the world can wash it off. "If you come, don't bring her."

"I'm coming, Lena. I just—"

"Don't bring her," I cut her off. "Eleven o'clock."

Then I hang up.

Family portrait:

Lou is over six feet tall and solid as a rock. She has skin the color of tree bark and none of us is exactly sure how old she is. She has told us all different ages on purpose, to keep us guessing and in our places. Children don't question their parents about things that are none of their business, so be seen and not heard, Lou likes to say. With my eyes wide open and clearly focused on her round face, I still manage to see with my heart. I don't see what is obviously a woman. I see Lou, who is the head of our family. Our father.

Denny is mama. Denny, with her gentle hands and long, silky hair. There is a wide streak of gray that snakes through it, like the bride of Frankenstein, and it is that streak that mesmerizes me when I am fortunate enough to have the pleasure of taking a comb to her scalp and scratching it for her. Unlike Lou, the years she has spent in captivity are etched on her caramel-brown face. Twenty-six so far and still so many to go. She pretends to be happy that I'm leaving, but in her eyes I see what she won't allow her lips to say. Denny's children were still babies when she did what she did to bring herself here, and they are all grown now. They don't come to visit and only one of them takes the time to write. In her mind, she is losing another child.

There are three of us children who belong to Lou and Denny; I am the youngest, though not in age. I was the last to join the circle, like a change of life baby, and after me, Lou and Denny decided they are done having kids. They had probably decided this before I came along, but after Lou found me in the shower room, abandoned with a symbolic note pinned to my ass and no one to claim me, she brought me home anyway.

On my last night here, I divide the few things I have accumulated in eight years' time between the women who are like my sisters. I give them the books that have kept me sane through the years, read cover to cover so many times that tape keeps the covers attached, and the few luxuries I have allowed myself. A small boom box and cassette tapes that I'm not supposed to have in my possession. I give one of them a sweater that she always coveted, and I spend hours braiding the other one's hair. She wants it this way and that way, parted here and there. I listen carefully and style it exactly the way she tells me to because I will miss her the most.

We cry. Even though Lou is dad and Denny has been through enough that her tears should have long been exhausted, we cry. Here in this place where none of us are really considered women, we cry like women. We are numbers with two-letter suffixes, and we are called animals and treated as such because we have done things to bring that label on ourselves, but we still cry. We sit up late into the night, passing a bottle of whiskey around, sipping slowly, passing our memories around even more slowly, and continue soaking each other in—for the last time. I am the one who is leaving the fold, so I cry the hardest.

I have to, because in the morning things will be different. They will have shut me out. I know it and I accept it, and I don't admit to myself just yet that I welcome it. It's hard to be happy about leaving my family behind.

The guards see what they want to see and pretend not to see what they don't. They don't see that none of us is where we are supposed to be after lights out. They don't see the contraband we pass around and they don't hear the sound of our voices as we talk and laugh and cry.

They don't see me in the middle of the night, holding still another woman as she cries as if the world is coming to an end. There are two others who belong to Lou and Denny, and both of them I will miss, but there is another woman I will miss too. As I hold her, we don't talk, and I don't let myself think about what I will miss the most. I wonder who she will love after I am gone and who will love her. I wait for jealousy and possessiveness to come, but they don't, and I know I am slowly wrapping myself around the idea of freedom.

Though we roam around the quads like unrestrained animals in a petting zoo much of the time, there are protocols to follow and rules to obey, when the people who matter are watching. The guards who pretend to be blind suddenly have sight. They remember that we are just numbers and that they have families of their own, families who count on their steady paychecks. Those of us who have learned this lesson early on know what is what and when is when.

As the sun comes up, I fall back into the role of inmate number 1250TN. I keep my eyes on the floor, I take the manila envelope containing the property I don't remember owning when I came here like I am grateful to have it, and I let myself be led meekly to the last stop. Jackie, a night shift guard, doesn't wish me luck, even though I kick her ass in Gin Rummy regularly and she has shown me pictures of her kids. I tell myself that I'm not offended by the fact that Tony, a swing shift guard, doesn't meet my eyes, even though I have stayed awake more than a few nights reading passages from what he hopes will become a best-selling novel. It's like they don't know me, like they don't give a damn that I'm leaving, and it hurts.

I want them to tell me they will miss me, that I have meant something to them, but they don't. I wait for them to impart last words of encouragement before the door, separating me from freedom, is opened and I am shoved out of it, but no words come. It's like I have never existed, like they want to forget they knew me.

I am so lost in my feelings of rejection that Tony's hand on my back doesn't register until he uses it to push me forward. I trip over my own feet, grab a chair in the waiting area to steady myself, and look back at him with fifty questions in my eyes.

Then I see it. A hint of a smile and traces of humanity in his eyes. He tells me, "And stay out," and then I get it. They don't want to remember that they knew me. They don't want me to miss them so much that I want to visit them here again. They don't want me to come back.

Something tickles my memory and I feel like giggling. Me and Vicky are kids again, partners in crime like only sisters can be, and we have devised the perfect plan. Mama is working and we are stuck in the house waiting for time to pass. For us, summertime doesn't officially begin until Mama comes home from work and we can escape to the outdoors with all the other kids. Mama leaves us by ourselves in the daytime, which is illegal, so we have to stay indoors until she comes home. We don't touch the stove, we don't answer the phone, and we don't open the door, no matter who it is.

I think the sun rises and sets on Vicky. She is the oldest and, therefore, smarter than I can ever hope to be. She convinces me that we can go outside to play with our friends and then come back inside long before Mama comes home from work. She'll never know we were outside, Vicky says, and I believe her. She pushes the house key deep in her pocket, takes me by my hand and off we go. I don't stop to remind her that she doesn't use the key to lock the door behind us. I see my best friend farther down the street and I am anxious to be down there with her. She has a Farrah Fawcett hair-styling head that I love to play with, and that is all I can think about at the moment.

Vicky is seven and I am five when Mama comes home and finds out that we no longer have a television or a hi-fi. Some of her clothes are stolen too, and she curses for hours about that. She says words I have never heard before when she sees that her record albums are gone. She beats the shit out of me and Vicky for leaving the house in the first place. She cries the longest over her photo albums, and finally drags herself off to bed, mumbling under her breath about our baby pictures being gone. "Who would steal pictures of my babies?" she wants to know.

The police aren't called, and I know it's because Mama would have to explain why we were left alone in the house to begin with. Someone might start asking questions that she can't answer, and she is too angry and disappointed to think up plausible lies.

We did it to ourselves. If we had just waited a few more hours, until Mama came home, she wouldn't have had to pick up the phone and call my grandmother on the scene. We go from the comfort of our own home to my grandmother's house, which smells like old lady and something else that I can't quite name. We get dropped off every morning and picked up every evening, and I hate it like I hate the homemade caramel and brownies my grandmother always bakes and makes us eat.

It doesn't take me long to realize that Vicky isn't as smart as I think she is, and it takes me even less time to come to the conclusion that we have made a big mistake. I don't think Mama ever really forgave us for being so stupid, and I don't even have to think about forgiving Vicky to know that I haven't. Like a lamb to slaughter she led me, and she was supposed to know better.

Vicky's arms surround me now and I smell her scent. It takes me back in time to a place I don't want to go. It takes me back to the claustrophobic little house my grandmother lived in, to the depths of her bedroom, where she kept an endless supply of White Shoulders perfume on her dressing table. It was her signature scent, and now it is Vicky's.

I catch myself before I open my mouth to tell her that her shoulders aren't white and the scent makes me want to puke. Instead, I hug her back and say, "Hey."

She pulls back and looks at me, sees that I don't have a relaxer anymore, that I have lost weight and gained muscle mass, and bursts out crying. I lift my locks from my shoulders and feel air on the back of my neck, watch her and wait. I won't hold her as she cries, won't offer her even a little bit of comfort, because I don't have it in me. She hasn't come to visit me in eight years and I don't know why. What I do know is that she wouldn't be so shocked by the sight of me if she had.

"Eight years is such a damn long time," she says when she can talk.

I catch her eyes and smile. "You know better than me. I owe you, what, about a million dollars and some change?" She put money on my books faithfully, kept me from having to beg, borrow or steal to survive.

We stare at each other. If I have changed, she hasn't. She still wears her hair long and straight, relaxed to death and hanging down her back. Still plucks the hell out of her eyebrows and lines her lips with a dark pencil before filling them in with bright lipgloss. She still looks like a deer trapped in the glare of highbeams, poised to run for her life at the slightest provocation. I wonder if she is poised to run from me and everything I represent.

"You look good, Vicky," I offer.

"You look . . ." She raises her hands, shakes her head and lets them drop. "Different. Damn, Lena. What do you press, a thousand pounds?"

She reaches out and squeezes my bicep lightly, looking awed. She is exaggerating, but I let it roll. I don't look anything like those tennis star sisters and she knows it. Smooth and tight, maybe, but nowhere near as buff. I'm working on it though.

"Just a couple hundred," I say. "Give or take. Can we get the hell out of here?"

My question catches her off guard, snaps her out of her thoughts and reminds her of where we are. "Oh!

Um . . . yeah." She looks at the envelope I'm holding.
"Is this all your stuff?"

"Everything else belongs to the state."

My eyes go everywhere at once as I follow her out to
her car. She is driving a shiny red machine, something
sporty and compact, and I like the look of it. I give the
leather seats and complicated-looking dashboard cur-
sory glances, and then I take my eyes back to the sky,
where they really want to be.

I like the look of the sun even better, love the feel of
fresh air on my skin. I can't get over how much brighter
the sun seems and how much lighter the air is on the
outside. As we drive off and pick up speed on the interstate, I push a button to lower my window. I stick
my head out and let the wind snatch my breath, stick
my tongue out and taste freedom. Vicky is right; eight
years is a long time.

Chapter Two

She catches me darting glances around her house and answers my question before I ask.

"She won't be home until later," Vicky says, referring to the person I most want to see and then again don't really want to see at all. "Around seven or eight, I think she said."

"She sets her own schedule?" I look around the room she shows me, in the rear of the basement, not far from the washer and dryer. Just outside the door is a carpeted sitting area, a big screen television and a treadmill. I look past her to the door, and see that it has a lock on it. I meet her eyes after it occurs to me that she hasn't answered my question.

"She decided to hang out with a friend. Maybe stay for dinner."

Vicky can't look at me. She does things to make herself busy. She straightens the covers on the bed, smoothes a hand over a pillow, and then adjusts the rug on the floor with the toe of her shoe. I wait for her to break out in a song and dance routine to kill even more time, wondering if she really thinks she's being subtle.

She is my daughter. The only child I have and the only one I will probably ever have. The one I spent seven hours of my life bringing into the world, and the one I haven't seen in eight hellacious years. The one who doesn't care that I am home. She doesn't want to see me, or maybe she isn't ready to see me. Either way, she isn't here, and Vicky being unable to look me in my face tells me more than I want to hear. I am hurt, and the feeling comes at me from out of nowhere, surprises me because hurt is something that I haven't felt in a long time. But I don't let my face bear witness.

"I guess she has to eat," I say.

"She wants to see you, Lena."

"I know."

"She just needs some time to adjust to you being home. It's been—"

"Eight years. I know that too." I point to the small closet across the room. The door is open, and inside I see boxes stacked against one wall. Three of them. My handwriting crisscrosses the cardboard like a cross-word puzzle I designed when I was drunk. Letters are jumbled together, scratched out and connected by thick dashes, making it impossible to guess what's inside. Might've been pots and pans at one time, and towels and sheets another time. Could be anything now.

"You saved my old moving boxes?"

"I saved your clothes," she says, moving past me to drag a box from the closet to the middle of the floor. "I found the boxes in a closet in your apartment . . . after you were already gone." She reaches inside and hands me a neatly folded nightgown that I immediately press to my nose, searching for a familiar scent. I find it and inhale deeply; my eyes close. "There's another box somewhere with shoes in it. I'll have to look for it." A smile touches her lips. "I wore some of them."

"The black slingbacks you always wanted?"

"Wore them." We laugh.

"The red stilettos . . ."

"Wore the hell out of those too."

"I think they were yours anyway." I sit on the bed and slide the box closer, dig in and sigh as I find several pairs of panties and matching bras. I was prepared to wash the ones I have on every night and recycle them, until I can get my hands on the money to buy more. It doesn't even matter that the ones I find in the box are a size too big or that my breasts could fit in the cups of the bras twice and still have room to breathe. "Thanks for saving this stuff. I need it like you wouldn't believe."

Vicky looks lost in thought for a moment. "All of your other stuff . . . we didn't know what to do with it. I wanted to save it too, but—"

"Didn't have much anyway," I say, letting her off the hook on which she hangs herself. Another day I will ask her for specifics. Who got what and what happened to this or that thing, but today I can only handle so much. For now I'll live with the lie.

I had furniture and household gadgets. A toaster and a blender that overheated and filled my apartment with the smell of burning rubber. I had a color television that I paid for over time and a VCR, which was high-tech back then. I had a stereo system with speakers almost as tall as I am, albums and cassette tapes, movies on VHS and a wicker basket where I kept spools of thread and needles for when I needed to replace a button or hem pants. I had books that I always swore I would die trying to save if a fire broke out. I had a top-of-the-line computer system that was like a second child to me.

I had a life and now I have nothing. Not even a daughter who cares enough to welcome me home.

Vicky asks me if I need anything else and I tell her that I don't. I watch her back out of what is now my room and pull the door closed behind her. After she is gone, I unpack the boxes and take stacks of clothes

over to the armoire. I pull out drawers and spend endless minutes trying to decide what goes where. I used to
have a system; now I can't remember what that system
was. Underwear and socks in the top drawers or the
bottom ones? Shirts and sweaters mixed together in
the same drawer or separately? Night clothes on the
left or the right?

The dilemma stumps me, sweeps my mind clear of
any and all thought. I can't understand what my problem is, why my mind won't cooperate and make things
easy for me. I am not a dumb person, I remind myself.
I have a degree in information technology, though I
have no idea where it is at the moment, and this isn't
advanced calculus. Something this simple shouldn't
require this much thought. So what is my problem?

Disgusted with myself, I leave the clothes sitting on
top of the armoire and push boxes out of my way with
my feet. I drop to the floor and lay on my back with
my arms crossed over my chest like I'm in a casket.
Inside, I was number 1250TN and here on the outside,
I am still number 1250TN. My mind has no problem
remembering that.

I start to do crunches, a hundred and twenty-five in
sixty seconds. I flip over to my stomach and do just as
many push-ups, wishing there was a bar bolted to the
wall or free weights sitting around for me to use. I can
lift a hundred pounds in one hand like it's nothing, and
before I got out, I was trying for a hundred and twenty-
five.

When I feel beads of sweat popping out on my forehead, I sit up and lean back against the bed, and stare
across the room at the clothes I don't know what to do
with. Then it comes to me slowly but surely. I realize I
have encountered my first obstacle.

I have to learn how to make decisions for myself all
over again.

***

They put me in a cell with a deranged-looking woman named Yolanda. She tells me to call her Yo-Yo, if I have to call her anything at all. She likes silence, she says, so could I please keep my mouth shut as much as possible? I look at the elaborately designed braids wrapped around her skull, the scar that stretches from her ear to the corner of her mouth, and wonder what she did to make someone do that to her. Then I decide I don't care one way or the other as she trains deep-set brown eyes on me and stares like a heathen. There are dark circles around her eyes and they are slightly misaligned. I come to the conclusion that she is more than a little touched in the head, and the confines of our cell suddenly seem smaller.

"Yo' ass got the top bunk." She leans against the wall with her arms crossed over her chest, taking me in from head to toe. Matching purple prison scrubs and thin-soled cloth sneakers make us twins, but that's where the similarities end. "That's all you got in here, too. Squatter's rights, girl. Don't shit in here belong to you but that space up there." She points at my bunk and then she uses the nail attached to the finger to pick her teeth. "Everything else in here belongs to me."

I climb up to my bunk and stay there until Yo-Yo leaves. I don't even let my legs dangle from the edge, I am so off balance and leery of her. One of her eyes has a tendency to wander away from the other one, and it rolls to the side of her face even when she gives me her profile. I'm not sure if she is staring at me, if she really is a mutant, or if she is simply unfortunate. The wandering eye follows me as she makes her way out of the cell and leaves the door open behind her.

I hop down and reach for the thing I have been staring at for the longest time—a stub of a pencil lying on the metal desk bolted to the opposite wall. The lead is dull and it's barely an inch long, but it is long enough for me to do what I want to do with it. Back on my bunk, I use it to draw on the wall, right where my head will lay when the time comes for me to pretend I can sleep. I make the letters of the name I draw on the wall fat and juicy looking, color them in carefully and then lean back to assess my handiwork. I decide it's my best work ever, and I toss the pencil across the cell, back to the desktop.

She pokes me in my back harder than she needs to and I realize that I have fallen asleep.

I jump like I've been electrocuted and roll over, meet her eyes and silently ask her what her problem is.

"Dinner," Yo-Yo barks at me. She motions to the tray in her hand like it holds filet mignon instead of four piles of colorized mush. I see what I assume is my tray sitting on the desk and roll my eyes. She leans to the side and admires my artwork on the wall. "What the fuck is that? You got a thing for beige shit, like the chick in that movie? What was the name of it?"

Women of Brewster Place, I think. I remember that one of the lesbian characters in the movie had a thing for beige bras, but I don't share my recollection with her. We are not in the process of making a love connection. "It's not a color, it's a name," is all I say.

"Thought you said your name was Lena?" she asks, helping herself to the roll on my tray.

"You gonna eat this?"

I shake my head. "My daughter's name is Beige."

"You got babies?"

"One."

"I got four of the little fuckers. Three boys and a girl, like stair steps. How old is yours?"

"Six," I say, listening to her eat like she doesn't know what food is.

"She with her daddy?"

Beige's daddy is so far removed from my reality that it takes me several minutes to conjure up a clear image of his face in my mind. He was an affair gone wrong, someone else's husband and someone I should've never looked at the first time, let alone twice. He doesn't matter anymore. "With my sister."

"Mine in foster homes."

"You miss them?"

Yo-Yo doesn't answer me for a long time and I wonder if she will. She eats her way through dinner until I hear the spoon scraping the tray, and then she tosses the tray up on the desk noisily. A few minutes later her voice comes at me from below. It hits the back of my head and I know she is stretched out on her back, looking up at me with the one eye that doesn't wander. She utters a loud belch and then farts.

"It don't pay to let yourself miss too much of shit in here," she says. "Heard tell you got a nickel." A nickel means five years, and I tell her she heard right. "Let me give you a piece of advice then, sweetstuff. Keep your head on straight and do your time. Don't be getting all caught up in fairytale land, 'cause that shit will get you killed in here. These hoes can sniff weakness like a dog can smell pussy. You don't need to be pining over no kid, 'cause believe me, she's way better off than you."

"You're saying you don't think about your kids at all?" My eyebrows climb my forehead in shock. I roll over and look down into her face, searching for the truth, one mother to another.

"I'm saying ain't nothing I can do for my kids in here and ain't nothing you can do for yours. You think these motherfuckers give a fuck about you missing your kid?

Hell no. Go out there and tell them you miss your kid
and they'll tell you, you should've thought about that
shit before you did what you did." Both eyes catch mine
and hold on. "Shit, give your kid a few more years and
she'll tell you the same damn thing. So you need to do
what you need to do for yourself. In here, you ain't no
mama, you an animal. And roll over and stop staring at
me, too. I don't like that shit."

I do as I'm told and take my eyes to the wall, to my
daughter's name. Beige. Like the color, but not like
the color. Once, I called an 800 number and ordered
something I saw on television. Had my order taken by
a woman named Beige and fell in love with the name
right then and there.

I fall asleep staring at my baby's name and wake up
with it on the tip of my tongue a few hours later. I watch
my feet kicking air at the other end of my bunk and see
my life flash before my eyes. I pull at the rope around
my neck and struggle to breathe, my eyes about to pop
out of my head. I'm convinced that my first night in
prison will be my last.

Yo-Yo controls the rope and her face looms over
mine in the darkness. Her breath leaves her mouth and
seeps into mine, a cloud of foul air that singes the back
of my throat. "See what I'm saying, sweetstuff?" she
whispers to me. "Caught you tripping, didn't I? You
better snap the hell out of it and real quick, too." I pull
at the rope and scratch my own neck, feel my nails digging into my skin. She smiles. "Told you, everything in
here belongs to me. You write on my walls again and
I'm cutting your goddamn throat."

And just like that, she is gone, leaving me gasping for
air and feeling like committing murder for the second
time in my life. I wonder exactly when the transformation from human being to animal occurs, how it starts,

and if I will realize it is happening to me. Then I realize it is probably not a matter of if, but when, and I pray like I have never prayed before. I am scared to death of turning into Yo-Yo.

I don't even think about what I do two weeks later. What I do think about is the feel of her breath in my mouth the night she strangled me. I think about the smirk that has been on her ugly face ever since, and it is what motivates me to strike back. After she is crazy enough to take me for granted and fall asleep in my presence.

I drop to the floor on the tips of my toes and have my pillow over her face in the blink of an eye. She fights like a jackal, but I come at her like a hyena, pressing my knee into the pillow over her face. She has fucked with the wrong one and I want her to know that. She pushes me off of her, and I go flying across the cell. My back meets the desk and my mouth screams in pain. We fight and fight and fight. Fists fly, hair is pulled, nails dig, and our cell is filled with the sound of heavy breathing and ferocious grunts and groans. She tries to kill me, and I try to convey the message that death is not a part of my plan.

Lights slam on and guards rush into our cell to wrestle us apart. I run my tongue around my teeth, make sure they are all still there, and smile. I don't even feel the billy club wedged under my chin, pinning me to the wall. I give Yo-Yo my shittiest grin and say, "Caught you tripping, didn't I?"

It messes with my head that she smiles and nods at me, and I think about what will happen tomorrow or the next day. I think I know why she is called Yo-Yo. Three days in solitary confinement gives me plenty of time to decide how I will stay awake around the clock, lying in wait.

They put my psycho cellmate in the solitary hole next to mine, and I hear the pattern of her breath all night and all day. There is nothing for me to do but listen to it, so I do. I recite numbers along with the huffs of breath I hear coming through the vent, count all the way to one thousand and start all over again. Sometimes she sings nursery rhymes, of all things, and sometimes she talks to me.

"Can you hear me over there?" Yo-Yo calls out in the middle of the night.

The first ten times she asks me I ignore her. Then I stop doing crunches long enough to give her what she wants. I am between fifty and fifty-one when I say, "I hear you. What the hell do you want?"

"How many years you say you got?"

"I didn't say."

"Well, say it now. How many you got?"

"Five," I pant, on crunch number eighty. "Five fucking years, and I hope I don't have to kick your ass every night, the whole time."

"You musta been dreaming you was kicking my ass, sweetstuff." She laughs like she is watching a hilarious television show instead of a concrete wall. I think about a show I used to watch on television every chance I got, and giggle too. *Mama's Family* was my all-time favorite.

"You ought to make your eyes focus on one thing at a time," I come back. "Then maybe you can see shit how it really happens." She cracks up even harder and I join in.

"Tell you what, sweetstuff. You got a decent right hook, but you need to cut out all that scratching and shit. Don't fuck around when somebody comes at you, either. Hit a bitch so hard you fart and make her think about coming at you a second time."

"I knocked your ass down," I tell her, feeling slightly competitive.

"Yeah, but I got back up. One thing you don't want a bitch on the inside to do is get back up." She huffs harder than I do, releases a steady stream of sharp breaths, and I wonder if she is masturbating and just psycho enough to want me to know it.

"What are you doing?"

"Push-ups. Two hundred of them motherfuckers. You?"

"Crunches." I wait a minute, so I can finish the set I'm on without losing count. Then I fall back against the concrete floor and swipe sweat from my top lip. "A hundred and ten."

"See how many squats you can do," she says, challenging me. "And then after that, run in place like you skipping rope."

I roll to my feet and get in position for the squats that she can't see me doing. "You ready?"

"Go on the count of three." We count together, and I make it to ninety-seven before I tell her that I have to stop and she calls me a lightweight.

We step out of our cells at the same time and catch each other's eyes. Three days in solitary seems like three months, but one thing I notice is that the food is better. Sandwiches with meat I can actually recognize and bread soft enough to chew. The food is the reason Yo-Yo claims she doesn't mind solitary, that and the fact that they actually make you sleep in pitch-black darkness as a form of added punishment. I look back into the emptiness of the cell and think about being safe as I sleep. That is what I don't mind.

"Jeffrey," Yo-Yo says to me a little while later. We are back in our cell, looking around like we have lost our minds. It's been shaken down, shaken up and shaken all around. Searched from top to bottom and side to side. My artwork is gone from the wall and I'm pissed.

"What?" I take my eyes away from the freshly painted spot on the wall and put them on her face, see she is looking where I'm looking.

"My oldest son's name is Jeffrey."

"My daughter's name is Beige," I say, "just like these walls. And she's gone . . . again."

Chapter Three

I suck in a breath as she comes back to me. It's been eight years and now she's back. I lie there and listen to her tip across the basement to my room. I know it's her because I have already memorized the sound of Vicky's footfalls. They are heavy, like she is stomping, leading with the heels of her feet and gripping the floor with her toes after the fact. The steps I hear now are softer, lighter, and I know their owner is slender and a little bit awkward.

Before I can stop myself, I begin to calculate the distance between me and my middle of the night visitor, to strategize on the best method of attack. If I move fast enough, I can be standing by the door with seconds to spare, time enough to catch her off guard and do my damnedest to snap her neck in two pieces. It is after three in the morning, and experience has taught me that late-night footsteps never mean anything good.

My eyes dart around my room and I gradually take control of my thoughts. I remind myself that I am in my sister's home and that I am safe. I stare at the doorway and know the exact moment that she fills it.

"Beige." It is the color of her skin as much as it is her name, and she glows in the darkness because of it. She is tall and thin, small-breasted and missing most of the curves girls her age usually own. Hers is a body that clings to childhood, stubbornly refusing to round out and fill itself in. There are no hips to speak of, only long arms and legs, with a swan's neck.

She is beautiful to me. A glorious sight to behold, like setting eyes on the Messiah and living to tell about it. I have seen her face in the pictures that Vicky mailed to me, seen the gradual disappearance of baby fat and the eventual emergence of dimples deep enough to swim in. In third grade, her teeth were scattered all over the place and crooked beyond belief. In the seventh, they were forced into compliance and neatly lined up next to each other behind the braces Vicky had installed in her mouth. I know she hated having them because in every picture I received after that her smile was missing.

I know she struggles in math. She will not eat cauliflower, even under threat of death. She bites her fingernails down to the quick. She first menstruated when she was twelve, and cramps incapacitate her each and every month. She is on the volleyball team. She thinks the rapper Nelly is fine as wine in a jelly jar, and she has been grounded at least twice for writing his name on her bedroom wall. Since she can't have Nelly, she has settled for entertaining the advances of a boy in her fifth period Biology class—a sophomore named Ulysses. Another boy, Darrick, is after her too, but she is undecided.

But that is all I know. I don't know what she thinks or feels. I don't know any of her secrets and life goals. I don't know what her favorite color is or if she likes chicken more than she does beef. I don't know her at all.

I raise up to my elbows and push my locks from my face. "Come in," I beg her. She does not move from the doorway, and I reach to turn on the bedside lamp so she can see me and I can see her. The sudden light blinds me, and I spend a few seconds with my eyes closed before I open them and look for her. I don't see her, and then I hear the sound of her feet hitting the stairs.

I am hallucinating, I try to tell myself, wanting something so badly that I have conjured it up. Then I tell myself to snap out of it. I know the sound of running feet when I hear them.

There is no sign suspended from the ceiling that says *Welcome Home Lena* and there are no celebratory balloons taped to every available surface to help me feel like I have made the right choice by coming here. Vicky's house is all Vicky, expensive furniture and gleaming glass tables. Spotless carpet and precise places for everything to go and to be. After I rifle through the bathroom for a spare toothbrush and use it, I take a shower and walk around naked, looking at what I didn't feel the need to see the day before.

Vicky graduated from college cum laude and her inevitable success shows in every room of her house. She likes shiny-looking things, and everything in her home reeks of newness, like the price tags should still be attached. I lift a lamp and check the bottom of the base for the tag just to test my theory. I remember when we were kids, she was always ready to tell people how much something cost when they complimented her on it. How she always measured the worth of something by how much it had set her pocketbook back. I'm convinced this is the reason she is still single, because she cannot conceive of a garbage man being worth more than the trash he hauls. I'll never admit it, but I think she lives in a dream world, doesn't see things for what they really are, and that is her greatest flaw.

There is a note for me on the kitchen table, held in place by two keys and the edge of a coffee mug. The sips of coffee still in the mug are cold and starting to thicken into something no one will want to wash out. Whoever was drinking it is long gone. The house is just waking up; it stretches and yawns around me, nothing like what I'm used to. Its quiet is slightly disconcerting.

I look at the note. *Lena, keys to the house and some money for bus fare. Or cab fare, whichever you prefer. Call your PO.*

I take a cup of yogurt with me down the basement steps and into my room. None of the clothes Vicky saved for me fit anymore, and I have to poke a whole new set of holes in the belt I loop through the outdated jeans I hop into. I don't own a single pair of sneakers, and I feel silly in the dressy loafers I have to wear. I feel even sillier rummaging through Vicky's closet, looking for a jacket to wear over my mismatched outfit. I come away from my scavenger hunt with a short Burberry raincoat, and I put it on with a frown on my face.

I try to remember if I have ever been like Vicky, consumed with the need to prove my worth with material things, and I can't. All I know is what I am like now, who I am now. I can't even decide if I am upset about the fact that I seem to have lost my past somewhere along the way.

Isolde Jamison looks nothing like a parole officer. She looks more like an aged porn star.

I watch her flip her blond hair from one shoulder to the other, see her rub her lips together to smooth her lipstick and then pick up a pen from her desktop. After all that, she gives me her eyes. "You were released yesterday?"

"Yes." I pull a folded envelope from my jacket pocket and hand her copies of my release paperwork. They have labeled me a dangerous felon, which means I am required to meet with her once a week, for the first three months of my parole. From there, she will decide if I merit a reduced visitation schedule. I stop staring at the way her red lipstick bleeds into the wrinkles around her mouth and look around her office. "It was too late to call or come by yesterday."

"Oh, well, you still could've called and left me a voicemail." She flattens the papers on her desk and reads them slowly. I notice that her lips move as she reads silently, and I wonder if there is any truth to the old saying about blondes. Then I remind myself that I am black and I should know better than to lend credibility to old sayings of any kind. She glances up and sees me staring. "Let's talk about the stipulations of your release, Helena."

"Okay," I agree, wondering if I have given her permission to call me Helena.

"It says here that the parole board wants you to complete an anger management class."

"I completed a year-long program in the joint."

"You'll need to do another one in the community, sort of like aftercare. You've also been ordered not to consume alcoholic beverages or to enter into establishments where they are the major items offered for sale. Oh, and a psychiatric evaluation too. Which one should we start on first?"

"If it's all right with you, Isolde,"—I call her by her first name on purpose and notice a slight widening of her eyes—"I'd like to find a job first. The evaluation probably costs money I don't have right now. Same for the anger management program. I need money to pay for those things." I can't help smiling. "I guess we could start with not consuming alcoholic beverages, since that's free, huh?"

I see her shift into guidance counselor mode as she pulls out a desk drawer and flips through file folders. She fans papers in a semicircle on my side of the desk, for me to seriously consider. I scan words like *temporary staffing agencies* and *job readiness programs*, and get stuck on the last page, which reads *GED programs*.

"You also have an order to obtain a GED," Isolde informs me.

"I noticed that," I tell her, scooting to the edge of my chair and angling my head, so I can read upside down. "I don't know why they—"

She cuts me off briskly, waving an impatient hand. "Most of the jobs you would qualify for will require a GED, so that's why the board wants you to obtain one. That makes sense, doesn't it?" She looks at me like she is debating whether or not I am able to follow a rational line of thought.

"It makes sense if I didn't have a GED, but the thing is, I have a high school diploma."

"What is your work history? What kinds of jobs have you had in the past?"

"I have experience working with computers," I say. "Data entry and things like that, if we're talking entry level."

"I think we need to start with entry level." She gives me a whimsical smile. "Have to crawl before you walk. Do you have a copy of your high school diploma?"

"Somewhere."

"You could enroll in a job readiness program, to help with deciding what sorts of jobs you'd like to look for."

"I taught those kinds of classes when I was inside," I say. "I'm not sure what I'll learn that I don't already know. I—"

She is a fan of interrupting people while they are talking, I see.

"You'll learn how to put together a resume and a cover letter," she is happy to tell me. "They'll also work with you on interviewing techniques and things like that."

"Well now, will I learn all this before or after I teach them how to take a computer apart and rebuild it? I know a lot of things have changed while I was away, but I've kept up with most of the advances in technology. I had a lot of time on my hands to do research and study, and I can still configure and design software programs with the best of them. I promise you, Isolde, the last thing I need is help creating a resume. I know it's been a while, but I think I can stand to pass on a job readiness program, if you don't mind."

"Software as in computer software programs?"

"At a minimum." She is skeptical and it shows on her face. "My background is mainly in graphic design, but I've dabbled in other stuff too. I'm not above washing dishes if that's what I have to do, but I was hoping I could find something a little more challenging, even if it is entry level."

"Okay," she says slowly, gathering her thoughts. She scoops up the papers she spread out in front of me and stacks them together neatly, fastens them with a paperclip. "With a high school diploma you might be able to find something in data entry."

"What about a master's degree in computer science?" I ask. "What will I be able to find with that?"

She stares at me, speechless. I have always felt it important to begin as I mean to go on, so I stare right back.

***

As a convicted felon and a dangerous one, at that, I admit to myself that a master's degree means nothing. I will be lucky if someone offers me a job washing dishes and I know it. And if they do, I will take it without thinking twice. I need money to put in my pocket, I need money to repay Vicky, and I need clothes that fit both my size and my life. I think about everything else I need as I reach up and pull the cord to signal the bus driver that I want to get off at the next stop.

Two blocks back there is a run-down print shop with colorful posters taped to the plate glass windows. A thousand business cards for twenty bucks, color copies ten cents each, and black and white copies a nickel a sheet. A smaller sign wedged in a corner of the window alerts passersby that they can also order rubber stamps and fax transmittals for a dollar a page.

The HELP WANTED sign taped on the other side of the glass door is what catches my attention. Crawling before I even start to think about walking, I step up to the counter, make eye contact with the elderly black man standing there and point to the sign. "I'd like to apply for the job," I say.

By the time I make it back to Vicky's house, I have also filled out job applications to wash dishes in a restaurant, to scrub toilets after hours in a daycare center and to work the counter in a dry cleaners. I let myself into her house, wondering if any of them will call me back for an interview and thinking, probably not. *Answering yes to this question will not automatically bar you from being considered for employment*, one application after another says. *Please explain the circumstances of an affirmative response.*

I smell frying meat coming from the direction of the kitchen and think, *yeah right*. How do I explain the circumstances surrounding my grandmother's death in three lines or less? Oh yeah, that's right. I can attach an additional sheet of paper, if necessary. Either way, I come out looking like the Grim Reaper and I have brought it on myself.

"How was school?" I try to make conversation as soon as I walk in the kitchen and spot Beige at the stove, flipping a sizzling beef patty in a skillet. The fire is too high and I instinctively step forward to adjust it. My arm brushes hers and she jumps like she's been stunned. I remember when she would force herself into my arms and refuse to let go, jump into the bathtub with me and take control of the bubbles. I wonder if she remembers.

"Lunch sucked," she says, staring into the skillet. "How was prison?"

After that, the kitchen is quiet as a tomb. I see what I couldn't see last night—the bony knobs of her spine down the length of the back of her neck. Round, hunched shoulders, pointy elbows two shades darker than the rest of her and a tight little butt covered in jeans so dark that I almost convince myself they are black. Her long feet are wrapped in orange socks, the same color as her tee shirt, and decorating the ponytail at the crown of her head is an orange scrunchie.

I am staring at the thin gold hoop in her ear, seeing her profile around the edges of my focus, when I say, "I missed you. Thought about you every day, all day."

"My friend Jerica, she said she has an aunt who was in prison for a couple of years, and when she came out she was funny." Her burger lands on half a bun and then on a plate. She flicks the eye off and turns to look me in the eye. The aroma of cooked flesh assaults my nostrils, but the reason I take two steps back has more to do with the expression on her face. I don't see my little girl anywhere in her face.

"Funny?" I know what she means, but I want to make her say it to me, want to see if she has the nerve to say it to me. My eyebrows climb my forehead as I wait.

"You know . . . *funny.*"

I want to slap the smug look off of her face, and I think about doing it—stepping to her and filling the room with the sound of my palm meeting her cheek. Then I think about the irony of the situation. The first touch of my daughter's skin that I am allowed in over eight years should be that of a slap? I don't think so. I decide to let her have her say, even if what she is saying is inappropriate.

"Your friend is wrong," I say. "Prison doesn't make you funny, as you say, unless you want to be. Or you already were. Is that the only thing you want to know? There's nothing else you want to ask me?"

We sit across from each other at the table, a glass monstrosity balanced on a hunk of off-white granite. I stare at her and feel something like anger fall around my shoulders like a cloak of fog. This is not what I expected. We should be falling all over each other, hugging and kissing everywhere our lips can reach. We should be making up for lost time, talking and laughing the way we used to. She should want to touch me and I should be touching her, tracing the lines of her face and smoothing my palm over her hair. I should be breathing in a scent that I never forgot.

I shouldn't be looking into the eyes of a stranger. "Didn't you miss me at all, Beige?"

"You don't look the same," she says, chewing a mouthful of bread and meat.

"Eight years is a long time."

"I forgot what you looked like."

"I didn't forget what you looked like. Couldn't even if I wanted to."

"How come you never tried to see me?"

"Was I supposed to break out of prison? It's not that simple, Beige. And besides that, I didn't want you to see me like that."

Her face goes from smug to cynical, wraps itself around anger and holds on tight. "You just didn't want to see me."

I open my mouth to respond, thinking that this moment in time is the maker or breaker. I will tell her how much I love her and how much I regret everything that's happened. How much I want the two of us to begin building a relationship. How my arms want to hug her so badly that they almost fly apart from my body and attach themselves to hers. She has no idea how I have craved her very essence, and I struggle with finding the words to tell her.

Keys jingle in the lock and then the front door opens and closes. Seconds later, Vicky floats into the kitchen like a dream. She is wearing pale pink scrubs and shoes so white they are blinding. A stethoscope hugs her neck, and the watch on her wrist is large enough that she has no trouble keeping track of the second hand. She is everything I am not—pure looking, reassuring and soft around the edges. A natural caregiver with all the answers.

She has been my daughter's caregiver for longer than I have. I guess this is the reason Beige's eyes light up as she enters the kitchen, a smile curves her lips, and her anger washes away on a tide.

"Hey, Mom," Beige says.

Vicky darts a quick glance at me and whispers "hey" back to her, touches the top of her head on her way to the refrigerator. It's like I am watching a television show, something so perfectly practiced it seems unreal. I feel my skin begin to peel away from my bones, hear my blood rush to my ears, and know that I am the odd man out. If I didn't know my place before, I do now.

I wonder if either of them notice me leaving the kitchen. Then I wonder what their quiet voices are saying in my wake, as I tip down the basement steps. For the first time I understand how a woman can be released from prison, enjoy one or two precious days of freedom and then find herself right back where she started—in prison. They call it institutionalization, the act of not being able to function in society and the de-sire to return to a controlled environment.

I call it not being able to cope with rejection.

Chapter Four

The goddamn jury doesn't even deliberate for a respectable amount of time. They hide in a room for two hours and twenty-two minutes and then emerge with the fate of my life in their hands. I rise along with everyone else in the courtroom and crumble to the floor minutes later.

"We find the defendant guilty of involuntary manslaughter," the foreman announces. He is a round man, short and balding. He combs the hair on one side of his head over the gleaming dome in the center, to connect with the hair on the other side. I have spent the better part of my trial staring at him, asking myself why he doesn't just go out and buy himself a toupee.

I wonder if he knows how silly he looks.

But the last laugh is on me. I am the one who will be going to the state correctional facility for women, and he will be the one looking silly, all the way home.

The buzzing noise in my ears is so loud that I don't hear the judge's words. I don't hear my attorney's response or the prosecutor's comeback. My head swivels around on my shoulders as I watch their lips move, and tears fill my eyes. I have yet to think about a future outside of the courtroom. I haven't stopped to think about prison.

I am sentenced to five years. Hands grasp at me, pulling my arms behind my back, and handcuffs appear from thin air. I hear a loud cry from somewhere in the back of the courtroom, and I turn to meet Vicky's eyes across time and space. She is dissolving right before me, like the wicked witch from the Wizard of Oz. She reaches out to me, but I can't reach back.

I let a single tear race down my face and swallow the others. "Get Beige," I call out just before I am hustled across the room and through a doorway. I know where I am going—to a tiny cell in the bowels of the courthouse. From there, I am going away for a long time.

"Vicky!" I scream, hoping she can hear me. "Get Beige! Take care of my baby!" She knows what I am saying to her. We have talked about this, about how she will take Beige in and keep her safe until I can get everything straightened out. Get myself out of the mess I have gotten into.

But not once did we talk about Beige calling her Mom.

The old man from the print shop doesn't call. Neither does the woman from the daycare center or the one from the restaurant. After two weeks of unemployment and knowing looks from Isolde, I find the list of temporary staffing agencies that she gave me, and I make appointments with three of them. Only one of them is accustomed to placing convicted felons, and their specialty is factory work.

It doesn't matter that I have a master's degree or that I can take a computer apart and put it back together before I have my morning coffee. I am assigned to a baked goods company, where I am put on the graveyard shift to fight with a giant machine that squirts creamy white goo into the center of second-rate Twinkie and Ding-Dong wannabes. I learn from experience that you get what you pay for, and I swear my allegiance to Hostess after only three nights on the job.

The pay is decent, and the job is supposed to last at least six months, which gives me some time to scout around for other job possibilities without feeling the heat of empty pockets and wasted time. I don't completely relax, but I do allow myself to shift from second gear into neutral. A steady job makes everything else I need to do seem like cake.

We are allowed two fifteen-minute breaks and an hour for lunch, but most of the regular employees do whatever the hell they want to do. It's all about the numbers, and as long as quotas are met, no one really cares how many smoke breaks you take or for how long. Right away I notice how much working in the factory is like being on the inside. White women stick together, black women join forces, and the ones fortunate enough not to belong to either group manage to get along just fine. The men find other things to define their allegiances, like bitchy wives and girlfriends, sports teams and sex talk. Skin color doesn't seem to matter to them as long as you can talk the talk.

The women compete for attention. Who has the best-looking hair or body? Who dresses the best, or whose significant other bought them what? I stay on the fringes of it all, pretending that I belong to a group that has yet to be defined, and take it all in. Wild mixtures of over-priced cologne always hang in the air and make my stomach turn. I concentrate on giving each pseudo Twinkie, Cupcake and Ding-Dong just the right amount of creamy white goo and tune them out. I'm so far beyond their day to day bullshit that I don't even recognize the language they speak.

It takes them exactly five nights of my presence among them to decide that I am strange. I do not smoke and, even though the temperature inside the factory often soars past seventy-five degrees, I do not step outside to catch a breath of fresh air like the other non-smokers. After my first night on the job, I don't go into the employee lounge when others are in there. I wait outside the restroom door until I am sure it is empty before going inside, no matter how badly I need to pee. Outdoors, there is too much space, too much room to move around in, and inside places like the lounge or the bathroom, there is not enough. Four times, the shift supervisor has to remind me that I can take a break and that I am entitled time to eat. Until then, I stay at my station, doing what I am told to do.

The one time I do go into the employee lounge while others are there, I find myself moved to violence that I am barely able to restrain. Sophia, another temp worker, steps up behind me at the soda machine, moves in close to drop her money in the slot and breathes in my ear. I have her face pressed against the machine's colorful shell and her arm wrenched up between her shoulder blades before I can think straight. I let her go and apologize like I really mean the words coming out of my mouth, but she sees that my eyes are wild.

I try, once, to walk into the ladies room as if the task is nothing, but I cannot make myself undress, even partially, knowing women surround me. They are too close, and I smell their scents, hear the elimination of their bowels and bladders, and feel myself drifting into a coma-like state. I have been in the sole company of women, against my will, for so many years that now I can barely stand to look at myself in the mirror, let alone suffer through another woman violating my personal space.

I am crippled and I know it. I think I do a decent job of covering my missteps and blending in as much as possible, until the night Stella sidles up to me as I squirt goo. I swipe sweat from my forehead and slide her a look. She looks around to make sure no one can hear us and leans in.

"How long you been out?" she asks.

"Excuse me?"

"You heard me. How long you been out?"

We stare, both looking at one and the same. She is older than I am by at least two decades, but our eyes still lock around the recognition simmering in the air between us. I wonder what she did, when, and if it was as bad as what I did. "Been out of what?" I say, just to make sure we are talking about the same thing. Beige thinks I should be funny, and Stella might too.

"You can play dumb if you want to, but you can't fool me. Like recognizes like." I keep squirting and she takes on the job of flipping the phony Twinkies onto their bellies on the baking sheet, which is the second part of my job description. We go on like this for several minutes, and then she speaks again. "They got seventeen years out of me before they finally decided they couldn't get no more. Took all my best years from me and then they put me out on the street. You, though, you still got some good years left in you."

"If you say so."

"I know so," she insists, backhanding her own sweat and catching my eyes. "It gets easier." I don't answer, but I do listen.

I try to take what she says with me on the bus, try to pick a seat next to someone instead of three seats away. Try to fight the need to stand, gripping the pole and swaying back and forth as the bus moves, even though there is a perfectly good seat a few feet away. If it is wedged between two people, I will not sit down. I cannot. *Easy* is a word that I don't remember.

I tell myself a joke: What do you get when you combine a fool, a jackass, and a lost cause? Me. But I don't laugh.

***

Beige circles around me like Sugar Ray Leonard, careful not to say too much, afraid of actually winding up in a conversation with me. She's always in my peripheral vision, so that I look up and she is part of the scenery. Beyond the pleasantries I force from her lips, she doesn't say much, but her eyes follow my every move. I feel privileged to have even that.

She crinkles her nose in distaste at the food I buy for myself and cook when the kitchen is finally clear. A meal without meat is inconceivable to her, and she sits across the table from me, pretending to do her homework, watching me crunch vegetable after vegetable. I watch her watch me and follow her lead, saying nothing. It is enough that she wants to be around me— though I probably couldn't pay her to admit it.

Beige struggles in math, and though Vicky is a nurse practitioner, she isn't much help when it comes to algebraic equations. Twice she warned me against the dangers of douching, and three times she has advised me on which painkillers are most effective for the migraines that sneak up on me. But, when Beige presents her with her math book for clarification, she looks cross-eyed.

She will eat her own foot before she asks me for help. Not once does she turn to me and ask if I know how to work out an equation. She has asked if I am funny, but she doesn't ask if I know anything about algebra. More than once, Vicky catches my eyes across the kitchen table, silently pleading for intervention, but I look away. I know the shit backward and forward, but I will eat my own foot before I tread where I'm not wanted.

This is my new freedom resolution: Beige will have to meet me halfway.

Vicky is an instigator though. Always has been, now that I think about it. "Leenie, do you remember what the hell *pi* is?" she says as if she doesn't have a clue. As if there isn't a formula key at the top of the page.

I take a soy burger out of the oven and slide it onto a waiting bun. Look at her like, *duh.* "Three point one four."

"How many damn exponents can one number have?" she complains another evening. I abandon the salad I am scarfing down and lean over her shoulder. I accidentally brush against Beige's arm, and she steps back so I don't have to touch her again.

I pretend I don't notice. Vicky has scribbled all over a sheet of scrap paper, and I can't make out anything she's written. "Give me the damn book, Vicky," I snap, irritated because she is mangling numbers beyond recognition. I work six problems before I realize that Vicky has disappeared and only Beige is leaning over my shoulder. Speechless, I hand her the book and the sample problems and go back to my salad, a little hurt that she flinches when my fingers touch hers.

The last straw is when Vicky drifts into the kitchen on a cloud of dreamy smiles and breezy breaths, and hands me what she calls presents. She found them in her papers, she says, and she thinks I should have them. Again. They belong to me, she tells me.

She waits to see what my reaction will be, but she is waiting in vain. I stare first at my bachelor's degree as if I don't recognize the name stamped on the paper, and then at my master's degree like it is capable of rolling itself into a snake and biting me. My face is blank, unable to twist itself into any particular expression. I wonder why I didn't think to ask where my diplomas were before now.

"What are they?" Beige wants to know. I feel her breath on the back of my neck as she curls her body around my shoulder to see for herself. She reads the words out loud, not knowing that each one is like a drop of cold water down the back of my shirt.

"Your mom's college degrees," Vicky says.

I don't say anything. And then I say, "I taught you how to read when you were four. You helped me study for this one." I hold up the master's degree and without thinking, touch her hand where it is wrapped around the back of my chair. "I wrote out test questions and had you read them to me while I made dinner or did laundry." I can't wrap my mind around the fact that she jumps away from my touch, looks at her hand as if it might be contaminated, but I make myself keep talking. "You might've been the only four-year-old in the city who knew what a motherboard was. It was . . ."

I trail off, suddenly tired of the sound of my own voice. She isn't really listening, and I am talking just to hear myself talk. Vicky pities me; I can see it in her face, and I don't want her pity. I just want my daughter back.

I swallow and stare at Beige until she has no choice but to give me her eyes. My eyes. "It doesn't rub off," I tell her. "It's not contagious." She looks doubtful.

Denny is the one who plants the concept of locking my hair into my mind. After what happens happens, I wear a short afro day after day and month after month, and discover that natural slips into my soul like butter on warm bread. I like the way my hair is a little bit curly and a little bit frizzy, but I don't like the way I have to wrestle it into a circle every day, after I sleep it into a square.

She sits me between her thighs and takes forever twisting carefully parted sections. I feel the warmth of her hands on my scalp and I fall asleep with my face pressed into her thigh. She shakes me awake and tells me to look at what she's done and I fall in love.

"They'll lock up if you don't comb 'em out," she warns me when I come to her straight from the shower, for her to tighten them up. This is not the first time I have come, wanting her fingers on my scalp and ready to doze off in bliss.

I settle myself on the floor between her thighs and lay my head back.

They drape my shoulders now, my locks, and a few of the more feisty ones race ahead toward the middle of my back. I find a shop not far from the factory that is full of chattering African women, and I give myself over to them. They flutter around me when I walk through the door, admiring my locks and commenting to themselves in a language that sounds angry and confrontational. Then one of them takes my hand and leads me over to the shampoo bowl.

Fingernails scrub at my scalp and I moan loudly. I can almost convince myself that the hard rim of the sink is Denny's thigh and the fingers running through my hair are hers—almost.

Out of the corner of my eye I see something that catches my attention. Pointing like a child, I look up at the woman looming over me. She follows the direction of my finger and then grins down at me. She adjusts the water and rinses my locks until I can hear them squeak, pulls the corners of my eyes toward my ears as she wrings them out.

"Cowry shells?"

"Yeah," I say. There is a jar full on a shelf across the room. "How much extra?"

"I put a few in for you, no charge. They bring good luck." Her face is serious as a heart attack. Makes me wonder if I still have the smell on me, if it really does rub off. "You need good luck, am I right?"

I am speechless, suddenly snatched back in time.

I tell Yo-Yo, for the third time: "Luck ain't got shit to do with it. I told you I learned how to do this kind of stuff way back when, so that's how I know what I'm talking about. Pay attention because we need to do this real quick and get the hell out of here."

We are using one of ten computers that the prison has for inmate use, and we are using it when we should be asleep. She won't even consider doing what she is doing during daylight hours, which puzzles the hell out of me, but I go along with the secrecy that she thinks she has to have. I teach her how to read at night, using the books I am never without, and we write letters to her children when no one is around to see.

She has written four of them so far, one for each of her kids, but she has no idea where to mail the last one. The oldest three are all in the same foster home and the foster parents are kind enough to send her pictures every now and again. Kind enough to realize that she might want to have the luxury of recognizing her kids if she ever passes them on the street. The youngest is twelve now, and Yo-Yo has no idea where she is. Somewhere in the state, we know that much, but exactly where is a mystery we are trying to solve.

I surf the Internet until I locate a search engine that I built. I am a hacker, which is against the law, but I am already wearing shackles, so what more can they do to me? It makes me laugh to discover that passwords have never been changed and security is easily breachable. My fingers fly over the keyboard and I frown in concentration.

"They want to adopt her," Yo-Yo says as if she is talking to herself. "We can't let that shit happen. They can't do that shit without asking me, can they?"

She wants me to tell her that they can't, but all I can offer her is a clueless shrug. Computers are my thing, and social service goings-on are like hieroglyphics to me.

"What's that fucking case worker's name anyway?"

"Scagnomilio," I remind her absently, still typing.

"Call that bitch tomorrow."

"And tell her what?"

I reach for the pencil I brought with me, slide a piece of paper in front of me and start scribbling. I finish copying the information the screen gives me illegally and pass it over my shoulder to her. "Tell her Fred and JoAnn Price, of sixty-two-eleven Crowder Street, can't adopt your baby without asking you first."

Yo-Yo whoops at the top of her lungs and dances around the room like a fool, clutching the paper to her chest in a million wrinkles. She makes so much noise that I hop up and cover her mouth with my hand. "You trying to get us time in the hole?"

"The food's better," she says, smiling. "And anyway, can't nothing touch us tonight. Girl, you my lucky charm. That's what I'm calling your ass from now on. Lucky Charm, like the cereal. 'Cept you ain't green and shit."

"Please don't," I say, already hating the nickname. I shake my head and go back to the computer, back my way out of the website I have violated and then shut down the machine.

"Too late." Yo-Yo reads the words on the paper the way I taught her, sounding out each syllable slowly and then saying the whole word in one breath. "I owe you one, Lucky."

"You don't owe me shit. And don't call me Lucky."

The African woman taps me on my shoulder to get my attention. She is done shampooing my hair and needs me to sit up. I zoned out, and she is wondering if she should be concerned. "Sorry," I mumble and let her lead me over to her chair.

"I'm Anta," she tells me as she clamps a hank of locks together and then reaches for a jar of beeswax. "What's your name?"

I open my mouth and out comes, "Lucky."

Anger management class reminds me of the drug education groups I attended when I was inside. A bunch of women sitting around in a circle, staring at each other and trying to look like they're listening. It's an hour and a half out of my life every week, for the next twelve weeks, but it is free. I can't recall anything else that I have to do from six to seven-thirty on Thursday evenings.

I frown when it is my turn to stand up and introduce myself, say why I am here and what I hope to learn. I want to say I am here because I have to be and I already know more than I ever wanted to know about anger and how to control it, but I don't. I mumble complete bullshit about wanting to learn new tools for controlling anger and that completing the class means one less parole violation. Everyone laughs and one woman shakes her head like she knows what I am saying. I take my seat, glad to be out of the spotlight, and wait for the woman next to me to stand and start talking.

I am totally unprepared for the facilitator's question when it comes at me from out of left field. "Why don't you tell us a little about some of the issues you've experienced with anger management, Helena?" Vivian is her name, and she has already told us that she is a clinical psychologist working on her PhD. She is short and heavy from the waist down, and she wears a bee-hive of elaborate-looking cornrows that are in need of a do-over. I don't like the way she seems to be looking into my soul, and I want to tell her not to waste her time because I don't have one.

"I can't honestly say I have had issues," I lie.

"So you're only here because your parole officer is making you come?"

"Exactly."

She holds my eyes and lets me see the wheels turning in her head. When they grind to a halt, she nods slowly and touches a finger to her lips. "I guess we'll see about that, won't we?"

"I guess we will." Bitch.

Chapter Five

"Do me a favor," I say to Beige as I come in the kitchen. She is fishing around in the refrigerator, and I stop just shy of the door and hold up the half-empty jar of cocoa and shea butter cream that I brought with me. "When you want to borrow something that belongs to me, ask first, okay?"

"I haven't borrowed anything from you," she says, careful not to look at me. She grabs a bag of grapes and bumps the door shut with an imaginary hip. I smell the unmistakable scent of incrimination in the air she stirs in her wake.

"Yeah, you did, and you just about used it all up, too. You don't want me touching you, but you want to touch the things I touch, things that belong to me. You don't think that's disrespectful?"

"It's just some cream," she drawls, and I want to pull her hair. One after another, grapes disappear into her mouth and she chews them slowly, as if she wants the taste of them to last forever. It is an evasion tactic and it pisses me off no end. This is the same strategy she employed after dumping a whole bottle of expensive cologne on the carpet in my bedroom when she was four. My room smelled like a whorehouse for months. Back then it was crayons and an upside-down coloring book. Now it is grapes, but the principle is still the same.

"What about the socks I suddenly can't find, the red ones? And the earrings I've been looking for since last week?" I buy myself one thing out of every paycheck— things I once had but that are long gone, like socks in every color except white. I have worn white socks for so long that I need an indefinite break from them, so I buy socks in vibrant colors. The red pair is my favorite. The two-tone gold earrings I am missing were favorites of mine too. They can't help but be, since they're the only pair I own.

She steals from me, but I know it's not really about possession of my things. Vicky has done what she can to see that Beige is materialistic. Everything she wears has someone's name stamped or sewed on it. She doesn't need the things I find on clearance and buy for myself, but she steals them anyway. I am not really angry, just puzzled.

"I don't know anything about any earrings," she says.

"Beige." My voice is soft and patient sounding. "You're wearing them right now." I give her five long seconds to come up with something to say and she doesn't. Then I leave her sitting there, eating grapes that she doesn't really want.

I go to my room and become restless, decide to go out and come back into the kitchen ready to roll. She takes in the sneakers on my feet, the jacket I wear and the shades on my face. I grab my keys from the table and a few grapes for the road, and treat her like she treats me. I don't even acknowledge her presence.

"Where are you going?" This is the first time she asks me that question.

"Out," I say over my shoulder. "You coming?" I think I hear a stampede behind me, too much rustling and rushing for just one person, but when I turn and look back at her, she comes toward me like she has all the time in the world.

It is chilly outside, not quite winter but too early for spring, and I can almost see my breath in front of my face. Beige zips her jacket all the way up to her neck, and I tug at the tab of my own zipper until I feel air poking at the skin on my neck and chest. I don't feel the cold so much as I do the liberation of it. As much as I want, I can have. I grin like an idiot as a gust of wind slams into me and picks my locks up from my scalp, holds them suspended in the air behind me.

We say nothing as we walk, cross streets, and walk some more. I know where I am going, but she has no idea. Twice I glance over at her and see confusion marked on her face. She wants to know but will not ask. Probably thinks I'm taking her to a place where all the funny people hang out. Wherever that is. She trails me across one last street, and then I turn into a doorway at the side of a brick building. Along the front of the building there are stores and small boutiques, but the doorway I choose is partially hidden, more suspect looking.

A bell jingles as I push the door open and bring Beige into another world. She sucks in a deep breath and smiles like she is in heaven. The smell of warm sandalwood is heavy in the room and soft music fills every available space. I can't decide what I want to look at first, there is so much to see. Shelves of fragrant body oils, bolts of patterned cloth and figures hand carved from rich woods. Every time I come, I find something different to capture my attention, and this time it is a wooden statue of an African woman, naked from the waist up and balancing a woven basket on the crown of her head. She is so intricate and realistic looking that I hold my breath and wait for her to walk right past me.

"I didn't know this place was here," Beige moves close and whispers to me.

"There's a lot of things you don't know." I glance at a rack of handmade earrings and necklaces and then at her. "Don't put anything in your pocket without paying for it."

"I don't steal." She is offended, and it shows on her face in the way she rolls her eyes to the ceiling when I narrow my eyes and contradict her. My earrings are still dangling from her earlobes.

This is what it's like to shop with my daughter, I think as Beige oohs and ahhs over everything she sees. I follow her around the shop, only looking away from her when I have to, to nod at the owner of the shop and her teenage son, who is too busy staring at Beige to notice me. I watch her smooth dabs of body oil on the backs of her hands and then breathe the scents deep into her nostrils. I notice that she fingers the dashikis we stop to look at and admires the soft material. I run my hands over the statues that she touches and agree with her when she says something smells good, even if I don't think it does. The sound of her voice mesmerizes me.

I buy more of the cream she likes and feel good about myself when our arms brush against each other's and she doesn't shrink away.

"What time is it?" I ask as we leave the shop. She falls in step beside me on the sidewalk and glances at the expensive watch on her wrist.

"Ten past four. How come you don't wear a watch?"

"Haven't needed one," I say and leave it at that. In prison there is no concept of time in terms of seconds and minutes. The only thing that matters is the day you go in and the day you come out. The in-between is a gray area of existence—untime.

"You don't talk much," she points out.

"Where I've been, the less you say, the better. One thing I've noticed since I've been home is that people on the outside talk too much. Everybody's always chattering about something, who's doing what, when, where and why. Makes my ears tired."

"You think I talk too much?"

I shake my head. "You don't talk enough."

"I don't know what to say to you half the time."

"Say anything. Tell me you hate me, tell me to go to hell, whatever you want to tell me. Just say something."

She thinks about what I have said for long seconds. "Can I ask you something?"

"Don't ask me if I'm funny again."

"Are you?"

"Should I be?"

"I don't know. You could be, I guess."

"I'm not," I say a few seconds later. Secretly, I wonder if I am lying to her and to myself. "But you're right, I could be. Is that what you wanted to ask me?"

"No, I was going to ask you what it was like."

An elderly woman bumps my shoulder as she passes and I reach out to steady her. She carries too many bags for her arms, and I help her shuffle them around until she has a firmer grip on them. I turn around just in time to collide with another shoulder, a man, and I go still as a rod. I see a hand come my way and move out of its path like I am dodging a projectile. He shrugs and keeps walking, and I breathe a sigh of relief.

"I'm not the same person I was before I went to prison," I admit to my daughter. It doesn't cost me anything to be honest. "It was like dying and still having to live."

Apparently what I give her is enough because she doesn't ask me anything else. We walk in silence until dusk settles around us and we are four blocks from

Vicky's house. I am in no hurry to get there, in no hurry to camp out in my room until it is time for me to sleep and then leave for work, so I reduce my pace to a stroll and push my hands in my jacket pockets.

Beige nudges me with her elbow. "You don't want to go back, do you?"

"I never want to go back."

Vicky is eleven and I am nine. We are both frozen with shock, sitting close together on my grandmother's porch, whispering back and forth. We have somehow made both of our bodies fit into one corner of the porch and it is uncomfortable, but I refuse to scoot even an inch away from her, nor she me. We have to be close, have to stick together.

We have been together so long it is first and not second nature. Where she goes, I go. What she does, I do. We experience everything together, suffer everything together. We don't know how else to be.

"Grandma came in the room and saw me," Vicky confides to me. Her lips are pressed so close to my ear that I feel the moisture her warm breath leaves behind. "She didn't say nothing."

"Did you cry?" I want to know.

"When I got through. She told me to get some tissue and blow my nose and then go outside and play. She said we gone have homemade caramel after lunch. She's making it now and I can't wait until it's done."

I can, I think.

The memory wants to linger, but I open my eyes and look around my room in the darkness. Push Vicky's phantom voice away from my ear and roll over in bed. I count to ten and then try to fall asleep again.

***

The telephone is something I don't use very often. Everyone I need to talk to is under the same roof as me, except for Isolde, and I can't think of anything that I would need to discuss with her, beyond formalities. Apparently, she feels the same way because she has yet to call Vicky's house to speak with me. I imagine it's because I'm probably the easiest client she has on her caseload. I'm not in the business of making waves, especially when I am the one who would be dragged under with the tide.

I am folding laundry, the jeans and loose-fitting shirts that I have grown accustomed to living in, when Vicky comes into my room and holds out the cordless phone for me to take. I stare at it like it is on fire and I am gasoline, wondering what the hell I am supposed to do with it.

"It's for you," Vicky says, inspecting the stacks of clothes on my bed. She flips through a mountain of soft faded denim and frowns, tugging on a pair of jeans toward the bottom of the stack. "Are these my jeans?"

"No, they're mine."

"Oh . . . well, they're cute. Can they be mine?"

"I don't think so." I laugh. Then I remember the phone and my frown matches hers.

"Who is it?"

"Mama. She wants to talk to you."

This is news to me. I have been home for almost two months and this will be the first time my mother has come looking for me. I realize that I have been waiting to find out what her reaction to me will be, to find out if it has changed in the five years or so since we last saw each other. In the beginning, she came to the prison at least once a month to visit me, and then she said the visits took too much out of her. Said she was having a hard time looking at my face after what I did. I have been waiting to see if she would come to me or ask me to come to her.

Vicky's face is unreadable as I take the phone from her. "Hello?"

"Helena?"

"Yes, Mama, it's me."

"Vicky says you're settling in okay, but I wanted to find out for myself. You're working now?"

"The night shift, and it's killing me," I say without thinking. Everything goes still and Vicky and me look at each other. I hear the sound of my mother's gasp in my ear. "I squeeze cream into snack cakes."

She checks back into the conversation a little at a time. "Nothing wrong with an honest day's work."

"No, ma'am, there's not, and at least it pays more than minimum wage."

"Well, you can't expect to start out making seventy grand a year, like you were before. That's pretty much done with. I have some of your stuff here, whenever you get ready for it. Some music and a few pieces of furniture, things like that. Been keeping them for you."

"Okay. How are you, Mama?"

"Cholesterol's a little high, but other than that . . ." she trails off, knowing she hasn't really answered my question.

She doesn't ask, but I still say, "I'm good too. Getting used to everything. A lot of stuff is different or else completely new. It's a little strange."

"Takes time," she says. "I was trying to let you get settled before I came down there. I've been wanting to come and see my grandbaby anyway. She keeps telling me about some outlet mall they built not too far away, and let her tell it, I got to get down there and check it out." She lives in Las Vegas, where there have to be outlet malls damn near on every corner, but she will make the trip to visit the one Beige wants her to visit. The outing is easily worth several hours of traveling, unlike visiting a prison.

"That sounds like fun," I lie. I have never particularly cared for shopping, and the idea of doing it now makes me think I have developed a phobia. Too many people in one place and too much noise. "Beige will like that, and it'll be good to see you. You like Las Vegas?"

"It's not home, but I guess it'll do. What do you think of that little town Vicky moved to while you were gone?"

"It seems okay."

I can't help feeling like I am being reminded that everything started with me and what I did. My mother is a big city girl at heart, and so are Vicky and me, I guess. We grew up with family in every part of the city and my grandmother close by. Some of the women more distant in relation even had men we called uncles in their lives. I pulled the trigger and caused a mass exodus. Without the matriarch, my family fell apart.

There has always been a woman at the head of my family. My grandmother birthed four children, two boys and two girls, each by a different man she never married. Neither my mother nor my aunt Dierdre ever married but, between them, they had enough illegitimate children to form their own football team. Vicky and I have different fathers, and neither of us can identify the mystery men since we were too young to remember what they look like. It is the thing to do in my family, have as many babies as you want outside of wedlock and not feel bad about it. As for my part, I added Beige to the mix. She is my mother's only grandchild and, like Vicky, I hope she breaks the cycle.

When my grandmother died, my mother relocated to
Las Vegas and my aunt Deirdre followed suit, making
her home somewhere in Mississippi. I embarrassed the
family and made it impossible for them to live in the
city they had both lived in all their lives. The stigma
was too much for them.

One of my uncles took the easy way out and died
before I could cast a pall over his life. Vicky took Beige
and ran. What my mother calls a small town is really
a good-size city with a cozy, small-town feel near the
Missouri state line. I don't think Vicky could bring
herself to abandon the state where she was born altogether, but she did a good job of separating herself
from everything that happened. Here, she can walk
the streets without being recognized as the hysterical
woman from the ten o'clock news all those years ago.
Here, Beige can go to school and have a normal life,
without being whispered about and pointed at, identi-
fied as the girl with the murdering mother.

Lines have been drawn and sides taken. Some think
I am a monster, and some don't think about what
happened at all. It is easier to sever the lines of communication than it is to open them up and hear what is
being said. I don't know where most of my cousins are
or what they are doing. I don't know if they know I have
been released, and I don't think they care.

"Well, I better get off of here," my mother says, slipping back into my thoughts. "Long distance is ridiculous these days. Before I go, you need anything?"

I look around my room at what I have managed to
accumulate and shake my head. I have as many pairs of
jeans as I need to have a clean pair for each day of the
week, socks in every color I can think of, and the earrings Beige finally returned. "No, ma'am. You coming
soon?" I don't need anything else except to see the look
on my mother's face when she sees me. I need that.

I hand Vicky the phone and go back to my laundry. She touches my shoulder softly and catches my eyes. "Hold on, Mama," she says, and then she drops the phone on the bed.

Seconds later, we are in each other's arms, squeezing like boa constrictors. This isn't a benediction and it isn't about forgiveness, but it is a long time in coming. She is saying something to me and I am all ears. I have always been able to hear what her mouth doesn't say, and I hear her now, though she is silent.

She is telling me whose side she is on.

Chapter Six

I have to take Isolde into the restroom with me because I have no choice in the matter. I have to allow her to watch me empty my bladder. I have to pee in a cup that is too small to accomplish the task without splashing my hand. She sees that I am wearing hot pink panties with little black monkeys all over them. I feel like a monkey, a circus animal made to dance on command.

She sees that I am menstruating, that my flow is heavy, and that it stains the urine she has requested. She wears thick gloves and holds the cup I pass her between two fingers with a look of vague disgust on her face. I feel two feet tall; humiliated, like a prisoner straining at my leash, promised freedom but still denied.

I feel like a criminal. My life is a joke, and I wonder if it will ever be funny.

She takes a long time wrapping up with her friends and I wait patiently. I remember being a teenager, and I know there is important bullshit to talk over before the school day comes to a close. She is probably discussing tomorrow's outfit and plotting on some unsuspecting boy she has her eye on. I see her laugh at something one of her friends says, and then she props a hand on her hip. She throws her hair from one shoulder to the other and strikes a pose.

She sees me standing on the sidewalk and makes her way over to me slowly, surprised to see me at her school. Her friends shoot me curious looks as they split up in different directions, but I only see Beige. I was out running and she lured me here.

I swipe sweat from my forehead, wipe it on the seat of my track pants and smile. Everywhere I sweat there is a dark, damp circle—under my arms, between my breasts and down the middle of my back. I must look a mess. "What's up with the rolling backpack? You have back problems or something?" I point to the black case she is pulling along behind her.

"I mean, I know when you were in school black kids didn't have actual books and everything, but these days one book weighs about ten pounds," Beige jokes and cracks a smile. "You expect me to carry all these books home?"

"You ride the bus," I say.

"Yeah, but I'm walking with you today, right?"

She doesn't have a choice. I don't have a car and her bus is gone, but I was hoping she would want to walk with me, was prepared to run back home if she refused. "I figured out a shortcut." She cuts me a doubtful look and collapses the handle on her backpack, shrugs it on her back, and falls in step with me.

Later on I say, "I didn't embarrass you by coming, did I?"

"No, but all this walking is going to have to stop. You exercise too much."

"It's good for you."

"If you say so." I reach out and press the button to change the traffic light, and she touches a finger to my bicep. "How come you're trying to look like a man?"

"You think I look like a man?" I look for the truth in her face and can't find it. Her eyes travel from the top of my head to the sneakers on my feet. She finally shakes her head, no. "Maybe like one of those sports women. Mia Hamm or somebody. Like you can kick some booty if you have to. You got into working out while you were in there?"

I don't pretend not to know where *there* is. "It was either that or sit around getting fat and lazy or mean and ugly. Did you try working out some algebra problems the way I showed you?"

"Yeah, my teacher didn't know what hit her. Tell me what else you did."

"I hope you're not gathering information, planning on finding out for yourself?"

"Please," she says, flapping a hand. "I'm not . . . I don't . . . I mean . . ."

"Good," I cut her off. "You want to take the bus from here?"

Beige grabs my arm and slows my roll, makes me meet her eyes. "No. I want you to tell me what you did in prison."

"Three days a week I taught computer classes, and when I wasn't thinking up new ways to keep from going insane, I read books. I had a crazy cellmate who didn't know how to read, so I helped her learn. And yeah, I got into exercising. Lifting weights and making myself look stronger than I really was. The harder you look, the less likely you are to be victimized. It's not like what you see on television, trust me. It's not like a resort, where you go and serve your time and people leave you the hell alone. It's not like anything you can ever imagine."

"I know it's not." She is angry with me, thinks I am patronizing her. She snatches her hand away and takes off walking. I have to skip a few steps to catch up with her. "I still wanted to visit you."

"I didn't want you to see me like that. In there."

"I thought you just didn't want to see me."

"I called every chance I got," I say, and it sounds pitiful to my own ears. "I made Vicky send me pictures all the time and I wrote letters, but you didn't write back. You stopped coming to the phone when I called."

"I was mad at you."

"I know. I was mad at me too."

"I'm still mad at you."

"I know that too."

"Everybody else's mama was at the school and going on field trips with us, but you couldn't." We turn the corner onto Vicky's street and she pushes ahead of me angrily. The look she shoots me over her shoulder is red hot and hard. "I used to make up stories when the other kids asked me where my mama was. You just don't know . . ."

"I think I do. What did you tell them?"

"It's not important."

"What did you tell them?" I say, really wanting to know. I think I have an idea, but I want to hear her say the words. Suddenly, it is important to me. I need to know exactly what I am dealing with, so I know how to fight it. I can't fight a demon I can't see. "Tell me." I take a page from her book and grab her arm as she goes up the porch steps. She tries to jerk away from me, but I hold fast. My eyes remind her that I am still her mother, and she simmers down to a barely appropriate level.

"I told them you were dead," she says in a strange voice.

I chew on what she said late into the night, turning it over in my mind and digesting it fully, looking for my reaction and eventually finding it. It is not what I expect it to be. It is not anger or even jealousy, not self-righteousness or self-pity. What it is, is understanding. I accept that I am not the only prisoner in the house.

"Listen," I say as I lean in Beige's bedroom doorway. It is past her bedtime, but she is wide awake. I have disturbed her in the middle of sneaking and listening to her MP3 player when she is supposed to be asleep. She pushes the headphones away from her ears and checks my face to see if I am about to start lecturing. I wish it were as simple as that. "I know you probably don't need me to be your mom now. You have Vicky for that, I guess. But what about as a friend? Do you need me for that?"

We stare at each other and I wait for a response, but she offers none. It's something to think about, to consider, I tell her and then leave her to her clandestine music. I should probably say something about her needing to get to sleep, but it would be hypocritical. I know what it is like when sleep plays games with your mind but won't completely take it over.

An exercise in self-flagellation is what this is. Twice, Vivian has had to intervene and call the session to order. Two of the women insist on sniping at each other, taking digs that cut so deeply even I feel the sting. One of them has committed some imagined offense against the other and she has to pay for her transgression. It is a matter of the strong against the weak, and we all know who the weak one is. I feel a little sorry for the target of the attack, but I feel even more sorry for myself. I'd rather be boiling in a pot of scalding water than made to put up with this shit.

Mary, the predator, narrows her eyes at Tanya, her prey, and points a shaky finger across the circle at her. "What do you think about that?" she challenges. She is of the opinion that Tanya is the lowest of the low, a woman who allowed drug addiction to be more important to her than her own kids. She has just announced that, instead of probation, Tanya should be in prison, rotting away.

Vivian's eyes dart around the group, from face to face, until they land on my mine. I am watching Mary closely and trying to decide if I have the energy to open my mouth and jump into the midst of the discussion. "Helena, you look like you have something to add," she says hopefully.

"I don't," I reply without looking away from Mary. Not yet, anyway. This is our ninth session, and other than the beginning introduction, I don't contribute anything meaningful to the group. I fill a chair and listen, which Vivian knows, but tonight she is hoping that I can help her take the group down another path, away from the violence hovering in the corners of the room.

"I don't think nothing about it," Tanya spits out, glaring at Mary. "I been clean for eight months and I see my kids every week. Ain't nobody in here that don't have something in their past they ain't proud of. Everything the child services folks tell me to do, I do, because I want my kids back."

"Shouldn't have never lost 'em in the first place."

For a second, Tanya looks defeated. She sinks in on herself and stays that way. The rest of us get a chance to see what giving up looks like. Then she draws in a mouthful of air and breathes fire. "Who the fuck are you to tell me about my life, you sanctimonious bitch? You have to be in this goddamn class just like everybody else, and that means your shit stinks, just like everybody else's. You're so quick to jump down my throat about my shit, but I notice you ain't too quick to talk about your own shit. Why the fuck are you here, huh? Where yo' damn kids at?"

"Why are we even talking about kids and shit?" We all turn our heads and look at Liz, the only white woman in the group. She is usually as quiet as I am, but now she is compelled to speak. She searches everyone's faces with her eyebrows raised, waiting for an answer that makes sense to her. "This is supposed to be an anger management class, but all we seem to do is sit around, putting each other down. Especially you, Mary."

"Watch yourself, white girl," Mary growls. Now she is on the hot seat and she doesn't like it. I smile for the first time since I walked through the door nine weeks ago. I like it when kingdoms fall and totalitarianism is overruled. "I'm talking to Tanya, not you."

"That's all you ever do is talk to Tanya, and I may not be black, but it seems to me you need to be concentrating on working out your own issues."

"How about if I work out my issues while I'm kicking your white ass?"

"I'm sensing anger," Vivian jumps in and sounds like an idiot. "Where do you think it's coming from, Mary? What's at the core of it?"

"I'm starting to get angry my damn self," a woman named Justine says, and the tone of her voice makes several of us snicker. She glances at her watch and slants an incriminating look at Vivian. "I got better shit to do than sit around, wasting time listening to Mary pick on people. I could be at home with my kids, 'cause I *know* where they are."

"Fuck you too," Mary tells Justine. "I asked a simple question, and all of you bitches are suddenly jumping on my case?"

"How is the situation with Tanya's kids any of your business?" Liz says.

"It's not," Tanya answers for Mary. "That's the point. It's not."

"Obviously something about the situation makes Mary angry," Vivian suggests evenly. "I think we should explore that. I'd like to go around the circle and have everyone say something constructive to Mary about where they think her anger comes from. Can we do that?"

"All right." Justine shifts in her chair and folds her arms across her chest. "I'm going first. I think Mary's anger has something to do with her own mother." She looks at Mary. "Seems like her own mama was a drug addict or something and she's putting her shit on Tanya. And I got your bitch, bitch."

Mary opens her mouth to object, but Vivian holds up a hand to stop the tirade that she knows is coming. "Wait a minute, Mary. Let's hear everyone out."

"Oh, so now it's jump on Mary time, right?"

"Doesn't feel good, does it?" I mutter.

"Excuse me?"

I am caught up in the simple task of picking invisible balls of lint from my shirtsleeve, and that is why I don't notice that I am the sole object of attention. I look up and run into Liz's curious gaze. If she has been unusually quiet, I have been even more so. She stares at me like it is just occurring to her that I am able to produce sound.

"Did you say something, Helena?"

I look around the circle and see several people scoot to the edge of their chairs, and don't know why. My response is a long time coming, and when I open my mouth I catch myself off guard. I haven't prepared a speech, but a speech is what I give anyway. "I was thinking about what you asked us to do. You wanted us to offer Mary constructive criticism on where we think her anger comes from, and I actually came up with a few plausible theories. Then I decided that I don't really give a shit where her anger stems from. I would be happy if she would just keep it to herself. I'm a little sick of hearing it, to tell you the truth."

"Well," Tanya drawls and snaps her fingers. "Take us to church now."

"Just because you sit your wanna-be-better-than-everybody-else ass over there and don't say shit, don't mean I can't talk. It's a fucking anger management class, genius. You supposed to talk."

"Yeah, but you don't talk. You sling your anger around the room and force all of us to deal with it," I say. "Not the same thing."

"Well, since you so smart, how come you sitting here with the rest of us unevolved sistas?"

"Excuse me, but you just told me I wasn't a sista," Liz points out comically. "So speak for yourself."

"Your ignorance is an embarrassment to me." Oohs and aahs fill the room. I utter fighting words, without meaning to, and start something I will have to finish. Mary is out of her chair and standing over me before I can get to my feet. I lay my head back on my neck and look up into her face. My stare renders her completely still. Her crime is forgery, petty bogus check cashing, and though she's been thrown in jail a time or two, she has no clue. There is a big difference between serving time in the county jail and serving time in prison. I don't think she knows this, but if she breathes on me the wrong way, she will. "You're in my personal space."

"What did you say, church mouse?"

"I said, your ignorance embarrasses me, and then I said you are in my personal space."

"Put me out of your personal space then."

"You don't want me to do that."

"I said I did, didn't I?"

"Yes, but I don't think you know what you're asking me to do. You want me to jeopardize my freedom for you. You consider yourself worth the price I'd have to pay, but you're not, and I think you know it. Which is one of the theories I came up with a few minutes ago— you have no self-worth. That's why you'll always be running around in circles, like a hamster, because you don't have sense enough to jump off the track."

She takes five steps back and spreads her hands. Looks around like she is in a trance and laughs, even though there is nothing funny. The rest of the group accepts that she is about to put on a performance, but the two of us know the truth. She has given me back my personal space in a way that allows her to maintain a fraction of dignity. In my chair, I step back from the ledge and let my muscles relax. I want to snap her neck and can visualize myself doing it—easily.

"Listen to the preacher, everybody," Mary announces. She makes a show of pulling an empty chair into the middle of the circle and folding herself into it loosely, props her head in her palm and stares at me condescendingly. "Go 'head, oh righteous reverend. Educate me."

I look at her long and hard. Take a deep breath and shake my head. "Get off the track, Mary," I say. "Just suck in a mouthful of air and . . . jump."

Every day I run the same distance and go the same route. I leave Vicky's house and take a left, then three more rights, and find myself on a busy main street. Tallahassee Boulevard, it is called, and I huff and pant my way down one block after another, until I am far enough away to consider myself lost. There is a park at my stopping point, and I always pause long enough to watch the joggers on the track there. I always consider crossing the grass and joining them, but I never do. It is a paved track, and I prefer the disorderliness of rough concrete under my feet. Don't want anything to do with something that will order my steps and force me into compliance.

I pause long enough to watch the building too. It is on the other side of the street, a three-story house that has been divided up into apartments. I like the wraparound porch and the cushion-covered chairs sitting on it, the plants lining the railing. I like the old-fashioned screen door and the fancy-looking numbers painted on a wooden plaque by the door. It looks like home and, for the umpteenth time, I debate crossing the street and knocking on the door. There is a FOR RENT sign in one of the windows, and I wonder how the landlord will feel about taking the sign down for a convicted felon.

I don't realize that I have been looking for a place of my own until I see the house and catch myself staring at the sign, hoping it is still there day after day, like it is waiting for me to get up the nerve to come and claim it. I think about my job and the fact that it is temporary. I think about Beige and how she will feel about me moving out. I think about Vicky and wonder if she will co-sign for me if I need her to. I have been locked up for so long that my credit is nothing, a blank page, which is just as bad as it is good.

I think about someone else beating me to the apartment and cross the street.

I am glowing with sweat and wearing shorts and a tee shirt that are more wet than they are dry, but the woman who answers my knock agrees to show me the apartment anyway. She tells me her name is Marlene and that her family has owned the house since before slavery. She comes from a long line of free blacks, has ancestors who were doctors and teachers long before it was the norm. The house is split up into five apartments. She lives in one and rents out the other four, usually to singles and college students. Her husband has been dead eleven years, and the extra income nicely supplements her social security.

By the time we make it to the third floor, I know more about Marlene than I need to, including the fact that she has diabetes and doesn't tackle the stairs very often. She is heavy-set and winded, trudges heavily down the hallway that runs from the front of the house to the back, and pulls a ring of keys from her pocket. There are two doors on the top floor, and one of them is the vacant apartment. The other is a storage closet. She pays her grandson to tend to the yard and the interior upkeep, and he keeps his equipment in there.

Already I like the fact that I will have no close neighbors, no one to run into in the hallway and have to converse with. I like the fact that I will be on the top floor instead of the bottom floor, wedged into a corner and hidden like an eccentric relative.

"Ain't no central air," Marlene says and pushes the door open. She motions for me to go ahead of her and then goes over to the row of windows along the front of the house and raises one. She points as she talks. "Bathroom's over there. That's the kitchen, and you're standing in the living room slash bedroom. This is the smallest apartment in the house 'cause it's really the attic. Space enough for one person though."

"How much?" I love it and I have to have it. The floors are hardwood and have seen their share of traffic. I smell fresh paint on the bare walls and something like bleach coming from the kitchen area, which is small enough to double as a closet. But there is a window on the outside wall, and sunlight will make all the difference. I decide right then and there that I will not hang curtains.

"Three fifty a month, plus the same for the security deposit."

The bathroom is just big enough for me to turn around in a circle. A compact tub and shower combo, a toilet and a sink, and no window. The stove is electric and the refrigerator is half my height, no freezer. But I am in love and it shows on my face as I meet Marlene in the middle of the living room slash bedroom. "I'm Lena," I say, extending a hand to her. "Lena Hunter. Is Friday soon enough for me to bring you the deposit?"

Vicky is stunned when I tell her that I am moving out. She opens her mouth and then shuts it, opens it again and reminds me of a fish up to the tank. "You're sure you're ready for this?" she says, as if I have never lived on my own before. "I mean, you just got out and . . ."

"Been out for almost three months," I say. "I'm ready."

"You know you can stay here as long as you want, don't you? I hope you don't feel like you have to hurry and get out, because you don't."

"I'm not moving across the world, Vicky. Just down the street and around the corner."

"What if I don't want you to leave? You just got here. Damn, I thought we could hang out like we used to and spend some time together."

"We can still do that."

"What about Beige?"

"Like I said, I'm just down the street and around the corner. She won't want to come with me anyway, if that's what you're worried about."

"She might think you're abandoning her again," Vicky says, damn near whispering.

I look at her like she is crazy. I can't believe what she has just said. Don't believe history is so twisted up in her mind that she could fit her mouth around the words, let alone utter them. "Did I willingly abandon her in the first place, Vicky?" She doesn't answer and I keep pushing. "Did I?"

"You know that's not what I meant."

"I don't know shit." Suddenly I am breathing hard and mad as hell. "Oh, wait a minute. I do know a little something. I know she told people I was dead and she didn't have a mother, and you let her. You stood back and let her say that shit. Like what I did was nothing."

"What you did wasn't right, Lena."

"Was it wrong, Vicky?" She looks everywhere but at me. Checks the wall clock for the time, eyes the day's mail spread out on the counter and sees dishes in the sink that need to be loaded into the dishwasher. "Was it one hundred percent wrong?"

"No," she finally hisses at me.

I walk out of the kitchen and leave her sitting there, thinking about what I did and why.

Chapter Seven

Sometimes there is the homemade caramel that Vicky loves so much and sometimes there is cake or brownies still warm from the oven. We have come up with a system for knowing what each treat means. We step into my grandmother's house, sniff the air and know.

"It's brownies." Vicky looks at me with dread on her face, just as my grandmother comes out of the kitchen to meet us at the door. Brownies are my favorite, which means that today it is my turn to keep the peace.

My grandmother fills the doorway and leans out to wave at my mother, who is waiting in the car to receive a signal that we are safely inside. I hear her car drive off, the sound of the lock turning, and feel my grandmother's hand on my shoulder.

"Y'all gone be good girls today?" she asks, looking from me to Vicky. We nod in unison and lean into each other. We will be as good as we can be, but it will not be as easy to do as my grandmother makes it sound.

"Yes, ma'am," we say at the same time.

Satisfied she is in store for a good day, my grandmother wraps her hands around our heads and nudges us toward the kitchen. "Take your coats off and go on in the kitchen. I got some oatmeal on the stove for you. Brownies is for after lunch."

I start to follow Vicky down the hallway, but she catches me by the back of my neck and steers me in another direction. "Not you, Leenie. I need you to do something else for me first. And I got some extra brownies for you to take home with you if you don't cry."

She always says that, but I never take extra brownies home with me, because I always cry.

Music spills out of my apartment and into the hall-way. I approach it slowly, carefully, and frown as I realize it is rap music. The door is standing open, so I walk right in and set the bag I am carrying by the door. Today is move-in day and, as far as I know, I don't have any roommates. No one is supposed to be here.

"Hello?" I call out.

"Almost done," a male voice replies.

It catches me off guard and my step falters as I cross the floor toward the bathroom, where the sound comes from. I step into the room and see him kneeling on the floor, inspecting the toilet. "What are you doing in here?"

"Replacing the toilet."

"No, I mean, what are you doing in here? In my apartment?"

"Replacing the toilet," he says as if I am slow in comprehending. "You must be the new tenant. I'm Aaron."

"Miss Marlene's grandson?"

"Miss Marlene's grandson isn't worth shit, but don't tell her I said that." He rolls to his feet and brushes off his pants. "I'm one floor down, right under you, and I'm who she calls when she can't find him, which is all the damn time. Who are you?"

"Lena." I stare at the hand he offers me until he retracts it and clears his throat uncomfortably. This is how madness starts, borrowing eggs and cups of sugar, knocking on doors at inconvenient times. I don't want to start something that will drive me crazy in the long run, and I don't need any new friends, either.

"Okay," he sings under his breath. He thinks I am strange. I hear it in his voice and see it in his eyes. He is wondering if Miss Marlene has rented an apartment to a mental patient, if he should consider moving. "I guess I'm done here, so I'll get out of your way."

"That would be good."

"Then I will."

"Good." I track his progress to the door and close and lock it as soon as he disappears. He makes me think of abnormal gene pools and mutants, he is so tall and solid. He snatches my voice and causes me to forget basic manners. In a dark alley, he is the hulk who scares the shit out of the unsuspecting woman who is stupid enough to be there in the first place. Standing in the middle of my tiny apartment, he takes up all the space and makes me seem like a dwarf. I feel my power diminishing and I don't like it, won't accept it.

I look around what is now mine and sigh. I have forgotten what it is like to be in close proximity to a man who is not wearing a guard's uniform. Forgotten how I'm supposed to interact with them. And I am in no hurry to relearn what I no longer know.

Beige comes after school lets out. She drops her rolling backpack behind the door and informs me that, since it is Friday, she will be spending the night. I take the cell phone she passes me and use it to call off from work. Then she calls Vicky and tells her that we have some shopping we need to do and we need a ride.

I buy new kitchen and bath towels, four sets each, and a new set of sheets for the bed I don't yet have. Everything else I find in a thrift store, much to Beige's mortification. The two lamps I buy don't match. There is no justification for why I pay hard-earned money for mismatched plates, bowls and glasses, and I don't offer any. I just buy them. I buy an area rug and an iron that I plugged in and burned the tip of my finger on. Someone sets a cast iron skillet down and I pick it up. I find a few more pots and pans and smile when I haven't quite spent fifty dollars.

We are heading to the car when a pickup rolls to a stop and two men hop out. They are almost to the entrance of the thrift store, prepared to drop off the futon they are carrying, when I call out and catch their attention.

"If you're giving that away, can I have it?"

"Oh my God," Beige groans, embarrassed because I have no pride. She slinks into the backseat of the car and hides her face.

I tap on the window and wait for her to lower it. "Pride goeth before a fall," I tell her.

I stop thinking of myself as a victim when I see Yo-Yo. This is the essence of a victim, I think as I stare at her. She is sitting on the shower room floor, with her back to the wall and her legs stretched out in front of her, looking at nothing through open eyes. There is blood everywhere, and she sits in the middle of it, dead.

I wonder if Children's Services might have heeded her request not to allow her youngest child to be adopted if they had known the child was the only reason she lived. Then I think, probably not.

I don't think about all the blood or the razor blade lying on the floor nearby as I drop to my knees beside her and gently close her eyes. I reach up and shut the water off. She is heavy, but I manage to gather her in my arms and pull her close to my chest. I lose all concept of time as I rock her like a baby. All I know is that the water was warm a while ago and now the puddle I sit in is ice cold. Like my heart.

I am shivering as I look up and see a guard standing there. My teeth are chattering around the one word I say: "Help." And then I cry. Hard.

Vicky almost knocks me over as I come through the door. She has been standing behind it, peeking through the peephole, looking out for me. She falls into my arms and pushes her face close to mine, fills my nostrils with the smell of anxiety. "Mama's here," she hisses in my face.

It can't be any later than eight in the morning. Her house is the first stop I make before going to my own apartment to crash. Beige doesn't have school today, and my plan is to drag her out of bed and take her out for breakfast. I don't know if I'm prepared to deal with my mother without food in my belly and energy in my limbs. I am exhausted, and the thought of facing my mother right this minute makes me want to slide to the floor and drop off to sleep.

"When did she get here?"

"Five or six this morning." She looks around as if she is trying to think up someplace to hide me. "Can you do this right now?"

"I don't have a choice, do I?"

"I guess not," she says, grabbing my arm as I push past her. She searches my face for long seconds and then she takes a deep breath. "Just . . . be nice, okay?"

My mother is standing at the kitchen counter adding creamer to a mug of coffee. With her back to me I can see that her hair is nearly all gray, soft looking and curly. The last time I saw her it was more pepper than salt and draping her shoulders. Now it is a short cap on her head, exposing the back of her neck and the beauty mark there. I see her hands fluttering around the mug in front of her. The veins crisscross under her skin, and I know the years have been as long and hard for her as they have been for me.

I see her hands freeze in the air over the mug and know she senses my presence.

"Good morning, Mama," I say because I don't know what else to say.

She gives me her face and stares at me long and hard. Whatever she is looking for, she finds, and then she nods like she is satisfied. "Leenie. What's going on with your hair?"

"Locks. You cut yours off."

"Didn't have no choice." She pats her Afro to give her hands something to do, and then she crosses the kitchen in my direction to give her legs something to do. "Most of it fell out, so I had to do something. Let me see what in the world you did here."

I stand still and let her fingers walk all over my scalp. She takes me back to childhood, to the days of sitting between her knees and having my scalp oiled and my hair braided. I can see myself there, borrowing a few inches from the pillow under my butt, with my arms looped around her calves and a wad of bubble gum in my mouth. Her hands are still soft and warm like heat lamps, and I feel myself blossoming under her touch, opening up like a rosebud.

"Can't comb these things out, can you?" she says, running her fingers through my locks until her hands settle on my shoulders.

"No, ma'am."

I am a child again, unable to maintain eye contact and tearing up under intense scrutiny. I have done something wrong and I know it, and now I am await-ing my punishment. She can scream at me, slap me or knock me to the floor and I will do nothing to defend myself. I will let her do what she wants to do to me be-cause, in doing what I did, I hurt her beyond my own comprehension. I made a decision for which she is sorry but I am not. I cannot be.

She sees my tears, watches me wipe them away with my hands and releases a stream of warm breath in my face. It is the *what am I going to do with you* breath that mothers save for their hardheaded children. "Leenie," she sighs tiredly. "I know you're sorry. I know you didn't mean to do it."

My mother does not see the cringe that takes over my face. She isn't looking for it because she does not expect it. It is there though. She folds me into her arms, and every second that I am there my arms tighten around her and a war rages inside of me. I know I should let her have this one thing, but I can't. It is a lie, and eight years in prison have forced me to look at all the lies in my life and vow to tell the truth from here on out. I can't be tried twice for the same crime, not even by my own mother.

"I love you, Mama," I say close to her ear, praying she accepts my words and leaves *sorry* out of this moment.

But she doesn't. "I love you too, Leenie. And I'm try-ing real hard to forget what you did. I want you to know that. I don't hate you, okay? I know you're sorry."

I pull away slowly and catch her eyes, shaking my head like I am in a trance. I need her to understand, need her to finally ask me why. We have never done that, talked about why. "I'm sorry I hurt you, Mama, but I'm not sorry about what I did."

She cannot handle my truth, and she leaves the kitchen to get away from it. I let her go because if she can't handle it, then I don't know what else we have to talk about.

Vicky is furious with me. She lurks in the shadows of the hallway, watching what she expects to be a Walton family reunion, but things haven't quite turned out the way she wanted. As soon as my mother takes off down the hallway, she walks up behind me and pushes me across the kitchen, deeper into the room, so we can have it out.

"What the fuck was that?" she demands, ready to slap the shit out of me.

"She wants me to lie and I can't do it."

"You can't pretend to be sorry for doing the crazy shit you did for five minutes, Lena?" She paces the floor and shakes her hands like her nails are wet and she wants them to dry faster. "All you had to do was keep your mouth closed and quit trying to be a superhero."

"Excuse me?" My eyebrows shoot up and my mouth drops open. "A superhero? Superheroes don't get caught, Vicky. They don't go to prison. But then again, they don't kill innocent people and neither did I, so I might just be a damn superhero. You know what this shit is about, so don't come at me like that. She can pretend she doesn't know, but you don't have that luxury and you know it."

"Yes, I know what this shit is about, but nobody asked you to take the law into your own hands, Lena. Nobody told you to go running over there with a gun. You made that decision on your own."

"And what was I supposed to do? Keep being a good girl, like you?"

"What happened was in the past." Vicky sinks down in a chair and covers her face, shakes her head. "You don't know what this shit has done to her. You weren't the one who had to see how this affected her. Her hair falling out was just the beginning."

"Making Mama's hair fall out was the last thing I was concerned with," I say and mean it.

"Seems like you were only concerned with yourself, Leenie." My childhood nickname falls from her lips with traces of venom hugging the first and last letters.

I feel the venom sting my skin and convince myself that I hate her. I hate her for saying what she is saying to me, but most of all, I hate her for being so weak. She has always been weak. "You know what? I don't need this shit from you. I don't need you to tell me about the rights and wrongs of what I did, because I already know about them. I had eight years to figure the shit out for myself. Been living with the consequences and surviving on my own all this time, so fuck you, okay?"

"You took a life. You didn't have to take things that far. They didn't need to go that far."

"God . . . I can't believe after all these years you're still as blind and clueless as you were when we were kids. Ignorance is not bliss, Vicky."

"There were other ways . . ."

"You never thought about it?" I say, cutting her off. My voice drops down to the bottom and I sound like Satan whispering in Eve's ear. I ease over to the table and sit next to her. She wants to look away from me, but she can't because I won't let her. "You never thought about grabbing a knife and hiding it in your clothes somewhere? Taking it with you when you had to go in the room? It never crossed your mind that you could stop those hands from touching you and keep that mouth off of you? You never thought about standing up for yourself?"

"You know I did. We talked about it," she confesses softly. "We used to plan what we would do."

"And then we'd go there and be good girls. Good little wimps. We didn't stand up for ourselves and we didn't tell anybody, we were so damn afraid of what would happen. I couldn't let that happen again. Don't act like you don't know what was at stake, Vicky."

"I never said I didn't. I just don't think you did."

"Maybe not." I can't sit any longer, so I stand. The counter digs into my back as I fall back against it, but the pain is nothing in the broad scheme of things. It is like a bee sting and I know what a battering ram feels like. "I lost Beige. I lost Mama. Lost myself and then I lost you."

"I supported you," she says, and I can see that she truly believes it. "I took Beige and loved her like you did, and I still do. I love her so much, Leenie. I missed you so much, but I had her, and she reminds me so much of you. I made sure you had money for the things you needed too. I didn't know what else to do for you."

"I needed you."

"I was there."

"But you never came." This is what hurts me the most. "Eight years I sat there and waited for you to come and you never did. The one person who knew my heart better than anybody else and you never came. I waited and waited, and every day I died a little more inside. I needed you to come and tell me you understood."

"How was I supposed to face you? How was I supposed to look you in the face and not feel like shit? I'm the oldest. I'm your big sister and I was supposed to protect you, but I didn't. If I had done my job maybe I could've saved you. It's my fault you had to do what you did." She lays her head on the table and cries.

A shifting of light catches my eye and I look up at the doorway. There is Beige, and she is crying too. I don't consider going to her and trying to comfort her because I am too busy wondering how much she heard. And how much she remembers.

***

I don't know enough to think it feels good or even that it should. In normal, healthy relationships maybe it does. But here in this room, it feels like a thousand snakes slithering all over my skin. They wiggle into my ears and into my eyes, fill my mouth and steal my voice. My lips are frozen into a perfect circle, but no sound comes out.

Being a good girl means saying nothing as I am violated again and again. As I am taught to do things I have no business knowing how to do. I can give pleasure with my mouth and with my hands. I can produce sounds like the women in the nasty videos I watch, can make believe that what is happening to me feels like heaven, when it really feels like hell.

I will learn, years later, that what we are doing now is called a sixty-nine. That many women enjoy the feel of a wet mouth on their breasts and between their thighs. I will know that sex is not filthy and sickening, something to be dreaded. Something to make me vomit for hours afterward. But I don't know this now.

I don't know anything except what I am told to do and I do it. Like a good girl.

I write a report for school and the assignment is to tell about something people don't know about me. It is supposed to be a fun assignment, a way to learn about my classmates and for them to learn about me. But I wonder what my teacher's reaction will be if I write that I know what oral sex is, if I write that nothing about it is fun.

I wonder if there will be any other kids who will admit to knowing the same. Other than Vicky, that is. I am dying to know if we are the only ones.

***

Isolde takes the certificate of completion that I pass her and smiles. She reads it in its entirety, then she sets it aside, reminding herself to make a copy for my file before I leave. She thinks I will take the original home and frame it. Has no idea that it will be in the trash before I can leave the building.

"I'm so proud of you, Helena," she tells me as if I should care. "It's been, what, six months? And you've accomplished so much."

"You received the results of my mental health evaluation?"

She nods. "No treatment was indicated, which is good. The only thing left for you to work on is getting your GED. Do you still have the information I gave you?"

"No, but I do have these." The next thing I pass across the desk is a manila folder. She still doubts that I am who I say I am, so I have brought her proof. In the folder are the degrees I earned, plus my high school diploma. I think about taking it from her and shoving it in her mouth, literally making her eat her words.

Isolde takes a long time looking at the papers in front of her. She scans my degrees like she has never seen degrees before. Then she drops the folder on the desktop and scrubs her hands across her face. She searches my face and I think I see water in her eyes where there was none before.

"It's just such a damn shame," she finally says.

He is not as tall and frightening as I first thought. Since it is me approaching him and not him approaching me, I am able to see clearly. And what I see is this: He is just a man. Intimidating hulks, I can't deal with. When he opens the door and sees me standing there and I see him, I know I can deal with him.

"You left these in my apartment," I say, thrusting his tools at him. "Kept waiting for you to come and get them, but you never did, so I brought them to you."

He takes the tools and cracks a smile. "You thought I was coming back up there? After the way you threw me out the first time? I don't think so. I did miss these though."

"Well, you've got them back now."

"Be right back," he says and clears my line of vision.

While he is gone from the doorway, I look around his apartment and notice how much more spacious it is than mine. Then I remember that my apartment is a converted attic and his is not. His living room is my entire apartment, and he has very little furniture: a sofa and loveseat and a coffee table, two floor lamps and an area rug. Everything color coordinates and makes the other thing taking up space in the room stand out even more.

I stare at it in awe, feeling my mouth water and my fingers itch to stroke it. At the same time, I miss what it can give me the way I miss a medium rare steak from time to time. The way I miss country fried chicken and greasy gravy, because I gave up meat years ago and took up working out. I swallow because there is too much moisture in my mouth and force myself to look away from it.

"You lift?" he says, coming out of the kitchen and noticing the direction and intensity of my gaze.

"I used to. That thing would probably swallow me whole." I am rooted to the spot, staring. He laughs and motions me inside.

"You can take a closer look if you want to. I don't think it bites." Hesitation is all over my face and he sees it. "I don't either."

I am like a child on Christmas morning, touching everything at once. I tell myself not to do it, but I still sit on the bench and lift a free weight. I still release a shuddering breath of satisfaction as I feel my bicep making its presence known. "That feels so damn good," I say before I can stop myself. I take the weight up and over my head, do a full set and then dance with embarrassment. I have gotten entirely too comfortable. "Sorry."

"No problem. Looked like you were enjoying yourself. How much do you press?"

"Used to be a hundred solid, but it's been so long since I did it that it has to be less now. Too damn long." Something like a whine wants to come out of my mouth, but I don't let it. I hop up from the bench and look everywhere but at him. "I should go. I'll be late for work if I don't leave right now."

"You want to take a weight with you?"

He makes me smile. "Thanks anyway. And thanks for letting me drool."

"Anytime."

He walks me to the door and I take one last look around. One last look at his face before I take off down the hallway and disappear down the stairs. I join the group already waiting at the bus stop and remember that his name is Aaron.

Chapter Eight

My new cellmate is a woman named Patty, and I know immediately that she does not want to live with me. She is white, newly transplanted from the South, and very afraid of that which she does not understand. I am black, not in the mood to be bothered, and ready to drive her crazy. It is something I cannot help, my behavior, and I think I am channeling Yo-Yo.

Prison makes me territorial without even realizing it. One side of the cell is mine and the other, hers. I claim the bottom bunk and force her to fall asleep staring at the ceiling. I take the dinner roll from her tray and make her wipe her hands on her scrubs because the napkins belong to me. I don't ask her anything about herself and I make her repeat herself three times before I respond when she speaks to me, which is not often.

I tell myself I am angry with her because she is a white woman, daring to be prejudiced in a place where she wears the same shackles that I do. But the truth lives in me, in a deep, dark cave that I have forgotten how to access. I don't hold her ignorance against her, because she cannot take something from me that I will not give her. It is much more basic than that, much more simple.

I am angry with her because her newness makes me remember what I have forgotten. She is in genuine distress when she sees that working in the laundry

room makes her hands crack and peel. The stress of
four walls and not enough space to pass gas in private
causes her to bite her nails to the quick. And before
long she gives up the habit of treating her hair to a
hundred brush strokes at lights out. It doesn't matter
anyway because the shampoo they give us is as watery
as baby piss and does not lather worth a damn.

I am angry with her because she reminds me that I
used to be a woman. Before I became an animal, I was
a woman. She hasn't yet shed the skin of the outside,
though it shrivels a little more every day, and I am impatient for the transformation to be complete. Twice,
she has been run off to our cell, trembling and crying,
by one bully or another, and I can only watch as she is
broken down. After the first time, I feel sorry for her.
After the second, I know what I have to do.

She never hears me leave my bunk and hoist myself
onto hers. The scrape of contraband, sharp and lethal,
is what snaps her eyes open and fastens them onto
mine. We stare at each other, upside-down. My face is
so close to hers that I smell her fear, right along with
the scent of hot urine leaving her bladder. It makes me
smile.

"Listen to me, bitch," I whisper to her soothingly.
"I don't want your ass in here anymore than you want
to be in here. But I'm all about making the best of the
situation, so here's what we're going to do. You listening?" I pause and wait for her to shake her head, but I
don't ease the pressure of the switchblade that I have
pressed against her neck. She tries to shake her head
and winces as she is nicked. "Good. Now, the first
thing you should know is that there are rules that have
to be followed, no matter what. Rule number one is,
don't touch my shit. Okay? Rule number two is, don't
fucking touch my shit, right? And rule number three

is, don't even fucking *think about* touching my shit.
You got it?" She doesn't dare risk nodding, but I smell
agreement seeping out of her pores.

I use her shirt to clean her blood from my switchblade and tell her, "Touch my shit again and I'ma cut
your fucking throat. You ain't nothing in here, so you
better hurry up and get used to it."

I fall asleep feeling good about myself. She cries herself to sleep, and I know I have helped her in the only
way I know how. She cannot be a woman in this place.
It won't let her be, and the sooner she knows it, the better. She will either kill herself or she will succumb and
become an animal. The choice is hers.

"You keep this up and we're going to have problems,"
Aaron says as soon as I open the door and find him on
the other side. He leans there and smiles engagingly.
Looks over my head, into my space, and sucks in a
deep breath. "My mother is from the South, and she
can cook her ass off. Judging from the smells coming
through my vents, you can too. You have to either cut
it out or feed me. Either way, I'm not leaving until you
tell me which it's going to be." I lift the bowl I'm holding and bring a forkful of vegetables to my mouth and
hold his eyes as I chew slowly. He laughs and shakes
his head. "You ain't right."

"I'm not trying to be," I say and leave him standing in
the doorway. I hear the door close and then he finds me
in the kitchen that isn't really a kitchen. "It's just brown
rice and steamed vegetables in a Creole sauce." I start
to fill a bowl, think better of it, and reach for a plate.

"Whatever it is smells good as hell, and beggars can't
be choosy." He helps himself to a fork from the dish
drain and takes his plate over to the futon. The televi-

sion is on, and he sits back to eat and watch it. There is no place else to sit, so I move to the other end of the futon and perch on the edge.

He eats like he is starving, pausing every few seconds to make an appreciative sound and to shake his head as if he is having a silent conversation with himself. It's funny to watch and I laugh. "Were you hungry?"

"Hungry isn't the word," he says. "Been up all night working on a story. Think the last time I ate was sometime yesterday afternoon. I forget food exists when I'm in my zone."

"You're a writer?"

"Columnist." He waits for recognition to light my face but it doesn't. "I write a column for a local newspaper. The *Sentinel*. You ever read the business commentary section?"

"I've never read the *Sentinel*."

Aaron looks at me like I am crazy. "Woman, where have you been?"

I almost tell him where I've been, and then I catch myself. I reach for his empty plate and take it to the kitchen. "You been doing that long? Writing?"

"As long as I can remember. Been with the *Sentinel* for six years now, but I'm thinking it might be time for a change."

"Another newspaper?" I hand him a bottle of water and sit down again.

"Another type of writing. I'm playing around with an idea for a novel, but then again, who isn't?"

"I'm not," I say. "What do you want to write about?"

"That's the thing—I don't know yet. I just know I want to write about something. Maybe science fiction or true crime. I'm still figuring it out. What about you, what do you do?"

"Squeeze cream into snack cakes," I say sarcastically. It is easier than being embarrassed, which is an emotion I have little time for. "I'm on a temporary assignment at the Snack-Rite factory."

"You like it?"

"I hate it."

"So quit. Find something else."

"It's not that simple. I'm working on it though. I know a little something about computers, and I'm hoping I can make something happen with that. I'd be happy if I could get a job that allows me to just look at them all day."

"Don't tell me you're a computer geek," he teases.

"Nothing but. I used to do it all—build them, take them apart, graphic design, whatever. Now I'm in charge of sticky goo and fake Twinkies."

"It's never too late to make a change."

I look at him long and hard. "Sometimes it is too late."

He tells me more about himself. That he grew up in Mississippi and was a registered nurse for nine years before deciding that journalism was his true calling. He wasted three years, he says, at a smaller newspaper and then he moved here to take the job at the *Sentinel*. I tell him that I will get a newspaper as soon as I can and check out his column.

I tell him as little as possible about me. That I recently moved to the city and that my sister lives nearby. He doesn't press for more information, and I am relieved. I haven't taken the time to think up stories to fill in the blank spaces in my life. Haven't needed to until now, and I think that if it is not him who asks questions, it will be someone else, somewhere down the line.

I need to have plausible answers ready.

I start to relax and get into the conversation. Then Aaron reaches out and touches my hair. I freeze and stare at him. "How long have you been growing your locks?"

"Almost four years." I can't take the invasion of my personal space any longer and I lean away from him. "Please don't."

"I like the shells," he says as his hand retreats.

"Thanks."

"So . . . I should go." He stands and stretches like a panther. "Thanks for breakfast. I think I can sleep now."

"I'm not looking for a man," I blurt out and take him by surprise. "A boyfriend, I mean. I'm not looking for that."

"Okay."

"Just thought you should know."

"I didn't ask, but if you thought I should know . . ."

"You touched my hair."

"Is that secret code for asking you to be my girl-friend? Because if it is, I didn't know."

"I'm just saying," I say, starting to feel silly. He is watching me like he thinks I might be developmentally delayed, and I am not helping my case. "I don't want any problems with you."

"What kinds of problems?"

"Just . . . problems."

"No problems here. Except for when you cook." Aaron laughs. "I can't be responsible for my actions then."

"I'll make you a plate and leave it outside the door."

"Cool. I'll let you lift when you want to."

"Promise?" Instantly my eyes are liquid and plead-ing. He hits me where it hurts and I think he knows it. He sees the raw yearning on my face that I don't try to hide, that I cannot hide, and knows we have struck a deal. I am already planning tomorrow's menu.

"Fish," I say. "Tomorrow."

"Fried?"

"Baked."

"Whiting?"

"Orange roughy."

"Damn, you make it hard for a brotha. Did I mention that I also own a Bowflex?"

I lay my head back and laugh.

Vicky is the worst kind of backseat driver imaginable. All I have to do is blink and she is screeching like a banshee and working my nerves. I remember that she is the one who taught me how to drive years ago and that I swore I would never ask her to teach me anything again, ever. I don't know how I managed to forget and let her talk me into getting behind the wheel of her car. She is even getting on Beige's nerves, and we share exasperated looks in the rearview mirror every few minutes.

"I can't concentrate with you screaming like a damn fool," I say as I ease to a stop at a red light. "Please shut the fuck up or else take the wheel yourself." We are on our way to my mother's house, to get the things she has that belong to me, and we are still a couple of hours away. I don't think I can last that long.

Beige snickers and earns herself a roll of the eyes. "These interstate cops don't play around, Leenie. You need to pay attention to the speed limit. That's all we need is to get pulled over and you don't even have a license."

"I have my learner's permit and there's a licensed driver in the car with me. Everything is under control. Did you forget that I have driven a car before, Vicky?"

"Things have changed since the last time you drove. People drive crazy these days."

"I know about crazy, so just relax. Take a nap or something."

"A nap?" Her voice is suddenly soprano and it makes my head hurt. She is such a drama queen. "That's your idea of a joke, right? I go to sleep and wake up and we're in Florida somewhere."

"Florida is back the other way," I remind her.

"My point exactly."

We stop at a service station to use the restroom and fill up on snacks for the road. Beige and I leave the mini-mart at the same time, carrying tall sodas and bags of sour cream and onion chips. She waits until Vicky goes to the restroom and then parks her lips close to my ear.

"Do you think we'd get in trouble if we threw her out of the car and left her stranded on the side of the road? She could hitchhike to Grandma's house, couldn't she?"

I almost choke on a swig of soda. "The Lord doesn't like ugly, Beige." But I am seriously considering her question. We could possibly make it work.

"The Lord doesn't have to ride in a car with her. Who's driving the U-Haul truck back?"

"She doesn't know it yet, but I am."

"Well then, I'm riding back with you." We both stare at the restroom door through narrowed eyes. She wishes she were Samantha Stevens so she could wiggle her nose and zap Vicky back home, and I wish I were Jeannie, so I could banish her to a bottle for the remainder of the trip.

"We could stuff her in the trunk," I suggest playfully.

"We'd still be able to hear her through the seats though."

"You've got a point."

***

Stella is a mess, I think as I listen to her talk non-stop. She manages to sound serious as a heart attack as she is talking much shit and making me laugh until my sides hurt. I wonder why she hasn't made it big as a stand-up comedienne, she is that funny. I suck in mouthfuls of second-hand smoke as I throw my head back and howl like an idiot the entire time it takes us to reach our destination.

The bond of prison time has glued itself between us, so we have become something like friends. With her, I will go into the ladies restroom and outside to keep her company while she kills herself, one cigarette at a time. We don't go deep with each other, don't talk about our past lives, and I still don't know what her crime is. She doesn't question me about my crime, and the absence of this information, on both of our parts, keeps our friendship superficial and comfortable. It is all I'm equipped to deal with right now.

She owns a beat-up pickup truck that is on its last leg but that she swears runs like a top. I don't argue with her as I crawl across the bench seat and unfold myself on the passenger side. I have done it so many times that it is no longer awkward but slightly funny. I ride home from work with her every morning, and sometimes we stop for breakfast or to do some shopping. She reminds me of Yo-Yo, and I can be myself with her.

This morning she is not taking me straight home though. Somehow she has talked me into coming along with her to have her future predicted. There is a psychic in town, one she heard about on the radio, of all places, and she is eager to know what the woman will tell her. I agree to go along just in case she learns something that messes her up so badly that she needs me to take control of her piece of shit truck and drive her home.

We pull up just in time to see a woman rushing out of the house, crying uncontrollably, and we take a second to look at each other.

"What the hell is that about?" Stella wonders out loud.

"Maybe she just found out her husband is leaving her," I speculate.

"Shit." She flaps a hand. "She should be scratching her ass and thanking whatever the hell god she believes in. That's good news, if you ask me."

"I don't think she asked you."

"Remind me to tell you to kiss my ass when we leave out of here, okay?"

"First thing."

Inside the house, the living room has been converted into a waiting area. Stella gives her name to a teenage girl who looks like she should be in school and takes a seat next to an anxious-looking woman with a fidgeting toddler on her lap. I sit in the middle of a row of empty chairs and dig the business commentary section out of my bag, settle in for a long wait.

"Lucky," Stella snaps. I look up and see her pointing to the empty chair next to her. I roll my eyes and slink over to her. "Eat this and act like you have some sense." She takes an orange from her purse and pushes it in my hands.

"You act like we're in church or something."

"This is a sacred place."

"*Pfft*, this is a con game gone horribly wrong. Can't believe you're spending money on this shit. When we leave, I got a bridge I want to show you. You might want to buy it and I'll give you a good deal." I break off a section of orange and pop it in my mouth, wink at her when she scowls at me.

"Keep playing with the spirits, if you bad."

"What's going to happen? Madam Sula's coming out here to put a hex on me?"

She doesn't have time to answer me because we are interrupted by the woman of the hour and we stare for long seconds. Stella's psychic is round like a statue of Buddha and dark like my television remote. Her hair flows down her back and over her shoulders like water. She wears the ugliest muu muu I've ever seen, which is cause enough to stare, but what catches my attention are her eyes. They are almost translucent, a light gray color, and focused on my face.

"Who is talking about me?" she asks, but she already knows.

I am pinned to my chair, convicted. And Stella gambles with her life. "She is," she says, pointing at me. "But I got a feeling you already knew that."

"Are you here for a reading?" the woman asks me.

"No, she is." It is my turn to point.

"Come with me," she orders me and like a fool, I go.

I follow her into her inner sanctum, sit in a straight-backed wooden chair that isn't designed for comfort when she waves her hand and tells me I should do so, and watch her carefully. The room is cold, unnaturally so, and I find myself balling one hand around the other and stuffing them between my thighs. The tips of my fingers are freezing and so is my nose.

"You don't believe in heat?" I ask, meaning to sound like a bitch and pulling it off quite nicely.

"Circles, not squares," she says. She sits across from me at a wooden table and tunes me out while she prays. I wait impatiently, and she finally opens her eyes on my face. "Never squares again. Am I right?"

"No, no squares. I mean, yes, you're right." I have vowed never again to be forced into the middle of a square, with no way out. I nod my head and give her one bonus point.

"Circles don't have corners, where you can be trapped, but circles go on forever. You could find yourself running around in circles, if you're not careful."

"Where are you going with this?"

"Where do you want me to go? You want me to tell you about your grandmother? If her soul is burning in hell?"

"I already know it is."

Voodoo woman shuffles a deck of tarot cards and slaps them down on the table like she is dealing blackjack. "Usually I have to use these at some point, to give my clients the most accurate reading possible. Plus, it makes them feel like something is really happening out here when what is going on up here is what it's really about." She taps her temple with a curled finger. "But I don't feel like I need to use these with you. I can read you like a book."

"The cards are for show, just like that crystal ball over there. And where did you manage to buy a degree in metaphysical science?" It is framed and hanging on the wall behind her, directly in my line of vision. I squint and try to make out the name of the college or university, but I can't make the words jump off the paper and meet me halfway.

"Same place I bought the tarot cards, where else? Who is Victoria?"

"My sister."

"And Beige?"

She pronounces my daughter's name wrong, like the first syllable of the bread roll with a hole in the middle of it. Baygue. "Beige," I sound it out for her. "My daughter."

"I want you to listen to me, all right? Because as sure as your sister's name is Victoria and your mother's name is Ellen,"—she sees my eyes widen and smiles, but does not pause—"I can read you. I know what you did and I know why you did it. There is one who doesn't know though, isn't there?"

"Tell me something I don't know. Convince me you're not a con artist and tell me something I don't know." But I am already convinced. I don't like this woman's aura, don't like the way her eyes seem to light up in her face. She scares the shit out of me, and I don't like feeling scared.

"Did you know your grandmama is here with you right now?"

I suck in a breath. Just like that, there are tears in my eyes and rage on my face. "Go to hell."

"You wear her like a cloak. Everywhere you go, she goes, because you take her with you. She let you go a long time ago, but you can't do the same for her. You need to ask yourself why . . . Leenie."

"Don't call me that."

"Can I call you Lucky?"

"No. If she's here, ask her why she did it."

"She says she doesn't know."

"She's lying." My voice is hot and hard, sharp like a razor and shaky like an earthquake. I think about lunging across the table and taking voodoo woman down. She is the closest target and the one who speaks complete and total bullshit to me. "Ask her how she could do that to me."

"She says you should let her go." She pauses to listen to voices that I cannot hear, looks like she is allowing something or someone to whisper in her ear. "Something about being trapped right along with you. Set her free and set yourself free at the same time."

"Is she in hell?" I need her to be in hell, need to know she is suffering.

"You are."

"You don't know shit about me."

"You turned out all right."

"What?"

"That's what she says, that you turned out all right. She says she has watched over you through your hell. Now she needs you to let her go, so she can go through hers."

"Whatever," I spit out, leaning toward her aggressively. "What the fuck ever, okay? Is she in hell? That's all I need you to tell me."

"She comes to me in black and she is anguished. In pain. Her soul has been requested in hell, but you won't let her go."

The door flies open and slams against the wall, announcing the fact that I am done being bamboozled and hoodwinked. I snatch my bag from the chair that I will never sit in again and damn near trip over Stella's legs as I march to the door. "Let's go," I snap.

"I still gotta get my reading," Stella protests.

I give her a look that has her following me out the door like she is hypnotized and I am the only one who can snap my fingers and bring her out of it.

"You know you ain't right, Lucky," she says, hopping up into the driver's seat and rolling her eyes in my direction. "I was gone ask that bitch for some winning lottery numbers."

I don't say anything and she pulls out into the street, a speed demon pushing the truck to the limit. Taking out her disappointment on a fifteen-year-old Chevy that has done nothing to deserve the abuse. She leaves me alone though, knows I cannot take anymore. That I am struggling against becoming like the woman we saw earlier and struggling hard.

We only make it two blocks down and one block over and then I give in. I fist my hands in my locks and push my chin into my chest. Scream at the top of my lungs and rock myself. Then I let the tears come. I cry until there is saliva down the front of my shirt and snot dripping from my nose into my mouth. I make savage noises because I am angry and feeling violent and then I scream again.

The loss of control frightens me in a way that I haven't been frightened in a long time. It isn't that I have never cried like this before, because I have. And that is precisely it. I am frightened because of what happened the last time I cried the way I am crying now. History could very easily repeat itself.

Stella doesn't know what to do with me, so she does the only thing she can think of doing. She knows who and what I am, knows that if she does anything more I will not accept it.

She pulls the truck to the curb and lays a warm hand on my back.

"Aw, Lucky," she says as if I have just broken the code. I am not as together as I have led her to believe.

Chapter Nine

Slumber parties are for children and silly teenage girls who think they have secret business to attend to after grown-ups are asleep. I have never cared for them, have never willingly been to one. Not once in my entire life. I think about Madonna and wonder how many young girls use the event as an excuse to satisfy sexual curiosity, exactly how far curiosity takes them before sexual orientation kicks in. I relive being corralled with hundreds of women at once, a perpetual slumber party, a feast for the senses and death for the soul. I know exactly how far motive, means and opportunity can push a person.

Beige is a typical teenager, wanting to order pizza and indulge in buttery microwave popcorn as we watch one rented movie after another. We let out the futon and lay on our stomachs, pushing the popcorn bowl back and forth, and I tell her three different times that I'm sure I don't want a slice of pepperoni pizza. She cannot conceive of not eating meat, of not tearing into flesh and loving every minute of it. She teases me about what I am missing, and I educate her on clogged arteries and insane cholesterol levels. She aims the remote at the television and adjusts the volume to tune out the lesson.

I listen to the way her personality has evolved as she kneels behind me and plays in my locks, her mouth going a mile a minute. There is a boy she likes but she isn't sure if he likes her. She has kissed another boy once, on the mouth, and she doesn't know if she appreciates the feel of human tongue in her mouth. She doesn't hate it, she just doesn't know if she appreciates it. She is considering studying drama and becoming an actress. Otherwise, she wants to be a dancer.

Beige giggles like the little girl I once knew as she whispers that she can't dance worth crap. Then she comes up with a brilliant idea. "I brought Vicky's makeup bag with me," she says, hopping off the futon and racing across the floor to her overnight bag. "Let's make each other's faces up."

I look at her and silently quiz her. Does she remember that I am her mother? That I am pushing forty and not fifteen? Does she feel that I love her so much I can smell it, thick in my nostrils? The desire to be a mother again is like undigested food, stuffed inside my intestines and adding ten extra pounds. It won't be eliminated because it is not waste, but I can't absorb its healing properties either. I notice that she calls Vicky *Vicky* and not *Mom,* but I don't point it out.

She slathers my lips with gloss called Red Hot Seduction, and I frown as I inspect her handiwork in the bathroom mirror. It is not my color, and she has neglected to apply lip liner first, before painting me up like a two-dollar whore. I scrub at her artwork with a wad of toilet paper and reach for the makeup bag. I spy a razor blade and pull it out.

"You can't start painting on all that gunk without laying the foundation," I say to my daughter in the mirror. She watches me arch my eyebrows like a pro, like I have been doing it every day for the last eight years. If she knew what I can really do with a razor blade, she would run like hell.

"Oh, you have to do mine next," she whines prettily and her reflection is gorgeous. "I hate this unibrow thing. Can you cut it off for me?"

I finish with my brows and then I sit her on the toilet seat and do hers. I show her how to apply skin cleanser to her face, how to let the tingle of pores emptying stimulate her senses, and then I talk to her about patting her skin dry, instead of rubbing it. I go through all the motions with her—moisturizer, a light blending of foundation and then translucent dusting powder to set her makeup. I pencil in the outline of her heart-shaped lips and blend two colors until they are shimmery and gold tinted.

She nearly faints when she sees what I have done with her eyes. I watch her watch herself in the mirror and laugh, shaking my head. "You played dress up all the time when you were little," I say softly. "Used to dance around the house like a little diva. Had so much blusher on, it was crazy."

Her eyes swerve over to mine in the mirror and lock. "You still do the best lips. Make your face up for me."

Vicky is a shade or two lighter than I am, somewhere around butter, where I am coffee with creamer. Medium brown. She has occasional acne in her T-zone, and foundation creates the illusion of flawless skin. For me, good health and the consumption of plenty of water means I have no need for illusions. I add liner and earth tone shadows to my eyes, stroke mascara on my lashes and take the longest time with my lips. When I am done, Beige and I have matching pie holes. I step back and look at the stranger staring back at me in the mirror. I try to remember who she is and where I know her from, but can't.

Beige moves up beside me and stares. "I remember you," she says.

I take my first hug from her since I have been home.
I pull her into my arms and hug her so tightly that she
struggles to breathe. She wraps her arms around my
waist and pushes her face into my neck. I don't care
about the makeup she is smearing onto my nightgown,
don't care that it probably won't wash out. All I care
about is that she is touching me and not flinching. That
she is pulling my scent into her nostrils and feeling me
do the same.

"I remember you too," I say and kiss the side of her
face.

We do hair next. I sit her between my thighs and do
cornrows across her scalp, send her to the bathroom
to shriek and coo at herself in the mirror. She tells me
that I have created a work of art on her head, and my
fingers cosign with her. Then she fiddles with my locks
until they are twisted together against my scalp in a
complicated-looking contraption that I think I like.

On her toes she puts nail polish called Mango Fe-
ver, and for mine I choose Tiki Punch. I paint her
fingernails after I give her a manicure, and then I shift
around impatiently when it is her turn to shape and
buff and polish for me. We put another movie on and
blow our nails as we watch, sitting close together on
the floor.

She falls asleep before I do, pushing her freshly
cleansed face deep into the pillow and her knee deep
into my back. She has always slept like a hurricane, no
telling where she will land or how much devastation
she will leave in her wake. I scoot closer to the edge of
the futon and hope I won't have to scoot any more. But
the night is long and the probability that I will wake up
on the floor is strong.

Just before I start falling asleep, I start to feel something I haven't felt in a long time. It taunts and teases

me, this feeling, and for the longest time I can't grab hold to it and make it be still long enough for me to see what it is. I watch it flutter around the room, land on my skin, and then dance away again. It pisses me off that it can be so cruel, and I curse it under my breath. Then it finally settles around me, and I realize that I don't want it after all.

This is when I start to feel like a woman.

My phone hardly ever rings, and when it does it's usually Vicky or Beige, so the unfamiliar voice on the other end throws me off balance. It is male.

"Lena?"

"Yes," I snap. "Who is this?"

"Aaron. I need you to get down here quick."

I look at the clock and curse like a sailor. He laughs. "It's eight o'clock in the morning and I just laid down. What the hell is it?"

"There's been a death in the family. Come now."

I am looking a mess, and he whistles under his breath when he sees me on the other side of his door. I am wearing my nightgown with a pair of jeans pulled on underneath it and no shoes, locks all over the place and pre-sleep crud in the corners of my eyes. Breath kicking like Van Damme. I push past him into his world and look for dead bodies. "I know some places you can hide a body and buy yourself some time," I say, only halfass joking.

Aaron lays his head back and cracks up. "Not that kind of death, but damn, are you serious?"

"Shit yeah. Out by the freeway. Who the hell died, and why do I give a damn?"

"That's cold, Lena." He closes the door and locks it, checking out my sleepwear. Thousands of little pink flowers greet him, and possibly my nipples, too. "I think Sophia is dead."

"Who?"

"Sophia."

"And you got me out of bed because you *think* she's dead? You don't know for sure, you just *think*." I pause and think about what I'm saying. I'm about to get riled up about a possible death and I don't have all the facts. "Who in the hell is Sophia?"

"My computer." He is barefoot too, and the soles of his feet kiss hardwood noisily as he crosses his living room, motioning for me to follow. He leads me to the second bedroom, his home office, and points accusingly at the archaic machine set up across the room. "She's dead."

Even from where I'm standing I can see that Sophia is old and tired. Once upon a time she was top of the line, but now she is about to cross the line into extinction. She is so old that she has wrinkles and age spots, but there is something regal about her. She deserves respect.

I approach her slowly, reverently. I am a third of the way in love. "They don't make these babies anymore. Where did you find her?" I stroke the ridiculously large monitor and then I push a few letters on the keyboard.

"My first computer. The love of my life. Had her for I don't know how many years. Can you save her?"

"Might need to call the morgue," I say. But I am pulling up a chair. "She sign a DNR order?"

"You're funny."

"And you're a sentimental fool. How many overhauls has she had?"

He shrugs, trying to think up a lie. "Two, three." Then, "I don't know, ten?"

"Tell me what she was doing before she died."

"She was fine one minute," he says, and I wonder if he is actually about to start crying over Sophia. "I was typing and then she made this funny noise. After that, the screen went black and she wouldn't do anything else."

"What kind of noise?" He tries to imitate the sound and makes me laugh. I look at Sophia and we share a moment of silent female communication. Let me die in peace, she begs me. And like a doctor playing God, I tell her that I think I might be able to gift her with a little more time among the land of the living. I think I know what ails her. She calls me a heartless bitch. I tell Aaron, "Go away and let me work. Don't come back in here until I call you. This could get ugly."

He leaves me alone with his pride and joy, and I go to work, losing myself in a strange kind of nirvana. An hour passes, and I don't even notice him sneaking back into the room and peeking over my shoulder. By now I am sitting on the floor, with the heart of the computer exposed to my prying eyes and fingers, in seventh heaven.

"Lena . . . what the hell?"

"Shhh," I say, shooing him away. "I think I know what the deal is. Give me a minute."

"She has PMS?"

"No, menopause. You need a new hard drive. Matter of fact, a new computer."

"Can we put a new one in?"

"We could, but no telling how long it'll last before you'd have to do it again. Read my lips, Aaron. Sheila is tired. She wants to die in peace."

"Sophia."

"Whatever. Let this pile of crap die. Damn."

"Why are you objectifying her?"

"Can't objectify an object." With a flick of my wrist, I pop the hard drive out and set it on the floor beside me. He flinches like I've slapped him. "What do you want to do? Because I can help you haul her out."

He looks like he wants to hurt me. "I'm getting a new hard drive. Don't touch another hair on her head."

"You know you're taking this way too seriously, right?"

"I don't play when it comes to my woman."

"Again. Whatever. Who's popping the new hard drive in?"

"You," he says as if it is a foregone conclusion.

We stare each other down. He says Sophia is the love of his life but he trusts me to save her, believes I have the power to do so. I don't have to talk him into it, don't have to give him a spiel about my qualifications, and he doesn't point out the obvious discrepancies. Like, why am I squeezing goo into snack cakes if I am a computer guru? He doesn't concern himself with any of it. I said it and he believes.

I stretch out a hand and he takes it, pulls me to my feet like I weigh two pounds. I wipe my hands on the seat of my jeans and look at Sophia one last time. We will meet again and I can't wait. "Thanks," I say.

Even now I cannot stand to watch it, but I am unable to look away. Here, three decades later, I see it and I still can't digest all that is rolling around in my gut. I want to get up from where I sit, frozen on the sofa, and help my sister, but I do not know how to help. Don't know what I can do or say that will make a difference. Part of me suffers because she is suffering. The other part suffers because I know that tomorrow will most likely be my day, and I feel the guilt that comes along with being relieved that today is her day and not mine.

Vicky is like a wild animal, kicking and screaming, her language barely intelligible. I think I must be the only one who understands what she is saying. One word: *No*. Loud and clear, no. But my grandmother is a force to be reckoned with. Vicky's strength is nothing to her. Vicky's cries fall on deaf ears. My grandmother has a job to do and, like the worst Jim Crow Negro imaginable, she will do it. Yessuh, she says in her mind. Right away, suh.

My hate is visceral. It fills every empty space inside me, until there is no place left for it to go. It pushes itself out of my body through my eyes. Makes itself water and slides down my cheeks like a river. I watch and pray that some hidden shred of goodness in my grandmother will finally take over and make her do what is right. What is not sick.

"No, no, no!" Vicky screams. My grandmother has Vicky's hands trapped inside hers, pulling Vicky up from the sofa. Huffing and straining to catch her breath when Vicky will not be lifted. "I don't want to. Stop it. Please, stop it. I don't want to."

"You stop this foolishness, Victoria. Right now. You hear me? I said stop it!" Vicky kicks out at her, swings her legs wildly and almost dislocates my grandmother's kneecap. I can't help wishing she would drop dead of a heart attack or a stroke, right then and there. I pray harder than I have ever prayed in my life, but she doesn't drop dead.

She slaps Vicky so hard that I feel the impact myself and Vicky is momentarily stunned into submission. Her tongue darts out to taste the blood in the corner of her mouth and then she loses it completely. She goes insane on my grandmother, scratching and clawing, kicking and swinging her fists. She leaves the couch willingly, to face off with her nemesis and win the battle. Instinctively, I stand too, ready to jump into the mix and help my sister take the old woman down. I ball my fists and take a step toward them. Then I freeze.

Another slap knocks Vicky on her ass, right back where she started, on the sofa. She holds the side of her face and cries a pitiful cry. She knows she will not win. Not today and not any day. She is not big enough and not strong enough. I watch the fight drain out of her.

"Now get your tail up and do what I told you to do," my grandmother snaps. She is winded and breathing hard. Feeling like she has been rammed by a Mack truck when it was really a compact car. She is too old to be tussling with children and she knows it. "Get up right now and go, Victoria."

Vicky gets up and goes. Her head is hung low and her spirit is crushed, and a few seconds later, a door closes down the hallway. My grandmother heads for the kitchen, has a thought, and then she turns to point a last-minute finger at me. "Don't you get no ideas about clowning like that, Leenie. You so small I can break you in two, and I'll do it, too. So don't even fix your mind to think about trying me, you hear?"

Behind a closed door, Vicky screams and I don't think about trying her. I think about killing her.

"Oh, that feels so damn good."

"You like that?"

"Shit," I pant. "Love it."

"What does it feel like?"

"Like good sex." We giggle together and catch each other's eyes. "I heard."

"You heard right."

Aaron takes the weight bar from me and sets it in its brackets. He has been spotting me as I push myself.

My muscles are singing, sweat is peeking out and rolling down my chest and the back of my neck. My scent rises to meet my nostrils, and I know my deodorant is talking too much and telling a few of my secrets. If I keep this up it will tell everything it knows. I would be embarrassed if he weren't sweating just as hard as I am and starting to smell just as bad.

"You pressed one-twenty," he says, reaching for the bottle of water sweating all over the floor by his foot. He takes a long pull and sighs. "Making progress, and progress is always good. You beat down yet?"

I roll to a sitting position and gather my locks from around my shoulders, use the sweatband on my wrist to make a ponytail high up on my head. I allow myself one good stretch, and then I lean over and curl my fingers around ten-pound hand weights. "Little bit more. I'm loving the sting. I needed this today."

He leaves the room and I hear the refrigerator door open and close. More water. Probably why his skin is as clear as a baby's and even-toned everywhere I look, which is most places. When we work out together he wears loose sweat shorts and wife beaters. Sometimes just the shorts, and his chest is nice to look at. He seems unaware that he is a black Adonis, seems unaware of my eyes as they follow him around his apartment.

I almost tell him to find a shirt, and then I catch myself. This is his space and I am the interloper. I close my eyes and keep lifting, my concentration deep.

The heat at my back shifts and intensifies, bringing me out of my trance of pleasure and putting me on alert. I stiffen and suck in a breath as his thighs hug mine from behind. His chest cradles my back and his arms come around mine. "Aaron," I say.

"Relax. Your form is a little off." His mouth is near my ear and then his hands are on my thighs, easing them farther apart. I am like a block of granite, unwilling to yield and wanting him to back off. "Lena?"

"Yeah?"

"Relax, okay?" His fingers squeeze my thighs, relax, and then squeeze again. "Feel that?"

"Yeah."

"Tension. Resistance. Let it go. You're working against yourself. The only thing that should be tense is this right here. Feel that?" His hands move from my thighs to my biceps and stay there. "Your thighs are straining, which means you need to reduce your weight. You're taking too much."

I lean over and switch to eight-pounders. Sit back against his chest and start over. "Better?"

"You tell me. Are your thighs tensing up?" He puts his hands there to feel for himself and makes a satisfied sound. "Pretend you're pulling through mud. Yeah, like that. And sit up straight. Good."

He gets up and leaves me alone again, and I breathe a sigh of relief and flow like water into what I do next. I spread my thighs wider, cross the weights over my chest and bend, rotate and circle my upper body slowly. He comes back and catches me looking like I am about to kiss the bench and sits back down behind me. He watches me help the definition of my chest along and leans back with me as I lean and support my spine. At first we move like Siamese twins, and then we move like shadows.

I roll forward, feel his palm on the small of my back, where my tee shirt exposes me and freeze. Silence greets me as I sit up and feel his breath heavy on the back of my neck. It whispers to me, tells me that he knows something, but what, I am not fully certain.

I wait.

"How much time did you do, Lena?" Aaron finally says and it is a done deal. He knows, and I know how he knows. He is a writer, a researcher, and he has seen the mark of the beast before.

"Eight years," I say and hold my breath. On the small of my back is a telling tattoo, an hourglass filled with black sand that escapes from one chamber into another, signifying the passing of time at a snail's pace. What is sand in one chamber becomes tears as it trickles down, and there are nine tear drops, one for every year I was imprisoned, and the last one for the year of parole release that I was finally granted. "Eight years, but it might as well have been eighty."

I put the weights back on the floor, run my hand around my neck, and wait for him to tell me to get out of his space. To tell me that I stink and he can smell me.

"Interesting."

"How so?" I don't know whether or not to be insulted. His voice tells me nothing.

"Just is. Explains a lot."

"Like what?"

"A lot. Like why you're doing the kind of work you're doing and not the kind of work you should be doing. It explains why you count to ten before you turn a corner, like you're waiting for the other shoe to drop because you just know it will."

"It always does. The tattoo told on me, huh?"

He makes a sound like a yes and then gives me an umph, umph, umph. I don't turn around and look, but I know he is shaking his head. "I contributed to a story on prison life a few years back. Saw a tattoo like yours during a prison tour. It was an enlightening experience, seeing the way women cope with being in prison."

"Bet you would've never suspected that I was hiding a criminal past in my closet," I say, giving him my profile.

"Are you a prior and persistent offender?"

"No, just a one-time breakout convict. I've been arrested once in my whole life, but when I do it, I do it big."

"What did you do?"

"I'm not ready to tell you that yet."

"Tell me this then," Aaron says, calm as still water. "Tell me about your family."

"You know I have a sister. She lives here in the city."

"No, I mean the one you had while you were in prison."

"Who said I had a family in prison?" He is treading on sacred ground and making me uncomfortable. Answering his question will bring him further into the place where the core of me dwells. It is a solitary place and it holds all of my deepest secrets, my deepest fears. Admission is not open to the general public, and I haven't decided if he is anything other than that.

"Did you?"

"I'm starting to see why you went into journalism. You don't have a problem asking nosy questions."

"You want me to back up?" Everything about Aaron withdraws. I feel him physically edge away, feel his breath become lighter on the back of my neck, and hear his mind begin retracting its tentacles from mine.

I say nothing for the longest time and then I say, "My mommy's name was Denny and my daddy's name was Lou. And I had sisters, women who were like sisters to me. We were closer than any blood family. We'd do anything for each other. That's what I regret most about being on the outside, that I had to leave them on the inside."

"You can't keep in touch with them?"

"Doesn't work like that. Once you're out, you're out—and I'm out."

"You trying to go back?"

"Never."

"What did you do, Lena?"

"No. Don't ask me that. I told you I was in and I told you about my family. Okay? Don't ask me that."

"Did you rob a bank?"

"No."

"Too many DUIs?"

"No."

"Drugs?"

"Hell no."

"Child abuse?"

I jump up from the bench and look around for my keys. His curiosity is natural, but it still pisses me off. The last thing I want to become to him is a source of entertainment, a spectacle any more than I already am.

"Hey, hold up a minute," he says, hooking an arm around my waist and stopping me in my tracks. He eases me back to a sitting position and grabs my eyes. "Forgive a brotha for being in awe of you, okay? You seem pretty well put together for somebody who just got out of prison. I guess I'm trying to reconcile what I see with what I've heard. Was it as hard as they say it is?"

"Probably ten times harder."

"Tell me about it."

"You know how a Vietnam vet can't put the words together to tell you about the action he's seen over there?"

"Yeah."

"It's the same for an ex-con. Ain't no words in the English language to describe what prison is like, so I can't tell you because the words don't exist."

Aaron looks at me long and hard. "That bad?"

"That bad."

Chapter Ten

The flashing lights take me back in time. Blue, red and white, all swirled together, looking pretty against the night sky, but still making my heart skip a beat. Suddenly, I feel the need to get home as fast as I can, to lock myself inside my apartment and close what is happening out of my mind. I turn my head and stare at Beige's profile, see her sitting as still as a portrait, refusing to meet my eyes. I need her to look at me, so that I know everything will be okay, but she doesn't.

There is a tap on my window and I am afraid to move a muscle. I might be shot if I go to press a button and lower my window, but the officer standing outside my door might break the window if he keeps banging on it with the metal flashlight he is holding. It is a toss-up, and I eventually opt to chance a bullet rather than risk Vicky's wrath.

"Yes, officer?" I say as the window clears my mouth and disappears completely. He shines strong light in my eyes, and I turn my face away from the abuse. Beige is next, but he is forced to study her profile.

"Are you aware you were going forty in a twenty mile per hour zone?"

"Um . . . no, I didn't know that. I guess I wasn't paying as much attention as I needed to be."

He looks around the inside of the car. There are grocery bags on the backseat, a Target bag full of shit, shower and shave stuff on the floor behind my seat, and a box of paperback books that I bought earlier from a flea market on the floor behind Beige's seat. We look exactly like what we are, two people on their way home after shopping. One of them driving twenty miles over the speed limit.

"Let me see your license and registration," the officer barks. Beige goes to retrieve my purse from the floor between her feet, and he puts her in the spotlight. "Keep your hands where I can see them, young lady."

"She was getting my purse," I butt in. I don't like that he snaps at my baby. Don't like it at all. "It's on the floor and the registration papers are in the glove compartment." At least I hope they are. I want this to be over like yesterday.

I hand him my driver's license and the registration paperwork for Vicky's car, watch him walk back to his patrol car, and let out a long stream of nervous breath. I am like millions of other people in the world: I don't like cops. But my reasons go beyond having superficial issues with authority.

"This will be over and done with in a minute or two," I say to Beige. "Damn, I hope Vicky didn't buy this piece of shit from Bey-Bey the crackhead." She giggles and I feel better about what is happening. I feel like an average, run of the mill Joe being stopped by the police. The urge to throw the door open and take off running lessens.

The cop comes back and I think Beige and I are about to be set free. I give him a mildly expectant look and get a frown in return. "I'm going to need you to step out of the car."

"Why? Is something wrong?"

"I'm not going to repeat myself again, lady. Get your ass out of the car. Now."

I'm not getting out fast enough for him, and he grabs my arm and hustles me toward the back of the car roughly. He spins me around and takes my head to the trunk. I feel cold metal against my cheek and wonder what the hell is going on. He has his hand pressed against the side of my head to hold me in place, so raising my head to look around is out of the question.

"What's going on?"

"Where'd you get the car?"

"It's my sister's. Please, what's going on?"

"I'm asking the questions here, all right?" His nightstick makes contact with the backs of my knees. "Spread your legs. Come on, you know the drill. Spread 'em. How long you been out?"

"S—Six months," I manage to say. The lining of my throat is raw and cold now. "Almost seven months. We weren't doing anything wrong. Trust me, this is my sister's car."

"Is that your sister in the passenger seat?"

"My daughter."

Another cruiser screeches to a stop near us, lights spinning all over the place, and another officer hops out and comes toward us. My keeper motions him closer and tells him to get Beige out of the car, to shake her down. I stop being afraid for myself and become afraid for my child.

"She's a child," I say, but no one is listening.

"Don't look like no child to me," the other officer says. I roll my eyes up in my head and see him marching Beige around to my side of the car, making her watch what is happening to me. They make her spread her legs and submit to a body search. My breath is humming in my throat as I watch alien hands glide along her legs, smooth over her ass and linger a second too long. A hum turns into a moan as those hands go near her breasts. She still won't look me in the eye.

"She's a child," I repeat, ready to commit murder. Again.

Her keeper orders her to sit down on the curb and to keep her mouth shut. It is my turn to talk, to explain why I thought I should partake in liberties that others take for granted. Shopping is as normal and non-threatening as it gets, but apparently I have no right to it.

I answer the questions hurled at me. "We were out shopping." Then, "Yes, I'm sure this is my sister's car. Call her. I'll give you her number." Then, "No, I'm not high or drunk. I don't drink or do drugs. Never have." And then, "No, there's nothing in my bags I'm not supposed to have." And then, "Yes, I have a parole officer and I keep all my appointments." They radio in to dispatch and have the owner of the monotone voice dial the number I give them. They check with Vicky regarding the whereabouts of her vehicle and I am cleared. They should let me go, but they don't.

Batman and Robin move from bad to worse. They are angry because I have no outstanding warrants and my breath doesn't reek of alcohol. My box of books is dumped on the sidewalk and every page flipped through. My groceries are tossed here and there, right along with the books. A loaf of bread is stepped on, a dozen eggs dropped without a second thought. They rifle through a box of tampons, rip open a package of toilet paper and then dump both of our purses on the ground in the space between the cars. Beige's lipgloss rolls away and disappears down a sewer drain.

They find nothing out of the ordinary, and I am slapped on my ass for my trouble, given a ticket for speeding, and allowed to come away from the trunk of the car and stand upright. Finally, Beige meets my eyes, and what I see there makes me feel like shit.

"This is my fault," I say after the officers have driven away and left us to clean up their mess. I throw food back into bags without worrying about economics and logistics. My hands shake. "This is all my fault. I should've let Vicky do the shopping and this shit never would've happened. What the fuck was I thinking?"

She helps me gather my books and takes the box from me, puts it on the backseat while I find the twelfth roll of Charmin and toss it inside the car. I will have to go back to the store and buy more salmon steaks. They are Aaron's favorite, and I promised to broil them for him tomorrow. My thoughts are scattered and out of sync. I think about Beige's lipgloss and feel tears hit the back of my throat. It is such a small thing, but in this moment, it is everything.

I see the confusion on her face, and my eyes slide closed for the space of five seconds.

"Bey, I'm sorry," I say. "I'll buy you more lipgloss. Friday, as soon as I get paid, I'll stop somewhere and buy you more. I'm . . . I don't know what . . . This is my fault."

I start the car but we don't move. I can't make myself shift into drive and give the damn thing some gas. I can't make my hands and feet cooperate with my brain. I am scared and shaking like a leaf. I'm so thoroughly fucked up I can't seem to get it together. Everything is a blur. I can't see through the tears standing in my eyes. Can't stand the fact that they won't stay there. They have to betray me and spill down my cheeks.

"What the fuck was I thinking?" This is where I'm stuck like a broken record. I fall back against my seat and stare out the window, see a group of people standing on a corner, waiting for act two to begin. Rubberneckers looking for their nightly entertainment, and unfortunately, we are it. I will always be someone's entertainment, I think. The epitome of an ex-con try-ing to live a normal life and blend in, and doing a lousy job of it.

I am not the woman I was eight years ago. A comput-er guru, making good money and being middle class. A concerned and attentive mother, dragging tired bones into school houses to meet teachers and talk grades and performance. Lecturing my motor-mouth child about talking too much in class. Cooking a balanced meal every night and giving baths. I am none of that. What I am now is a convict, and I will never be able to escape the consequences.

"This is what it's going to be like from now on," I tell Beige. "This is my life."

"Because you've been to prison," she says, and it is not a question.

"Exactly. Because I've been to prison. I can't even vote in the next election."

"Didn't you know?"

I give her my eyes. "What?"

"I mean, I'm just saying, Mom. If you knew this was how it might be, then why did you do what you did?"

I have no answer. I am speechless, and we stare at each other for the longest time. If I could talk, I would attempt to answer her question. But I can't, and the cause of my sudden deaf, dumb and blind state is easy to diagnose.

She called me *Mom*.

He thinks he has worked a miracle in the kitchen, and he wants to show me the fruits of his labor. Says he wants to give me a treat, for all the delicious food I cook and he consumes greedily. I laugh and tell him that he does eat faster than anybody I've ever seen, but repayment is unnecessary. He lets me use his workout equipment whenever I want, which is several times a week. If anything, I should be upping the ante on the food I cook for him. I am not feeling taken advantage of, I say and laugh.

Still, he insists on showing me what he has done and then sharing whatever it is with me. If I have ice cream, we can have a feast and then work out together to get rid of the evidence, he says.

I hang up the phone and meet him in the hallway on the stairs, midway between his apartment and mine. I am anxious to see what the big surprise is. I don't think he is prepared for the way my face shuts down and my smile slides sideways. It turns into something ugly and obscene. I feel my bowels loosen and I clench my ass cheeks together to keep from losing myself all over the stairs. I push the pan away from me, back to him, and he notices that I am falling apart right before his eyes.

"Lena?" he says softly. His face shows concern.

"No. Get that shit away from me."

"Baby, what's wrong? They're just brownies. I didn't—"

"Fucking brownies," I roar like a dragon. My voice fills the hallway and bounces off the walls around us. I breathe fire and brimstone. I shape-shift into the biggest, brownest, ugliest bear at the zoo and keep roaring. "I don't want that shit! How the fuck could you think I'd want brownies? Fucking brownies?"

"Lena, I don't understand. What did I do? Tell me what I did." He never raises his voice, and that hits me the wrong way. He thinks I am insane, speaks to me like he works on a psych ward and I am an uncontrollable patient. Calm and soothing is not what I need right now.

Aaron tries to hold on to the pan and reach for me at the same time, but anger gives me speed. I slap his hand down and slap the pan out of his hand. It hits the floor. Brownies fly all over the place and land on the floor at our feet. I stomp them like a maniac, grind them into the floor until I am breathless and spent, and then I leave him standing there, calling my name.

I don't go back to his apartment for two days, and when I finally do, we don't talk about what happened or why.

This is what he says when he opens the door and sees me standing there holding a pan of apple turnovers, still warm from the oven: "I want to write your story."

He takes the pan, sniffs appreciatively, and smiles. All is forgiven. He snatches up a turnover, eats half of it in one bite and offers me the rest. I push his hand away. "I don't eat sweets," I say, smiling back. "Sorry about your brownies. They made me sick to my stomach."

"You didn't even taste them."

We lock eyes. "They made me sick to my stomach."

"Past experience?"

"Past experience."

"Tell me about it."

"No."

"Why not?"

"Why?"

"You don't trust me?"

"It's not about trust. It's about boundaries and peace of mind. Some things are better off being left for dead."

"Your story might inspire someone, Lena. Might help the next person going through the same thing."

"You don't know anything about my story. You don't have a clue."

"And that's a good thing?"

"Ignorance is bliss in this case."

He is about to say something but then he thinks better of it. He takes his sweets to the kitchen and comes back to me. "I want to show you something. Come."

In his office, Sophia is already booted up and ready to roll. Since I performed open-heart surgery on her, she is reborn. I think I see her smile as Aaron pulls up his chair and settles himself in front of her. It's a tired smile though. He will still have to give her a decent burial before too many more moons come and go. I stand behind him and wait to see what he has to show me.

He accesses the Internet and types my name in the search box. My hands land on his shoulders and my nails dig in. I moan disgustedly when I see that he has his choice of several responses to click on. My story is everywhere it shouldn't be, and now he has it. He selects the first choice, a newspaper article from over eight years ago, and I see my picture unfold on the screen. I stare at myself and try to place it. I think it is a professional portrait of me and Beige, with Beige photoshopped out of the image.

"You just couldn't leave it alone, could you?"

Aaron studies the picture. Looks over his shoulder and catches my eyes. "Ignorance is not bliss, Lena. This shit makes you seem like a monster, and I don't think that's who you really are."

"You have no idea who I really am."

"Then tell me."

"Why is this so important to you?" My voice rises and takes us into argument territory. "You didn't even know me six months ago and now you want to know everything about me. You want to know things I don't tell anybody. Things that aren't your business to know. Why do you give a shit who I am and what I'm about?"

"I think you've got a story to tell." It's simple for him. As easy as one, two, three.

It's as hard as eight, nine and ten for me. "You don't get paid to think."

"Who doesn't want a book written about them?"

"I don't, that's who. I don't need you digging around in my business."

"You're saying you don't care about telling your side of the story?"

I have his number, and the look I give him tells him as much. "Oh no, you're not twisting me up with that shit. Forget it."

"How many times will you say *shit* before you think up another curse word to toss around?"

"Fuck you."

"Try another one because that one's not working for us right now."

I look at him. I mean really look at him. I see the same things I always see, but they come at me differently with the introduction of new tension in the room. He is not someone to glance at and forget about. He is a man who makes a woman do a double take, makes her pause somewhere in the flow of her conversation and take a moment to ponder and appreciate. Makes her look for a wedding ring and flirt when she sees none.

But I don't do any of those things because I tell myself it isn't like that between us. Nothing happens to me when I see him, when our eyes catch each other's and hold on. We are easy with each other because I look past his eyes. They are the color of melted chocolate and intense. I don't stutter when he licks his lips and clears his throat before he speaks to me. His voice is not Barry White's, but it is smooth and deep, like a body of water that appears to be a placid river but is really a bottomless ocean. Yet, it is just a voice to me.

I have my own muscles and my own body definition, so I don't need to be concerned with his. Don't need to think too much about how wide his palms are or how long his fingers are. There is no need to fall into his heavy eyelids because they are just eyes. I don't have time for a man in my life, and even if I did, he is not my type.

When I first started coming to his apartment, I waited for a woman to come onto the scene and start asking questions. Though nothing is happening between us, if I were his woman I would have so many questions that he'd have to write his responses down and spell check them. We look suspicious, and I can't deny that. We look like we are having some sort of affair, and if I were his woman I would not stand for another woman hanging around him all the time.

No woman comes, though, so I have come to a few conclusions of my own. "I thought you might be gay," I finally say.

"Because?"

"Because I don't see a woman coming and going."

"You come and go."

"I'm not your woman."

"That's true," he concedes with a tight smile. I have offended his masculinity, and his eyes tell me that he wants to fight. "I don't see a man coming and going in and out of your place either. Does that mean you're a lesbian?"

"Oh, you gotta go there, right?"

"You went there."

"Tit for tat?" I roll my eyes and walk out of the room. He catches up with me at the door.

"I'm not gay, Lena, and I never have been." I cannot say the same, so I don't say anything. "Did you hear me?"

"I heard you. I'm just not speaking to you right now. I'm being mad at you for the next little while."

"It's like that?"

"It's like that." I'm halfway up the stairs when I remember something important. "But if I *were* speaking to you, which I'm not, I would tell you not to forget that I'm using your car tomorrow afternoon. Gotta go back to the store. And in exchange, I will have stuffed salmon to seduce your palate and maybe a baked potato or two. But there will be no talking while we eat."

He laughs and shakes his head. Leans in his doorway and watches me disappear up the stairs. "Lena . . ."

"No book, Aaron. No, no and no. Don't ask me again." I close my door and try to forget about seeing my face plastered all over the Internet.

Chapter Eleven

Three quarters of the way through my sentence I am transferred. Moved closer to my hometown in preparation for the release that I am sure is coming. Five years has never seemed so long, and now that my sentence is drawing to a close, I start remembering how to spell freedom. I have another year and a few insignificant months left.

It starts over, only on a larger scale. I am the new kid on the block, the fish, and I find myself on the top bunk, but I don't complain. Women are women, and they will be bitches regardless of where they are. The transition from maximum to medium security means nothing when hundreds of disgruntled vaginas are running the show. I share a cell with three other women and pretend that I am content. I have learned to ignore propositions to have my pussy sucked or to suck one, and I'm not shocked when the offers come my way. This is my life, and I am still waiting for it to be funny.

I meet Anna, and together we come to the conclusion that we are the only sane ones in a world of madness. I live in B dorm, the medium security pod, and she lives two floors up, in D dorm, where the hardened criminals are housed. She is a menace to society but during meal times, when they mix us all up in one room like vegetable soup, she is just Anna.

She tells me that she tried to do some *Burning Bed* shit, that she started a fire in the trailer home where she lived with her boyfriend and she used his sleeping and unaware body as kindling. She got twenty to life for thinking she could pull off a Farrah Fawcett and play the battered wife card. She has only been inside a little over a year, but it is starting to take its toll on her.

Anna is ten years younger than I am, but she is deep. She likes to read and then discuss what she reads. She breathes life into the characters she reads about and reminds me that reading truly is an escape from reality. We bond over books. And then the bond grows deeper.

I have said that prison is another world, and the same holds true from one prison to the next. This one is no different from the one I just left—inmates roaming around freely, doing whatever they want to do under the guise of darkness, and guards seeing what they want to see and turning their heads when they are tired of looking in one direction.

Anna comes for me one night. With her long black hair and slanted half Cuban, half Taiwanese eyes, her small waist and high breasts, she comes for me. She takes me to the prison chapel and we sit close together, looking through a book that neither of us is really reading. There are others in the room with us, their voices like soft sighs and their throaty demands in the air around us, but we don't turn our heads to search them out. We don't peek into dark corners to see for ourselves the images created by our own minds. The chapel is the one place that guards don't invade very often, if ever.

The book is a prop and we both know it. We know Anna's hand is resting softly on my thigh because it wants to be there and mine on hers because it cannot be anywhere else. I am not surprised when she reaches down and pulls her shirt over her head, shows me her breasts and wants me to touch them. I take my mouth there and love her the way I once liked to be loved, letting myself be bold and hungry. The dominant one. The man.

She kisses me with everything she has, and I take her tongue deep into my mouth. It is different; it tastes and feels different, but not wrong. I have been without taste, touch and stimulation for so long that this is not wrong. Soft feels luxurious and wet feels like fire. We cannot touch fast enough or taste long enough. We cannot be close enough. Our kisses turn rougher and deeper, our orgasms cut like knives and make us both tremble long after they have subsided.

We know we want to do this again and we know we don't want to do it again with anyone else. This is the beginning of our affair. The moment we become lovers and chart our own path, which is the path of least resistance. Abstaining from sex is gruesome to one who knows the pleasure of it. We accept that we have loved men and that we still crave the fullness that only they can provide, but what we do is enough. More than enough in this time and place. We explore and learn each other's bodies the way we know our own bodies, and we make it a beautiful experience.

I am ignorant of the rules, though, and my relationship with Anna means that I will have to pay. I learn about the woman Anna avoids, the one she rejects and doesn't desire, out on the yard. She stares at me—hard. Makes her presence known and her intentions clear. She wants Anna, and I am in the way. I ignore her, and it is the second worst mistake I have ever made. Sending myself to prison is the first.

Guards can't come fast enough to prevent what is happening. I hold my breath and pray they come soon. I wish for them to save me from the crazy bitch I am faced with and then to save me from myself. Everything happens in slow motion, which slows their progress even more. In my mind, the seconds tick by, a minute seems like an hour and an hour is a lifetime.

My stomach sinks in on itself as I fall back and away from the blade she thrusts at me. I hear the wind her arm leaves behind; she wants to cut me so badly. She swings and swipes at the air with the blade and takes ten years off my life each time, until I think I am a new-born baby again. I can see myself falling to the ground in a puddle of blood, dying in prison and leaving my daughter an orphan in the truest sense of the word.

I don't like the image and it fuels me. We circle each other warily, and she tells me that I am a dead black bitch, that I should've stayed in my place and left her woman alone. I tell her to suck my black pussy and then I say I think that is what her problem is. She wants to suck it.

That makes her mad and stupid at the same time. She flings the blade to the ground and charges me. Suddenly we are just women again, slapping and scratching, gouging and biting. She slams my head into the concrete over and over again and I see stars. I pull her hair so hard that her eyes are slits in her face. We roll and I do some slamming of my own. I trap her cheek between my teeth and draw blood, almost take a chunk of flesh with me as I retreat. She screams like a fallen warrior, and an arm flings out to pat the concrete around us.

She finds her blade and brings it between us. We struggle over possession of it, and neither of us is the victor. I end up with a neat surface cut that stretches down my side, and she ends up with a gut full of metal. The blade ends up exactly where she wanted it to end up, except it is her intestines that are visible to the na-ked eye, instead of mine.

She spends six hours in emergency surgery, she comes out stitched up and humbled, and I am awarded another four years in prison for my trouble. They say I have committed the offense of assault first degree with a deadly weapon, but I say I have defended myself. It does not matter that the weapon is hers. What matters is that her blood is on my hands. Word on the block is that her heart stopped beating during surgery but that she was revived, which means I have narrowly avoided another murder charge and possibly, life in prison.

I spend a month in the hole, where the food is not as good this time around, and then I come out labeled a dangerous felon and in it for the long haul. Anna no longer has to sneak down to B dorm to visit me because I am in D dorm with her. We go on like nothing has changed, still a couple.

Anna comes with me to the chapel, but we are not here to make love. I am here to throw myself on someone's mercy. I walk up to the altar and fall to my knees, fold my hands under my chin and pray so damn hard that God has no choice but to hear me. I pray for everything I can think of. I pray for Beige, for my mother, for Vicky. For starving children all over the world, for Yo-Yo, for Patty. Everything and everybody.

And then I pray for the salvation of my soul. I admit to God that holding that blade struck a chord deep inside of me and that at some point, holding it felt good. I ask Him to remove the taste of violence from my mouth and the stench of blood from my nostrils.

I ask him to please find a way to let me know that my grandmother is burning in hell, because if she isn't, none of this is worth it.

***

"I have groceries in the car," I say helplessly, looking over my shoulder to where Aaron's car is parked at
the curb. My face tells the stranger in front of me that
this isn't on my agenda for the day, stepping inside
and chatting like milk won't sour and cheese won't
melt. This is Aaron's fault, and I will be sure to slap
him when I get back home. I glance down at my wide-
leg jeans and rainbow-printed dashiki, back up at his
sharply creased slacks and tasteful tie, and step inside
the lobby of the *Sentinel* newspaper. I don't want to,
but not doing so means I have to be unnecessarily rude.

I remember the CD in my hand and thrust it toward
the stranger who is so hospitable.

"I'm supposed to drop this off to Don Hughes."

"I'm Don," he says and smiles at me. "Aaron told me
to expect you this afternoon. Let's go in my office."

He does most of his work from home, Aaron does,
and this is why I am following a man named Don to his
office, even though I have no idea why. I take in my sur-
roundings as I go, glance at the motivational posters
framed on the walls and stick my finger in the soil of a
potted plant desperately in need of watering. It will die
soon if it doesn't receive some much-needed attention.
"Your plants are dying," I say.

He drops into a captain's chair behind a massive
desk and reaches for the telephone. "Darla," he says
into the receiver, "the plants are dying. See about some
water for them, would you?" Then he is motioning for
me to take a seat and grinning from ear to ear. "I'm
Don Hughes. Did I say that already?"

"I think so. I'm Helena Hunter. I don't think I said
that already." I pass him the CD with Aaron's latest
submission saved on it and hike my purse strap higher
on my shoulder, ready to take my leave.

"Aaron tells me you know everything there is to
know about computers."

"Not everything. Aaron exaggerates."

"Tell me what you do know."

"Is this an inquisition?" Milk is damn near four dollars a gallon. Too expensive to be sitting around in a hot car while I sit around in a chilly office.

"What if it is? Tell me what you know."

"Graphic design, some typesetting," I say. "I've designed and built a few websites, done a few software programs."

"Which ones?" He sits up and folds his hands on the desktop, searches my face.

"Which ones what? Websites or programs?"

"Both."

"Websites? Okay. You've heard of Crichton Pharmaceuticals?" He nods. "Grambling and Rochester, the company that makes all the household cleaning agents? Those websites are examples of my work. As far as programs go, you probably use Winstar Express or you've heard of it."

"Word processing software," Don says, thinking.

I smile. "Mine."

"Aaron says you rebuilt his computer in a matter of minutes."

"I did what I could, but she's got one foot in the grave and the other on a banana peel. It won't be long." I think I know where the conversation is going, and I lean sideways and eye the laptop sitting on a table behind him. "Oh, I see . . . you've got a computer emergency too. Give it to me, let me see what the deal is. It's a newer model, but they're all the same inside." My mind is clicking, wheels turning. "There's probably an issue with your cookies settings or a firewall discrepancy."

"Can you get around firewalls?"

"I can hack with the best of them." I think about what I have said and my lips snap closed. "I don't actually *do* that but I have *heard* it's fairly easy, if you know what to do."

"You've *heard*?" he leads me with a sneaky sparkle in his eye.

"I've *heard*."

"Why are you squeezing goo into snack cakes?"

Our eyes meet across the desk and do a complicated two-step. I watch him watch me and I wonder if I should lie. His is a personal question, and I don't do personal questions. Still, there is something about the way his eyes bore into mine that tells me he is looking for a lie. Looking for me to shift in my seat and look away from him. If I do these things, then I will have truthfully answered his question, no matter what I make my mouth say.

Something else is there too, and it makes me want to tell him the truth. I have nothing else to lose, except for my integrity, and that I will not relinquish under any circumstances. "It pays my bills."

"Is that the only reason?"

"Because I am a convicted felon." I wait for his porcelain skin to redden.

It doesn't. "I think I recall Aaron mentioning something to that effect."

"I think Aaron talks too much."

"Your crime?"

"Involuntary manslaughter and, before you ask, eight years. That's how long I was locked down. Any more questions?"

"Just one. When can you start?"

I scoot my chair closer to his desk and extend my hands. "Right now. Pass me your computer and leave me alone, so I can work in peace. I can probably fix it real quick."

"I don't think you understand," Don says. He drops a hand on my arm, sees my eyes land there like missiles, and pulls back. "I mean, when can you start work?"

"Excuse me?"

"I need a junior typesetter. Aaron suggested to me that you could handle the job in your sleep. I'm offering it to you, if you're interested."

"A job," I say slowly, carefully. "As a junior typesetter."

"As I said, it's a junior level position, but there is room for advancement. We have computers here, and from time to time they do require servicing. What do you think?"

"Why me? Why hire a felon when you could pick somebody off the street?"

"I have picked somebody off the street. I picked you. Now, do you want the job or not?" He glances at his watch and sighs. "It's my lunchtime and I'm half starved."

"Oh, I want it, but are you sure you want me?"

He rises from his chair and walks around the desk toward the door. Shakes his head like I am trying his patience. "Miss Hunter, I believe you'll fit right in around here. Give your job two weeks' notice and report at eight sharp on the twenty-third. Do you need anything in writing?"

"I'd feel more comfortable with a firm offer."

He goes back to the phone. "Darla? Prepare a letter of intent for . . . get a pen and paper, would you? Helena Hunter. Yes, like a deer hunter, and Helen with an *A*." He cuts his eyes at me and makes an exasperated face. Good help is hard to find. "The typesetter's position. The twenty-third, and bump the starting salary up two grades. She has experience. She'll wait."

I think about mentioning the milk that I'm sure is coagulating in the backseat of Aaron's car, and then I think, to hell with the milk. Right now I need that letter from Darla worse than I need my daily dose of calcium.

Aaron is ready for me when I storm into the apartment building lugging a gallon of warm milk and a soggy grocery bag. I know he hasn't been to sleep since early this morning, when he crawled away from his computer and came to me in search of food. He is waiting up for me, pacing up and down the hallway with his hands stuffed deep in his pockets.

"Well? What happened?" he says, eyebrows high up on his forehead.

I skid to a stop and punch him in his chest with the milk I am carrying. "What the hell were you thinking?"

"Did you take the job or what?"

"I took it, but you could've given me a heads up, Aaron. Had me going in there in these funky jeans, looking like one of the Black Panthers. What's the matter with you?"

"If I told you I was planning to help you find a better job, would you have gone?"

I don't even have to think about it. "No. You should've asked me first."

"So stay at the snack cake factory. Forget about working with computers and keep squeezing fake goo into fake Twinkies. It's your life."

"I know whose life it is." He pisses me off, being sarcastic. I don't need that right now. Especially since I'm beginning to feel like things are turning around for me. Finally. Today I look a man in the eye, tell him I'm a felon, and I still get a respectable job. I need Aaron to get that I'm trying to say thank you without having to come right out and say it. I don't know if I remember how.

I figure out that he gets me when he sighs like he's tired and says, "You're welcome, Lena."

"My mama always said a hard head makes for a soft behind."

"Let you tell it, your mama co-wrote the Bible, the dictionary, and the lyrics to most of Marvin Gaye's songs. You need to stop lying on the woman."

"Don't talk about my mama."

"Whatever."

"Loosen up, Lena. Damn."

Aaron's hands are large, and they are swallowing mine on the weight grips. He stands directly behind me, breathing down on the top of my head and doing his part to prevent me from dislocating my shoulders. I pull down on the grip and watch the metal pulley ropes angle across the front of my body, see the blocks of resistance lift into the air and know he is doing most of the work. I should've let myself be talked out of lifting weights standing up, but like he said, my head is hard.

"I am loose."

"Liar," he says. "Here, hold the grips down at your waist." He takes away his hand, and I feel myself being pulled to the right like a marionette. I giggle and he groans. "Hold the damn things at your waist, Lena."

"They are at my waist."

"Don't bend your knees. Here . . ." Behind me, Aaron drops to a squat and takes his hands to my kneecaps. "Your feet need to be shoulder width apart. That's why you keep getting jerked around. Your center isn't grounded." He doesn't notice the muscles in my calves going rock hard at his touch, same with the muscles in my thighs as his hands climb higher. He puts my feet where he wants them and fits his chest against my back again. "Use your muscles to pull the weights, and stop letting the machine call the shots. Either that or get back over there with the kiddie weights."

"I got this," I say, talking much shit.

"Right." He releases the weights and watches me jerk sideways and almost collide with the frame. His hands on my waist are the only things stopping me from taking flight.

"I'm just not used to lifting standing up, that's all."

"If that's what you need to tell yourself. Pull."

Concentration eludes me, but I do my best to bring my hands to my center and feel the burn I crave. I'm lifting a total of fifty pounds, twenty-five on each side, and I can't understand why it is suddenly so hard. My biceps tremble like they are overworked and my breathing is choppy like I am asthmatic, which I'm not. I tell myself that I am having trouble performing because Aaron's hands aren't steadying mine, because my palms are sweaty, but I think I know better. I can't perform because he hasn't taken his hands off my waist since we started and there is heat where he touches. It drains my energy.

"What's going on up here?" Aaron says, feeling along the length of my raised arms.

"I can't . . . I don't know."

"Do I make you uncomfortable, Lena?"

"A little, yeah."

"Why?"

"You're a man."

"As opposed to a woman?" I don't answer. We are treading into territory where I'm not sure of my footing. "Lena?"

"Yes, as opposed to a woman. Are you trying to ask me something, Aaron?"

"You know what I'm trying to ask you."

"You think I'm a lesbian?"

"I'm more interested in what you think."

"And why would you be interested in something like that?" I'm tired of lifting weights and I stop. I turn the hand grips loose and let them reel in with a loud clank. I step around Aaron and find space enough on the floor for me to stretch out. Crunches seem like a good idea.

"Maybe I'm interested in you."

"I told you in the beginning that I wasn't looking for a boyfriend."

"Are you looking for a girlfriend?"

"I'm not looking for anything, right this minute. I'm still trying to adapt to life on the outside and get my life in order."

"Like you adapted to life on the inside?" Aaron steps over me and goes over to the weight bench, stretches out on it and studies the ceiling. He folds his hands low on his belly and waits for my response.

"When in Rome," I say, and he chuckles under his breath. "What?"

"Nothing. I'm just trying to picture you with a woman."

"It's different."

"Better?"

"Different."

"Take me there with you. Tell me what it's like."

"You don't know?"

"I know what I know, and you know what you know. I want to know what you know, see how it compares with what I know."

"Translation, you want to be nosy."

"That, too."

"Is this conversation off the record?"

He smiles at the ceiling. "What conversation?"

"If I read this shit somewhere, I'll know where it came from and I'll never speak to you again. And I'm only saying it once."

"Were you, like, a pimp with a string of different women, or . . .?"

"There was only one." I fall back against the floor and catch my breath a little at a time. I haven't thought about Anna very much since I got out, but I let myself think about her now. She comes into the room with us and takes a seat, ready to listen to what I will say about her. How I will make her come alive for Aaron to experience with me. "Anna."

Chapter Twelve

"You loved her?"

"I cared about her, but I don't think I loved her. It's hard to love someone else when you can't figure out if you love yourself. There's no room for love in prison."

"What was she like?"

I think about the question before putting words together. I have to get this just right, have to make him understand what I need him to understand. "She was younger than me, still energetic and optimistic. Very pretty. Slender and shaped like a Coke bottle. I don't remember the exact moment that I knew I was attracted to her. I just woke up one day and knew I was. Never thought I'd swing the other way, but it was happening before I could stop it."

"You would've stopped it if you had seen it coming?"

"Probably not," I admit softly. "It's true what they say. Prison is a microcosm of the larger, free society. There's racism and class systems, crime and drugs. Violence. All that shit happens every day, and depending on who you are and what you're about, you react differently to it. But in a women's prison, two women being together doesn't get the same reaction it would in the larger society. Nobody looks twice because it's normal, or if nothing else, it's accepted. It's a choice you make."

"Did you choose her or did she choose you?"

I stick a finger into the midst of my locks and scratch my scalp, thinking. "I'm not sure. Seems like we chose each other. To her I probably seemed safer than some of the other options and I felt the same way. I guess I thought, if I'm going to do this, it has to be with someone safe. It has to be with someone I desire."

"It was about more than being a victim of circumstance then. You wanted another woman."

"Truth?"

"Nothing but."

"I don't think there's a woman on earth who hasn't thought about what it would be like to be with another woman. If you find one who says she hasn't, even for a second, she's lying. Could be she just thought about kissing or touching, naked or fully clothed, but she's thought about it. Prison sets you free from just thinking, if you want to be set free."

"Hold up," he says, pushing up to his elbows and staring down at me. "You make it sound simple as hell. What about men who go to prison and end up being somebody's bitch? You're saying they've been set free?"

"There are women who are raped in prison too, Aaron. I'm not talking about rape or fucking by force, and I don't know shit about what it's like for a man in prison. I'm talking about your everyday housewife or real estate agent, secretly wondering what it would be like on the other side of the fence, if what's on the other side is appealing to them in some way. Women see other women who are attractive to them in some way too."

"So what keeps your average, everyday housewife from finding out?"

"Fear of the unknown," I say without hesitation. "The hush-hush factor. What if she tells someone and everybody finds out? What will my husband or boyfriend think? My kids or my friends? Total secrecy isn't guaranteed, and some women aren't willing to risk it, so fear keeps them in line." I grab his eyes. "Not the church, not your mom or your dad. Fear. Being trapped in a cage with nothing but women eliminates the fear."

"And now that you're not in prison anymore?"

"I'm not afraid of anything—except going back. I'm petrified of that. If I wanted a woman, I'd find one to be with. Wouldn't give a shit what people thought if that's what I needed to be whole. You ever been with two women at the same time?"

He chokes on his own breath and laughs. "Damn, where did that come from?"

"You don't get to ask all the questions," I remind him. "Have you?"

"Once or twice. It was . . . very erotic. Very stimulating."

"Tell me."

"There's something about watching two women make love to each other that takes it to a whole new level. You get to watch your fantasy come true right in front of your eyes and then you get to wiggle into the middle of it and play a leading role. You get the right mix and it's . . . quite interesting."

"Is that something you would want to do every night?"

His head rolls around on the bench and we lock eyes. "When a man finds the right woman, one is enough. You and Anna had a relationship, so you know what I'm talking about, Lena. Was being with her enough?"

"In that time and place, yeah. It wasn't about degradation or control. It was about making each other feel good in a place that makes you feel so bad. One of the first things people do after a near death experience is run home and fuck somebody's brains out or else wear out their vibrators. People need to be reminded that they're still alive, that they haven't died, no matter how close they come. You take what you can get, when you can get it."

"You still keep in touch with Anna?"

"No." I shake my head. "When Anna walks out of prison, she'll either find herself a good man and have a baby or two while she still can, or she'll find herself a good woman and live her life the way she wants to live it. Prison does one of two things, Aaron: It shows you what you aren't or what you really are, and that's across the board, on every level."

"That's deep. Answer me this, though: If lesbians don't desire men, why do some of them buy penis-shaped vibrators and dildos and use the hell out of them?"

"You probably need to find a lesbian and ask her," I say. "Hell if I know."

"Am I asking a lesbian right now?"

"I don't know," I tell him, "but I don't think so."

"Explain yourself. A bisexual man is considered a conflicted gay man who is in denial. How can you come out of a lesbian relationship and not think you're a lesbian?"

"It's different with women, with me anyway. All I know is I'm not a lesbian right now. If I was then, I'm not right now. I can't explain myself, and I can't speak for anybody else."

I don't relive the horror of the experience often, but when I do, I relive it fully. I go back in time and feel every touch like it is happening in the here and now. I smell every breath and hear every voice as if I can reach out and wrap my fingers around them. Reliving it makes my face crumble into a mask of outrage, makes my insides liquefy and my entire essence crush in on itself like a tin can under the weight of a giant foot.

It comes when I least expect it. When I am in the basement laundry room waiting for my whites to dry. When I am swaying in time with the bus's motion, on my way to work. When I am standing at my window, watching children play in the park across the street. I look at them and wonder which one of them will grow up to be a predator. Odds are, one of them will.

Sometimes the horror comes to me when I am in bed, sleeping off a long night at work, and those are the worst times. The times when it catches me off guard and makes me suffer through it from beginning to end, as if I didn't pay close enough attention the first time. I'm too tired to force myself awake and out of it. Too tired to fight it off.

Always after reliving it, I run to the shower and stand under the hot spray until I have used every drop of hot water there is. I don't care who needs the water I steal from them or how long they have to wait for the hot water heater to refill. I have to scrub myself, have to clean the residue off of my skin before it settles there and eats me from the outside in.

Ironically, the shower is where it happens, the one and only time it does. If Beige is sleeping over, she humors me and sits on the toilet seat while I shower. She talks to me and tells me all kinds of off-the-wall stuff, her voice raised over the roar of the water, and I listen and stay grounded. Bringing her into the bathroom with me is a way to spend every possible minute with her, which is what she thinks my motive is, but it is also a way to make sure I am not ambushed. To make sure I am safe.

When she is not with me, I check the locks on the door and on the windows. I lock the bathroom door behind me and pray.

A man is warned about the dangers of dropping his soap in prison, but they don't pass the same wise advice on to women.

And they should. Someone should write a book and fill every page with the credo, *Don't drop the soap*. It is the single most important thing a woman in prison can learn, especially one who has enemies that she isn't even aware of.

I close my eyes and relive.

I don't realize that the shower has cleared out until I shut off the water and look around, see that I am the only one left. I step off of tile onto concrete and reach for a towel, and this is when I am jumped.

My arm is wrenched behind my back and my face is pummeled. I see stars as I fall to the floor and curl my body into a ball. There are feet everywhere, kicking me from every direction, and the pain they cause feels like nothing I have ever felt. Nothing I will ever forget.

There are four of them, bitches that I have seen before but that I don't really know, and I do what I can to defend myself against them. When they want to punch, I punch back. Pull hair, I pull back. Bite, I bite back. I almost take possession of someone's nipple, smashed between my teeth, and I rip out a fistful of hair when the opportunity presents itself. I feel the skin on my knuckles split open as they connect with someone's teeth.

I am not without my own wounds though. I have been viciously kicked in the vagina and stomped along the length of my body until I can't see straight. I have been bitten in the same places that I bite, and the warm heat on my scalp tells me that I am bleeding there. I think my wrist is fractured and one of my toes broken.

I see my attackers through a haze of tears, sweat and blood. I blink a million times to keep them in my sight, but I still miss one. She is the one who circles around behind me and takes me back to the floor with a home-made billy club—contraband she is not supposed to have—and for this very reason I go down the way I'm supposed to, with little to no fight left in me.

"Black monkey bitch," I hear someone croak in the seconds before everything goes dark. I know what spit feels like on my skin. Urine, too. And I hear the scrape of a blade near my scalp when the ponytail that hangs down between my shoulder blades is confiscated as a trophy.

I don't know how long I am unconscious, but when I open my eyes again, they are violating me. Holding me down on the floor, with their knees digging into my arms and legs like shovels. One of them takes her turn and I swing an arm or a leg. It is someone else's turn and another leg or arm is free to protest. But I can't stop them from doing what they are doing to me, can't stop the screams from coming out of my mouth either.

There is no gentleness here. There are teeth and hands, fists pounding into my abdomen and face, pel-vises floating in front of my face. I turn my head, refus-ing to have unwanted pussy in my mouth, and take so many slaps across the face that I lose count. I become so unsettled that I vomit and damn near asphyxiate myself.

I think it is over, but then I discover that it has re-ally just begun. I have never seen anything like the grotesque-looking apparatus that is used to torture me, have never imagined that something so heinous could exist. Shock, disbelief, and then electrifying pain makes me slip underneath a sheet of blackness again.

"That's for Laura," I am told. For the one who took the blade in her gut.

An eternity passes before someone thinks to look for me, and when someone does finally come for me, it is Anna. I hear her footfalls on the concrete and think the worst. They have come back for round two and maybe brought along a few more of their friends this time. "No," I say. "Leave me the fuck alone. Get the fuck out."

She sees me crawling across the floor like a serpent, leaving a blurry line of blood in my wake, and she screams. And screams and screams. She throws herself across my body and cries like someone has died. I lie still and wait for her to stop. I will not tell her that her weight causes me more pain.

Anna is still screaming as she runs to the doorway and falls to her knees outside the shower room. Talking is difficult for her, but she manages to scream one word: "Lou!"

Lou is tall and wide, thick with muscle and frightening to me. She crashes into the shower room and hovers over me like a statue. I stare at her buzz cut hair, at the tattoos riding the length of her arms, and then I focus in on her round face.

I remember my voice and scream.

"Shhh, now. Ain't nobody gone hurt you no more. Can you stand up?" She bends at the waist and reaches for me, and I go wild. I try to swing my arms and kick my feet, but they won't cooperate. She doesn't waste time ducking and dodging because I pose no threat.

"Don't. Touch. Me." I spit. "Nobody is fucking touching me again."

Lou takes a step toward me, and I stop her with a look. "I mean it. I'll cut your goddamn throat."

She stares at me until she can stare no more. Then she turns her head, sees Anna in the doorway and says, "Go get Denny. And tell her to bring some clothes."

***

Aaron barely gets his door open and I am pushing past him, taking over his space like it is mine. I go straight to the weight bench and lie down. I don't even stop to check how much weight I am about to take before I lift the bar and start punishing myself. I do five reps alone, and then he is standing over my head, spotting me.

"Lena," he whispers, and I shake my head.

I don't want to talk. I don't want to think. I just want to sweat. Reliving it does this to me, makes me antisocial and hateful. Burns up my tongue and fills my mouth with the taste of acid. I am hoping that lifting will cause me to sweat the stench from my pores because I cannot face the shower just yet.

"No," I whisper back to him.

"No, what?"

"No talking. Just this." He closes his mouth and keeps watching me.

I lift until my arms tremble. I do two hundred crunches, sixty squats, and a hundred push-ups. Then I leave his apartment and take my feet to the pavement. I run until I think I am lost.

Stella laughs at me, laughs until I think she's about to piss in her pants. She says I dance like a funky chicken and smile like a second-rate actress in blackface. Personally, I think the Electric Slide slash Four Corners that I am doing is pretty damn good for somebody who hasn't danced in years. So what if the version of the slide I'm doing went out with big hair? I'm still doing it. And I'm killing it, too.

I can't help the smile that stretches from one side of my face to the other, either. It comes out of nowhere as soon as I catch sight of my new car pulling to a stop in front of me. Even though it is gently used, it is new to me. It has four wheels and two doors, a few dings here and there, but it is mine. Bought and paid for.

"Girl, quit acting silly and unlock the door so I can sit down," Stella complains around a giggle. She joins me in a quick dip and sway, and then she flops into the passenger seat dramatically.

"You know what, Stella?" I wave one last time to the salesman who talked me into buying the Chevy I am driving and ease my way into the thick of traffic.

"I know you gone tell me anyway, so what?"

"I used to drive a pretty little BMW. It wasn't quite top of the line, but it was still a BMW. Had a sunroof and leather bucket seats too."

She doesn't say anything for a long time, and we ride in silence. This car, the one I have spent most of my savings on, doesn't even have a radio. But the engine is clean, and it is as quiet as a church mouse. It doesn't jerk and shake when I give it gas. She nods her head, agreeing with thoughts that I can't hear, and reaches over to pat my arm.

"What color was it?"

"Silver bullet," I say, and we crack up.

"Well, this here ain't no BMW, but I guess it'll do. You miss it, your BMW?"

"I miss all of it. Everything I had back then that I can't even pretend I'm going to ever have again. I miss my life." I stop at a red light and look at her. "Don't you miss your old life?"

"This is my old life," she says quietly. "Before I went in, this is what I had. A factory job and a little apartment, some worrisome-ass relatives who was always borrowing money. Bills that was always overdue. Wasn't too much to miss, Lucky."

"Did that have anything to do with you going to prison?"

She looks away from me and thinks her own thoughts. For all the talking and horsing around we do, we don't talk about crime and what we know about it. She isn't on parole, but I am, and we don't discuss the fact that I am constantly in violation of the stipulations of my release simply because I associate with her. We pretend that we are drawn to each other solely based on personality likenesses.

"I was a thief," Stella tells me. "And I'm not talking about no half-stepping booster either. Go, Lucky. The light's green."

I step on the gas and divide my attention between her face and the street. She has caught my attention. "You were on lockdown for seventeen years for stealing?"

She laughs sarcastically. "You think driving a BMW was something, try pushing a Cadillac Seville. Those babies ride so smooth you don't even know you moving, and that's the truth. Used to mess around with this dude who had one, and that's what they finally caught my ass driving. Chased me down twenty miles of interstate like I was a serial killer or something, and all the time I'm tossing shit out the windows. Five hundred dollar bags and thousand dollar shoes. Loose diamonds, all kinds of shit. Figured the less I had in my possession when they caught me, the less they could do to me.

"Anyway, I was so busy trying to get away from them motherfuckers that I was pushing that Caddy to the limit. Shoulda been paying attention to what I was doing, but I wasn't, and I ended up running into a few cars along the way. Hit this one car and paralyzed a lady I didn't even know. Ran into a minivan carrying a bunch of little kids and made a mess of everything. You don't even want to know what happened with that."

"Damn," I say because I can't think of anything else to say. "That's fucked up."

"After that, I figured I needed to go to prison, you know?" She stares at me and waits for me to agree with her, but I don't. She finally gets tired of waiting and takes her eyes out the windshield. "I guess you think I'm some kind of monster, huh? Stupid bitch running around stealing and crashing into innocent folks."

"I don't think shit. You feel like you paid your debt to society?"

"I feel like I paid mine and somebody else's too. Prison fucks you up so bad you don't know if you coming or going half the time. If it ain't nobody around to tell you when to wash your ass and when to eat, you forget to do either one of them. Took me a long time to get my head on right after I got out. That's how come I recognized you like I did."

"I'm walking around with a sign on my back, letting people know I've been to prison?"

"Just like one whore knows another one, an ex-con knows another ex-con, Lucky." She sees my look and grins. "You ain't gotta look at me like that. It ain't a permanent condition, if that's what you worried about, but it does take some time to shake off. You should see somebody, to help you get it out of your system."

"Somebody like a shrink?"

"I did."

I'm seeing her through new eyes, trying to picture her sitting in a room with a head doctor and pouring out all her dirty little secrets. I can't get the picture together in my head. "It'll be a cold day in hell before I let some quack-ass doctor get inside my head. Sonofabitch would probably be crazy by the time I got through with him anyway."

"They done seen and heard it all," she says, pointing at a fast food restaurant farther down the street. "Let's stop. I'm hungry."

We go in and join a line that is almost out the door. When it is my turn, I order a side salad and a baked potato. Stella looks at me like I'm crazy and orders a triple cheeseburger, fries and a chocolate shake.

"That's why you look like a strong wind would blow your little ass over," she jokes. "You don't eat worth shit."

"Shut up, carnivore, and pass me the salt. Have you seen the stuff passing for meat they serve on the inside?"

"Seen it? Hell, I cooked it for nine years. Them bastards found out I could cook, and guess how I ended up serving my country."

"You were in one of those *Nightmare in Badham County* prisons," I joke.

"All of 'em are nightmares."

"True."

"You planning on telling me what you did?"

"I killed my grandmother, Stella." While she digests what I have said, I steal a couple of her fries, dunk them in ketchup and watch her face go from surprise to shock. Several minutes pass before she is ready to hear my next words. "Now it's you thinking I'm the monster, right?"

"I think you musta had your reasons."

"I did."

"How you live with something like that, Lucky?"

"I don't. Most days I just pretend like I can forget about it."

"You need to talk to somebody. Get it all worked out in your head, so it makes sense to you."

"Bullshit. I need to talk to somebody, so it makes sense to *you* and everybody else, but I don't need it to make sense to me. It made sense to me the day I pulled the trigger. All this other shit, this new world I have to live in, that's what doesn't make sense to me."

"Join the club," Stella says around a mouth full of flesh.

Chapter Thirteen

Beige sees the anxiety on my face and pushes her face close to mine, searches my eyes. "You okay?"

"I'm good. What'd you say you wanted to see?" I look at the display board and become confused. Too many choices and too much room for error. None of the movie titles sound familiar, though I'm sure I must've seen a preview of at least one of them somewhere. I already know I'm not up for inexplicable violence, and I hope she isn't either.

The line moves up and we move with it. I shift to the side to avoid being directly in front of the man behind me. He is too close, breathing down the back of my neck, and it feels like he is getting closer and closer the longer we stand here. Twice he has bumped into me from behind and not bothered to excuse himself, and twice I have put enough space between us that it shouldn't happen again. But it does and it bothers me.

"I've been wanting to see that new movie everybody's been talking about. I think I want some nachos too." Beige rubs her belly and grins at me.

I think I want air to breathe and space to move around in. "As long as it's not rated R."

She gives me a long-suffering look and shakes her head like I am old and decrepit. "It's PG-13, Mom, okay?"

"It better be," I say, fishing money out of my pocket and handing it to her. Standing in one spot is driving me crazy, and I have to move. "Do you mind getting the tickets? I'll be right over there."

"You sure you're okay?"

"I said I was good, didn't I?" I point to a spot not too far away. "Right over there."

The truth is, I don't know if I'm okay or not. It is Saturday night and it seems like the whole city is out in full force to see a movie. The lines are congested and people are stacked on top of one another; personal space is nonexistent, and I feel like I'm about to lose it. No one else seems to mind all the accidental touching and bumping, the occasional brush of asses against asses, but for me, it is a violation of the highest order. I can't understand how people can let themselves become so complacent with having their bubbles popped, can't comprehend that I was once one of them.

I keep my eyes on Beige, see her buy two tickets and count the change carefully, and then stuff it in her pocket. She is stopped by a man wanting to know the time, and she smiles as she tells him that it is just after seven. So polite and comfortable in a world full of roaming animals, she doesn't consider that he really isn't interested in the time so much as he needs an excuse to invade her space even more than he already has and initiate conversation. She is a pretty girl, fresh and lush looking, like a peach just plucked, and he knows enough to appreciate what even she doesn't know she has.

She makes her way over to me, and I keep my eyes on the man. He watches her the way men watch women, and it makes the underside of my skin burn, right next to my bones. He feels my eyes on his face and looks up just in time for me to silently tell him that I will slit his throat and sacrifice him to the gods. That I will go back to prison with more blood on my hands and more hate in my heart. He is nothing and no one to me, but Beige is everything to me. It doesn't take him long to do the math in his head and find something else to look at. Smart man, my eyes tell him.

Grown men have no business lusting after little girls, no matter how well developed their bodies are. They should be able to look in a little girl's eyes and see that she is not ready to enter the world of adult sadism, no matter how round and juicy her ass is, and regardless of how tight and succulent her breasts are. Everything is tight and succulent at one time, like fruit on the vine that is pleasing to the eye but left on the vine until it is mature enough to be consumed. We know enough to let nature take its course where fruit is concerned, but we don't know shit about kids.

Beige and I get looks as we join the line at the concession stand. People study us and wonder if we are a couple because her arm is draped around my shoulders and mine hugs her waist. We whisper silly things to each other and share giggles that don't include the rest of the world. For a while, I forget that I am unsettled and feeling threatened. I think she does what she does on purpose, knowing that I am not entirely human and that I am still part crouching tiger, hidden dragon. In her own way, she offers me her protection, and I can't help thinking that it should be the other way around. That it was the other way around.

"You want to be at home, don't you?" She orders nachos and a jumbo Icee, and leans against the counter with one side of her mouth tipped up at the corner.

I order popcorn and a large soda and tell her, "I want to be wherever you are."

We are seeing a movie called *U Got Money*, which is supposed to be funny, and I think I am the only person in the theater who isn't laughing. I am too preoccupied with the fact that the person sitting next to me has claimed the armrest. Her arm is pressed into my side

and her cologne is overpowering. She crunches popcorn and crosses and uncrosses her legs so many times
that I lose count. I am transfixed by the fact that I can
hear the conversation she is having with the man on
the other side of her.

In the row behind us there is an elderly woman doing
her best to corral three children into behaving. I hear
her tell them to shush, to hush and then to flat out shut
up when nothing else works. I know she is Big Mama
because one of them calls her constantly, says he has to
pee and makes her curse under her breath. They stand
to leave the aisle and sweep my locks off the back of my
neck as they pass. It takes me ten minutes to regulate
my breathing.

Two rows down, in front of us, a group of teenage
boys are tossing kernels of popcorn across the theater
at unsuspecting people. They think it is funny to watch
people squirm in their seats, scratching places that
do not itch. It is hilarious to them to see their targets
turn in their seats and verbally abuse the people behind them, instead of the true culprits. They sit there
and hold their breath, impatient for the inevitable
outbursts, while I sit in my seat and count the seconds
until someone starts shooting. This is how simple nonsense escalates into complete chaos.

I am like a child with ADHD. My mind is so polluted
with extraneous stimuli that I cannot focus on the task
at hand, the movie I have paid to see and enjoy. Beige
laughs and lets herself be seduced by the big screen,
but I cannot be seduced while I am being violated.
I talk myself out of claustrophobia by staring at her
profile and stealing some of her innocence for myself.
I keep myself from screaming by choosing a cheese-
soaked nacho from the tray she holds and stuffing it in
my mouth. I count the minutes until I can escape.

At some point I do laugh at what I see on the screen. A large part of the movie is about parody. Making fun of people and exposing their ridiculous behaviors for what they really are.

An actress is confronted by two men who are unaware that she is PMS'ing, and they push her buttons until her eyes roll back in her head and she turns into a monster. The fight scene is comical, and I almost forget that I shouldn't be laughing. PMS is nothing to play with.

The noisy kids behind me are back. They shuffle past and locate their seats just about the time popcorn kernels start coming our way. Something flies past my head, and then Beige swats the air in front of her face.

"Are they stupid or what?" she whispers, irritated.

"I think so," I say. "You want me to go down there and knock some heads together?"

"Mom, please . . ."

"I'm serious, I'll—"

"It's cool, sista," the man two seats down from me cuts in. He is talking loud and sounding angry. "You ain't gotta go down there and do nothing, 'cause in a minute I'ma put some fire in somebody's ass. Let another piece of popcorn come up here."

Instantly, the popcorn tossing stops and peace is restored. Even the noisy kids behind us settle down, and I am reminded that men do serve a useful purpose, after all. I don't stop to think that I will be the next unwanted distraction.

It happens before I have time to prepare myself. What is a parody turns into a disgrace, and it is nowhere near funny to me. I grip my knees and watch four men trap a woman in a dark alley. I suck in my breath, hold it, and watch the woman's clothes being torn away from her body. I think she is saying something, maybe screaming for help, but the buzzing in my ears keeps me from hearing her. She is thrown to the ground, still begging and pleading, and the men start beating her.

"What is this shit?" I ask no one in particular. "How is this shit funny?" I look at the people around me, waiting for someone to explain it to me, but no one says anything. Beside me, Beige goes still and looks at me like she is worried that I will flip out at any minute.

"It's all right," she says. "Look . . . nothing's happening to her."

I take my eyes back to the screen and I see that the woman has turned into a female version of the Incredible Hulk, complete with a string bikini and generous breasts. She tosses her attackers every which way and laughs as each one of them meets gruesome fates. A few people laugh with her, but I don't. I am still frozen.

"That's not the way it happens in real life," I blurt out. "That's not real life. You know that, don't you?"

"I know, Mom. Are you okay? Do you want to leave?" I am embarrassing her without meaning to. Her eyes beg me to settle down, and I make a concerted effort to do so, for her sake.

"No . . . I'm good. It's just . . . who thinks shit like that is funny?"

I think that maybe I have played my hand to Beige, given her a first peek inside the fractured and fucked-up life I've lived. She doesn't tell me this, but I see something shift in her face, a look come over her features that confirms it for me. She realizes that I am damaged goods, that I am a little bit coo-coo and slightly crooked in the head. She wants to know what prison is like and I show her, though I want nothing more than to keep the reality of it as far away from her as I can. But she cannot be around me for any length of time without the stench of it rubbing off on her.

Her nostrils are full of the stench as she grips my hand in hers and laces our fingers together. She squeezes my palm to hers until there isn't room for air to pass through them, mixes the sweat in my palm with the sweat in hers, and shifts in her seat so she can lay her head on my shoulder. She pities me.

"It's okay, Mom," she says.

"No, it's not," I say back. She has no idea that it will never be okay. That I will never be okay. "No, it's not."

My grandmother spends extra time wrapping my scarf around my neck and tucking the ends. Next, she helps me separate my fingers inside my gloves and pull them on snugly. It is one of the few memories I have stored away that brings a feeling of warmth with it when it comes to me. Most of the other ones bring along with them anger and numbing cold.

She is hardly ever doting, but she is today because she senses that her hold on me is loosening, that she is losing my allegiance. Rebellion is written all over my face, and she is smart enough, cunning enough, to know that she needs to do something to assure my continued cooperation. I am a loose end that she cannot afford to leave hanging.

She zips my coat and then tries to kiss me on my cheek, but I spin away and leave her kissing air. Leave her wishing she had the right to put her lips on my skin in love and affection. I hate her, and I think she can smell the hate wafting from my armpits like musk. She thinks kissing me will neutralize the odor, but she is wrong.

"All right now, Leenie. That's enough of your foolishness, you hear?"

I pretend I don't hear, and I keep staring at the door and counting the seconds until a car horn sounds. My mother is always punctual. She drops Vicky and me off at seven every morning and picks us up at four-thirty every evening. It is four-twenty-nine, and we know to be wrapped and ready to run out the door at the sound of her car horn. She never comes inside.

I wish she would come inside, just once, so she can see what we do all day, while she is working. Mothers are supposed to be psychic, and I just know that if she comes inside she will sniff the air and know. She can save us if she comes inside.

The horn sounds, and Vicky rushes over to the door like she expects Santa Claus to be on the other side of it. The way she wobbles in her coat would be funny if there wasn't something so desperate about her need to escape. She, too, is wrapped as snug as a bug in a rug, and her mittens slip off the doorknob many times before she is able to grab hold of it and turn it.

My grandmother's hand is weighting my shoulder down, and as I go to follow Vicky out the door, it clenches tight enough to keep me in place. She puts her face in mine and forces my chin up with a finger, makes me look in her eyes.

"You fix your face, Leenie. Ain't nothing in the world that bad you gotta look like that," she says.

"I hate you." To my grandmother's face, I say this. And I feel like I have lost twenty pounds afterward. It is finally off my chest, out there for her to look at and to consider the ramifications.

I expect her to apologize, to say that she knows she is wrong, to ask me what she can do to make me stop hating her, but she doesn't. What she says is this: "I hate you too."

And I never look at the world the same again.

***

My mother answers on the fourth ring. She is in the middle of a nap and my call wakes her up. I hear low levels of irritation in her voice, and I clear my throat, clamp the receiver to the side of my face with a trembling hand. If I cannot sleep, then neither will she.

"Why didn't you ever come inside?" I say as soon as she says hello.

She says nothing for long seconds, and then she releases a strong breath. "Is that what you called to ask me, Helena?"

"Yes. Why didn't you?"

"This is ridiculous, you know that?"

"Ridiculous like it was ridiculous when I told you what was going on inside that goddamn house?"

"You were a child and you liked to make things up. You—"

"Vicky backed me up. She said the same thing I did."

"Vicky was always easily influenced. You could always talk her into doing or saying whatever you told her to say and do. What is this about?"

"It's about you never coming inside." I'm pissed and she hears it in my voice. "If everything was a figment of my imagination, why didn't you ever come inside?"

"Because I had worked all day and I was tired. Okay? What else do you want to know?"

"How could you do it?"

"How could I do what, Helena?" She is out of sorts and patting around on the nightstand for her cigarettes and lighter. She pauses to fit a cancer stick between her lips, and then the flicker of death ignited comes through loud and clear. "How could I do what?"

"Be in such a state of denial that you didn't even hear your own children's cries for help?"

"Look, I don't have to listen to this. It's been peaceful while you were gone, and now that you're back, don't think you're about to turn my life upside down just because you messed yours up. It doesn't work like that."

"You could've saved us. You could've kept us away from that place and saved us."

"And then did what with you? Neither of you cows had sense enough to stay your asses inside the house like I told you, so what was I supposed to do with you? All I needed was somebody calling the police because my kids was running the streets and at home by themselves. If you had listened to me and stayed inside, you could've saved yourselves. So how is this my fault?"

"You made me kill her. You did nothing, so I had to do something."

"Oh my God"—like she is in a state of disbelief—"Leenie . . ."

"Don't call me that."

"Girl, you have lost the last little piece of your mind you still had. I knew something wasn't quite right about you the last time I saw you, but I couldn't put my finger on it. Are you insane?"

"It's the truth. You made me kill her because you didn't do anything to stop me from wanting to. You knew." She tries to interrupt me, but I roll right over her words and keep going. "Don't interrupt me when I'm talking, Mother. You knew about the sick shit going on in that house and you can't tell me you didn't. That's why you never came in. You sent us in there day after day, but you wouldn't do what you were making us do. How are you looking at yourself in the mirror every day?"

"The same way you manage to look at yourself, Leenie."

"Oh, is that so, *Ellie*?" I use her childhood nickname and stop her flow with a gasp. She knows that I know. "Are you still there, *Ellie*? Are you listening, *Ellie*?"

"You're crazy," she hisses into the phone. "I'm hanging up now."

"Hang up then, *Ellie*."

"Good-bye, Leenie."

"Good-bye, *Ellie*. And thanks for nothing." I give her the click first.

Aaron and I are testing out the hypothesis that a man's hands grow a woman's hair. He shows up on my doorstep, claiming to be in the throes of writer's block and aggravated because of it, so I put him to work moisturizing my scalp. I hand him a bottle of pre-warmed hot oil treatment and curl up on the floor between his knees. Twenty minutes after he finishes, I am in no hurry to leave the cave his long legs provide, and he likes the way my fingernails scratch through the hair on his calves. It is a mutually satisfying compromise, a safe coven to take shelter in, in exchange for endless minutes of scalp massage and follicle stimulation.

He leans back against the futon and purrs like a big cat, but I'm not sure if he is responding to what I am doing or what I am saying. With him, it is hard to tell what's going on inside his head.

"I think about her sometimes," I say after several minutes of thick silence. Our conversation is heavy, and it makes the air in the room heavy too. I feel my voice pushing through the density of it, ignoring the signals to remain trapped inside me and struggling to be heard. I think it wants to be heard even though what I am saying is not fit for human consumption. "I don't think I'm saying it right. I don't really think *about* her,

don't feel sorry for her as an individual, but I think
about her. About what happened to her. Does that
make sense?"

"Does it make sense to you?"

"I guess it does, yeah. You really had to be there to
know what I'm saying. It's like laughing at a joke that
goes right over your head, if you weren't there."

"Now, that makes sense to me," he says. He leans
forward and stretches an arm around me. His hand is
shiny with oil, and I catch the hot oil bottle before it
falls to the coffee table and makes a mess. I smell pep-
permint gum on his breath as he retreats back into his
reclining pose.

"Did you know her?"

"Only by sight. She was one of the aggressives. A
chick named Nicky."

"Aggressives?"

"What they call a woman who is more like a man
than a woman." I look over my shoulder and catch his
eyes. "You know what I mean—a woman who might as
well be a man."

Aaron chuckles under his breath. "Oh, like a woman
who could kick my ass?"

"And take your woman."

"That's pushing it a little bit, but I see what you're
saying. So Nicky was a man's man. What did she do
and who did she do it to?"

"I can't remember now, but it seems like it was
something really silly."

"But you can remember what happened to her?"

"At least twice a week." My fingers leave his calves
and find his toes in his slides. I pluck at the hair on
the tops of his big toes and release a shaky breath.
"I can still hear her screaming all the way over on D
block, where I am. She's on A block, but I can hear her

like she's in the cell next to me. I remember thinking, where the hell are the guards when you need them? Why don't they come and help her?"

"They pretended like they didn't hear her?"

"I don't know how they couldn't have heard her, when I can still hear her right now."

"That tickles."

"What?"

"Playing with my feet," he says softly. "Tickles."

"I'll stop." I discover the skin on the undersides of his knees and linger. "She was this big, ugly woman. Her voice was deep and rough, like a chainsmoking man, and she was always hacking and spitting like a damn thug all the time. But you know what? She screamed like a woman."

We sit with the quiet for a while. He lets me get lost in my thoughts and doesn't interrupt me as I navigate through them, find my way out and back into the room. His fingers get twisted up in my locks, and my scalp is putty in his hands. He is working my demons loose and coaxing them out of my mouth.

"What did they do to her?" Everyone from my time in prison is relegated to the ambiguous category of *they*ness. The guards, the other inmates, the violators and the victims. They are all *they* and Aaron helps me keep them there.

"I don't know, but even if I did, you wouldn't want to know the specifics. In some ways women are ten times more vicious than men."

"You think so?"

I recognize his tone. It is the one he uses when he wants me to elaborate. The one he uses when he thinks he is being covert about prying. He doesn't know what bag I will come out of, so he reverts to the tone. "I know so," I say, deciding to indulge him because I need to indulge myself. "Men aren't evolved enough to give a shit about weaknesses that they can't taste, touch and feel. They get caught up in surface shit like money and physical strength, whose dick is bigger. Women go deeper. You think I care if another woman's tits are bigger than mine are if the goal is to bring her to her knees? I'm looking for the core of her, what makes her thinks she is who she is. That's where I want to start attacking. Nobody can tear a woman up like another woman. It's instinctive."

"Sounds like you know from experience."

"Experience is the best teacher, Aaron. I'm a woman, or at least I was before I went inside, and I'm telling you what I know. I don't know what I am now."

"Go deep with me, Lena. Tell me who you think you are now."

I take a deep breath and shake my head. "You don't know what you're asking."

"I think I have pretty good idea." He nudges my head from one side to the other, collecting my locks in his fist and making a ponytail at the top of my head. "I don't think you know what I'm asking though. Don't think you know who you are."

"Now you're just trying to piss me off."

"Am I lying?"

"How are you going to ask me something like that? Who do I think I am? What kind of question is that?"

"It's a simple question. Who are you?"

"No," I blurt out, spinning on my butt until I am looking up into his face. "That's not what you said. You said who do I *think* I am."

"Same thing."

"No it's not."

"It isn't?" He cocks his head to one side and stares me down, knows he's talking about two different things and wants to see if I am mentally flexible enough to keep up with him.

"You know damn well it's not. Don't play with me, Aaron. Don't patronize me, okay?"

"Is that what I'm doing? Playing with you?"

"Hell yeah. If I know you, you've got my hair sticking straight up in the air, looking silly as hell. Sitting here asking me questions and acting like you don't know what you're asking. You think I'm a joke or something, like I don't know about your psychology shit?"

"I think you haven't answered my question."

"It's a stupid question. Who am I? Who do you see? What you see is who I am."

"That's your answer? What I see is what I get? Like Coronet?"

"I don't owe you anything."

"You owe yourself something though."

"Go where I've gone and then come back and tell me that. Live with animals like I've lived with them and then tell me that."

"*They* are animals now?"

"*They* have always been animals. Guess that makes me one too, right?"

"If you say so."

"Okay, well then that's what I'm saying." He spreads his knees to make room for me to hop to my feet, and I use them as leverage. I call out, "I'm an animal," on my way to the kitchen. "You ever seen a caged animal in action?" I don't hear a response, but I'm not really expecting one. I nod my head as I stick it inside the refrigerator and push things around on the shelf. Come out with a bottle of water that is half gone in one gulp. "I didn't think so."

Aaron materializes in front of me as I back out of the refrigerator and stand. "What does a caged animal do?" He takes my water bottle and puts it to his mouth without dropping my eyes.

"Kill, steal and destroy." He offers me the water and I take it, put it to my own mouth.

"You did that?"

"What if I did?"

"What if you did? Did you have to do it?"

"I thought I did at the time. I had to survive. Kill or be killed."

"So rather than be killed, you did the killing."

"Still ended up dead though."

We stare and then his lips open in slow motion. "What are we talking about here?"

"Survival of the fittest."

"No, I mean right here and now. What are we talking about, Lena?"

"I don't understand the question, Aaron."

"I think you do. Are we talking about you hearing another woman's screams or your own?"

I suck in a sharp breath and open my eyes wide to glare at him. "That's a fucked-up question."

He shrugs nonchalantly and hisses through perfect teeth. "Open your mouth and tell me you never screamed. Nobody ever made you scream. Tell me."

I don't open my mouth and tell him what he dares me to tell him because I can't. My heart is beating too fast, throat too dry. What I tell him is this: "Get out."

"Coward."

"Fuck you. Get out."

"I don't think so."

"Excuse me?"

"You still owe me, so you need to keep your word and oil my scalp like you promised."

I look at his low 'fro and roll my eyes. "That nappy shit. Oil it yourself."

"And you can get a comb through yours?"

"Fuck you," I say again because it feels good coming out of my mouth. It sounds vulgar, but it hits the tip of my tongue just right. Gives me power.

"I dare you."

It stops me, what he says. Makes me pull up short and reevaluate my stance. Makes my eyes fall into his like a ball into a mitt. I push past him and flop down on the futon, spread my knees and point to the floor. "Sit down, boy. I swear I can't stand your ass."

A few minutes later, he snatches the comb from my hand and does a one-eighty to stare at me. "Are you trying to pull my hair out by the roots?"

"I'm trying to comb the nappy shit. Turn around so I can get through."

"Whatever. Do me some of those braids. I think I might go for the hug-a-thug look this week."

"It's too short to braid, and you're too old for that shit anyway. What you need is a haircut."

"How many times will you say *shit* before you find another curse word to throw around?"

"It won't be *fuck*, I know that much."

He stalls my progress and lays his head back in my lap and cracks up. Makes me laugh with him and pop him on the shoulder with the comb at the same time. It takes me almost an hour to get through oiling his scalp because he insists on thin parts and meticulous application. Not too heavy but not too light. Doesn't want to jeopardize the fluffiness of the 'fro he is too old to be sporting anyway. I talk about him bad as I lift the pick through his hair and shape it into a perfect halo around his head. When I am done he destroys my hard work and rests the side of his face against my thigh, finds my toes on the floor with his fingers.

He takes my feet with him as he stretches his legs out in front of him and fits his head between my thighs. The soles of my feet find balance on the tops of his thighs and we relax together. This is new, this closeness we are sharing, but it doesn't feel threatening, so I let it be. I try to recall if anything about Aaron feels threatening and I can't.

"Hey," I say, gently squeezing my thighs together on his neck. "I'm not your woman. You're getting a little too comfortable. Go home."

"Somebody's got jokes," he says, looking at me upside down.

"No, somebody's got work tonight and somebody needs sleep."

He doesn't raise his head from my thighs and leave for another hour, and I don't have the heart or the desire to make him.

Chapter Fourteen

Lack of sleep is to blame, I think. It is the reason I can't keep up with the assembly line tonight, the reason I have neglected an entire tray of fake Twinkies and sent them down to Stella, missing goo. She thinks I am on my job and doesn't check behind me before switching on the machine she controls and sealing the defective goods in cellophane. Some unsuspecting consumer somewhere will be disappointed with their purchase, but I will be long gone by then.

I forget to put on gloves before I pick up a tray of cupcakes, and the metal singes my palms. I scream and drop the tray on the floor. I stand there and watch the night manager inspect the damage and decide that over half of the cupcakes can be salvaged. I shake my head and squeeze goo into contaminated snack cakes, send them down the line to be sealed and tell myself I should call somebody to report what is happening.

I do that twice, drop trays, and then I take a break. I come back to my station ready to work, and my hands won't stop shaking. They are in cahoots with my overactive hearing, working together to wreak havoc on me, and slowly succeeding. I can't stop the screams from ricocheting through my head and deafening me. They are the same screams I have told Aaron about, but they are different. They aren't hers anymore, that other woman's. They are mine, and I almost hate him for reminding me that I screamed for help and that when help came, it was too late.

Stella hears my screams. She can see them flying around inside my head despite my best efforts to keep myself in check and make it through the shift in one piece. I keep forgetting that she has something like second sight. That she is just as much of an animal as I am. I can't hide from her for long. She is on me the minute we break for lunch, hovering outside the stall door as I empty my bladder and peering over my shoulder as I wash my hands. Dogging my heels, with her fingers poking me in the small of my back, making sure I don't veer off course as we make our way outside.

"I know you got a new job and everything, but you keep fucking around with those machines and you won't have any hands to fool with them computers," she says the minute the door closes behind us. "Ain't no reason to start showing your ass."

I sit on a makeshift chair that is really a milk crate turned bottom side up with an old plastic cushion on it, and lace my fingers on the back of my neck. "My head's kind of messed up tonight, Stella."

"Look at me." She waits until I do. "Who you think you talking to? You think I don't know?" She digs around in her mammoth purse and pulls out a flask, passes it to me like it is the Holy Grail. "Take yourself a sip and calm your nerves."

As soon as the vodka lights the tip of my tongue I start choking. The hairs in my nose catch fire, and heat spreads through my nasal passages. I cough and suck in long pulls of fresh air. "I'm already in violation of my parole by virtue of hanging out with you, Stella," I find my voice and croak. After a few more seconds of coughing, I wipe tears from my eyes and look at her. "The last thing I need is Isolde showing up and smelling liquor on my breath."

"That bitch ain't leaving her comfy bed to come and check up on your ass. Them sons-of-bitches don't know shit about violation." She takes her flask back and tips it to her lips. "You come out of the joint all rehabilitated and shit, all taught up how to act right, and they still treat you like shit every chance they get. How is that giving us a second chance?" The flask makes a wide arc in the air as she spreads her arms and looks around. "Look around you, Lucky. We still ain't got our forty acres and a mule."

The liquor makes me giggle. I have seen her like this many times before, and now I know why. "There is no such thing as second chances, Stella. You know that."

"You use that card I gave you?"

"Hell no. I don't need a shrink to tell me that my life is out of order. I need my old life back. The one I had before I fell down the rabbit hole and woke up."

"Take your ass back to sleep and see if you can find it then." I burst out laughing, and she finishes what is in her flask and joins me. "That's what I thought. You had some emancipation dick, yet?" I laugh even harder and damn near choke. "Okay . . . well, what about some pussy? You flow like that?"

"You are out of control, Stella. Just put the flask down, walk away slowly, and don't look back. Don't be like Lot's wife."

"Shit, I'm putting this sucker in my purse until next break. Here, I think it's one more swig left. Take it."

I push it away and shake my head. "I don't drink."

"If you don't get some help, Lucky, you will." She hikes her purse higher on her shoulder and uses her fingers to tick off her points. "This is what you gotta do. First, get some emancipation dick or pussy, however you flow, because that'll help keep your skin clear. Then you gotta find you somebody you feel comfortable talk-

ing to and talk. Get the poison out so some other shit
can get in. Like busting a boil. And then"—she pauses
as I groan loudly—"*and then* you gotta get on with your
life, Lucky. Don't waste your time trying to figure out
how I know what I'm saying, just do it."

"How many times have you pulled that flask out tonight, Stella? I think you might be drunk. Let me get
up so you can sit down." I think I see her wobble on her
feet and I pull her arm. "Sit your old, drunk ass down
before you fall down."

"In Africa they listens to the old folks," she tells me,
settling herself on the cushion. "Think they wise."

"This ain't Africa," I say.

"You goddamn right it ain't Africa, but if this ain't a
jungle just the same, I'll eat you. And I don't flow that
way, you hear me?"

"Stella . . . please." I try not to laugh but she makes it
hard. "Just sit here and chill out for a minute. Get some
fresh air."

"I'm telling you, Lucky. I seen some of them come
out and turn to drugs and sex, or else they turn right
around and go back inside. Like they can't survive
without some kind of crutch to lean on. Now you, I got
you pegged for a drinker. Can't see you shooting no shit
in your arms or sniffing nothing, but I can see you taking a sip or two. That's what'll make your hands stop
shaking, make you sleep easy at night."

The image she creates disturbs me in ways that I am
not ready to explore. I touch her shoulder with one
hand and push the other one through my locks. "Stop,
okay?"

"You ain't hearing me, girl. You ain't."

"I am. But I need you to stop now."

"You didn't know I had a daughter, did you?"

She won't stop, so I sit on the ground next to her and wrap my arms around my knees. "I can't handle this shit right now, Stella." She is drunk, I know that now. Not getting there, but already there and riding it out. Coming down and wanting to talk, requiring me to listen. She knows I am not going back inside without her. Knows I won't let her go back inside until I think she is okay.

"I said *had* because I don't know where the hell she is, right to this day, Lucky. I been in and out of lockdown so many times I lost count, and this last time, when I decided I wasn't going back, I couldn't find her." Stella slaps her hands on her knees and rocks herself, looks somewhere in the air in front of her face at something that I cannot see. That I know I don't want to see. "She got herself pregnant six times, which means I got six grandbabies out there somewhere and I don't even know where they at. Can't even begin to tell you. But you know what I do know?"

I open my mouth to ask her what she knows, but she isn't expecting an answer and she doesn't wait for one.

"You reminds me of her a little bit. Something about the eyes, I think. I don't want you to end up like her though. Last I heard she was shooting that shit in her veins and living in a fantasy world from sunup to sundown. She ain't had nobody to talk to and tell her right from wrong, 'cause I was too busy ripping and running. But you, you can be talking your ass off, getting that shit out of you before it eats you up."

"I'm all right, Stella," I say and squeeze her arm.

"I'll see your ass this time next year and you'll have a handy dandy little flask, just like mine. Might be gold instead of silver, though, 'cause you strikes me as a gold flask kind of person. Don't do that, Lucky. Get some help for your demons."

"There's no such thing as demons. The Boogeyman either."

"Shit, girl, you need more help than I first thought. That's when you know you really in trouble—when you can't see the demons riding on your back. Them motherfuckers sneaky like that."

"Did you get rid of yours by talking to somebody?"

"Lucky." Stella says my name like she is tired. Her shoulders sag as she digs through her purse and presents me with her flask. "My demons is at the bottom of this thing. I drank 'em up. Now . . . I'ma ask you again. Do you want to be like me?"

I stare at the flask and say nothing.

Nothing about it is intimidating, Vicky tells me. She shares her first impressions of what she sees in her professional nursing voice, which I think is strange, but I don't comment. She describes the landscaping around the building like she is talking about blood pressure levels and the associated dangers of letting them go unchecked. She judges the staff coming and going in the same voice that she uses to explain the side effects of medication. I listen to her voice clip itself off at the end of each word, feel it emphasizing periods after every couple of syllables, and wonder exactly when the transformation from woman to automaton occurred.

Before coming here, we spent part of the afternoon sitting around a car dealership lobby, cackling like old hens and sipping bargain store coffee, while her car was being serviced. Then we roamed around in a high-end shoe store, trying on shoes that we didn't need and wishing there was a clearance rack in sight. In Target, she bought a battery for her cordless phone and I bought a cordless phone, a Tom Jones CD, and a bag of

Cracker Jacks. She was fine, relaxed and loose, smiling and laughing embarrassingly loud.

She is tight now. Uptight, upright and tense in the driver's seat. Fixated on every detail of the single-story building across the street from where we are parked at the curb. She describes to me what I can see with my own eyes, like I am blind and she is my sight. I see brick and glass, an entrance and an exit door, and cars in the parking lot. As an afterthought, I glance at flowers and shrubs because she makes such a point of mentioning the million different colors some gardener has mixed together.

I tell her that I don't give a shit about flowers, and she makes herself smile. "What are you going to do while I'm in there?" Fifteen minutes from now I will be inside the building, meeting with a counselor for the first time in my life. I'm worried about how things will go and curious to find out what I have to say to someone I don't know, but I am even more worried about the look on Vicky's face.

She ignores my question and asks one of her own. "What are you going to do in there?"

"Stella says I need to get some stuff off my chest, so I guess I'll do that."

"What does Stella know, Leenie? I mean, who is she to say you need therapy? What makes her think that?"

"I think she's a closet alcoholic," I say and silently apologize to Stella for setting her business out on front street.

Vicky throws her hands up and rolls her eyes to the roof of the car. "Oh, well, of course she's qualified to judge your mental state. God knows she's got her shit together."

"You don't understand. She—"

"I understand you're taking mental health advice from an alcoholic ex-convict, Leenie. I understand that perfectly. What I don't understand is why you're even stooping to her level."

She goes on and on and doesn't realize what she has just said. I watch her face shift and wrap itself around every emotion she feels, let her run out of steam slowly. "I'm an ex-con too, Vicky. Did you forget that?"

"Your situation is different from hers," she snaps.

"How?"

"You know how, Leenie. Look, I don't want to argue about this. I just don't think you need to be telling all your business to some stranger who doesn't have a fucking clue, okay?"

"What if something is really wrong with me?" I put up a hand when she grips the steering wheel and grits her teeth. "Just listen for a minute. What if I do need to talk to someone about some of the stuff going on in my life?"

"Like what? What's going on in your life that isn't going on in anybody else's?"

"Nothing," I say. "I think that's the point. I hardly ever leave the house if I'm not going to work or with you or Beige."

"Neither do I."

"Except for Stella, I have no friends."

"Neither do I. And Stella is suspect, if you ask me. You can do better."

"I don't know who I am anymore, Vicky. I don't even know where to begin looking for myself."

"None of us really knows who we are. That's why life is such a bitch. You don't start knowing yourself until it's time to die, and by then, what's the point?"

"I'm scared damn near all the time and I don't know why." The admission takes a lot out of me and puts a lot in me at the same time. Until now I haven't given a name to a large part of what I feel on a day to day basis. Finally, I face it and call it what it is: Fear.

"What are you afraid of?"

"Living. I've been away for eight years, and everything is new and strange. Everything feels different, like I'm supposed to be doing something, but I don't know what."

"You need to give yourself time to adjust, Leenie. I tried to tell you that before you moved out, but you wouldn't listen to me. You had to—"

I cut her off. "Don't do that."

"Do what? Speak the truth?"

"Don't minimize what I feel. Don't try to make everything have a nice, neat explanation, because it doesn't. What's going on with me doesn't have shit to do with me moving out of your dungeon and you know it. My shit goes way deeper than that, Vicky. And you are the *last* person I should have to say that to."

"Oh, so that's it," she says, flopping back in her seat and staring at me. She looks at me as if she has finally figured out the mystery and doesn't like the conclusion. "That's what you're going in there to tell those folks? All our family business?"

"Have you ever told anyone about what happened?"

"Hell no, and why would I?" She looks at me like I am crazy.

"Why wouldn't you? It wasn't your fault. Mine, either."

"I don't need people looking at me like I'm some kind of freak, whispering and giggling about my business and thinking, poor, poor Victoria. Did you hear what happened to her? I don't need that shit, Leenie. And neither do you. The old bitch is dead. Let the shit stay dead with her."

I look at Vicky long and hard. Give her time to get her emotions under control before I say, "You don't have friends, either."

"How in the hell do you know what I have? I have friends all over the place. Work and everyplace else."

"Beige says the phone hardly rings, and when it does, it's mainly Mama."

"Beige talks too damn much."

"You don't socialize the way you should."

"Now you're Oprah?"

"Why aren't you dating anyone?"

"Lord," Vicky drawls sarcastically. "Please don't tell me you're about to suggest hooking me up with one of your butchie girlfriends?"

"You think I'm a lesbo?" I almost laugh out loud.

"Shit, don't you think you're a lesbo? What's with all the scruffy jeans and tee shirts? No makeup, no nail polish, no nothing. You don't even wear earrings."

"Beige stole them again and she won't give them back."

"Well, here." She snatches diamond cut hoops from her ears and pushes them into my hands. "Put these on."

"You know that was a low blow, right?" I flip the visor mirror down and check myself out after I put on the earrings. "You were wrong for that *butchie* crack."

"Am I right though? Are you attracted to women, Leenie?"

"Would you blame me if I was?" I catch her eyes and raise my eyebrows. "I mean, with all the shit we've been through, odds are one of us would turn left. Would it be so strange if I was the one who did? Would it really?"

Vicky snaps her mouth shut and her eyes dance away from mine. "Are you going in there or not?"

I reach over and squeeze her hand to bring her eyes back to mine. "You should come with me." My words make her snatch her hand away and use it to massage the wrinkles out of her forehead. She closes her eyes on a long hiss and shakes her head.

"No, Leenie. You're not the only who can be scared and that"—she points out the window and shakes her head again—"scares the shit out of me. Stay out here with me. Will you do that?"

I don't have to think about my response. I have been saying it for so long that it comes automatically and it feels at home on my lips. "Don't I always stay with you?" I ask softly.

For the third time in a week I stand on Aaron's doorstep at the crack of dawn, with my pillow bunched under my arm and thick sweat socks hanging off my feet. He hears my knock and opens the door without bothering to look through the peephole. He knows it is me and he knows what I want.

We don't speak as he stands back from the door, making ugly faces as he stretches, and I tip over to his sofa to spread out. He locks the door and walks back into his bedroom to resume what I have disturbed. He is a night owl, and knowing him, he hasn't been asleep long. Probably just long enough for the sleep to get good and then I show up, dragging my pillow behind me.

There is a blanket folded over the back of the sofa waiting for me, and I reach for it instinctively. I am too lazy to sit up and shake it open, so I kick it open with my feet and curl up underneath it, sighing when my head hits the pillow. His space settles around me in a way that mine will not when I am having trouble sleeping. I hear the kitchen clock ticking and his fax machine click on and go into receive mode. Feel my lips becoming slack and my eyelids gaining weight.

I am asleep in minutes, and Aaron's voice rips me out of my silent void the way a baby is ripped from the womb.

"Lena." He stands in his bedroom doorway, wearing gray boxers and scratching his bare chest.

I wipe saliva from the rim of my mouth and wait for my eyes to uncross. "What?" He moves away from the doorway and leaves me wondering, and it doesn't take me long to find my way to his room. I stand at the edge of his bed and tug on my locks. "What did you want?"

Aaron doesn't say anything, just shifts around in bed and tosses the covers back. He creates a space for me and pounds the pillow under his head. It bunches into submission and he nestles the side of his face into it and stares at me, waiting. I look at him and then at the bed, at the bed and then at him. Then I turn around and walk out of his bedroom.

I come back ten seconds later with my pillow.

"There's an extra pillow," he says, yawning.

"I know. I need mine too." I give him my back, pull the covers up to my waist and hug a pillow to my chest. I push my arm underneath the pillow on loan from him and close my eyes. I take a deep breath and scratch the tip of my nose. Try not to move too much as I bend my arm back and search for the spot between my shoulder blades that is itching. He becomes still and clears his throat.

"Right here?" His nails scrape over the surface of my tee shirt and land in one spot.

"Lower." I sigh as he scratches lightly. "Harder."

"Here?"

"Yeah."

"Better?"

"Yeah. Thanks."

"No problem." His breathing evens out and I know he is drifting off. "Did you have a bad dream?"

"Little bit."

"Scale of one to ten, how bad?"

"Seventeen and a half."

"Do you want to talk about it?"

"No." And then, "I heard the screams again."

"Hers or yours?"

I am silent for several seconds. He knows what he is asking me, and I do too. "Mine."

"How many times, Lena?"

"Once." I hug my pillow tighter and squeeze my eyelids shut. "Can't sleep sometimes."

He scoots across the mattress and curls his body around mine, parts his calves for my feet and then crosses his ankles around them. His arm is like a weight around my waist, solid and strong, and I don't worry about being yanked out of bed if I don't want to be. I know I won't be attacked and sleep is safe.

But just in case I don't know, he says, "Sleep now."

I lose contact with the world and sleep.

Aaron is still snoring when I open my eyes again. It is almost one o'clock in the afternoon, time for any sane person to be up and about. I move away from him slowly and ease off the mattress. He is sleeping so hard that he doesn't even realize I'm missing. I cross the living room, look at the blanket I abandoned on the sofa, and go into the kitchen.

The smell of sizzling bacon does what missing body heat couldn't. It wakes Aaron up and brings him stumbling into the kitchen, sniffing the air. I pass him a mug of Colombian blend and watch him take a seat at the table. I flip bacon over in the skillet and get my thoughts together.

I gather my courage and open my mouth. Something has been on my mind for the longest, and I am finally ready to satisfy my curiosity. "Why don't you have a girlfriend? Or a wife?"

His mug stops halfway to his mouth and he eyes me warily. "Broke up with the last woman I was seeing not too long before you moved in."

"How long before?"

"About two weeks." He takes a sip and shakes his head sadly. "Couldn't deal with her son. He's sixteen and so out of control it isn't even funny. Had to keep asking myself if I was sleeping with her or if he was. I'm too old for pissing contests."

"You never wanted kids?"

"I always wanted kids. I want to be married first though."

"So you're holding out for a ring?"

"I'm getting too old to be holding out for anything right about now. It didn't happen, and that's cool with me. Can't miss what you never had."

I crack eggs on the rim of a bowl and add salt, pepper and a dash of milk. "None of the women in my family ever got married, either. Guess we were all too fucked up to try living normal lives."

"Normal is subjective," he says.

"No, it's not. There's normal and then there's fucked up. Two completely different things. The women in my family were fucked up. Still are."

"If you say so." He bows his head over the plate I slide in front of him and prays. I watch him and wonder what his god's name is. If his god really has his eye on the sparrow or if he only sees the good and righteous people. I wonder if I am even in his god's peripheral vision, and then I try to picture what a sparrow looks like.

"Stella thinks I need to talk to somebody . . . about my issues," I blurt out. "What do you think?"

"Do you care what I think?"

"Yes, tell me."

"Truth?"

"Truth. Slow down before you choke yourself."

"Yes, ma'am. I think you have a story to tell. I think it might help somebody else."

"You're just saying that shit because you want a best-seller."

Eyebrows go to the ceiling and lips curve. "Oh, your shit has the makings of a bestseller?"

"If you can write worth a damn, it does."

"So tell it to me. Let me help you tell your story."

"No."

"You chicken?"

"Maybe." I drop slices of bread in the toaster and turn the heat up. They can't brown fast enough, and I waste time rooting around in the refrigerator. "Strawberry jam or apple butter?"

"Plain butter," he says. "And then strawberry jam. Do I scare you, Lena?"

"You did at first."

"Why?"

I think about my answer as I spread butter and then jam. I take a bite out of one of his slices and hand it to him. "Big and tall," I tell him. "Man. Foreign object. It's been close to ten years, Aaron." He whistles behind his teeth and looks at me through new eyes. "Things like hairy chests and hard-ons, I don't know anything about."

"You felt that, huh?"

"Yeah."

"Did it scare you?"

"A little bit."

"What was scary about it?"

I surprise myself by blushing, something I haven't done in years . . . since before. "Nothing. Everything. I don't know."

"It might be interesting to find out."

We stare each other down. "It might be a nightmare too."

"But eventually you might be curious?"

He chews purposefully and watches me watch him. My eyes won't stay on his face. They go to his chest and count the hairs there. They float along the length of his arms and ride the muscles, then drop to his legs and remember the hardness there. They snap back up to his and dig in. "I already am. But I need to get things straightened out in my head before I can even think about going there with you."

"Then talking to somebody might help."

"So you think I should?"

"I think you should think about it."

"And while I'm thinking about that, what will you be thinking about?"

He catches my eyes and swallows a mouthful of coffee. Finally, he says, "You tell me."

Chapter Fifteen

Vicky has the radio blasting so our conversation can't be heard on the other side of our bedroom door. We finish plotting and planning, and then we sit on our beds and wait for the inevitable confrontation. An old Temptations cut keeps us company as we both deal with our own personal demons and search for courage. We don't have long to ruminate, but we know this already and we are ready.

The door flies open and my mother stomps into the room, twists the knob on the stereo and brings silence to our space. The three of us take turns staring at each other and then smoke starts pouring out of my mother's ears. Vicky and I are still wearing our pajamas, and we are nowhere near ready to walk out the door with her. I haven't brushed my teeth and Vicky's hair is sticking out from her head like she stuck her finger in a light socket. My mother is beyond pissed.

"What the hell is this?" she roars. "I thought I told you heifers to get your clothes on damn near an hour ago."

Vicky looks at me and I look at her. She is supposed to take the lead on this, but as always, I am the one who grabs the reins and smacks the horse on the ass. "We're not going," I say.

"Excuse me?" A hand goes to a hip and her neck rolls. She dares me to repeat myself, gives me the evil eye and lets me know that an ass-whipping is in my very near future.

"We're not going. I'm not, anyway. Can't speak for Vicky."

"I'm not going either," Vicky finds her voice and speaks up. She tucks her feet back under the covers on her bed and lies on her back. Folds her hands on her stomach and looks at the ceiling. "I hate it over there."

"I have work, goddammit. I don't have time for this shit. I need to be rolling in five minutes, and the two of you need to be rolling with me." She snatches the covers off of Vicky and grabs her arm. "Get up and get some damn clothes on. You too, Leenie. I don't know what the hell kind of games you're trying to play, but making me late for work is out."

"Leave her alone," I say. "We're not going and you can't make us."

"Oh, I can't make you?" My mother pulls her shirt up and starts in on her belt. She twists it loose and eases it out of the loops, holding my eyes to make sure I see what she's doing. "Is that what you just said? I can't make you?"

"I don't care about a whipping. I'm still not going."

She comes toward me, about to snatch me up from the bed and put a hurting on me. "Girl, you better—"

"I'll call the police and tell them you beat me if you make me go over there. I'll run away and I'll go so far away that you'll never find me," I promise. And I will, because it is the only option. I have been pushed into a corner, and the only way I can get out is to come out swinging. At this point, I don't care who gets hit. "I'm not going."

"I'm not either," Vicky adds. She sits up on the edge of her bed and grips the mattress. "If Leenie runs away, I'm going with her. You want us to do that?"

"I want you to get some clothes on so I can go to work," my mother screams. I duck as she swings the belt and it lands with a loud whack on the bed next to me. "All of a sudden you're on strike, when you know I can't afford to lose my job playing around with you?"

"So go to work. We can stay here, like we used to do."

"We tried that once, remember?" She glances at her watch and curses like a thug on the street. Says words I have never heard uttered in anger. I've heard them uttered under other circumstances, but she doesn't know that. She pushes her hair off her forehead and looks around wildly. I think I see her counting to ten, and then she points a stiff finger. "How long have you two been planning this shit? All weekend? And you just now decided to pull this shit on me?"

"We decided we don't need to go over there anymore." This is Vicky's answer, and judging from the look on my mother's face, it doesn't make the cut.

"You just decided."

"It stinks," I say.

"And it's junky."

"There's roaches." It is a lie, but she never goes inside, so it's plausible.

"She doesn't feed us stuff we like to eat."

"And it's boring. I'm staying here."

Vicky darts a look at me and swallows. "Plus, we want to stay home from now on. School starts back in a little while anyway. We know to stay in the house."

I look at the alarm clock and can't help the smile that takes over my face. "You gone be late for work, Mama."

"I swear to God, if I come home and your little asses even look like you been outside . . ."

"We won't," Vicky tells her.

"And don't fool with my stove or the door. Don't open the door for nobody."

"We won't."

"Leenie?" She narrows her eyes at me, thinking I am the missing link. "You hear me?"

"Yes, Mama."

"If I come home and shit is out of order, I'm kicking some ass. Starting with you, Leenie. You're always the mastermind behind everything anyway."

Vicky rolls to her side and hugs her pillow, yawns like she is so sleepy. "Have a good day, Mama."

My mother slams out of the room, mumbling under her breath and slinging her purse around. Her head rotates on her neck and snaps back into place as she snaps at the air in front of her. She is so out of it that she forgets to put her belt back on. I sit still and wait for the sound of the front door closing and the locks twisting. When I am sure she is gone, I stroll around the house and double-check. I come back and see Vicky dancing around in the middle of the floor, grinning from ear to ear.

"Thought you was punking out on me for a minute there," I say.

She laughs and flops back on the bed. "I can't believe she didn't beat the shit out of us."

"Nothing she can do with both of us at one time. I told you that. Present a unified front and she has no choice but to back down. I was gone slit my wrists if she would've made us go over there. She would've had to drag my ass out of the house, kicking and screaming and butt-ass naked. And she would've really been late for work, stopping by the emergency room and everything."

Vicky is cracking up, laughing so hard that she holds her stomach and struggles to breathe. "I can see you doing some stupid stuff like that, too." We slap fives because we have won our first scrimmage.

"You think I'm playing, but I'm serious." I go over to the window and raise it halfway. Find my stash and light a cigarette. I squat down and blow smoke through the screen into the morning air. "If she brings her ass over here looking for us, I might just slit her wrists instead."

"She ain't coming over here."

I don't say anything, just look back at Vicky over my shoulder and raise my eyebrows.

Around lunchtime, Vicky tips up behind me at the front door and whispers in my ear.

"You was right. That bitch came over here looking for us."

"Told you," I whisper back and press my eye to the peephole. My grandmother is pounding on the storm door and calling out for us to open up. To let the lion into the lamb's den.

"Victoria! Leenie!" she shouts, still pounding. "I know y'all in there. Open this damn door and I mean open it right now!"

"She's out of her fucking mind," I tell Vicky. The pounding starts to get on my nerves, and before I know it, I am yelling along with her. "Go away! I'm not opening the door, so go home!"

"Leenie?" Like she doesn't recognize my voice. "You open this door right now. Y'mama told me 'bout this morning. I'm here to bring you two back to my house so I can keep an eye on you. Now, open up. I ain't got all day."

Vickie pushes me aside and takes over where I leave off. "Mama said not to open the door for strangers," she calls out in a sweet voice.

"Strangers? What the hell?"

"We don't know you," I say. "So go away."

"How 'bout this?" My grandmother gets bold and sassy. "How 'bout if I call the police and tell them you in the house all by yourselves?"

Vicky is fourteen and I am twelve. Together, we are more than old enough to be home alone. "How 'bout if I call the police and tell them what I know?" I check the locks and make sure they are secure. I have considered the fact that she might have a spare key, and that is why the storm door is locked and the safety chain is in place. I tell myself that if she makes her way inside my sanctuary, they will have to carry her out. I have drawn the line.

I step back from the door and look at Vicky. We decide to ignore the pounding until it goes away. "You want the bathroom first?"

"Yeah, but you're coming with me, right?"

"I was gone smoke another cigarette," I say.

"Leenie," she whines and stamps her foot. I think I see tears collecting in her eyes.

"I don't want to look at your naked ass." The truth is that sitting on the toilet seat while she takes a bath is boring as hell. I can think of a million other things I would rather be doing, but she doesn't like to be in the bathroom alone.

"You can sit outside the door and read one of those nasty books you got hidden in the room."

"Harlequin Silhouettes are not nasty."

"Does Mama know you got them?" She never considers that smoking at twelve years old is a much worse transgression. It is the nasty books that she focuses on, and they aren't even nasty.

"No, and she better not. Damn, you get on my nerves. Why you need me to go in there with you?"

She takes off for our room and comes back a few minutes later with clean underwear and her housecoat bunched in her arms. "I don't know," she says. "But you gone stay with me, right?"

I grab my book, follow her down the hallway to the bathroom, and slump to the floor outside the door. "Don't I always stay with you?"

Half an hour later the phone rings, and she calls out, "You still there?"

"Yeah, and hurry up. My butt is falling asleep," I answer, turning a page. She knows I'm not going anywhere.

He wants to celebrate my first day on my new job, even though all I did was sit in orientation and fight to keep my eyes open. The transition from the graveyard shift to day shift messes with my head, and staying awake all day is a challenge that I am proud to have met head on. He wants to celebrate that too.

He meets me on the porch when I get home from work and tells me to hurry up and change into something loose and comfortable. Some shorts and a tee shirt, he says. And that is what I do, pull my locks into a ponytail and jump into denim cutoffs and an Abercrombie and Fitch tee shirt that I stole from Beige because it looks better on me than it does on her. I hope leather slides are decent enough for wherever we are going.

The minute we get to our destination I kick off my slides and crunch grass between my toes. I help him pick a spot to spread a blanket, and then I claim the spot in the vee of his thighs for my own. My spine curves to his chest and he takes my weight, lets his hands hang from his knees and gets barefoot with me.

In a park is where we are, and there is an outdoor jazz concert underway. Hundreds of people are scattered around on the grass, doing the same thing we are doing, listening and enjoying. Scandalous-smelling smoke wafts past us and the hiss of beer cans being sneaked open is loud in the evening air. We sniff and glance at each other, giggle like kids.

The sky turns dark and stars peek out, and I have a thought. I lean into his chest even harder and tilt my face up to his. "Did I ever tell you that I used to smoke?"

"Wacky tobacky?" His eyebrows climb his forehead and a smile takes his mouth.

"No, cigarettes. I was twelve. I quit when I was thirteen."

"Nah, you never told me that."

"Well, I'm telling you now."

"And I'm listening too."

"Do you hear that?"

"What?" He slaps at a mosquito and curses under his breath.

"That horn. He's tearing that baby up. I love it. Listen."

"I'm listening," Aaron says and touches his lips to the back of my neck. "I'm listening."

I beg him to let me stay until the concert is over. The music goes on and on, and it is after midnight when I finally stumble into my apartment. I will be exhausted in the morning, but I don't care. I haven't heard good jazz music, live and unfiltered, in years, and if I suffer, it will be worth it.

Denny gives a guard the signal, and a loud buzzing noise fills the air and shakes B dorm up. It is somewhere around three in the morning and we are awake, the six of us, my family and Anna, when we should be asleep like most everybody else. But this is not the time for sleeping; it is the time for revenge. This is Lou's brainstorm, but I am her wingman, the one who was wronged and the one with a point to prove. If I don't follow through, she says, then I will forever be a victim, and victimology has no place in prison.

This is why, after a row of cell doors slide open, I am the first to go charging inside cell number nine, swinging a pillowcase filled with sharp hunks of granite. I know who my target is, and I make a beeline for her, drag her down from her bunk and kick her around on the floor. I do my best to bash her head in with the pillowcase. Her cellmate tries to help her, but Lou grabs her and throws her against the wall like she weighs a lot of nothing. She finds herself with a blade pressed to her neck and, like a good girl, she doesn't move.

This is the bitch I want. The ringleader. The one with the super-size homemade dick that bled me out like a stuck pig. Lou says she has pull and people listen when she talks, so she is the one to silence. The others are insignificant, nothing but minions, and my eventual revenge on them is sweet. But this is much sweeter, by far.

I have dreamed of the four of them, have seen their faces as I feared closing my eyes and sleeping, and imagined their demise. In the end, I push two of them into tubs of scalding hot water in the laundry room and watch their skin bubble on their limbs like soup. I know enough not to earn a murder charge, but permanent disfigurement seems appropriate. It appears to be an accident, which earns me nothing more than a stiff reprimand.

The cameras have blind spots, and one of those spots is where I am waiting with my sister for the fourth person on my list. We throw her to the floor and kick her any and everywhere. One of her arms is broken and she is missing three teeth when we are done with her, and I make sure she remembers me.

This one will too, I think as I aim for her face again and again. I try to wipe it away completely and almost take her life with me. Lou clamps her hands around my arms and pulls me out of the cell. She tosses the pillowcase inside the cell and goes back in after it. I don't hear what she says to the woman I have beaten to within an inch of her life, but I do hear what she says to her cellmate.

"Put the word out," Lou says. "Lucky is part of my family now, and that means nobody fucks with her from here on out. Make sure everybody understands, okay?" Her voice is low and smooth, like she is asking what color the sky is, but I have seen her choke a woman and use the same tone. She is a lifer, which means she has nothing to lose and we all know it. She has no soul.

Not long after I inflict senseless violence, I scream like I have lost my mind. Being a member of Lou's family means I have to take the mark, and I do it willingly. Anna wipes sweat from my forehead and tries to distract me with soft touches and sweet kisses, but nothing can erase the pain I feel. I breathe through my mouth and growl like a lion the entire time that it takes Denny to draw the hourglass on my back and then to color it in.

"How many years?" Denny wants to know. She already knows, but she wants to hear me say it.

"Nine." I get nine teardrops, and each one of them feels like fire on my skin. I don't consider it abuse though.

I consider myself lucky.

***

Isolde studies me curiously. She has changed up lipsticks and now she wears a crazy color purple to match the lilac eyeshadow on her eyelids. Everything she wears is from the purple family, her pants, her blouse and her shoes. Even the sterling silver ring on her index finger has a purple stone perched on top of it. I stare at her, and in my mind she looks like a giant grape. Reminds me that it's lunchtime.

"Is it as bad as they say it is?" she asks. We are talking about prison life. "I mean, I've seen that show *Oz,* and it makes prison seem like hell on earth. But is it really like that?"

"Television dramatizes everything," I say, choosing my words carefully. "But a lot of what you see is really what it's like. Only worse. People have no idea what goes on behind those walls, and most people don't have the stomach to find out. It takes a certain kind of person to survive it, which isn't necessarily a good thing. Weak people go crazy."

"You seem okay."

"I'm not weak. I'm not crazy either, which is why I asked you what I asked you."

"About therapy." She remembers the information I requested from her the last time we met. Referrals to low-cost counseling centers. She shuffles papers around on her desk, and then she swivels around in her chair to flip through a stack of files. "You said you wanted something economical but still sort of private." She removes a paperclip and passes me a sheet of paper across the desk. "I think I found something that might work for you."

I read the paper, and then I read it again to make sure I am comprehending. "A pilot project?"

"There haven't been very many programs developed to assist women who are just coming out of prison and

returning to society," Isolde explains. "But with the in-
crease of females who are convicted and sentenced to
prison, people are starting to take notice of the obsta-
cles women face. Things like child custody and housing
resources. This project is aimed at working with female
offenders and helping them reintegrate into society."

"I've reintegrated just fine."

"Yet you asked me to locate places where you can get
therapy." Her face says she is skeptical. "I think if you
give this place a chance you might be surprised."

"I don't want to sit in a waiting room full of ex-con-
victs, with everybody knowing why I'm there."

"The project sponsors therapists in private practice,
Helena. I don't think it'll be quite like going to the free
clinic and having sick babies sneeze all over you."

"I can pay for what I need."

"But why should you have to pay for something
that's here for the taking?" She folds her hands on the
desktop and stares at me. "It's free, so use it. Plus, I've
heard some good things about a few of the therapists.
One of my other clients sees a guy by the name of Kimmick and she says—"

I get hung up on one word. "A guy?"

"Yes, a guy. Would you rather talk to a woman? Because I'm sure they have some women working on the
project too." That makes me laugh. I sit back and pinch
my nose, shake my head, and look at the paper again.
"What?" She smiles, ready to hear the punchline.

"Nothing. It's just . . ." I laugh again. Shake my head
some more.

"What is it, Helena?" Now Isolde is giggling. "Tell
me."

"It's just . . . I've been around nothing but women for
the last eight years, and I swear to God, if I don't ever
have to talk to another woman for the rest of my life,

I'll be satisfied." The punchline is not what she expects, and her smile slips sideways. I put up a hand. "No offense."

"None taken," she grunts. "I think."

"You don't understand."

"I guess I don't." She points to the paper in my hand and nods. "But I bet they will."

"You said Kimmick?" If there has to be an evil, a man is the lesser of the two. Considering.

"Kimmick. Tell him Sollie sent you and he'll give you a discount. Oh, wait. It's free, so forget the discount."

I can't stop laughing. "Sollie?"

"What, don't I look like a Sollie?"

Actually, she looks more like a big, juicy grape, but I don't share my observation. I remember that I'm on my lunch break and I am starving. If I leave now, I'll still have time to grab something quick to eat on my way back to work.

"Yeah, you look like a Sollie." I fold the paper and slip it in my purse, reminding myself to have Aaron do some digging and check the place out for me.

Chapter Sixteen

Beige is stunned. It is the only word I can come up with to describe the vacant look on her face as she walks into my apartment and sees Aaron sitting on the futon flipping through CDs. She has heard me mention his name, knows he is my friend from downstairs, but she has never seen him. She stops a good twenty feet away from him and eyes him warily, like he is the Cookie Monster and she is a giant coconut macaroon. He looks up from a Nona Hendryx CD and locks onto her scrutiny, gives her a taste of her own medicine.

It is a weird moment and I stand there, watching them watch each other and waiting for someone to speak. Finally, I figure out that I should be the one to introduce them to each other. "Beige, you remember me mentioning my friend Aaron," I say, closing the door and reaching for her backpack. She is spending the night with me and her backpack is stretched to the limit, full of all the things she thinks she needs to survive for twenty-four hours.

"The guy from downstairs," she says slowly. "Your friend with the weight machine."

"Right. You finally get to put a name with a face, huh?" She doesn't see my smile because she is busy staring at Aaron. I look at Aaron and he is looking at me curiously. "Aaron, this is—"

"Beige," she cuts in. "Beige Hunter. Nice to meet you."

Aaron sets a stack of CDs on the coffee table and rolls to his feet. Standing, he towers over me and Beige, looks imposing and not to be played with. Like a black Mr. Clean with hair. Beige's eyes travel over him from head to toe, and then she takes a small step backward. She remembers her manners and slips her hand inside the one he offers.

"It's a pleasure," he says. "I've seen you come in and out of the building a few times. Didn't know you were visiting Lena."

"I come a lot. Mostly on weekends, when school is out. She says you're a writer."

"Newspaper columnist. What term are you?" I can see the wheels turning in his head, can see the dots connecting. He does a good job of keeping surprise out of his face, but I know him well enough to know that the wrinkles in his forehead mean he is slightly irritated. He wants to choke me, but he wants to confirm his suspicions first.

"Just a freshman." Beige swivels and takes my eyes. "My mom didn't tell you?"

"Your mom," Aaron says, nodding slowly. He smiles like he is just figuring out something that he should've known all along, and then he runs a hand around the back of his neck. "She mentioned a few things. You look a lot like your mom."

"I'm cuter." She ends her statement with a flirtatious smile.

"I don't know," he hedges, playing along. "She's got a little something going on too."

"If you say so."

"What is it the kids say, don't hate?" I roll my eyes at Beige, and then I let Aaron see me roll them toward the ceiling. "Did you bring your math book?"

Suddenly, she is fourteen again. Shoulders slumping and lips long. "Yes, but we don't have to do my homework tonight, do we? Some of the other kids are going skating, and I was gonna see if you could take me."

"You mean like drop you off and pick you up?"

"You can stay there with me and skate too. It's a family skate night thing." I go over to the phone and pick up the receiver, start punching in numbers. "Who are you calling?"

"Mr. Rork, or whatever his name is," I say, serious with a capital *S*. "I need to tell him that your fantasy is ridiculous and he should shut the island down."

"Mom . . ."

"Yeah, *Mom*," Aaron says. "Take the girl skating, and you skate too."

"Keep dreaming. And shut up, Aaron. I'm baking salmon tonight, remember?"

"You can bake it tomorrow night." He pretends not to see the silent communication I am sending him, and I want to get him in a headlock. "Do you know how to skate, Lena?"

"Do you?"

"I do a little something."

"Well then, you go."

"Mom . . ."

I look at Beige. "He can take you and I'll stay here and make dinner."

"You know you're being silly, right?" He turns to Beige and shrugs.

"Just a little," she cosigns.

I am outnumbered and I know it. "How long does this thing last?"

"Five to eight." Beige sizes Aaron up once more and hooks a thumb in his direction. "You can bring him if you want to."

"I'm not skating, so get that out of your head."

"Okay. Probably there will be some other old heads you can sit around talking to," she says.

An hour and a half later, Aaron is making me sick and I stick my tongue out at him for the third time in a row. As he rolls around the rink and does a crazy leg move for my benefit, I think about giving him the finger. We stare at each other, and then Beige is directly in my line of vision, her face less than six inches from mine.

"Mom, I need money."

"I just gave you money." I hand her the soda I am playing with and pat my pockets. "How much more can you eat before you throw up?"

"I'm planning on stuffing myself so I won't have room for salmon." She drinks half my soda and trades me the cup for a ten-dollar bill.

"I think you're planning on loitering around the concession stand until that acne-plagued boy behind the counter notices you." Her face turns bright red and gives her away. "Told you some things are timeless, didn't I?" She giggles and rolls off, disappearing inside a circle of sweaty-faced teenage girls making their way over to the concession stand.

I turn around and almost run into Aaron. I didn't hear him roll up behind me. "You look like one of those roller skating dudes from the seventies."

"I never noticed it before, but you look like a mom," he says and skates backward over to a bench to sit down. He pats the spot next to him and unlaces his skates. "You should see me in my own skates. These are rentals, so they don't know my feet on a personal level. I can really get down in my own shit."

"Is that why you're sweating like a pig and looking like you're about to pass out? All that getting down you were doing?"

"Hey, at least I was doing it." He changes back into his Nikes and sits back. "She seems like a good kid, Lena."

"She is. Vicky did a good job with her."

"Must have killed you to have to be away from her for so long."

I stare into my cup and swallow. "It was my punishment. For doing what I did."

"I thought that's what prison was," he sounds impatient. "Repaying your debt to society doesn't stop there though, does it?"

"I don't think it ever stops. Are you angry because I didn't tell you about her?"

"I'm wondering why not, yeah."

"I can't answer that. Maybe because she's mine and I don't want to share her just yet. I haven't had her in so long."

"What about her father? Where is he?"

"I told you the women in my family are fucked up, didn't I? He was never a factor. She doesn't know who he is, and it's been so long, I don't even know if I remember, myself."

"That's sad."

"That's my life." I drop a hand on his thigh and squeeze, wanting to make him smile. His face is entirely too serious right now, and I need to move away from serious for a while. "Come on, Aaron. Cut me some slack. I was going to tell you, okay? I just need to do things in my own time and in my own way." I wait for him to give me his eyes, and then I smile an apology.

"You're a pretty woman, you know that?" He sees me blush and chuckles. "You know that."

"Nothing about me is pretty."

"Are you serious?" He searches my eyes, looking for hints that I am teasing him and fishing for compliments, and it doesn't take him long to see that I am telling him my truth. He snorts in disbelief and shifts on the bench, bends an elbow on the back and props his face in his hand. "You are serious. Damn, Lena. Can I just say that I disagree? I mean, I can't speak for the next man, but I think strength is pretty, in its own way. Courage is sexy as hell, and perseverance is straight up hot. In the right woman, of course. I see all those things in you. Plus, your skin is so clear and smooth I can damn near see through it, and you've got a really nice ass."

I choke on soda and swipe the back of my hand across my mouth, unable to look Aaron in the face. "You shouldn't be looking at my ass."

"You don't mind, do you?"

"I can't stop you, but . . ."

"Look at me, Lena."

I keep talking and don't look. "I'm just saying, you shouldn't be looking at my ass. I don't ogle your body."

"You don't?" He knows I'm lying and it shows on his face.

"Okay, I saw your chest a few times and you have nice legs, but that's only because you never have clothes on."

"Maybe I'm trying to tempt you."

"Aaron, please. I had to make you put on shoes before we left the house."

"So?"

"So you're a caveman. Temptation has nothing to do with it. You have no home training."

"You like a caveman, no-home-training-having man. Don't you, Lena?" He flicks a finger down the side of my face and I wave it away. "You like me."

"I didn't say I didn't."

"I like you too."

I set my soda aside and blow out a strong breath, wipe my palms on my thighs and look at him. "*Okaaay*. What do we do now that that's out of the way? Exchange phone numbers and meet in the hallway between classes?"

We stare at each other. "You're cute when you're nervous."

"I'm not nervous. I just . . . this is . . . I know there's a way to do this, but I can't seem to remember what it is. I'm out of practice."

"It's like riding a bike, Lena."

"It's been a long time since I've been on a bike, Aaron. I don't know if I'm ready for you."

"What do you think I want from you?"

"I don't know, sex? Men like sex."

"Intimacy doesn't have to be synonymous with sex, and in this case, I don't think it should be. I'm trying to be close to you."

"You are close to me. How much closer do you want to be?"

I am unprepared for his hand on the back of my head, for our lips to meet in the space between us, and I freeze. I keep my eyes open and on his. He does the same, and we look cross-eyed to each other, with our faces so close and our lips resting against each other's. From beginning to end, the kiss is chaste and it lasts only three seconds, but it seems to end too soon. It takes me that long to discover that his lips are soft and that I like the weight of them on mine. I like the feeling of his nose mating with mine.

He pulls away and I squeeze his thigh, signaling to him that I want him to come back. My tongue darts out and wets my lips, and then we connect a second time. There is more pressure this time and I sink into it, take the kiss beyond one I would give an elderly relative, and give as good as I get. I tilt my head and part my lips slightly, inviting Aaron to come inside.

He ends the kiss with a hard peck and shakes his head. "Not yet," he says, pushing off the bench to his feet. He looks at me long and hard, and then he grins. He walks away and leaves me wondering if I have turned him off by not knowing how to kiss.

I tell myself that I will not embarrass myself even more by asking him what he thinks of the kiss, but the question is out of my mouth before I can stop it. I glance at the staircase and make sure Beige is way ahead of me, out of sight and on the third floor, and then I touch his arm. "Did I do it right?" I whisper.

Aaron ducks his head and puts his face close to mine. "Do what right?"

"The kiss. You didn't say anything."

"I should be asking you that, instead of the other way around. I was given the privilege of kissing you, Lena. So you tell me, did I do it right?"

"Mom," Beige calls from the floor above us. Her voice is sharper than it needs to be. She does not like to be kept waiting, but I'm ninety-nine percent certain it's because she isn't all that fond of Aaron.

"I have to go," I say and jog up the stairs.

Beige leans against the wall, fidgeting with the zipper on her shirt as I unlock the door. She has been unnaturally quiet since we left the roller rink, but she comes back to life as soon as I close the door at my back.

"He's kind of fine," she says, stepping out of her shoes and setting them by the door. She stretches her toes in her socks and pretends like she's not interested in my response. "You didn't say he was cute."

"I didn't think being cute was a prerequisite for being a good friend. And why are you noticing that he's cute anyway?"

She rolls her eyes like I am dense. "Seems like you spend a lot of time with him."

"I guess I do. He's a nice person."

"If he's so nice, then how come you didn't tell him about me?"

The question stops me cold. I drop my purse on the futon and scratch my fingers through my locks, thinking. "I don't really know how to answer that, Bey. I guess I didn't tell him because I wasn't ready to tell him. The subject never came up." I realize a second too late how that sounds. "I didn't mean that the way it sounds."

"Sounds like you kept me a secret from him. I walked in here and he didn't have a clue who I was. But I knew who he was because you always talk about him."

"I don't always talk about him."

"Yes, you do. It's always, 'Aaron says this' or 'Me and Aaron went here or there.' You talk about him all the time."

"Okay, so he's my friend. So what?"

"I think he wants to be more than just your friend." She flops down on the futon and aims the remote at the television. "Can we order pizza?"

"Yeah, we can order pizza—after you tell me why you're pissed with me."

She makes me wait while she channel surfs and plays with the volume of the television. She doesn't look at me and I don't think she's really seeing the television either. She tries to tune me out, and I don't appreciate her efforts. I walk over to the television and stand in front of it, making it impossible for her not to see me.

"I'm not pissed."

"You were a little rude when we got back home tonight," I remind her. "Had to remind you to say thank you to Aaron for driving us."

"I'm surprised you even noticed I was there, the way you were hanging all over him and ignoring me."

My eyes get big and offended. "What is your problem? You were the one who said it was okay for him to come with us in the first place."

"That was before I knew he was your boyfriend and everything."

"He's not my boyfriend," I say, wondering if that is exactly what he is and if I have been too preoccupied to notice him slipping into the role.

"I saw you kiss him, so that means he's not just your friend. I don't like him."

"Has he done something to you? Said something out of the way to you?"

"No . . . I just don't like him."

"And you don't have a reason?"

"Nope."

Too many years of dealing with women and the myriad attitudes that come along with them tires me out. Beige isn't yet a woman, but she will be one day, and she is practicing all the techniques she will stock her arsenal with on me right now. She avoids my eyes, lifts her chin in the air and sniffs disdainfully. She crosses her arms under her breasts, props an ankle on the opposite knee and starts her foot to tapping the air. She opens her mouth to say something and catches herself. She remembers she is still a child, not equipped to deal with me on my level, and even if she were equipped, she would be crossing a line that she is afraid to cross. The realization renders her mute.

I put up my hands in surrender and move away from the television. "I'm taking a shower. Can you thaw out long enough to come and talk to me?"

"Who comes in there with you when I'm not here?"

"I lock the door," I snap. "You know what? Forget it, okay? I'll save you some hot water." I cannot believe we are arguing, cannot understand exactly what we are arguing about, and the more I think about it, the less I care about the particulars. She is about to make me lose the religion I never had.

I leave the bathroom door standing open so I can hear her if she decides to talk, and I break records soaping and rinsing myself. I drop a gown over my head, wrap my locks in a scarf and find Beige still sitting on the futon, looking mutinous.

"Did you call the pizza in?"

"No, I called Vicky to come and get me," she informs me curtly. "She's on her way."

"You're not spending the night with me?"

"I changed my mind."

"Oh, so now I'm on punishment, Bey? What kind of shit is this?"

"You really want to be with him anyway, so I might as well go home."

"This is your home too."

"No, it's not. It's only big enough for you. You picked it out all by yourself."

I take a deep breath and count to ten. Look at her and feel my shoulders slump in defeat. I have forgotten how to beg—and good riddance. "What is this really about, Beige?"

"If this is my home too, then why don't I have a room here and why didn't you get a place big enough for both of us?"

"I got what I could afford at the time. I guess I could get something bigger now, but I like this neighborhood."

"And Aaron is right downstairs."

"We're back on that." I pace the floor and scrub a hand down my face. "You don't want me to have friends? Is that what the issue is?"

"It's supposed to be just you and me." Her eyes fly up to mine and lock in. "This is supposed to be my time with you, but it's not. I come second to everything else in your life and I should be first. You should be all about me right now, not having a boyfriend."

"Wait a minute," I say, pointing a finger. "Last weekend I wanted you to come over and you couldn't because you had a thing you absolutely couldn't miss. I wanted to take you shopping the other day and you blew me off then too. It's okay for you to have a whole other life that doesn't include me, but it's not okay for me to have friends? It's okay for you to tell people that I was dead, but I neglect to mention you to someone and I get put on your shit list? You're being immature, Beige. And unfair.

"I'm doing the best I can here, baby, okay? You think it's easy for me, having to be with you like this? Sitting here, waiting for you to come over and then dropping you off when it's time for you to go home? I hope you don't, because it kills me a little more each and every time I have to do it."

"You wouldn't have to if there was room here for me to live with you." She pushes her feet into her shoes without bothering to unlace them, and her heels hang over the backs.

"You said you didn't want to come with me. I asked you and you said you wanted to stay where you were. Was I hallucinating, or didn't we have that conversation?"

She says nothing as she pushes her arms through her backpack straps and slings it across her shoulders. There is a knock at the door and I assume it is Vicky, come to collect what is hers and no longer mine.

"Are you going to answer that?" I ask after the second round of knocking.

Vicky comes storming into my apartment, looking from me to Beige curiously. "What is going on over here?" Her house slippers slap against the soles of her feet as she walks to the middle of the room and puts herself in between us like a referee.

"Apparently Beige is angry because I have friends and because she doesn't have a room of her own here and because I don't have a bigger place, even though she said she didn't want to live with me." I blow air through my fist and watch Beige push past Vicky and disappear into the hallway. "I've done something wrong. Again."

Vicky looks out the door. "Beige, you did say you didn't want to go with Lena when she moved."

"Well, maybe I changed my mind," Beige calls from the hallway. "She didn't ask me if I changed my mind."

I take one, then two breaths. And then I lose it. "How was I supposed to know you changed your mind, little girl? A few months ago, you didn't even want me touching you, and now I'm supposed to guess the precise moment you finally decided that I was worth your time?" My voice is loud and the entire scenario is moving into ghetto territory. Vicky covers her face and mumbles something about God helping us, and I roll my eyes. God stopped looking our way years ago.

"Beige," I shout, "get your narrow ass back in here and look me in my face while you talk your shit. You want to talk like a woman, then be woman enough to face me."

I give her ten seconds, and when she doesn't come back inside the apartment, I go out into the hallway after her, with Vicky right on my heels. "Leenie, calm down please," she whispers, and I swat her away like a fly. "You know how you get."

That makes me turn on her. "How do I get, Vicky?"

"All I'm saying is—"

"Fuck that. Don't try to backpedal now. Tell me how I get."

Somewhere below us, a door closes. Vicky looks around nervously and licks her lips. "Could we go back inside and discuss this rationally?"

"There's nothing rational about this situation. I mean, I know you're rational and everything. You think everything to death and you find excuses for why things are the way they are, and that's fine because that's just who you are. I have always accepted that about you. But Beige isn't being rational right now, and we know damn well I'm not, because *you know how I get*, right?"

Vicky's hand is shaking when she raises it to smooth the wrinkles from her forehead. She glances at Beige, and then she turns pleading eyes on me. "Leenie. Please. She's fourteen. She doesn't know the way you and I know. I think what she's trying to make you understand is that you were gone for eight years and she missed you. That's all."

She wants that to be all. Wants me to grab hold to that simple piece of the puzzle and leave everything else out of the equation. Her eyes beg me to keep my mouth shut and let things be, and I know it is the right thing to do, the best thing for Beige. But I don't know if I can continue being the sacrificial lamb for everyone else's peace of mind and at the expense of my own. It is a tiresome job.

"You should tell me what you feel," I say to Beige. "If you missed me and you want to spend more time with me, then tell me that. If you changed your mind and you want to come and live with me, then tell me that too. But don't give with one hand and take back with the other. Don't be selfish with your affection and make me beg and grovel for it, because I won't. I've lost enough already. I won't give anybody my dignity. Not even you. I worked too damn hard to earn it back."

Beige gives me attitude, shifts her weight to one side and stares at the wall. "I'm ready to go home now, Mom."

I feel myself stretching to the point of snapping in two, and can actually see myself snatching her by her collar and shaking her until her teeth rattle. I take a step in her direction. "Which one of us are you talking to, Beige? Me or Vicky?"

"You act like you don't want to be my mother," she says, still staring at the wall.

"Everything I've ever done in my life that was worth anything, I did because I'm your mother. I got myself in the situation I'm in because I'm your goddamn mother. You think you know so much, but you don't know shit. You don't have a fucking clue."

Vicky touches my arm. "Leenie."

I shrug her hand off and back away from the cliff. If I jump I will take my daughter with me, and no matter how angry she makes me, I don't want to do that. I sacrificed myself to protect her from the cliff. "I don't need this. I can't deal with this right now." I catch Vicky's eyes. "Take her home. She doesn't want to be here."

Beige takes off running down the steps, and after she is out of sight, Vicky is in my face.

"She doesn't know," she repeats for my ears only. "She doesn't remember anything, and I don't know about you, but I hope she never does."

"And why did I do what I did, Vicky? Was it because I want her to have nightmares every night and piss in the bed until she's seventeen?" She colors beautifully, ashamed of the memory that belongs to her. "Or did I do it because I want the same things for her that you do? I don't want her to remember, either. And *maybe* I want that just a little bit more than you do, since I'm the one who brought her into this fucked-up universe in the first place."

"Leenie . . ."

"Take her home," I say and close the door in her face. In a secret place inside myself, I am devastated over the fact that Beige still prefers Vicky over me. Angry that Vicky broke records getting here to save Beige from me. And scared to death that it will always be this way. I'm terrified that, after everything I've been through, wanting a fledgling relationship with my child will be what ultimately destroys me completely. Beige has no idea what I would do for her, what I would do to keep her with me, but Vicky does.

Chapter Seventeen

I disturb Aaron's workflow when I knock on his door a few minutes later. I follow him into his office and see that he is in the middle of putting a column together. His half-dead computer is working overtime, and he has stress wrinkles in his forehead. He sits down at his desk and slips back into his zone.

I curl up in a recliner, pull my gown down over my knees and chew on my thumbnail. Watch him work and steal some of his quiet. Minutes pass and then hours. At ten to one in the morning, he rears back in his chair, hits the save button and scratches his head.

"She'll call or come by after she calms down." He slips a blank CD into the drive and looks at me over his shoulder. "This too shall pass, Lena. You'll see."

"She's jealous of the time I spend with you. She thinks I love you more than I do her."

"It doesn't work like that, does it?"

"In her mind it does. I almost let loose on her."

"Well, I'm glad you didn't because *you know how you get*." We stare at each other for several seconds. Then he cracks a smile and I throw my head back and crack up.

When he's done working, we do something different. We don't sleep. At three o'clock in the morning, we leave his apartment and cross the street together. He challenges me to a race, loser buys breakfast, and I forget that I am chasing him around a track that goes

round and round in a circle, with no set destination,
like a hamster's wheel.

We run until our clothes are wringing wet and then
walk our sweaty asses into the Waffle House and sit at
a booth like neither of us leaves foul odor in our wake.
He orders enough food to feed three people, most of it
animal flesh, and I make do with a waffle and low-fat
syrup. Still hungry, I finish my meal off with a bowl of
fresh fruit and a glass of orange juice. I prop my elbows
on the table and watch him put away more food than I
will eat in a week's time.

"What did you write about this week?" I say as he
puts a whole sausage link in his mouth and chews exactly thirty-two times.

"I responded to some reader questions. IRAs versus
money market accounts, 401Ks and stock market questions. Stuff like that." The waitress leaves our bill on
the edge of the table and he pushes it closer to my side.
I push it back to him and he chuckles. "It's like that,
huh? You're a sore loser?"

"I didn't lose. You cheated. You took a shortcut you
didn't think I saw you take."

"You've got eyes in the back of your head?"

"Front, back and both sides." A memory creeps to
the front of my mind and my smile turns into a giggle.
"I used to have a cellmate named Yo-Yo who had one
lazy eye and one that rolled around to the side of her
face. You couldn't sneak up on her for shit."

"Yo-Yo?"

"Because she was crazy. Up and down like a yo-yo,
you know? Her real name was Yolanda." I roll her
name around on my tongue and taste it, and then I say,
"Yolanda Maria Callahan. She was my first friend in
prison."

"Where is she now?"

"Dead. She killed herself and left me to find her body. I wanted to bring her back to life and kill her all over again for leaving me."

He thinks my words over as he crunches ice. Wipes his mouth with a napkin and follows a waitress around the restaurant with his eyes. "You made other friends . . . after she died?"

"A few. Pigpen and Squirt." I give him names. "White Girl Julie and Don Juan."

"Pigpen?"

"Her cell was always a mess."

"And White Girl Julie?"

"She had skin pigmentation issues. Had more white spots than black, so we gave her that nickname."

"Do I even need to ask about Don Juan?"

"Probably not."

"What about you? What was your nickname?"

"Lucky," I say and hear the pride in my voice. "I was Lucky."

"Lucky Lena."

"No, just Lucky. Lena didn't exist." I flip the bill over and reach into my sock for the money I stashed there. "Yo-Yo gave me that name because she said I was a lucky charm, and it stuck."

"Sounds like there's a story there. Leave it. You're right, I did cheat a little bit."

"There is a story, but it's not mine to tell. It's Lucky's. She's the only one who can tell you about her life in prison. Lena wasn't there."

"Where is this Lucky woman? Have I ever met her?"

I look around, over my shoulders and behind my back. Smile at Aaron like there's still a few feathers hanging out of my mouth. "She was just here. You didn't see her?"

"You're playing with me."

"No, I'm not. I'm trying to tell you that you're going to have to be a little quicker on the uptake, writer man. If you want to talk to Lucky and get her to tell you her story, then you're going to have to learn how to tell when she's looking right at you. Learn what questions to ask and when. She comes and goes and she's cagey like that."

"I know another woman who's kind of cagey too," Aaron says, narrowing his eyes at me and looking deep in thought. "Her name starts with an L. Can you guess who I'm talking about?"

"Comes from being caged like an animal for so long. Living in a zoo."

"There are a lot of different animals in the zoo, so help me out here. What are we talking about—lions, tigers, bears? What?"

"I was something like a cross between a wolverine and a lion cub. I had fangs and claws, but I didn't like to use them unless I had to."

He tilts his head to one side and lets his eyes land all over my face. "Am I talking to Lucky right now?"

"That's for me to know and for you to find out. The first thing you need to know is that you're dealing with two different people and they need to stay separate. One is past and one is present. Some of the things you might hear . . . they're pretty rough. Might change the way you think about . . . some people . . . and you need to be prepared for that."

"Is this the part where I get scared and decide to leave you alone before things get too deep?"

"This is the part where I remind you to be careful what you ask for because you just might get it."

***

Beige plays phone pranks, thinking that I don't know it's her. She calls and hangs up when I answer. Sometimes she holds the phone and sounds like she is struggling with speaking, and then she hangs up because she does not know what to say. She knows that I don't have caller ID, and she thinks she is safe from detection. She does not know that I have learned to identify a person's intent just by listening to the pattern of their breath. It is a survival instinct, the same way that interpreting the sound of an oncoming person's footfalls is, and her intent is to make me suffer.

A week has passed since she reverted to acting like a toddler and I jumped into the sandbox along with her. We are both being silly, and since I am the adult, I know I should be the one to make the first move toward reconciliation, but I am moving in slow motion. I am punishing her as she punishes me, though she doesn't know what she is being punished for or why. I can be cruel, but I'm not cruel enough to ever want her to know.

So I punish her by not giving her what she wants, which is for me to be the first to speak and make it easier for her to follow suit. She hurts me by rejecting me, and that is a bitter pill to swallow. Every time she calls, I listen to her breathe anxiety, immaturity and confusion in my ear, and I say nothing for several seconds.

Then I say, "I love you," and hang up the phone first.

Kenneth Kimmick ushers me into his office and tells me to have a seat. His voice is rough from too many years of cigarette smoke, and he reminds me of a drill sergeant, the way he clips his words off at the ends and makes each one sound like a sharp command. He looks like one of Santa's helpers on steroids. Short and round, with a long gray beard that stops in the middle of his chest and a smooth dome of a head surrounded by tufts of shaggy salt-and-pepper hair.

I sit in the middle of a worn leather couch and drop my purse on the floor by my feet.

Motorcycle memorabilia is everywhere, covering the walls and littering the surface of his desk with no rhyme or reason. I think I have stepped back in time, right into Hell's Kitchen.

"Do you still smell it?" he asks out of the blue.

I look away from the clock on the wall and focus on his face. Only forty more minutes to go. "Still smell what?"

"The stink of prison."

"Prison has a stink?"

"Doesn't it?"

"How would you know?"

"I don't know. How would I?" He cracks a smile and pisses me off.

"This is funny to you?"

"No, not this." He points to the floor between his knees. "Not the situation. You are though. Look at the way you're sitting right now." His finger turns on me and makes me look down at what he sees. "You've got your arms wrapped around yourself like a python. Like you're scared something might slip out if you relax."

"And that's funny to you?"

"It's funny in the future," Kimmick tells me. "The day I remind you of this day and you can sit back and laugh about it with me, it'll be hilarious then. Tell me something about yourself, Helena. Something you feel safe telling me right now."

"Nobody calls me Helena, except the woman who gave birth to me. It's Lena, and how are you so sure I'm going to be here in the future?"

"Will you be?"

Impatience has me throwing my hands up and then slapping them on my knees. I roll my eyes to the heavens and ask somebody to give me strength. "Here we go with the twenty questions again. Is this what it's going to be like every time I come?"

"Works every time." Laughter makes his belly jiggle.

"What works?"

He points at me again. "You're not wrapped up in a cocoon anymore. Maybe now you can tell me a little bit about why you're here."

"Aren't you supposed to be able to figure that out?"

"I don't know. Am I?"

I wrap myself back up and stare at him. I don't think I am ready for this, and I don't think he is ready for me. He stares back at me, and then he smiles and says our time is up. I hate him.

Madame Sula's real name is Thelma, and she tells me that her family is from the Louisiana Bayou. The sight, she says, swung from limb to limb on her family tree and hopped on her back quite by surprise. It came up in time from before the cotton fields, landed on her grandmother's head, skipped her mama's head and then was gifted to her. She has two sisters and a brother, but she is the only one who can see beyond what is in front of her face.

She remembers looking into people's souls as early as age six, and she says she scared the shit out of more than a few of her school teachers over the years. She knew the church pastor was fucking the choir director, who was a man, way before his wife stopped by the church one sunny afternoon and caught him in the act. She knew her father was keeping a second family three

towns over, long before her mother loaded a shotgun
and went to see for herself late one night. And she says
she has always been able to speak with the dead. As an
afterthought, she adds, in case I care, that she didn't
start charging people money to look into their souls
until she was over the age of eighteen.

I sit across from her, stare into her crystal ball, and
pass her a crisp fifty-dollar bill. I came alone this time
because I am slightly embarrassed about being here
and I'm unsure of where my head will be by the time I
leave.

She says, "Phoenix rising," and that is all.

"What does that mean?"

"It means that as one soul burns for an eternity, another rises from the ashes to live again. Who is Aaron?"

"A friend."

"Do you love him?"

She catches me off guard, and I wonder what corner
of my soul she finds Aaron in. "Does he love me?"

"Do you think I am like the motorcycle man?" She
laughs. "I won't play twenty questions with you. You
know he does, but you spend too much time trying to
figure out what he sees in you that is lovable. Ask him
who Nettie is, and then you will begin to understand.
The world is not simply black and white for everyone.
Some people pay attention to the gray areas."

She scribbles something on a piece of paper and
pushes it across the table to me. When I don't pick it
up, she nods at the paper and lifts her eyebrows. "Are
you afraid of what it says?"

"Should I be?"

"I don't know. Depends on what it means to you.
Read it and see."

I read and then I frown. "Let sleeping dogs lie?"

"Stop calling your mother Ellie. You taint a relationship that should be healing. She can't help what she's been through any more than you can. You think she doesn't understand you, but she does. Admitting she does is a whole other issue, though, and she won't, so stop trying to make her. Just accept and move on."

"Easier said than done."

"Why is it easy for you to accept Victoria's weaknesses and not your mother's? Not your own? Do you think they hurt any less than you do?"

"She could've saved us." This is the point I think I will always be stuck on.

"She couldn't save herself any more than you thought you were saving Beige."

She still pronounces my daughter's name incorrectly, but this time I don't waste my breath correcting her.

The phone rings three times and I get hung up on three times before I pick up the receiver and hear my mother's voice.

"Helena? This is your mother."

"Yes?" Ellie.

"I'm calling about Beige. She tells me that you won't speak to her."

I clamp the receiver between my head and shoulder and keep washing dishes. "If she would call and not hang up, I'd speak to her. What does this have to do with you?"

"Vicky is upset and so is Beige. Apparently, you lost control and said some things you probably shouldn't have said."

"I'm upset too. Do you care about that?"

She sighs disgustedly. "Why do you always attack me, Helena? This is why I never call. You always want to argue with me, and I don't have the energy for it."

"You never call because you *think* I want to argue with you, but I don't. Just once you could call to see how I'm doing or just to say hello. That would be nice."

"It works both ways, you know. You could call me too."

"I suppose I could," I say slowly.

We hold the phone for several seconds and then, "I heard you got a new job."

"A couple of weeks ago, yeah. At a newspaper."

"You like it better than the factory job?"

"Much."

"Beige says you have a boyfriend. Eric, I think she said his name is."

"Aaron. And he's not my boyfriend." Aaron moves up behind me at the sink and hangs his head over my shoulder. He makes an *excuse me* face and winks. I push him away and dry my hands on a dishtowel. "He thinks he is though."

"They always do," my mother says and chuckles. "I guess everything's going okay for you then?"

"So far so good. You?"

"No sense in complaining. All this heat messes with my sinuses, but other than that, I guess I'll make it. How long is this thing between you and Beige going to go on?"

"I don't know. I'm tired of it though. I'll have to fig-ure something out."

"Well, please do because I'm getting tired of listening to her whine every hour on the hour. And don't even talk about what my phone bill is going to look like when it comes. Whatever it is you did, just say you're sorry and let it be."

I start to snap, start to say something that will end with me calling her Ellie in the ugliest tone I can man-age, but I don't. Instead, I count to ten, run a hand over my locks, and bring Aaron a glass of juice over to the futon. "Okay, Mama. I'll do that, all right?"

"All right. Now, I'll talk to you later."

"Okay."

"And Helena?"

"Yes, Mama?"

"Vicky usually calls me on Sunday evenings, when the long distance rates are cheap. Just in case you didn't know about the rates and everything."

"Okay, Mama. I'll keep that in mind."

"It'd be all right if you did."

I hang up the phone and look at Aaron. "Tell me about your mama," I say.

He paints a picture for me. Describes a heavyset woman with two chins and a head full of thick hair. He says she reached back and got her hair from the Indian blood in their family. I smooth my palm over his head and tell him that he did too. Then he says she never made it past the eighth grade because his grandmother died young and she had to help take care of his aunts and uncles. She earned a living as a maid and she never missed a day of work for as long as he can remember. She beat his ass when his grades didn't look good enough to her, and she never let him out of the house without clean underwear on his butt or without making sure his teeth were brushed.

She still lives in Mississippi, along with his sister and two brothers, and they all live within minutes of each other. They are close like I wouldn't believe, and he misses them pretty much every day.

"Have you ever thought about moving back home?"

"To Mississippi? I don't think so. It's a nice place to visit though." He takes my hand and lays it on his thigh, runs the pad of his thumb over my fingernails one by one. "I was thinking about maybe going down for a visit later in the summer. Have you ever been to Mississippi, Lena?" I shake my head. "Would you like to go?"

"With you?"

Aaron makes a show of looking around the room, checking out the space surrounding him and then the space behind me. "You see somebody else in here wanting you to meet their mama? We can pack Beige up and throw her in the car with us. She needs to go ahead and start liking me anyway."

"I'm on parole, Aaron. I can't just leave the state whenever I feel like it."

"How much longer do you have? What, three or four months?"

"Three, I think. But . . ."

"Like I said, the end of the summer." He makes it sound so easy. Like a definite plan.

Chapter Eighteen

Vicky winces as I grab her hand and squeeze it like my life depends on it. She starts to say something, but I slap a hand over her mouth and tell her to hush. I pull her into the household cleaners aisle and stick my head around the end display of Tide so I can see without being seen.

"What are we hiding from?" she wants to know.

"Not what, but who."

I watch Kimmick separate a shopping cart from a line of carts and push it in the opposite direction. He walks slowly, as if he has all the time in the world, looking at everything he passes and scanning price tags. He drops a bundle of toilet paper in his cart and turns down an aisle, out of sight. I drag Vicky with me as I go after him.

"Who are we following, Leenie?" She jerks her sleeve from my grasp and refuses to budge.

I think about slapping her, but she would probably make too much noise. Give me away before I can find out what I want to find out. "This guy I've been seeing. I just want to see what he's up to."

"Did he come in here with another woman or something?"

"No, he's alone." I peek around another corner and the coast is clear. "I'm just being nosy."

"If he's alone, then what's the—"

I wave my hands in front of her face like a thousand swarming bees. "Would you just come on? There you go, thinking everything to death. Shut up and come on."

"What about my cart?"

She has two things in her cart: tampons and dissolving dishwasher tabs. Things she can live without or pick up again, but she wants to work my nerves. "Bring the flipping cart, Vicky, damn. We might need it for distraction anyway."

I send her down one aisle and up another one, give her explicit instructions for the information I need her to bring back to me. I pretend to be looking through stacks of throw rugs while she pushes her cart down the aisle where Kimmick is and then comes to find me.

"What?" I ask as soon as her cart squeaks to a stop in front of me.

"Preparation H, some of those socks old men wear, and toothbrushes."

"That's it?"

"Wait, I think I saw some women's underwear in his cart too, and they looked big enough for him to wear."

I gasp and my eyes bug out. "Seriously?"

She rolls her eyes and looks like she is tired of my foolishness. "No, Leenie. Why are we following this dude again?"

"I want to see if he is who he says he is. If he's for real. Come on."

I pick up Kimmick's scent near the electronics department and follow him from there. He takes ten minutes selecting a cell phone case, and he eventually chooses the first one he picked up, the cheapest one. He flips through country-Western CDs and debates with himself over whether or not to buy Faith Hill's latest. He decides against buying a CD and tosses a DVD movie in his cart. After he gets ink refills for his inkjet printer, he leads the way to the shoe department.

I leave Vicky trying on a pair of house slippers that look like ballet shoes and peek around a corner at him as he slides a size eleven men's shoe from a shelf. They are boxy-looking corduroy slippers, the kind old men in nursing homes wear, and I mentally tell him that I like the red pair better than I do the black pair he is holding.

Vicky taps me on my shoulder and scares the shit out of me. "What do you think? Pink or blue?" She holds out two pairs of slippers and waits for me to pick one. I roll my eyes and pick blue. Kimmick circles around my orbit and I snatch her in front of me, hiding from him and breathing a sigh of relief when he doesn't even look up.

He picks up Rembrandt toothpaste, so I know his teeth aren't false. He passes right by the adult diapers, so I know he doesn't shit or piss in his pants. He picks up two bricks of Irish Spring soap and a stick of Old Spice anti-perspirant, so I know he washes his ass, even if he does smell like a mixed-up French whore afterward. I drop a brick of Dove soap in Vicky's cart, add a tub of coconut-mango body butter for Beige, and continue on my quest.

"Where do you know this dude from?" Vicky eyes the body butter, and then she gets a tub for herself.

"He's a motorcycle freak." We follow him to the men's clothing department.

"Since when do you care about motorcycles?"

I motion for her to be quiet, and then I tiptoe to the other end of the clothing floor. I end up in the misses department, flipping through a rack of pajamas to have something to do with my hands. He searches through stacks of folded khaki pants until he finds his size, and then he chooses a tan pair and a gray pair. I choose a mint green pajama set for Beige and a matching robe, and follow him when he is done.

Vicky is all over my nerves. "Stop being Sherlock Holmes and tell me who this dude is, Leenie. What's he got on you that we have to trail him around Target?"

"He doesn't have anything on me, and please lower your voice." I see Kimmick get in line at the checkout. "Do we have everything we need?"

"I wanted to get some Special K and some soda," Vicky says, consulting her list.

"All right." I check the basket. "Get the cereal and soda, grab a pack of disposable razors, and meet me at the checkout."

He is in lane three, so I get in line in lane twelve, which is a safe distance away. He can't possibly see me from where he is standing, and he has no reason to look my way as he leaves the store. I stick my face in a magazine and bump the cart forward with my hip as the line moves up.

Vicky and I are tossing our bags into the backseat of her car when a horn blows nearby. She looks up first and then calls my name. I back out and look at her across the roof of the car. She points and wiggles her eyebrows.

Kimmick sits in his car, holding up traffic and smiling at me. "I thought that was you, Lena. How's it going?"

For a second, I can't speak. I clear my throat and nod stupidly. "It's going okay. Thanks for asking."

"Funny running into you here, huh?"

"I guess so. Kind of funny."

"Did you find everything okay?" His smile disappears so suddenly that I'm not sure it was ever there. We stare at each other, and I see that he is not angry about being spied on, but curious. "Find out everything you needed?"

I don't pretend to misunderstand. "For the time being, I guess."

"Good. See you around?"

"Maybe."

He drives away, and then I have to deal with Vicky. "What the hell was that all about, Leenie? That guy gave me the creeps. All that gray hair and that beard. Ugh. You think he spills food in it and carries it around with him without even knowing it?"

"He's a therapist, Vicky. And nobody says the word 'creep' anymore." I snap on my seat belt and pretend I don't see her staring a hole into the side of my head.

"I thought you weren't going to do that."

"I have to."

She slams the car into gear and backs out of the parking space without looking first. Almost crashes into the car across the lane from us because the driver of that car has the same idea. "You could've at least picked someone who doesn't have hemorrhoids," she says.

"Sometimes I have them, from giving birth to Beige," I point out, and she pops me on the back of my head.

"Shut up, Leenie."

Stella calls me, needs me, and I come running. Her piece of shit truck is in the shop and she needs a ride to work. I don't even let her finish telling me why she is calling me before I am sitting in front of the apartment building where she lives, blowing the horn for her to bring her ass.

She gets in the passenger seat eating fried rice right out of the carton and offers me a forkful of MSG. "Thanks, but I'm laying off clogging my arteries this week. You need to stop off anywhere else before work? You got cigarettes and all that?"

"Think I got everything I need," she says. "What's your deal, miss thang?"

I pull into traffic and glance at her. She is staring at me and grinning from ear to ear. "What?"

"Look at you."

"Look at what?" She makes me blush.

"Something's different about you, Lucky. You look good, girl. Peaceful."

"I've been meeting with this guy. He's . . ."

"So you do like dick."

"I'm not talking about dick, Stella. I'm talking about meeting with someone." I chance taking my eyes off the road and catching hers. "You know, talking to someone. Like you told me to."

"Oh."

"It helps."

She sits back in her seat and folds the box of rice closed. Bounces it on her lap like it is a fretful baby. "I'm glad for you, Lucky. I was worried about you for a while there."

"I owe you for that," I say.

"You don't owe me shit. I knew you was gone get it together for yourself. Got yourself a good job and everything. Got a decent man friend, even if you ain't giving the poor sucker none." She cackles like intimacy without sex is inconceivable. "I'm proud of you, girl. Real proud." She hears me sniffle and curses under her breath. "Don't start that shit, hear? You just pay attention to the damn road. All I need is the police pulling us over and I got me some MD 20/20 in my purse."

We ride in silence until the factory's sign pops up on the horizon. I feel time slipping through my fingers and I clear my throat. "Stella?"

"Hmm?"

"Do you ever think about looking for your daughter again?"

"Can't lie and say I don't. Sometimes. But after so much time goes by, Lucky, you figure it's best just to leave well enough alone. I don't think I could stand to see her strung out on that shit anyway. I'm already half dead, and seeing her like that would kill me dead, for sure. I told you, you reminds me of her, didn't I?"

"Yeah, you told me. What's her name again?"

"Crystal." Pride rolls off her tongue along with the name. "Crystal Sanchez."

"Sanchez? You had you a Mexican man?"

"Girl, had two or three of them smooth-talking devils. I got a whole 'nother reason for why they call 'em wetbacks, too. Lord forgive me, 'cause that wasn't nice. Don't nobody hate that stereotyping bullshit worse than I do, and you know that, Lucky. But still, the truth don't need no support." She gathers up her stuff and gets ready to climb out of the car. "Lord knows I don't feel like it tonight."

"You behave yourself, all right?" She waves my words away and lights a cigarette. "I mean it, Stella. And you call me if you need me too."

"I need you to quit talking to me like I'm the kid and you the old head, 'stead of the other way around. That's what I need. Can you get me tomorrow night?"

"All you gotta do is call."

"Well, I'm calling now. Can't you hear the phone ringing? Ring, ring, ring. You hear that shit?" I fall back against my seat and laugh long and hard.

Kimmick is a sneaky bastard. He gets me to talking and I don't even realize he's done it until it is too late and he is in my space. Always, he begins our sessions with a question that he says has been on his mind since the last time we met. Something I have said in the previous session makes him think of the question, he claims, and he presents me with it as soon as I walk into his office and lie down on his beat-up leather couch.

There is a pattern to the way we do things. He makes fun of the fact that I lie down, says I am being theatrical and melodramatic, influenced by too many television movies. I tell him that it is easier for me to look at the ceiling rather than at his funny-looking mug, and we laugh a little bit. And then he puts it to me, the question that has been on his mind all week.

This week I flip the script though. There is something that has been on my mind all week, and I don't want to be distracted, so I come out with it as soon as I cross the threshold into his universe.

"I want to talk about my family," I say as I kick off my shoes and swing my feet up on the couch.

He lays a peanut butter cup on his tongue and eases back in his chair. "You want one of these before I put 'em up?"

"No, thanks." We finished off a whole bag last week and I figured out then that he is bad for my diet. "Did you hear me? I said I want to talk about my family. You asked about them once before."

"And you told me you came to Earth on a space ship from Krypton," he reminds me, tongue in cheek. "Said you were a stowaway on the same ship that brought Superman here." "It wasn't Krypton." I find a water spot on the ceiling and stare at it without blinking.

"It was another planet. One where women rule and there are no men. One woman makes the rules, and everybody else falls in line. Disobedience is punishable by death. A bunch of crazy bitches with penis envy and fucked-up levels of consciousness."

"There had to have been some men around," he speculates around a mouthful of chocolate. "Babies were born."

"I think they broke into sperm banks and stole sperm to procreate. I never had a father and I never thought I needed one. Never thought the absence of one was strange."

"You think it's strange now?"

"Now I'm too old to give a damn."

He is quiet for several seconds. And then, "So . . . no men. What else?"

"The women in my family don't need men. We are a self-contained unit, like an evil sorority."

"Do you count yourself as an active member of the sorority?"

"I count myself as the black sheep of the family. The one who would not conform. I went to prison because I refused to repeat the chant and fall in line."

"I thought you went to prison because you killed your grandmother."

Kimmick gives it to me straight, no chaser, and the force of his words snakes through my body and bounces around inside my head. When I can speak, I look at him and say, "It amounts to the same thing."

"I'm confused."

"So am I."

"Your grandmother led the evil sorority?"

"She had to be stopped."

"By any means necessary?"

"By me," I say and go back to the ceiling. "I didn't have a plan to kill her. She was in my way and she wouldn't budge. Wouldn't admit to me that she was wrong. Wouldn't say she was sorry or even fix her lips to accept the part she played in everything."

"So you shot her."

"So I shot her," I confirm gravely. "She wouldn't move."

"You say she wouldn't move. What was she standing in the way of, Lena? What was she hiding?"

"A black heart."

"Elaborate?"

"No. I want to talk about my family."

"Who were we just talking about?"

"People from the place in outer space. My family of origin. I have another family that I don't belong to anymore."

"Who are they?"

I smile as I remember. "Lou and Denny, my parents. Pigpen and White Girl Julie, my sisters. And Anna. She was my lover. Does that shock you?"

Kimmick braces his elbows on his knees and tilts his head to one side. "The price of gasoline is what shocks me, if you want to know the truth. Do you fancy yourself the only woman who's ever taken another woman as a lover, in prison or anywhere else?"

"Hardly. Do you have any idea what goes on in the sanctuary while church services are supposed to be going on?"

"I'm Catholic. Spare me the details." We laugh. "Are you trying to shock me?"

"I think you should be," I say. "You might as well get shock and repulsion out of your system now."

"As opposed to later?"

"Later gets ugly. Later could have you running out of here without your peanut butter cups."

"Will you still be here after I run out?"

"I have nowhere else to go, so where else would I be but lying right here?"

"Then I'll come back," he says. "Assuming I run out, which I doubt I will. You don't scare me, Lena."

"I should."

I issue the same ominous warning to Aaron, and he laughs in my ear. He listens to my tale of an evil sorority and asks many of the same questions that Kimmick asks. But the second time around, I am expecting them, and they are easier to answer. Kimmick breaks the ice and makes me wade into water that is freezing cold. Then I climb out of the whirlpool and Aaron is waiting, ready to wrap me in a warm towel, and after I stop shivering, I leave him with the wet towel that is Lucky, so the two of them can become better acquainted.

There is a process by which what happens between Aaron and me happens. I am still getting used to the ways he has of getting me to talk, so different from Kimmick's ways but just as effective. I am still wrapping the concept of unforced and undemanding intimacy around my mind, sinking into it and letting myself speak from my mouth what I feel in my heart. There is no mulling over and censuring. What comes to my mind is what comes out of my mouth, and he rolls with my flow and takes it as I give it to him. He tells me that what I give him is priceless and makes me wonder if he is the one who should be consulting with a shrink.

He slides an arm around my waist and pulls me back against his chest, makes a pillow for my head with his elbow and kisses the back of my neck softly. This, too, is a process, the one we go through when it is time for sleeping, and we are making our way there together.

He eases his knee between mine and makes me think about what it would be like to cross the line we have not crossed, to experience all of him. I wonder what he would say if I peeled off my tank top and pressed my bare chest against his bare chest. If I offered him a cradle for his sex, without cotton tap pants as a barrier between us. If I asked him to remove his underwear and meet me halfway.

He is hard and he does not want me to know it. He puts space between us from the waist down and drops a hand on my waist when I try to fill the space. His breath backs up in his throat and he chuckles.

"I want to be closer to you too," I say.

"This is enough for me, Lena."

I don't believe him, and I have to see his eyes. I roll over on my back and search his face in the darkness. "What if it's not enough for me? You know it's been ten years since . . ."

"Are a few more months going to make a difference?"

"Months?" My voice goes high and tight with shock. He throws his head back and laughs. "How much longer do I have to wait for you to kiss me?"

"We kiss all the time." He proves his point by warming my belly with his palm and dropping a kiss on my lips. "See?"

"You think I'm a child?"

"I think you deserve all the space you need to move around in. I'm not trying to put pressure on you to do what I want to do, Lena. It's your world, baby. We do what you want to do and when you want to do it."

"What do you do?"

"Become accustomed to cold showers."

"Shit." The darkness is my friend, and Aaron does not see me coming until it is too late. I pull his face to mine and push my tongue in his mouth before he knows what hit him. He gasps and I go deeper, make him kiss me back. He doesn't need much provocation, and a few seconds into it, we are breathing hard and competing to see which one of us can open our mouths the widest, who can swallow who whole.

"You taste good to me," I tell him after we pull apart. "I love the way you kiss."

"Love the way you kiss too. Knew I would though. Goodnight, Lena."

"Goodnight." It takes me a few minutes of tossing and turning, and then I fall asleep.

When I do, I dream of Yo-Yo. She is so clear and so real to me that I can smell the bergamot she uses in her hair and bubble gum on her breath as she hovers over my shoulder, irritating the hell out of me. She is the only person in the world who can make me want to do harm to a computer. Make me want to pick it up and toss it out the nearest window and send her flying out after it.

She works my nerves.

"For one of them college girls, you sure is dumb, Lucky. You ain't even looking in the most obvious places," she says for the fiftieth time. It makes perfect sense that she is at the *Sentinel* with me, in my tiny office. She sits on my desk, next to the computer monitor, and helps herself to the jar of M&M's there.

I look at her and roll my eyes. "I'm looking everywhere I know to look, Yo, damn. Point both of your eyes in the same direction and shut up talking to me, okay?" She knows that I have been searching for Stella's daughter during my lunch breaks. Knows that not being able to find her is driving me crazy, and she thinks riding my ass about it helps.

"Oh, now you want me to shut up? You came looking for me; I didn't come looking for your ass. You always was a pain in somebody's booty hole, Lucky. But you know what? I'ma forgive you 'cause I know you love me."

"I don't love you," I say and shake my head.

"You can't say that shit to save your life, can you? If somebody offered your ass a million bucks to say it, you'd take your ass home broke as a joke, wouldn't you?"

"Kiss my ass. Oh, wait, you'd have to be able to see it to kiss it, so forget it."

"You got jokes?"

"Shhh." I motion for her to be quiet and concentrate on the search results lining up on the screen. One of them might lead me to Stella's missing daughter. Yo-Yo crunches candy by the handful and cranes her neck so she can see the screen too. I catch a whiff of hair grease and swallow the lump in my throat. "I miss you, Yo. I don't know why, but I miss you all the time."

"I feel you missing me, Lucky," she says. "I been telling them about you up here too. Making sure they have your back, like I used to. Told 'em about how you helped me find my babies and got you a few brownie points."

I cut her a sharp glance, and she winks at me with a shitty grin on her face. She knows I hate brownies and she knows why. "I wish I could find them for you now. Wish you could see them again."

"I see 'em all the time. They doing real good, too, Lucky. Don't worry 'bout me, girl. It's all good now, you feel me? You just do your do and do it right. You got to represent for all the ex-cons coming along after you. Let 'em know we people too."

"I wish you were here to help me represent."

"Shit, you don't need me no more." She hops down from my desk and empties the last of the M&M's into her hand. "Speaking of which, I gotta go. They calling me. I'll be around though, looking out for you. Meantime, you need to open your eyes and look around you.

Been a snake, it would've bit you right on your ass. And you say I can't see."

"Don't go, Yo. Stay with me a little longer." I reach for her, but she slips through my fingers like air, grinning like a fool and chomping on candy. "You have to go right this minute?"

"Right this minute, sweetstuff. They make you earn your keep up here, but it's cool. The food is extra special. Way better than what we had in the joint."

"I love you," I say.

"I know you do. Just wanted to hear you say it." She blows me a kiss and then she is gone.

I run out of my office and look up and down the hallway. I want to catch her before she can get away because there are things I want to ask her. Things I need to tell her. I don't see her, and I call her name over and over, but she doesn't come. Then I start to cry.

I wake up crying, but I am not in pain, not grieving. What I feel has nothing to do with sorrow and death and everything to do with living. There is pleasure so sweet that I cannot help my tears. I find Aaron's hand where it rests against my core, run my fingers along his arm, and cradle his head against my chest. Let myself feel his sensual touch.

Aaron takes his hand away a little at a time, presses his lips to my mouth, and then to my forehead, where there is dampness. "Shhh." The storm he created in me while I was sleeping is over. He tugs my tank top down and over my breasts, kisses a spot low on my stomach as he finds my panties and rights the wrong I have done to them. I have twisted and turned so much that they are riding my thighs. "Better?"

"Better," I whisper, drifting off again. My vagina is still pulsing. "What about you?"

"Doesn't matter. Relax and get some sleep."

"It felt like I was flying." I think I can feel wind beneath my wings, carrying me back to the clouds. Think I hear Yo-Yo asking somebody why she can't have her damn wings yet, and I giggle when I hear the response she receives. The voice is like velvet, smooth and soothing, and it tells her that she still has work to do on her mouth.

"Hey . . . Giggles," he curls up behind me and snatches me back from sleep. Pushes his knee between mine and fits his lips to my ear. "You listening?"

"Yeah. What did you say?"

"I said I love you."

"Love you too." I charge back into sleep and search for Yo-Yo. I want to tell her that I can say it, and I plan on asking her where I can collect my million dollars.

Chapter Nineteen

Family Portrait:

Who can see that a holiday celebration is really just a farce? That it is simply a gathering of people who are related by blood, but who would rather be anywhere else in the world. Anywhere that didn't require sitting around a ceremonial table, shoveling food into their mouths and reciting preordained snippets of the family chant in installments. Who is brave enough, courageous enough, to push their plate away, to stand and speak out against the hypocrisy of celebrating a holiday linked to a man we call our holy savior, when we are all so full of satanic obedience that the smell of smoke fills our nostrils?

It is like this each and every holiday—the dreadful trek to my grandmother's house, dressed in our finest and clutching Mama's hand the whole way. Sometimes she cannot drive properly because her hands are shaking or else she is fumbling with her cigarettes and the ever present lighter. And sometimes she has to wrestle with either me or Vicky, whichever one of us claims the front seat, because we are constantly groping for her hand, wanting to hold it for reasons that she cannot or will not understand.

I accuse her of never coming inside the house that smells like old mothballs and shameful secrets, but that is a lie now that I sit down and think about it clearly. There are times when she can bring herself to step into the portal of hell and bear the heat for short periods. Usually on holidays and only for a few hours, the time it takes to consume a meal and to recite the chant that has no words.

The chant is really a delicate dance that we all do. Me and Vicky, my mama, my grandmother and my mother's sister Deirdre. We do it with our eyes, and it goes something like this: Bounce your eyeballs from one person to the next, always keep them in your sight and pay attention to what they do. Take your cues from them. Don't speak unless you're spoken to, don't forget to smile when someone says something they perceive as funny, and don't forget to say please and thank you. Absolutely no spontaneous conversation and no un-necessary fidgeting. Eat everything on your plate and say how much you enjoyed at least one thing on your plate. Above all else, children should be seen and not heard.

Dierdre's children are heathens, a handful of nappy-headed boys who are always playing practical jokes and being left back a grade, with a few girls added to the mix to serve as guinea pigs for their brothers' lunacy. But on these occasions they are perfect angels because they don't have a choice in the matter. The house speaks to them, tells them that they must not take the freedom they have for granted, and it stunts their wayward nature. If that isn't enough, Dierdre threat-ens them within an inch of their lives. She manages to make them afraid of something they can't see or feel, but that she is all too aware of.

It takes me years to figure it all out, but when I do and I think back on the holidays, I realize that Deirdre knows. I see her face in my mind's eye and I recognize the expression that lives on my face as the same one that owns hers. She does not want to know what she knows, but experience is the best teacher, the only one, really. Except for holidays, she keeps her children far away from this house, and I have always respected her for being strong enough to do at least that much for them.

We are Vicky and Leenie, but before us, they were Ellie and Dee-Dee. Before homemade caramel and brownies there was pineapple cake and lemon drop cookies.

What I cannot understand is why no one ever pushes their plates away and renounces their membership. Why anyone volunteers to be tortured and comes of their own free will. There must be a way to excommunicate from the sorority, and if street gangs allow their members to take a beating and walk away from them, then we must have some rule in the handbook for walking away from this.

Who will stand?

In the end, Vicky will. She wipes her mouth with a napkin, gets to her feet, and smoothes her dress down the front. It is her first big-girl dress, cream with a tasteful floral print and a matching three-quarter sleeve cardigan, in honor of her being fifteen. She no longer has to wear patent leather buckle shoes. She wears low-heeled pumps and sheer hose, and she looks pretty with her hair curled and lying around her shoulders.

My fingers curl around the butter knife beside my plate and I wait for her to say something inflammatory. I will use the knife if I have to, will force the dull blade through someone's skin without a moment's hesitation. All she has to do is give the word and we will be like the Lone Ranger and Tonto. I see her lips open and hold my breath.

"I have to pee," Vicky says, and my mother frowns in disapproval. The boys giggle, and Deirdre sends them a hooded look. Vicky has just committed a cardinal sin. *Pee* is not a word children should say. They can say *dick* and *pussy*, *fuck* and *suck*, but not *pee*. What is she thinking?

Vicky doesn't wait for permission to leave the table, and neither do I. I scramble out of my chair and follow her out of the dining room. "Sit down, Leenie," my grandmother barks. "She doesn't need you to wipe her behind, does she?" I stare at my grandmother and she stares at me. We hate each other, and it shows on our faces. Ten seconds pass and I am still not in my chair. "Did you hear me, girl? I said sit down. There's still food on your plate."

She thinks I come back to the table to resume my seat, but sitting down is the furthest thing from my mind. I come back to knock my plate to the floor and watch it shatter into a thousand pieces, to see food smear across the floor and drip from the tablecloth to the chair cushion. I come back to pick up a butter knife, toss it back down, and pick up a fork instead. It is sharper and will do the most damage, if it comes down to that.

At the other end of the table, she stands and glares at me with her mouth open. I grip the fork and never look away from her. I dare her to come. The air at my side shifts, and then Vicky is there. She looks from one face to the other, and she wants to keep her eyes on Vicky because Vicky is the lesser of two evils, but she can't. She cannot help being drawn back to me. Vicky still has good left in her face, and I don't. Like recognizes like.

The memory leaves me feeling cold and angry. To get away from it and warm up a little, I blink, roll my head to the side, and look at Kimmick's face. I wait a beat and then ask him the question that is on the tip of my tongue. "Do you think my grandmother could see her death in my eyes?"

"You mean like a premonition?" he says.

"Yes, like a premonition." I relax the muscles in my shoulders and ass, and cross my ankles at the other end of the couch. "Do you think she knew that I'd be the one to exorcise her?"

"But you said you didn't plan to kill her, Lena."

"God threw Lucifer out of heaven," I say. "I don't think He planned to do it; He just knew it had to be done. You do what has to be done."

"How are you like God?"

"The whole scene, it was like the Last Supper." Needing to make my point has me sitting up and swinging my feet to the floor, facing Kimmick and talking with my hands. "I'm Jesus, right? Vicky and my mama are the other dudes sitting at the table. Seems like Aunt Deirdre is Mary Magdelene . . ."

"Who?"

"The woman sitting at Jesus's right. Don't act like you haven't read *The DaVinci Code*." A smile curves my lips. "Own your truth, Kimmick. This is a safe place."

"Now we're about to get into a discussion on religion?"

"No, we're about to discuss the fact that the remains of the first human being were found in Africa and Jesus was a black man, or at the very least, Middle Eastern. He didn't look shit like you, but that's neither here nor there. Why do you think Mary Magdelene smiles at me?"

"Mary Magdelene is Deirdre, correct?" I nod. "And she smiled at you?"

"Yeah, she smiled. Why do you think she did that?"

"I'm more interested in why you think she smiled at you."

"How come you never answer my questions?"

"How come you never answer mine? You always answer a question with a question. So who, I ask, has issues with owning the truth? You or me?"

"My truth is the truth," I say.

"And what is that? Why does Deirdre smile and who is your grandmother? We're talking about the Last Supper, aren't we?" Kimmick uses his fingers to tick off names as he calls them. "There's Peter, Paul and What's-his-face. Doohickey and Whatchamacallit. You say there's Mary Magdelene—"

"I don't say, I know," I cut in.

"Wasn't there a Lancelot or a Michael or a Job or something? And then there was—"

"Judas." I am triumphant. "Deirdre smiles because I have called Judas out. I still get nailed to the cross though."

Kimmick watches me crack up at my own joke, and I look so funny to him that he joins me. "You're killing me, Lena," he says, shaking his head.

"You wouldn't be the first." That makes him laugh even harder.

I recreate the scene for Aaron, thinking that he will laugh the way Kimmick and I do, but he doesn't. He looks at me like I am crazy and drops a metal strainer in the sink irritably. I see him truly angry for the first time, and it intrigues me.

"It was a joke, Aaron," I say for the second time. He pretends not to hear me. He checks the marinara sauce bubbling on the stove, shreds a little more Parmesan cheese and then drops pasta in a pot of boiling water. "Where's your sense of humor?"

"I guess I'm not in the habit of playing with God, Lena."

"Oh, and the joke you told me about the priest, the rabbi and the—"

"That was a stupid joke, baby, and it wasn't even that damn funny. This shit is not a joke and it's not funny at all. What happened to you had nothing to do with God." He wipes his hands on a dishtowel and goes to the refrigerator. "We're talking about a couple of sick motherfuckers fucking with people's lives, and to me, that's not a laughing matter."

"You're angry with me?"

"No, I'm angry *for* you. You tell me this shit and it makes me want to snap somebody's damn neck. It hurts me to know how you were hurt."

"So I should stop telling you then," I say.

He blows out a harsh breath and massages his eyelids with stiff fingers. Looks at the floor and then gives me his eyes. "That's not what I mean, Lena. Don't ever stop talking to me, telling me who you are and why, okay? Just don't expect me to find anything in it to laugh about. Right about now I'm feeling like running out and killing somebody for you."

"I know how that feels," I say without thinking.

Aaron turns down the fire under the marinara sauce and then adjusts the flame under the pasta. He points a finger at me and narrows his eyes. "You take the jokes too far," he says and leaves me in the kitchen.

He disappears into his office, and I wander around his living room. I turn on the stereo and find a song I remember, a slow and sensual song that is at least twenty years old, and I start my hips to swaying. I sway over to him as he crosses the room, and I lace my fingers around his neck. "Dance with me," I say before I pull his mouth down to mine.

We rock around the living room, bump into furniture and almost knock a lamp over, but we keep dancing. Keep kissing, too. Long, wet kisses that have my breath coming faster and harder. Greedy kisses that have him pressing me against the wall and sighing into my mouth. I stand on the tops of his feet and feel his erection in the vee of my thighs, hum low in my throat.

"I want you inside me," I tell him, and my voice does not sound like my own. It is hoarse and thirsty sounding, like I will die if I cannot drink from his fountain.

"I want to be inside you," Aaron says and kisses me again. He sucks in a breath, presses against me, and kisses the side of my neck softly. "You feel that?" He knows I do. "That's a dragon, Lena, a greedy dragon, and I need you to be ready for it when it comes to you. I don't want you scared or confused or hurting." He pulls back and finds my eyes. "I need you whole and healthy and screaming because I'm making you feel so damn good that you can't believe it. I need you crying because you don't want it to end, not because you're wondering what you got yourself into. I want you to be sure you're ready."

"How much longer?"

"You tell me."

"Now."

"You love me?"

"You know I do."

"I love you too. Wait for me, okay? I need to be ready for you too. I like to plunder and devour, so I need to work on taking small bites because ten years is a long-ass time."

"Maybe I want to be devoured."

He laughs. "Oh yeah? You really are a wolf, huh?"

"I'd probably tear you up," I say, smiling.

"Oh, you're talking much shit tonight. Get on in here and make me a plate, woman. Better make yourself two while you're at it. I think you need to start building up your endurance because your days are numbered."

"Beige," Aaron says a long time later. We order scoops of ice cream to go and eat them as we walk home. He finishes his Rocky Road before I am even half-way through my Rainbow Sherbet and hooks an arm around my neck, ready to talk. "Is she still calling and hanging up?"

"Twice yesterday," I say, and suddenly my appetite is gone. He takes my cup and drops it in the next trashcan we pass. My arms are free, and I slip one around his waist and match my stride to his. "I miss her."

"Call her."

"And say what? I don't feel like I'm the one who should be apologizing."

"How much does she know, Lena?"

"As little as possible. Not what you know," I say. "You think I should tell her?"

"Up to you. But personally? No. Not yet, anyway. She's a kid and she needs to be one as long as she can get away with it."

"I just want her to be okay with me, you know? I mean, I know we're not the Partridge Family, but why can't she just accept me for who I am and be okay with it? I fucked up; I know that. Nobody knows that better than I do."

"She doesn't want to share you, which is understandable under the circumstances."

"She says she wants to come and live with me. I wanted her to in the first place, but she said she didn't want to. Now she does."

"Have you changed your mind?"

"No, she did."

"So tell her to pack her bags and come. School's almost out."

"My apartment is barely big enough for me, and I like it." I take a deep breath and glance up at him so he can see what I'm feeling. "I like your apartment."

"I wouldn't mind a house," Aaron says slowly. "Definitely outside of the city, maybe somewhere out in the country. A horse and a dog or two would be nice too."

"And then what, I take your place?"

He shakes his head and looks at me like he wants to ask me if I hear air between my ears.

"You like the country, Lena?"

"I never gave it much thought."

"Do me a favor and start thinking about it, would you?"

Tammy turns sideways and two-steps through the door. Then she moves through the office we share like half of a wall. She is wide and round, tall, and six minutes away from a massive coronary. She sits down in her chair and scoots up to her desk like she is just finishing a marathon, breathing like she needs oxygen, and smiles at me. I smile back.

"Can I ask you something, Tammy?"

"Do I have to answer?" She turns her computer on and taps the mouse.

"Um . . . I guess not, if you don't want to. It's just about the M&M's I had on my desk. Did you eat them?" The jar is empty, and I know I'm not the culprit, so it has to be her.

"Didn't touch them." She sees the skepticism on my face and repeats herself more forcefully. "I didn't touch them. I know it might be hard to believe, but I'm not much of a candy eater."

"What do you usually eat?"

"Oh, I don't know . . . pizza, pasta. A little cake here and there. But I don't eat too much candy. It's bad for your teeth."

I look at the empty candy dish again and run a hand over my head. "It's just . . . I don't care about the candy, I really don't. I mean, I put it there to be eaten. I just need to know who ate it."

"Well, it wasn't me," Tammy says. She ignores me in favor of her computer, but I can't stop staring at her. She feels my eyes on her and looks at the ceiling. "What do you want? You want me to buy you more M&M's or something?"

"You really didn't eat them?"

"Read my lips. *N-O*. Maybe we've got ourselves a crazy ghost with a sweet tooth or something. Besides, I'm on a diet."

"Good luck with that," I say and turn on my own computer. I think I know what I need to do.

Beige is surprised to see me waiting at the curb when she finally comes out of school. She thinks I am here to rip her a new one because she plays pranks on my phone and hangs up in my ear. It takes her five minutes to cover two minutes' worth of distance, and her eyes touch down on everything except my face. She doesn't know which bag I will come out of.

"Do you have something you want to say to me?" I say as soon as she stops in front of me. She looks exactly like she did when she was four and I caught her painting her fingernails. And her jeans. And the wall. And my drapes. I wanted to shake her then, and now I just want to hug her. "Do you?"

"What am I supposed to say?"

"You call and hang up on me when I answer."

"If you know it's me, then why don't you say something?"

"I do say something. I say I love you every time."

"Then you hang up," she points out and props her hands on her hips.

I drop my head and push wrinkles out of my forehead. We are going back and forth like children, and it's getting on my nerves. I lean back against my car and fold my arms under my breasts, spread my feet on the curb and purse my lips. "Look, I love you and I miss you."

"I love you and I miss you too."

I feel a weight lifting off my shoulders and then, a second later, the hair standing up on the back of my neck. "Who's this little cat hanging around the fence, eyeing you like a stalker?" I point off in the distance, where a tall boy with round glasses lurks, watching my daughter hopefully and looking downright pitiful.

"That's Darrick. He's um . . ." She shifts from one foot to the other and turns an impressive shade of pink.

"Um . . . your boyfriend? Spit it out. And who said you were old enough to have a boyfriend anyway? Call him over here. I want to meet his little four-eyed ass."

"Mom . . ."

"Call him." I look away and wait for Darrick to haul ass over to me. He is not little, but tall and lanky, with long hands and even longer feet. A trumpet case swings from one arm, and his glasses are tilted on his face clumsily. I look him from head to toe, stick my tongue in my cheek and grin. "What'cho name is, boy?"

Beige goes from pink to red and throws her hands up. "Mom! Oh my God."

Darrick has a sense of humor. He bursts out laughing and pushes his hands in his pockets. "I'm Darrick, ma'am. Nice to meet you."

"Don't try that *ma'am* crap on me, boy. I've been around the block a few times. I know the score, okay? Beige isn't old enough to be having a boyfriend."

"W—We're just friends."

"That's all you better be, too. You look like a decent enough little cat. You play the horn?"

"A little bit."

"Wait a minute. Either you play or you don't. Which is it?"

"I play."

"Are you in the band?"

"Yes, ma'am."

"What grade are you?"

"Freshman."

"You're a little tall to be a freshman, aren't you?"

"Mom . . ."

"All right, all right. My work here is done." I wag a finger between Beige and Darrick. "Tell your . . . friend bye and get in. Two minutes." I hop in the car and count the seconds.

She sulks her way into the passenger seat five minutes later and rolls her eyes at me.

"That's what you're supposed to be doing," I tell her. "Rolling your eyes and being pissed with me because I make your life miserable, not the other way around. It's a little late in coming, but believe me, this is the way things are supposed to be. I'm the old head and you're the one with milk still behind your ears. You don't get to punish me, so let's be clear on that right now."

"I wasn't trying to punish you."

"What were you doing then?" A red light catches me and I stop reluctantly. I reach over and turn her face toward mine. "You know I love you and you know I've missed the hell out of you all these years. And you know I feel like shit for having to be away from you and bringing it on myself. You can't seriously think that us wasting time like this is healthy. I need to be with you every second I can, Beige."

"You have time for Aaron," she pouts.

"You don't have time for both me and Darrick?" A car horn sounds and reminds me to drive. "Look . . . I love that you want me all to yourself, but you know that's not life. I want you all to myself too, but I know you have school and friends and other stuff to do besides look at my face all day. Doesn't mean I don't love you. I think loving you too much is what started all this anyway."

"How can you love me too much?"

"I would run out in front of a speeding bus to drag you to safety," I say and flip on the blinker. "If you needed a heart and they couldn't find a donor, I'd tell them to put me under and take mine. When you love someone the way I love you, sometimes you don't think clearly. Like with that little cat, Darrick. I thought about punching him a few times, just because he was looking at you."

Beige giggles and blushes. "You embarrassed me enough for one day. He said you were tight though. Couldn't believe you're old enough to be my mom."

"Tight?"

"Fine, Mom. Duh."

"Oh, well, there might be some hope for the little four-eyed drummer boy yet."

"He plays the trumpet."

"Whatever." I flap a hand.

She is hungry, so we go through a drive-thru. Then we call Vicky from Beige's cell phone to tell her that

Beige is with me. No telling what time I will bring her home, so don't wait up. School is almost out for the summer and the homework is light. We drive to my apartment and park, cross the street and venture into the park. Spread her books open on a picnic table and pretend to study.

I am trying to remember what I know about probability and coming up with blanks when Beige lays her pencil down and says, "Is that why you did what you did to Great-Grandma, because you loved her too much?"

"No. Love—true love—should never hurt. Do you understand what I'm saying to you?"

"I think so."

"Good, because if someone says they love you and they hurt you on purpose, they don't love you. Get away from them, get out of the situation any way you can, and get on with your life. Wait . . . that's not quite right. Definitely get out of the situation, but don't send yourself to prison doing it. Promise me you'll do that. Get out, I mean."

"Okay, but I don't understand—"

"I didn't love her," I say. "And it didn't seem like she loved me. I hated to be around her."

"I remember going to her house a few times when I was younger," Beige confesses in a low voice, as if someone might overhear what she is saying and accuse her of being mean for saying it. "I didn't like it."

I am holding my breath. "Why?"

"It just didn't feel right to me. I didn't like the way it smelled, and she made me feel funny. Always staring at me and calling me Bee-Bee. I told her my name was Beige, but she kept calling me that. . . . I cried every day after you left."

"I cried too. Probably every day for a year straight. I decorated the walls of my cell with your name. Put your pictures up everywhere, so I could see your face every day."

"Nana said you wasn't in your right mind when you did what you did."

I am not ready to go there with Beige. I need a few minutes to get my thoughts together and put them in order. "My attorney thought I would get a few months in jail, at the most, and then probation," I say. "He said he'd had a few other clients with cases similar to mine where the guys got probation, and he knew the judge pretty well. I wasn't supposed to go to prison, but I did. And I definitely wasn't supposed to be there for as long as I was. That part I didn't do on purpose, Beige."

"Nana said—"

"Your grandmother is so deep in denial that she can't think straight. She remembers what she wants to remember and to hell with the rest. Kimmick says that's common with victims of sexual abuse. Do you know what that means? Sexual abuse?"

I watch her face lose shape and form. She clamps a hand over her mouth and quickly makes her way from a moan to a cry. She is a smart girl. She knows what I am saying to her and what it means. She reclaims the breath she lost in her struggle not to fly apart, and fists her hands in her hair. Looks at the table. "Who is Kimmick?"

"This guy I hate but that I talk to sometimes. He says that people can only take so much before they reach a point of no return. Some people know enough to seek help right away, and some just want their shit to go away, to deny it ever happened. That's your grandma's deal. They're calling it familial dysfunction these days." I ease her hands from her hair and wrap them in mine.

"Other people find a gun and pull the trigger. That's my deal."

Beige pulls away from me and pushes away from the table. Stands in the grass like she is ready to charge me. She is angry and she doesn't know why. Or maybe she does know why and she doesn't know what to do with what she feels. Her chest heaves, and I think, if she has a heart attack, I will never forgive myself. I will throw myself to the ground and curse God until He takes me along with her. I will die before I ever know what life is really all about.

I shrug helplessly and swallow the tears in my throat. I can't do anything about the ones falling from my eyes. "I did the wrong thing, Bey. I did. But I couldn't take any more. I lost the ability to think clearly. All I knew was that I had to make somebody hurt the way I was hurting. I didn't think about the consequences of what I was doing. I didn't think about what would happen afterward, and I should've. It never crossed my mind that I'd lose you. I just knew I had to make it stop, couldn't let it keep going on. Don't be mad with me anymore, Bey, please. Don't keep punishing me like this, because I don't think I'm strong enough to take it. Not from you."

"Why did Great-Grandma do that to you?"

"I don't know."

"Will you tell me about it?"

I shake my head and reach for her. She comes to me without hesitation, sits on the bench next to me and falls sideways into my arms. "Maybe one day, if I ever really have to." If she ever remembers, I think, and hope she never does. "For now, I want you to hold on to childhood as tight as you can. This should be the best time of your life." I lock her up in my arms and kiss the top of her head.

"Childhood sucks," Beige decides a few minutes later. She is suddenly inspired by the topic and probably grateful for something else to grab onto. I listen to her go on and on about getting her own apartment and a job, so she can shop all the time. "I'm not having bills," she swears heatedly and makes me smile into her hair. "I'll eat out all the time, so I won't need a refrigerator and stove, and I'll never be home, so I won't need gas or electric. I'll come to your house to do my laundry."

Her cluelessness about adulthood makes me feel joy for the first time in a decade. I squeeze her tighter, in no hurry for her to grow up any more than she already has. I have missed so much. "Was it good to you, Bey? Childhood?"

"It was okay," she says. "Still is. Except for when you embarrass me in front of my friends. Wait until you get old. I'm coming up to the nursing home and clown you in front of your friends every day. Watch and see."

"Oh, so I'm going into a home?"

"Probably not. That just sounded good. I love you too much to put you in a home like that. They don't treat the old folks right in those places. I think I'd kill somebody if they hurt you." She realizes what she has said seconds after I do, and the moment passes in silence. I am the first to giggle. "Sorry."

"You were always warm and safe, Bey? Nobody ever hurt you?"

"No."

Then, I think, my living is not in vain.

Chapter Twenty

Beige thinks it is corny that we all wear the same blouses in the same color, but Vicky thinks her idea is the best one since sliced bread. She beams proudly when the photographer compliments her color choice and asks where we bought the blouses. I tell her the wheel and dirt came long before dry silk was ever thought of and shoo her over to where my mother and Beige are standing, already in position. I have never quite developed an affinity for having my picture taken, and I can't stop glancing at my watch.

We take family portraits for the first time since Vicky and I were teenagers. Then, it was just the three of us, and now there are four of us, posing stiffly and pasting wooden studio smiles on our faces. We split up, and Vicky and I pose together, then we flank our mother and rest loving hands on her shoulders. Then it is Beige's and my turn, and the photographer doesn't have to coach smiles out of us. We are giddy for the camera.

"I want a ten-by-thirteen of that one," Beige says, staring at the proofs of her and me.

My mother looks over Beige's shoulder and smiles. "Me too," she says. Her smile widens when our eyes meet.

***

There are no secrets in my house. I will not allow them, and if I cross boundaries in ensuring that what I will not allow does not occur, then it is for a good cause. Boundaries can be established later, but secrets will ignite and burn in hell before they ever have a chance to invade my sense of security.

From the moment Beige is able to string two words together, I tell her that she must tell me everything. That I am her mother and I will keep her safe. I tell her never to answer a knock at the door and never to allow a stranger into our home. I tell her never to go with a stranger and never, under any circumstances, to allow anyone to touch her in ways that she does not want to be touched.

I make her repeat after me as I recite the parts of her anatomy to her. "These are your arms," I say and point. "These are your legs and your feet. Do you know what this is?"

She looks like an adorable little ghost when she smiles. An ethnocentric Casper. She slaps a dimpled hand on her belly and giggles. "This is my belly, Mama," she squeaks.

She thinks we are playing a game, but I know we are not. "What about this?"

"My bottom." Another giggle. "My butt-butt." She slaps her butt cheeks and cheeses at me.

"This?"

"My piracy," she informs me, suddenly serious. "Nobody touch it."

She means her privates, but she is close enough. "That's right. Nobody touch it. You tell me if they do, all right?"

"A'wight." She hops on the tips of her toes as I pull a nightgown over her head and tug the hem down over her legs. I sit back on my haunches and feel around for her slippers. I finally find them and help her push her feet into them. She is like a little monkey, wrapping her fat little arms around my neck and wrestling for control of my face. She wants me to look at her, and I do.

She talks so close to my face that her lips brush mine. "Ceral, Mama. Want some ceral."

"You just had dinner," I say, but she knows cereal is in her future.

"Ceral."

In the kitchen, Beige spies a bag of cherry licorice that I have forgotten to hide, and she dances a jig. Tries to snap her fingers in time to the beat she creates. "Canny," she chirps. "Canny, canny, canny." Cereal is a distant memory now.

"Thought you said you wanted cereal."

"No. Canny."

I peel a rope of licorice from the package and stoop down to her level, tap my lips and pucker up. "Kiss first." She comes at me with all the force she owns. Almost knocks me on my ass as she kisses my lips with gusto. She chews her candy, and I stare at her, thinking that she is the most beautiful thing I have ever seen. "Bey?"

She focuses on my face without missing a beat chewing. "If anybody else ever tries to make you kiss them on the mouth, you tell me, okay?"

I can't let it go.

Aaron goes over on his back when I push. Still half asleep, he spreads his arms for me and then wraps me so tightly that I sigh from the relief of it. I spread out with him, my face finds his neck, and I breathe in his scent. It calms me, but I still can't stop shaking.

I shake like a leaf, like I am in the middle of a blizzard wearing a bikini. My teeth chatter, and the only warmth I can find is the warmth I steal from him. He pulls the covers over me and rubs my back. Massages me back to sleep.

"She was my baby," I whisper to Aaron. "She was my baby, Aaron. Mine."

"Shhh," he pats and rubs, kisses my chin and then my shoulder. "I know. It's over now. Shhh."

My session with Kimmick runs over, and I am five minutes into his next client's session when we are finally done. I use up another five minutes, blowing my nose and getting my face together before I step out of his motorcycle haven into the waiting room. There is one other person in the room, and I don't make eye contact. I hurry toward the door.

"Lucky?"

I freeze and turn in slow motion.

"Patty?"

She looks like Patty, but then she doesn't look like Patty. Her hair is shorter, stylishly cut, and she has gained a few pounds. She stands, touches her mouth and is about to cry. I walk over to where she stands and search her face. I am looking for anger and resentment where there is none. Her eyes tell me that she knows I did what I did because I wanted to help her. That she was helped.

"I thought you were going back to the South."

"I was, but you know . . ." She touches her stomach and I see that what I first thought was a few extra pounds is really a baby growing. "I got engaged to a truck driver, and his people are from around here. You know how that goes."

I nod. "I see you went back to wearing nail polish and stuff."

"You've got on lipgloss," she points out. "Looks good. How you doing, Lucky?"

"Good. You?"

"Good. Better. Kimmick's fat ass works a number on you, huh?"

"He's no joke," I say and smile.

Patty gasps and claps her hands under her chin. "That's the first time I've ever seen you do that."

"First time for everything, right? This is your first baby?"

"Yes, and I'm supposed to be having twins."

"Congratulations. Two reasons not to go back."

"You got kids?"

"One."

"Then you got a reason not to go back too."

"Got about a hundred of them," I say. "Maybe I'll see you around, Patty."

"Maybe," she says and waves.

We are not friends, but the fact that we both survived a war makes it easy for us to hug before we part ways. We hug each other a long time, smelling the scent of freedom on one another's skin. Once upon a time, she didn't know if she was going to make it, and I was sure I wouldn't. But we did. Both of us. And that means something. We both swallow the lumps in our throats when we pull apart.

"Baby, look at this," Aaron says.

He walks over to the weight bench, takes a free weight from my hand and replaces it with a sheet of paper. I read it slowly. "You found her." Stella's daughter is so close that I can reach out and touch her. If she were a snake, she'd have bitten me a long time ago.

Beige and I find her twenty minutes west of the city, where she has been living for the past two years. Hers is one of four apartments on the second floor of a women's transitional housing complex. Because of Aaron, I know she was arrested for stealing and sent to prison to complete an institutional substance abuse program. She is clean now, working with Children's Services to regain custody of her children, and working part-time at a nearby grocery store as a cashier. She is this close to getting her babies back, to getting her life back, and I hope there is room in it for Stella.

Beige juggles a bag of potato chips, a soda and four candy bars, and elbows me in the side. She whispers, "What if that's not her?"

I set a fruit cup and a bottle of juice on the conveyor belt and nod my head. "That's her. She's got Stella written all over her." Stella lives in her daughter's face the same way I live in Beige's face. She is there, in her daughter's eyes, her lips, and the tilt of her head as she checks the register tape for errors. They have the same fingers.

The line moves up and we move with it. I curse under my breath when the woman in front of me takes forever filling out a check. I toss a pack of the gum Aaron has to chew while he works on the belt and tell Beige to put back three of the candy bars she's holding.

"You're getting papaya juice," she complains.

"Fruit juice, candy. How are we talking about the same thing? If you had four cups of yogurt or something, you might have a point to argue."

"You used to let me eat candy all the time."

"Yeah, well, Gary Coleman used to be cute, but now? Not so much. What'chu talking 'bout, Beige? Pick one and put the rest back."

"Excuse me, ma'am. Is this your stuff?"

I stare stupidly, and Beige bumps me from behind, reminds me why I am here. I glance at Crystal's nametag and shake my head. "Yeah, this is my stuff. But not the four candy bars. I'm not paying for those."

"Mom . . ." Behind my back, Beige motions that the candy bars should be rung up too, thinking I don't see her.

"Um . . . should I add them, or . . .?"

"You look like her," I blurt out and sound simple.

"Excuse me?"

"You look like your mom."

She looks at Beige and raises her eyebrows curiously. Thinks I am two cards shy of a full deck. Beige shrugs and latches onto my arm. "Don't look at me. I ain't never seen your mom, but this is mine."

I slide her a look. She wants those candy bars badly. "Stella is your mom, right?"

"You know my mother?"

"Yeah, she talks about you all the time."

"They told me she was dead."

"She's not. Who told you that?"

Crystal looks at the line forming behind me and Beige and starts scanning our items. She moves slowly and lowers her voice. "The people at Social Services. They said they lost track of her some years back and she was probably dead."

That makes me mad. "Stella's not dead. What the hell is wrong with the system? She's not dead. She lives a half-hour from here, has a damn job and everything. She looked for you and couldn't find you." My hands are shaking as I scrub them over my face. "Damn. She wants to see you. All this time you thought she was dead?"

"Me and my mama ain't exactly had the perfect relationship. Ain't really had any kind of relationship for a long time. I didn't think one way or the other about her." She hands me a plastic bag and makes change for the twenty I give her. Pauses a few seconds to count out my change and lay it in my hand. Then she looks at me with eyes that are old and tired. "I'm glad to hear she ain't dead, laying in the ground somewhere by herself, but I don't know if I'm glad to hear 'bout her wanting to see me. I don't know if I really care."

"Stella's a good person."

"She might be now, but you don't know nothing about what kind of mother she was. I don't need unnecessary problems in my life right now. Got enough as it is."

"So . . ." I glance at Beige, my hands up and out. "You don't want her phone number or her address? You don't want to know where your own mother is?"

"I didn't say I didn't want to know." Crystal slaps her hand on her hip and surveys the line I am holding up. "I said I *don't know* if I want to know. What I do know is, I'm not gone have a job if you don't quit holding up my line, and I can't afford to be out of a job. Unless you planning on paying my bills and letting me and my kids come live with you."

Beige and I quickly get the hell out of line. I want to reconnect Stella with her daughter, but taking on extra roommates is out of the question. I'm still mentally working out how Beige and I will live in the same tiny space together and keep from strangling each other. I circle around the register and touch Crystal's arm. She scans a box of cereal and doesn't look at me. I have to make do with her profile.

"I'm leaving this for you, okay? It's Stella's address and phone number." Her uniform is a smock with big pockets, and that's where I stuff the paper that I am armed with. There is a possibility that she will slap the shit out of me for invading her space, but I will do myself much more harm if I don't finish what I started. I'm not leaving until she knows where her mother is.

After that, the rest is up to her.

I stay at Crystal's side, waiting for her to snatch the paper from her pocket and throw it on the floor, so I can pick it up and stuff it right back in her pocket. I'll stand here, stuffing and restuffing all day, if I have to. I've had all the loss and senseless destruction I can stand. I feel bad for Stella and even worse for Crystal, and I need to do something. I don't waste time dwelling on why I am putting myself in the middle of Stella's personal life, sticking my nose where I know it doesn't belong. I just know I need to do this. Maybe somewhere in the back of my mind I feel like helping to bring Stella and her daughter back together will make up for everything that I've done to tear Beige and me apart. If I can't have a happy ending, somebody has to have one.

Beige is nowhere near as patient as I am. She cuffs my arm and pulls me away from Crystal, to the exit door. I glance back one last time and look for scraps of paper fluttering to the floor and breathe a sigh of relief when I see none.

"You think she'll call?" Beige asks as we get into my car.

I toss my bag over into her lap and shift into drive. "I don't know. Maybe she'll ease into it. Call and hang up a few hundred times and then finally say something."

She rolls her eyes and looks away, embarrassed. "That was mean, Mom."

"Well, it worked for you, didn't it?"

Eight years of honing my response time is what saves Crystal from becoming a paraplegic. I slam on brakes

just as she appears in front of my car, and I barely
avoid taking her knees for a ride on the bumper. Beige
is gripping the dashboard and looking at me like I'm
crazy as I roll down the window and stick my head out.
It takes me a few seconds to find my voice and use it
because visions of going back to prison for vehicular
manslaughter dance before my eyes.

"You almost hit me," Crystal says as she rushes over
to my window. "Damn, I thought I was gone for real."
If she is careless enough to run out in front of a moving
car, then I am silly enough not to apologize for driving the car. I raise my eyebrows and wait for her to tell
me what is so important that it's worth risking life and
limb. She pats her chest and takes deep breaths. "Why
didn't she come herself?"

"She doesn't know where to come. Doesn't even
know I'm here," I say. "I looked you up on the Internet."

"And she couldn't do that?"

"Stella thinks computers are part of a government
conspiracy. She won't touch one coming or going. It
probably never crossed her mind that she could use
one to look for you."

"You think she really wants to see me?"

"Why don't you call her and ask her yourself?"

"Guess I could do that one day," she says. "You planning on telling her you found me? Where I am?"

"Do you want me to tell her?"

She gives my question long seconds of thought. Looks
out over the parking lot and crosses her arms over her
chest. Balls her fist and bounces it against her lips. Finally, she leans down and braces her arms on the car
door. "If she writes to me, she has to do it through the
leasing office, but she can call my neighbor's apartment
and she'll get me to the phone. I'm working on getting

my own phone. I'll write the number down for you, but tell her not to call me if she ain't got her shit together, 'cause I don't need no more problems. I'm trying to do it right this time, you know? Can't go left no more."

Beige digs a pen out of her purse and writes the number down, smiling. "This is good. Real good," she tells Crystal. "You should see your mama. Talk to her and get back with her if you can. You only get one."

"I'm off on Tuesdays and Wednesdays. You can tell her that too. What's your name, anyway?"

"Le—" I catch myself. I think about it and clear my throat. "Lucky," I say and smile. "I'm Lucky."

"You want to tell me about Lucky, Mom?"

We are on the interstate heading home. I switch lanes and glance at Beige. "She's just a woman I used to know." She looks like she wants to ask more questions, but she doesn't. She knows she might not be ready for the answers she will get.

Chapter Twenty-one

Aaron and I experience love differently. He is patient and nurturing, soothing and caring. Always careful to restrain himself and to give me the space he thinks I need. He listens with his whole body, talks with his mouth and his presence, and makes me feel safe. I need safe, and he understands my need. I need human touch, and he gives it to me, but he stays within the box he draws around himself. He thinks ten years of not being with a man makes me fragile and too soft to the touch. He handles me like there is an eggshell around me and if he presses too hard I will crack into a million little pieces that can't be pieced together again. Like Humpty Dumpty.

It is endearing, the way he treats me. Lovely that he can suffer through hours of sleep with an erection that won't go away and deny himself even a measure of release. He thinks I don't feel him slipping out of bed when I am supposed to be asleep, thinks the hard spray of the shower doesn't creep into my consciousness and make me want to be wet too. It never occurs to him that I am not made of glass, and that I share the parts of my life with him that I share not to cement his image of me, but to disabuse him of it.

Yes, I have been hurt. Yes, I have been abused. And yes, I am struggling my way back to life. All of these things are true. God, are they true. But his insistence on cherishing me frustrates me more than it fulfills me.

There is a time and a place for everything. Our relationship has gone through many phases, and all of them have led us to this point. I've held his hand and allowed myself to be brought here with him. I've enjoyed every minute of the process and then become content to let him keep leading our relationship where he feels it should go.

But it is my turn to lead now. My turn to take his hand and show him what I need and what I am ready for. I know the brand of anti-perspirant he prefers, the brands of cold cereal he eats and which ones he will not eat. I can order food for him without having to ask him what he is in the mood for. I can look at him and see that he has a headache and know the exact spot on his head to massage. I know he likes his khakis creased but not his jeans, he prefers boxers over briefs, and he likes broccoli better than he does sweet peas. I know he is careful to keep anything involving animal flesh away from the food he prepares for me, and I trust what he says. I trust him with me.

In every way that counts, I am his woman. Most of the time we live together, we eat together, we exercise together, we read and play together. And in the dark of night, we sleep together. But I don't know what it is like to really be with him. Making spiritual love is what he calls it, and I can feel the goodness of his spirit mating with mine, so I know what he says is true. In the dark of night, I am a lion cub, curling under a dragon to sleep, and I have never slept so peacefully in my life.

Still, he breathes fire and ignites my skin. He doesn't know that I crave him on a visceral level, that I need to be his woman in every way. He thinks I have missing pieces of myself that I need to find, and I do. But one of the missing pieces, he is in possession of.

Night after night, I feel like jumping out of bed and confronting him. Telling him that I'm a woman and any woman worth her shit needs to be able to satisfy her man. I need him to let me do that. The circle needs to be complete in order for me to be complete.

I don't jump out of bed though. I wait.

The shower sprays down hard on his head and shoulders. Through the frosted glass he looks like a supplicant statue, with his head bowed, his feet spread and his arms limp. He takes his punishment willingly and without fight. No steam, no heat, only ice cold needles against his flesh, meant to douse his fire and to scatter his concentration. It is a hard roe to hoe, I think as I slip my tank top over my head and step out of my panties. I leave them on the floor and slide the shower door open, step into a self-made Antarctica and twist my locks up on top of my head.

"Lena . . ." Aaron is surprised to see me. He wants to ask me what I think I am doing, but he can't stop staring at my breasts. He reaches around behind him and adjusts the water, adds hot water to the mix to accommodate me. "Baby, what . . .?"

"You want some company?" I tilt my head to one side and watch him become hard. My nipples are suddenly tight enough to coax a winsome sigh from my lips. His penis is huge and two-toned, pointed straight at me. I can't help staring at it, can't help the warmth that settles between my thighs or the way my belly does a little flip-flop at the mere thought that it will soon be mine.

"You know you shouldn't be in here. This is—"

"I shouldn't be in here, Aaron? Why not? This is where you are. We share everything else; why can't we share this?" I move closer to him and touch it lightly, feel it jump in my hand. I wrap my fingers around him and stroke slowly. His eyes lower to slits and burn into mine.

"We will share this. Eventually. Right now, you need . . ." A long hiss fills the space between us and his head drops back on his neck. He lets himself enjoy my touch for a moment, and then he captures my busy hand in his and threads our fingers together.

"I'm getting kind of tired of you telling me what I need, you know that? Tired of you telling me how this is going to go, too. Do you think I don't know what I want, what I need? Who I want?"

"Nobody's questioning the fact that we want to be together, Lena. I just want to make sure you're ready to take things to that level. I don't want you hurt or—"

I snatch my hand back and swipe it through the air, point a finger in the middle of his chest. "Look, don't do that, okay? Don't come at me with logic and good intentions, because right now I don't give a damn about all that. I know you won't hurt me. I know you love me. I'm not standing here offering myself to you as a sacrifice, Aaron. I'm standing here telling you that I want us to make love. Tonight. Now. And you don't have much of a choice in the matter."

"Lena . . ."

"Am I your woman?"

"Yeah, but—"

"And you're my man?"

"Hell yeah, but—"

"Are you fucking somebody else?"

"No, but—"

"Is it that you don't want to be with me?"

"Don't go there."

"So you do."

"You know I do, but—"

"Then stop taking cold showers and let me do what I'm supposed to do for you. Do what you're supposed to do for me. You're not the only one with needs, Aaron."

"I—"

"I'm ready for you. Are you ready for me?"

"Been ready. I love you."

"I love you too, and I'm not trying to be with anyone else, but you're pushing it."

"Somebody else like who? Is it that motherfucker at the bank? The one I had to check the other day?" His sudden anger tightens the muscles in his chest and has him unconsciously flexing his arms, ready to start swinging. It makes me laugh, which makes him take a step in my direction. "Is something funny?"

He is not getting it, and I am getting more pissed off as the seconds pass. I stamp my foot and point to the shower floor. "Look, forget about the guy at the bank. I can't even see him for looking at you. Stop treating me like a child and treat me like a woman, okay? That's what I need. To be treated like a woman, a whole woman. Can you do that for me, Aaron? Can you take me there?"

"Baby, I—"

"Can you?"

"Damn, can I talk?"

I don't let him talk. I push myself in his arms and pull his mouth down to mine. Kiss him like it is my last chance to kiss him, like the tongue in his mouth belongs to me and I want it back. I learn new tastes and textures, grip his head and take the kissing deep and wild. His is the only flesh I will allow myself to eat, and I feel like I can eat him whole. The lion cub moves aside and lets the wolf come out. It is mating season.

We drip water all over the floor as we stumble out of the bathroom and into the bedroom.

My legs are riding his waist and my arms are locked around his neck. My mouth feasts on his neck and shoulders, and I can't taste enough of him to be satis-

fied. He growls and whispers in my ear, nasty things
and then silly things and then erotic threats. He asks
me if I am afraid, I tell him no, and he says I should be.
Says I should be very, very afraid.

There is wrestling, and it is uncoordinated and possibly comical. Mouths are everywhere, lingering here
and there, and teeth are sharp, lips soft and soothing.
When we are done with our animal-like foreplay, I
have tasted every part of him, reveled in his gratifica-
tion, and endured the ecstasy of reciprocity tenfold.
We make music together, and it is not beautiful and
unrealistic. It is not rose-tinted and washed over by a
hazy glow. It is timeless, off-key and so damn perfect
that I cry.

He is a large man, tall and hard, muscular and capable of strength that sometimes catches me off guard
and mystifies me. I think he will handle me the way
men like to handle women; think he will twist me and
turn me, flip me and flex me, and I come to expect it.
Even to anticipate it. I think I want to be handled and
I feel like I probably need it, since it has been so long.

But Aaron does not handle me. He spreads out on
the mattress and gives me dominance.

He eases his tongue in my mouth and sends words
down my throat. "Are you okay?"

"Yeah," is all I am capable of whispering. We are
slick with sweat and tension where our chests press
together, wet and oozy where our middles meet and
acquaint for the first time. I open like a flower for him
and cradle. Feel myself approaching a totally different kind of orgasm as my hips rotate slowly round and
round with a mind of their own.

"Ten years is a long time," he says and sucks my
bottom lip inside his mouth. He breathes hard and
fast, rocks his hips in time with mine. Makes my eyes

slide closed and my throat moan. "Like riding a bike, remember?" My forehead on his, I nod and then gasp because I can't help it.

"Ten speed or training wheels?" I say, and we giggle.

"It's whatever you want it to be. Get on it and get used to the seat. Take it for a test drive and set the pace." He spreads my arms out with his and threads his fingers through mine, grips tight. "It's your bike, Lena. You can ride it any way you want to ride it. Are you ready?"

I am more than ready. Strength against strength, I sit up and back, and I use our arms, our hands clasped in the air, for balance and resistance. I rotate my hips, and he is there, on the verge of everything.

"You're like a virgin." He growls at the ceiling and clenches his teeth. Squeezes his eyes shut and inhales so deeply that his nostrils flare.

This feels right like nothing has felt right in so long. "Then be my first," I say. Then I close my eyes and jump.

Stella curses me out, curses me out some more, and then she tells me that she owes me big time. I tell her she doesn't owe me shit, and then I tell her I have to go. I am in the middle of getting some emancipation dick. We howl like fools over the phone lines, say we will talk soon, and disconnect. I pass Aaron the phone so he can hang it up, and then I get back to the task at hand. He has completed six chapters of the manuscript he is writing, and I am his first advance reader. I am decked out in sweat pants that swallow me up, a tee shirt that hangs to my knees, and thick sweat socks that flop off the ends of my feet, curled up on his sofa with a stack of papers in my lap. In his space and in his clothes too.

Actually, I am getting comfortable—in my own skin, in his skin and in my life. I look up from a page that has me wrapped around its finger and thank him for the glass of juice that he slips into my hand. "Baby, it's so damn good that I can't believe it, but you didn't follow the outline we worked on. I mean, I see bits and pieces of myself, but you seriously changed some stuff around."

"I like it when you call me baby," he says and repositions me so that his head ends up taking the place of the papers in my lap. "It's fiction. We don't have to go straight true crime, do we?"

"I thought you wanted to tell my story."

"I wanted to know it more than I wanted to tell it. I want to know you. What do you think about the main character? Is she gritty enough?"

"She's fine, but you think I'm gritty?"

"Did you hear me say it's fiction?"

"That's what your mouth says, but I notice there's a character in here named Yo-Yo," I point out.

"I couldn't resist. What time are your people getting here? Because I'm hungry."

My people means my mama, Vicky and Beige, and they are all meeting us at Aaron's apartment later. From there we are going out to dinner. This will be the first time that he comes face to face with my mama and only the second time he meets Vicky. "Seven. You can wait."

"If I have to wait until eight to eat, then I'm having a steak to make up for my sacrifice," he complains. "And tell me now if your mama knows anything embarrassing about me, so I can be prepared."

"Are you nervous about meeting my mama?"

"Are you nervous about me meeting your mama?"

"Why should I be?"

"What if she doesn't like me?"

"Doesn't matter," I say, rubbing his head. "I like you."

"I thought you said you loved me."

"I do that too. Where are you going with the sub-plot about the old lady and the Bible?"

He turns the page in my hand and reads upside down. "Me and old Nettie go way back. You have to keep reading and see what happens."

"Why don't you just tell me who she is?"

"Who said she was a real person?"

"Sula," I blurt out. "She told me to ask you about Nettie a while back, but I'm just now thinking about it. So I'm asking, who is Nettie and where do I go looking for her if I need to kick her ass about my man?"

He starts to say something and then stops himself. His forehead wrinkles and puckers up. "Wait a minute. Who the hell is Sula?"

"A psychic lady Stella took me to see."

He chuckles and pinches his nose, shakes his head tiredly. He's crazy about Stella, but he thinks the two of us together is triple trouble. "You and that damn Stella. Did she have you burying potatoes with nails in them and sprinkling salt across doorsteps too?"

"Don't make fun of the gris-gris," I tease. "Sula knows if you talk about her, Aaron. She will find you and rock your world."

"I can see she rocked yours. What did she say?"

"She just told me to ask you who Nettie is." I am not so much lying as I am omitting a small portion of the actual truth. A woman shouldn't tell a man every damn thing. "I was skeptical about her powers, and giving me Nettie's name was supposed to prove to me that she was the real deal."

"Playing with God again," he murmurs.

"Just tell me who she is, Aaron!" My frustration makes him crack up, and I want to strangle him.

"Nettie Sugarwater is a legend, baby," he says, still giggling. "A family legend. According to my mother, she's a distant relative who was a slave down in Alabama somewhere. My grandfather's sister's uncle's cousin's daughter. Or maybe she was my grandmother's sister's uncle's cousin's sister's daughter? Hell, I don't know. She was somebody's daughter; we can speculate on that much."

Suddenly, he is fascinated with the evening news, and I am left staring down at him and waiting for the rest of the tale. When he is quiet for too long, I shake him. "And? What happened to her?"

"She was hanged in the town square when she was nineteen and pregnant with her sixth child. I added a few years to her age in the manuscript, as you can see."

"Damn, six kids?" This piece of information stops my flow. It is scary to contemplate pushing that many babies from my womb and then having to love and care for all of them simultaneously.

"Had to keep the plantation fully staffed." He aims the remote at the television and lowers the volume. Looks at me like we are about to swap ghost stories. "Legend has it that she was something else. Always in trouble for one thing or another. Slapping little white kids and talking back to the massa, refusing to nurse anybody's babies but her own. Shit like that. Now, you would think, with the way they did little Emmett Till for supposedly whistling at a white woman years later, that Nettie's ass would've been grass. But people claimed she was a witch, so nobody was too quick to tangle with her. She was into hexes. The gris-gris, as you call it."

"So why did they hang her?"

"Because nothing else seemed to work. She laughed when they lashed her and then kept right on doing what she was doing. They say she spoke in tongues and talked to the dead, scared the shit out of people. They said she wasn't human. And let my mother tell it, she never made a sound when she gave birth to her babies and every last one of them came out with a birthmark in the middle of their foreheads, like a star."

I throw my head back and laugh because I can't help it. I'm convinced that Aaron is making this up as he goes along. Trying to freak me out.

"I'm serious," he insists. "Nettie talked the massa into letting her learn how to read and write, and then she used what she knew to help other slaves escape. She wrote out fake travel passes and helped slaves passing through on the Underground Railroad. Some even say she knew Harriet Tubman."

"If she knew Harriet Tubman, why didn't she take her babies and get on the train too?"

"She probably would've, eventually, if she hadn't been so quick tempered and vindictive. She got caught up in a war of wills with a neighboring plantation's mistress, and that's how she ended up being hanged. Her children were little stairsteps and not really old enough for hard labor, but the massa hired them out to work on the neighboring plantation anyway, and that pissed Nettie off."

"She put hexes on everybody over there?"

He nods and cracks a smile. "Hell yeah, she did. She had the massa walking around like he didn't know if he was coming or going, had the slaves revolting, and caused a horse to throw the massa's son. So now you can add a crazy massa and a paralyzed son to the mix. Nettie was a mess, I'm telling you. She got to be friends with a cook in the big house, and she passed the woman some herbs to put in the food over there. That's how she messed with the massa's head and had his hair falling out."

"And nobody figured out it was Crazy Nettie doing all that stuff?" I think I love Nettie and I don't even know her. I don't even know if she ever really existed, but her legendary love for her children speaks to me like a lifelong friend.

"Oh, now she's Crazy Nettie?"

"You know what I mean. What happened after that?"

"She would go over to the other plantation and call the mistress out, spit at her feet and curse her out in all kinds of foreign-sounding languages, so nobody knew what she was saying. But you got the point.

"She was throwing down hexes all over the place. She'd sneak over there, grab her kids and bring them back home. Massa would come looking for them, and she'd have them in her shack, sitting in the floor shooting marbles like it was any other day, and she wasn't clowning.

"The lash was nothing to her. Some even say the scars she got disappeared from her back in a day's time." He snaps his fingers and catches my eyes. "Just like that. There one minute and gone the next, like she cast a spell and made them disappear."

"So . . . she was hanged because, why?"

"I'm getting there, Lena. Chill out and enjoy the story," he says.

"She was hanged because she turned the massa into a bumbling idiot and fed his wife enough poison to send her running out of the house, straight into the cotton fields, choking and gagging. They say the woman was speaking in tongues and stuffing her mouth with cotton as she died. Said that after she was dead, a star appeared in the middle of her forehead and there wasn't enough makeup in the world to cover it up for her funeral.

"They figured it was Nettie's doing and they figured the only way to stop her was to kill her. She was hunted down and brought to the town square for a public hanging because by that time, more than a few people wanted to see her dead."

He rolls up and off the couch, reaches for my hand and pulls me up too. "We need to start getting ready for dinner."

"I was excited," I say, looking anything but. "But now I feel bad for Nettie. What happened to her kids?"

Aaron shrugs and leads the way to the bathroom. "I don't think I've ever heard that part of the story. I'll sit in here with you while you take a shower."

"Come in with me," I tell him even though he's already taken a shower. "The woman died trying to save her children and nobody knows what happened to them?"

"I think they lived to tell the story. That's probably how it got passed down from one generation to the next, though I'm sure it's beyond tall by now. She was crazy as a road lizard, as my mother would say."

"Crazy about her kids, and I can't be mad at her for that. I don't blame her for doing what she had to do, even if she should've seen the future and taken her kids and ran behind Harriet Tubman way before it got to that point."

"My mother says that a mother's love for her child is incomprehensible." He turns on the faucet and adjusts the water temperature. I help him shed his shirt and then I get undressed. "Makes you do all kinds of shit you never thought you'd do, in the name of protection."

"Makes you lose what little good sense you thought you had," I say and step under the spray. I knot my locks at the top of my head and wait for him to take the hand I hold out to him.

He does and then he kisses my palm. I run my hands along his chest, press a kiss to his nipple and say, "Your mother was right."

Chapter Twenty-two

"I want you to explain something to me, Lena," Isolde says, looking from my face to the slip of paper that she holds in her hands curiously. "How is it that your paycheck is damn near twice what mine is and I've been on my job for twelve years?"

"You went to school for the wrong thing. Should've gone into computers or something. Maybe accounting or law. There's plenty of innocent people looking to avoid prison."

She stares at the pay stub I submitted a moment longer and passes it back to me. I think I see discontent in her eyes, and I don't blame her. She is overworked, underpaid, and unappreciated. Even in prison I kept up with the news, and I know it's been years since state workers have been given a decent raise.

"You just might be on to something." She closes my file and folds her hands on top of it. Closes this chapter of my life, the chapter where our lives have intersected for a brief period of time, and sits back with a wide smile. "So . . . this is it. It's over, huh?"

"It's over," I say. "No offense, but I hope I never see you again."

"None taken. I was just about to say the same thing to you. I hope I never see your face in this place again, Lena. It doesn't belong here, and I'm not sure it ever did."

I point to my file. "You've read the circumstances of my crime?"

"I have."

"Well, then you know that I did belong here." I take a deep breath and release it slowly. "But I don't anymore. It was nice knowing you, Isolde, and thanks for everything you did and didn't do. I appreciate it."

Isolde tries to look confused, but she doesn't quite manage it. "Was there something I was supposed to do that I didn't?"

"You know damn well you could've treated me like shit if you wanted to, but you didn't." I zip my pay stub in my purse, slip the strap over my shoulder, and stand. I extend a hand to her. "It means a lot to me that you didn't."

My hand is ignored and Isolde is hugging me before I know what is happening. "Good luck, Lena," she says close to my ear. "I think I'll actually miss seeing you every month."

I am hugging her back before I know I want to. "Me too," I say and mean it.

"The country?" Beige shrieks in a tone that I have never heard before.

Aaron is already in defense mode, circling around my apartment with his hands out and keeping his eyes on Beige, in case she makes any sudden moves. "Technically, it's not really the country," he says, sounding calm and extremely reasonable. "It's not the suburbs, but it's not the country either. More like somewhere in between the suburbs and the country. There will be running water and electricity."

"Where is this place anyway? And why is it called an unincorporated township?"

"That just means it doesn't belong to any specific city. But there's no need to start turning red in the face, Beige. It's only about thirty or forty minutes away, and they even have a Super Wal-Mart."

"Wal-Mart?" She damn near chokes. "I don't shop for clothes at Wal-Mart. Oh my God, Mom, are you even listening to this?"

"Aaron," I say and shake my head. He is not helping, and the lopsided smirk on his face tells me that he knows it. I go over to Beige and touch her arm. "You said yourself, there's not enough room in my apartment for both of us. Plus, Aaron won't let me leave him here. We need a house, Bey, and I like the one we looked at." I turn on Aaron and narrow my eyes. "And it's not forty minutes away, either. Probably about half an hour, if that."

She slaps her hands on her hips and paces the room. "Okay, well, tell me this: Do any other black people live in this town?"

"You can be the first," Aaron puts in and covers his smile with his hands. I shoot him a warning look and he shakes his head. He sits on the futon, turns his attention to the television, and pretends he's not listening and laughing.

"Bey, come on. I want you with me. I need you with me."

"Mom, please, you know I'm coming. Ain't no way you're moving and not taking me with you this time. But . . ." She stamps her foot and puts on her whining face, swings her arms from side to side. "It's just . . . what about my friends?"

"You mean, what about Darrick," Aaron singsongs like a five-year-old. Two sets of eyes train on him and snap his mouth closed.

"What am I supposed to do there? I won't know anybody, and I already know everybody at my school. I don't want to start at a new school. All the kids will be looking at me funny because I have on Reeboks and they have on cowboy boots with mud all over them."

"I think you're exaggerating just a little bit, Bey. You can—"

"She can stay at the same school," Aaron chirps like a parrot that's been trained to talk.

I tune him out and keep talking. ". . . make new friends and still keep in touch."

He clears his throat and coughs words into his fist. "Stay at the same school."

"There's email, and we might actually have a telephone installed for emergencies, you know. In case one of the pigs gets sick. Oh Lord, Aaron. What are we going to do if one of the pigs gets sick? Do you think people in the country know where to find pig doctors?"

"You're not funny, Mom. This is serious. If we move to the country, my social status is zero. I'll miss all the parties and I won't know the latest music. Probably can't even get the same radio stations. Next thing you know, my best friend will be a boy named Bubba, who stutters and eats his own boogers."

"Oh, now see . . ." I forget my train of thought and slap a hand over my mouth to keep from bursting out laughing. When Aaron looks up, I am in a corner, bent over at the waist, quietly cracking up.

"Look," he says and puts his hands back out. "What about this: Lena, you still have to drive in to work every morning, and some mornings I will too. We can drop Beige off at school and bring her home in the afternoons. It'll take some compromising though."

"Such as?"

He looks at Beige. "Such as, school gets out at two-forty and Lena doesn't get off work until four. You ride the bus to Vicky's house after school, get your homework done, and be standing at the curb promptly at four. I want my woman home with me as soon as possible, so you can't be bullshitting around and getting lost with your friends. Social events have to be planned and arranged in advance, and your grades need to stay where they are or better." He thinks about it for a second, dips his head and catches Beige's eyes. "I heard about that *D* in math."

She is outraged. "Math is hard, and why can't we get a house in the city? They're building all those new houses on the south side. They're nice looking."

"Because I want a yard where I can have a decent size pool installed, and I don't want to have to put up a fence around the three inches of land I own. I don't want my neighbors so close that I can smell what they're having for dinner with the windows closed and the curtains drawn."

"A pool?" She is listening now.

"Right. And I'm getting a dog, so if you're allergic, you better see about some medication or something now. Dogs need room to run and play."

Beige sees what I see. Aaron holds his own. He will not be easily intimidated by living in a house where he is outnumbered two to one. We stare at him and swear we can see him marking his territory.

"What about a cat?" Beige says. "Or some fish? A bird?"

"I'm not running an animal shelter," Aaron says. "Besides that, a cat will try to eat the fish and the bird, which defeats the whole purpose, doesn't it? And the dog will be kicking the cat's ass every other minute. So it needs to be one or the other. Cat, bird, or fish, plus my dog." He starts pacing, then he stops and drops his hands on his hips. "We could probably find a cat who can get along with dogs."

"Um . . ." I raise a finger like I'm in church and look from Beige to Aaron helplessly. "Did anybody ask me if I wanted a cat or a dog?" They look at each other and roll their eyes to the ceiling, decide to ignore me. "Excuse me? Is this how it's going to be? Two against one?"

"Lena might even be able to change her work schedule so you can get home earlier. We'll play with some time frames and see what we come up with. You think you can work with that?"

"I guess so. Do I have a choice?"

"Not really. It's either Podunk High or plan B. Those are the choices."

"And what are you guys doing, getting married or something?"

Aaron and I catch each other's eyes and stare. We've been making plans. Plans to live under the same roof. Plans to have Beige live with us. Plans to be together forever. But we haven't factored marriage into the equation. I am the first to look away because I have never factored marriage into my life.

"Would that bother you?" Aaron asks Beige, and I hold my breath.

"I guess not. You need to make an honest woman out of my mom. But don't think I'm putting up with a bunch of screaming brothers and sisters, because I'm too old for that." She gestures in my direction. "And you are too, Mom. You are *sooo* past your prime."

"Forty isn't old," I say. Aaron lays his head back and hollers with laughter. "And I'm not even forty yet, so watch yourself. There's nothing wrong with my uterus. I can have as many babies as I want."

"At least one more," Aaron mumbles under his breath.

Before I can demand clarification from him, Beige starts up again. "Mom, give it up, okay? What about a cell phone? The one I have is old, and I only get a hundred peak minutes a month. I need a new plan with more minutes, just in case something happens and I need to reach one of you guys."

Aaron reads her like a book, even though she schemes with a blank face and a coy smile. "We can discuss a new phone," he says after a minute.

"And if I'm going to be emailing my friends, I might need a laptop too."

"Oh yeah, and what about this: Don't push it," he says and then goes into the bathroom. He shuts the door behind him with a definite click.

Beige and I consider each other for long seconds. I wait for her to pick up where she left off, to give me fifty more reasons why the move will be the ruination of her life as she knows it. She scratches the side of her head and shifts from one foot to the other, purses her lips and thinks about something that I can only guess at. She scratches a spot on her arm and giggles, and then she sinks down to the futon and folds her legs yoga style. Hums under her breath and nods slowly.

"I like dogs," she finally says and reminds me of the little girl I love so much.

Vicky orders a mocha latte for herself and a shot of espresso for me, and gives a man sitting at the opposite end of the counter a shy smile. He's been staring at her since we walked into the coffee bar ten minutes ago, and until now, she's pretended not to see his wide-eyed, interested gaze. I see it, though, and it is not the look of a complete stranger wanting to make her acquaintance. He knows her, and the blush creeping up her neck tells me that she knows him too.

"What's the story?" I ask, sliding into a chair across from her at a little wooden table that is too small to be anything but cute and useless. I shoot a glance at the mysterious man, see that he is still staring, and smile into my cup. "You know him?"

"He works at the hospital in pathology," she says. "Do you think he's cute?"

She could do worse, I think. Mystery man is like my espresso, dark and full of impact. Perfectly shaped bald head, nice lips and capable-looking hands.

"Definite eye candy appeal," I say. "Have you been seeing him behind my back, or is he on the prowl?"

"On the prowl." Together, we angle our heads and check him out one more time. He sees our inspection and laughs, raises his mug and salutes us cheerfully. "I can't decide if I should go out with him or not. He's asked four times already, and I keep putting him off for one reason or another."

"Why? He's hot, Vicky." She blushes even more and stares into her coffee with more concentration than the drink calls for. I reach across the table and touch her hand. "Don't tell me you're scared of him. Oh my God, you are. What the hell? Why?"

"Look at him, Leenie. He's gorgeous." She takes a sip of coffee and glances over her shoulder like she thinks he might be standing there listening. "Plus, he's five or six years younger than I am. I think he's got kids, too."

"So?"

"So he probably just wants to have sex."

"And he has problems finding someone to help him out with that?" I am incredulous and I think not. "Vicky, please, the man obviously sees something he likes and he wants to take a closer look. You should go over there and say hi or something. Quit playing hard to get. That gets old after a while."

"I'm not. It's just . . ." Vicky is frustrated, can't find the words in her extensive vocabulary to express what she wants to say. I see fifty different emotions cross her face, and I can identify with every one of them. But I make myself wait for her to tell me what she feels, instead of telling her that I already know, the way I usually do. "It's been a long time since I've dealt with a man, Leenie. A *looong* time."

"It's like riding a bike," I hear myself say and smile. "You just get on and start pedaling. And don't look down to see how far you might fall."

"That's it? That's your sisterly advice? Get on him and ride until I fall off?"

"I said nothing about getting on the man, so get your mind out of the gutter. I'm saying take it slow, but definitely take it somewhere. See what happens. You deserve it."

"Too much baggage."

"He has?"

Vicky looks at me for a second, then she rolls her eyes and shakes her head. She thinks I'm not following her where she wants to lead me. She slaps a hand to her chest and falls back in her chair. "Me, Leenie. My baggage. All my secrets. If he finds out who and what I really am, he'll be gone so fast it'll be like he was a dream."

"How is he going to find out?" I say. "And what is there to find out? You're not the one with the sordid past; I am. Don't make my shit your tragedy, Vicky. That part of our lives is over and done with. What you are is a successful nurse practitioner, an attractive single woman, and up for grabs. Let him grab you."

"Part of your shit is my tragedy, Leenie, and you know it. I played a part too."

"Kimmick says I should start trying to reframe what happened to me. He says I should consider myself a survivor instead of a victim. I think you should do the same. It makes everything so much easier to look back on."

"I wasn't talking about that." We search each other's faces, and for once, I am the first to look away. "Not exactly, anyway. Kimmick knows everything?"

"Everything he needs to know."

"He knows about me too? That I was there and that I—"

I cut off her flow, wave a hand and dismiss what she is about to say next. "That you were there," I say and catch her eyes. "And that's all. It's about getting on with our lives, Vicky, not living in the past and rehashing it every chance we get."

"Does Aaron know?" Her voice is quiet. "I mean, about . . ."

"He knows," I say. "He says he has a newfound respect for the medical field. If he calls you Louise by mistake one day, just act like you don't know what he's talking about. His sense of humor can be a little over the top sometimes."

"He didn't run away." She looks hopeful.

"He didn't."

"Do you love him?"

"I do. So much I can't believe it. It's like I didn't know I was looking for him until I found him, and now I don't ever want to be without him. I thought I was through with men for good."

"Lord knows you have reason to feel like that. You and me both. Can he be trusted with what he knows, Leenie? I mean, I like him and I think he's a great guy, but—"

"I love him, Vicky, and you know that's not something I do easily. I couldn't feel like that about him if I didn't trust him with my life. I'm telling you, don't worry about it. I'll go serve another eight years if the subject ever comes up again, okay? I've got you."

She pushes her mug away and balls her fist against her lips. Looks at me for a long time and talks with her eyes. "You've always had me, when it should've been the other way around. You should've been the oldest and I should've been the scared little baby."

"There's nothing valiant about what I did. Look at everything I lost because of it. You tried to tell me she wasn't worth it, but I wasn't listening. Sometimes I wish I would've."

"I missed you so much, Leenie," she says and tears up. I see her tears and throw my hands up dramatically. That makes her laugh and swipe them away. "We've been through a lot together, me and you. I owe you so damn much that I don't even know where to begin paying you back."

"You don't owe me shit."

Mystery man is still looking in our direction, and I lock eyes with him. I refuse to let him look away from me until I see what I need to see in his face. He wants my sister and he wants her badly. His lip is almost dragging the floor and his eyes are begging me to be his wingman, to say something to her that will make her give him the time of day. He senses me, knows that I have the power to make it happen for him. He knows that Vicky and I are one and the same, closer than mere sisters can ever be, and my opinion matters.

It is not about wielding power though. My love for my sister is the first true love that I ever knew, and that makes me just as submissive to her as she is to me. The secrets we have between us make me her slave just as much as she is mine. There is no doubt in my mind that she will drive to the nearest body of water and jump in, if I ask her to. No doubt in my mind that I will dive in right behind her, because if she goes down, I go with her. I cannot stand by and watch her be destroyed and not reach for and take my share of the misery.

We have parts to play in life, Vicky and me, and we play them. Prison would have demolished her because she is weak, soft and malleable. She wants to please too many people for my tastes. She sees good in others where sometimes there is none, and she is a natural caregiver. She has scars on her soul that need tending, that need healing and a patient hand.

Me, I am the stronger of the two of us and I always have been. Doesn't mean I am better, just different. Yet, we are still one and the same. Two sides of one coin that has much value. One side without the other means nothing and is worth nothing. The scars on my soul make me harder than she is, able to withstand and to take more. I step in when soft is not what is called for, when good does not exist, and when pleasing others is not an option. We cannot be divided, no matter how much time passes or who comes onto the scene.

I stare at mystery man and size him up. I know Vicky, what she needs and what she does not need. And I know what I will not stand for her to have. In his eyes, I am looking for patience and understanding, tolerance and compassion. Something more than lust and sexual desire. She already knows about lust and sexual desire, and it is the something more that I want for her. I want her to find what I have found and to let the discovery heal her, the way it is healing me.

Thinking about everything chokes me up a little, so I sit with myself for a while and people-watch. Vicky does the same, and we laugh at a busy toddler and his harried mother, to keep from talking about our own stuff. We sneak more peeks at mystery man and giggle like teenagers, to keep from crying. And then we catch each other's eyes and end up back where we started.

"You did what I needed you to do, Vicky. You played your part." I am done swimming in mystery man's pool, and I take my eyes away from him and put them on my better half. "You took my baby and you cared for her the same way I would've. No second-best crap and no half-stepping with her. Somebody had to do that, and I wouldn't have wanted anybody to do it but you. Knowing she was with you helped me make it through. It was one less thing I had to worry about, so I think maybe I might owe you."

I reach across the table and wipe a tear from her eye and she smiles sadly. Misery and sorrow aren't the only things that we have shared. We have also shared motherhood, and somehow it feels like that was part of our destiny. I stop feeling resentful about my daughter's affection for her aunt and start feeling grateful for her aunt's affection for me. Grateful that I could be the one to give Vicky something that I know she wants but will never have, even if it was only for a little while.

"You were so good to her," I say. My words are thick with emotion and unshed tears. "I'm so grateful to you, Vicky. I owe you—"

"You don't owe me shit." She steals my words and gives them back to me. "I dropped the ball a little bit, but I tried to have you like you had me, as much as I knew how. I tried . . ." Her voice trails off, she shakes her head, and I can see that she still doesn't believe that she did enough.

"Do you love me?"

Vicky pulls in a long breath through her nostrils and they flare from the effort. She releases it out of her

mouth and gives me a watery smile, then reaches for
my hands and squeezes them so tightly they hurt. "Like
life, Leenie. More than life."

"Then forget about it, okay? Work our stuff around
in your mind some kind of way that helps you deal with
it, and then store it away. Let this be the end of our
tragedy and the beginning of the rest of our lives. Come
with me as I walk away from all of it and don't look
back. Can you do that? I hope so, because it doesn't feel
right without you with me."

She sniffles and clears her throat. "Damn, this Kimmick man is really helping you, huh?"

"Like you wouldn't believe. You should think about
talking to somebody too."

"I might just do that."

"One thing though. What we . . . our . . ." I search
for the words and eventually find them, take my hands
from Vicky's and flatten them on the useless tabletop.
Then I put my thumb and index finger together and
drag them across the seam of my lips as if I'm closing
a zipper. "The end, Vicky. What happened at the end,
that's what I need you to do with it. Let me have it and
you let it go, okay?"

"Aren't you tired of carrying it around? Of carrying
me around?"

"I'm tired of talking about it and I'm tired of you
feeling guilty about what happened. Things went down
exactly like they were supposed to. We carried each
other."

She is on her lunch break, and we are pushing it by
lingering in the coffee bar. After a few more minutes, I
remind her of the time and we get up to leave. She has
fifteen minutes left to make her way across the inter-
section and back up to the seventh floor of the hospital,
and I have just as long to make my way back to my

apartment to meet Aaron. We are doing one last walk-through of our house this afternoon, and we still have a few errands to run before we pick up Beige from school and get on the road.

My face changes when I think of Aaron; something shifts and gives my thoughts away, and Vicky can read me just as well as Sula can. She slings her purse over her shoulder and touches my arm softly. "Did you ever think you'd meet someone like him, Leenie?"

"No." I shake my head and feel my lips tremble. "I never thought I deserved to meet someone like him."

"You do. You deserve the best."

I am standing at the door, and I should open it and step out onto the sidewalk. Vicky comes up behind me and waits for me to do just that. Three more people are behind her and a line is forming. They all want to leave, but I am blocking the only exit, staring through the glass at congested traffic and people marching up and down the sidewalk, going about their business and living their lives. My eyes bounce from one person to another as they pass the shop, and I wonder how many of them have their own personal tragedies, how many of them manage to find their way over and around them, and go on with their lives in a way that fulfills them. I think there must be too many to count because there are a lot of people in the world.

I take Vicky's arm and pull her away from the door. "You remember what Mama used to say all the time when we were kids? Sometimes God doesn't send you what you want but what you need?" I nod in mystery man's direction. "What if God sent him for you?"

She looks at me like she doesn't recognize me. "You don't even believe in God."

"There you go again, thinking everything to death. Go over there and talk to the man, Vicky."

"And say what?"

"How about, where should I meet you tonight for dinner? Or, pick me up at eight? Hell, he's a little too fine to be missing out on the possibilities. If some other sista comes along and turns his head, your shit is over."

"Possibilities, huh?" She looks at him and he smiles his encouragement. His eyes tell her to come along, and I think I feel her body gravitating in his direction.

"Infinite," I say. "Go on and handle your business."

She damn near skips across the coffee shop. Is almost there when she has a thought and comes skipping back to me. "Stay right here, okay? Don't go anywhere."

"Don't I always stay with you?" She skips off again, and I smile with my whole face. She knows I'm not going anywhere.

Chapter Twenty-three

Aaron rolls over in bed and finds me gone. Then he comes to me in the same condition that I am in—naked, skin sticky with dried sweat and good loving. He presses into me from behind and wraps his arms around me. I welcome his touch and sink back into his body like it is an extension of mine, fit my head under his and give his chin a place to rest. We stand at the window in his apartment and look out over the park across the street.

"Couldn't sleep?"

"Not without you," he says. "What's on your mind?"

"Thinking about when I first moved in. My head was really messed up. Scary to think about how messed up. You think there's somebody over there in the park somewhere looking at my tits?"

He laughs and rearranges his arms so that my tits are covered. "There's no lights on in here and it's dark. You want somebody to be looking at your tits?"

"Nobody but you, baby. Nobody but you." A kiss lands on my shoulder and then on the side of my face. I lean into his mouth and slide my arm up and around his neck. I love the feel of his heat.

"It's your world, Lena. I just need to be in it with you. I was thinking about you today, when I was finishing up the manuscript. Thinking about how proud I am of you. Thinking to myself that I'm glad you picked this building to move into." He curls an arm around my neck and closes his fingers on the ball of my shoulder.

I cannot move even if I want to, which I don't. "I was waiting for you."

"I told Vicky that I never want to be away from you," I say. "I can't imagine it."

"I love you too." He squeezes me and growls like a bear, right in my ear. "You feel that?" I nod. "That's me telling you I feel the same way. Does that scare you?"

"What I feel for you scares me."

"Flow with it," Aaron tells me. "Flow with me, Lena. Marry me."

I take a deep breath and fight against the tears in my throat. "That's a big step."

"Bigger than making a home together? Raising your daughter together?"

"She's already half grown," I say, and a sob escapes without my permission. I hate myself for being weak, for crying when tears are useless, and I scrub a rough hand across my face to punish myself. "I missed all the years in between. All the important stuff."

"You have some important stuff to look forward to though. A lot of years ahead of you to make up for lost time."

"I can't get the time I lost back."

"You can cherish what you do have though. Some people don't even have that."

I tap into his train of thought and think of Yo-Yo and then of Stella and then of Denny. Scratch my nails through the hair on his arm and shake my head. "So much for feeling bad about myself. I can't do it with you around."

"And I plan on being around for a long time," he says and turns my face for a kiss. "Speaking of which, we're about to have five bedrooms to figure out what to do with."

"And?"

"And . . . we could put a few babies in them. Marry me, Lena."

"Aaron, please." I want to sound long-suffering but I don't quite pull it off. He touches me in a deep place and I know he knows it. "I don't know what to say."

"Say yes."

"I need some time."

"How much time?"

"Some," I say and step away from him. I come back a few seconds later, facing him. I pull his face down to mine and search his eyes in the darkness. "Just some."

"Not too long?"

"Not too long."

We go back to bed and we make love the way we always do. Hard and fast, hot and thick, and then slow and easy. It feels like we have been doing it for years. Like we know each other inside out, like we know what every sound and every touch means, and we can make each other hurt so good that it is almost shameful. I call out to him and he chuckles. He answers my call with one of his own and whispers to me that Beige's bedroom will have to be on the other side of the house. Otherwise we will corrupt her.

She might hear the headboard knocking and think someone or something is trying to get inside of our home, might hear the sounds we make and think we are being harmed in some way. Four walls and a closed door cannot keep our lovemaking confined. It has to be out there in the air around us, living and breathing with a life of its own. She is not ready for the power of it, and I hope she will not be for many years to come. It might scare the shit out of her if she is ever lucky enough to find it for herself. When I sit still long enough to think about it, it scares the shit out of me. I'm scared of having it and even more scared of losing it.

Fear makes me raise my head from the middle of
Aaron's chest and crawl up his body until we are face
to face. "Are you sleeping?" I know good and well he
is because he snores softly and breathes evenly, but I
need him to wake up.

"I was," he mumbles, rubbing his eyes. "You need
something? Did you have a bad dream?"

"A little bit. Can I tell you something?"

"Yes."

"Yes," I say and wait for him to get it.

"Are you saying what I think you're saying, Lena?"

"Yes."

"Yes, you're saying what I think you're saying, yes,
you had a bad dream, or—"

"Just . . ." I press my lips to his to stop his words. He
is starting to confuse me, and it is too early in the morning for confusion. I'm thinking more clearly than I have
in years. Thinking that maybe he is someone that God
sent for me, if there is a God and I am somewhere on
His radar. Then I think, no, not maybe, definitely. He
is for me and I am for him, regardless of who or what
placed him in my path. Something this good cannot be
bad for me, and I don't want to miss out on any more
possibilities. So I say, "Just yes, okay, baby? Yes. I can't
do this without you."

"Yeah, you can," Aaron says. "You can do it, Lena. But
you're not going to." He taps his lips and puckers up,
and I fall into him. I wait for him to catch me, and I sigh
when he does.

I tell Beige about Nettie, tell her about the legend of
the woman who loved her children so much that she
died trying to save them, and she looks at me like I am
losing my good sense faster than she had hoped. Like

I have been stricken with a mental illness that she is not ready to deal with. A typical teenager, she wants to see pictures of the mythical woman, wants to lay hands on tangible evidence that she existed in some time and place. I shrug helplessly and tell her what I know, that Aaron told me the story and that is proof enough for me. She is still less than totally convinced.

As bedtime stories go, she is not impressed. Her head rolls to the side and she giggles at me from her side of the futon. "Nettie?" she says. "Mom, please. What kind of name is that?"

"Probably short for something," I say and yawn. "Aquashanetta or something."

"And she had a star on her forehead?" Skepticism owns her voice.

"No, her kids did. Like a birthmark."

"*Pfft*. Whatever." She snuggles into her pillow and sends her knee in my direction. I push it down and we wrestle over sleeping space. She thinks the same thing I think: She can't get her own bed fast enough. Then she gives up the fight and scoots close to me, wants me to make a seat for her bottom and to drop an arm around her waist. She wants me to hold her like I did when she was small enough for me to push my nose into her hair and smell her all night long.

She isn't small anymore, but I still push my nose into her hair and I make a seat for her. "Don't make fun of the gris-gris," I tell her as she falls asleep, and she wakes up long enough to crack up.

There isn't anything close to laughter on her face when Aaron's mother opens the door and welcomes us into her home. Beige looks like she has seen a ghost, and I do too. We both stare at the star-shaped birthmark on the woman's forehead. It is not in the middle, but off to the side, near her hairline. It's not quite how Aaron described it, but it is there all the same. Apparently it got relocated as the legend and the genes passed from generation to generation.

Aaron's mother smiles and kisses me on both cheeks. She notices the direction of my gaze and sends her son an exasperated look over my head. "I see Aaron told you about Nettie," she says in her husky, accented voice. She smells like bread baking and freshly churned butter, like she is safe and warm, and I like her immediately. She touches the spot where Nettie lives and winks at Beige.

"Is she real?" Beige wants to know.

"Got a picture I can show you right now." She reaches for my baby's hand and disappears with her, deeper into the house. I look at Aaron and he winks. Then I take off behind my future mother-in-law and my daughter. It's not that I don't believe Aaron, not that I don't believe Nettie was real, but I have to see the picture too. Have to see if I can see myself in her eyes.

If I had known that I was going to be ambushed, I wouldn't have gotten into my car and driven right into it. If I had known that today was going to be the day that I break down and fall apart, I wouldn't have left the little patch of dirt that Aaron and I are making into a vegetable garden. I wouldn't have showered away my good mood and brought not one, but two bags of peanut butter cups with me.

He is not himself today, a little voice in the back of my mind whispers to me. Watch yourself. But I don't fully comprehend what it is that I'm supposed to be watching until I am halfway through the first bag of

candy and tearing into what has to be my thirtieth peanut butter cup in as many minutes. Until he says what
he says to me and I finally figure out that Kimmick is
the bastard of all bastards and he knows it.

He wants me to think that his questions are innocent.
That he only wants to gather more background information for future reference. But that is not his game
at all. He pushes and provokes me, wants to break me,
and he starts his attack by calling me a liar. I call him
a bastard, and it doesn't faze him in the least. He says
he's been called that and worse and lived to tell about
it. He reminds me that I have called him much worse,
especially back when I first started coming to see him.
By now I've been coming to see him every week for at
least six months, which means that I'm almost family,
and he has cousins that he hasn't seen as many times as
he's seen me. It's too late to go back to the way we were.

I get that he won't stoop to my level and let himself
be distracted, and decide to humor him. "How do you
figure I lied to you?"

"You told me that yours was a family made up entirely of women," he says. "That was a lie."

"No, it wasn't. I told you there's been a woman at the
head of my family for as long as I can remember. That's
what I said, Kimmick. Don't twist my words around."

"No, Lena." He says my name like I don't remember what it is and he has to remind me. "You said no
men. Break-ins at sperm banks and genetic mutation.
Things like that, that's what you said."

"So what's your point—or do you even have one?"

"My point is that you're evasive."

"I should spill my guts to you? Tell you everything
there is to tell about me?"

"That might help," he says and pops a peanut butter
cup in his mouth. He talks around a glob of chocolate

and clears his throat. "In any case, it would certainly help if you stopped picking apart the information you tell me before you tell it to me. You sift through it, decide what you want me to know, and you keep everything else to yourself."

"That's my prerogative, isn't it?" I sit up, and my feet drop to the floor like lead weights. I brace my elbows on my knees and stare at him. "I don't have to tell you anything I don't want to tell you, Kimmick. You can't make me do anything I don't want to do."

"That's important to you, isn't it? Having control over yourself and not doing things you don't want to do?"

"I've done all kinds of shit I didn't want to do to survive, so that's not even an issue."

"Like what? What kinds of things have you done?"

"Fight, steal, lie," I say. "Hell, whatever the situation called for. You can't be a parent and not do at least one thing you thought you'd never do."

He thinks about what I have said and nods his head in agreement with a silent observation. "What about going to prison? Was that something you thought you'd never do?"

"What kind of question is that? Do you think I would've wasted my time earning a master's degree and taking a good-paying job if I planned on giving it up to go and lay down for eight years?"

"Lay down?"

"Serve time."

"Oh. No, that doesn't make much sense, does it?"

"You know it doesn't."

"Why did you go to prison then, Lena?"

I look at him like he is crazy. "Did I have a choice?"

"We always have choices," he says. "They might not be the ones we want, but we have them. You shot and killed a woman. That was a choice you made."

"And if you already know that, then why ask the question in the first place? There's your answer: I went to prison because I shot and killed a woman. That was my choice."

"You had other ones."

"Not really."

"Let's talk about those choices, shall we?" He pretends that I haven't spoken, that I haven't said I had no other choices. He shows me his palm and ticks off his points on the tips of his fingers. "One, you could've called the police and let them handle whatever the problem was. Two, you could've cut yourself off from the situation and steered clear of it altogether. And three, you could've aimed the gun lower. Somewhere that wasn't fatal but that would've gotten your point across just as well. Did you think of any of those choices?"

My feet need to be in motion, so I stand and start pacing. I cross my arms over my chest and review the choices he lays out, one by one. They all sound overly simple and generic, too pat and not the way the world really turns. But they do have their merits. "I did aim the gun lower and I did call the police." I look over my shoulder and down at him as I pass. "On myself after it was over and done with. And steering clear of the situation wasn't possible. I had to face it head on and deal with it. Nobody else had the guts to do it."

"So we're back to the fact that you planned to kill your grandmother?"

"I told you I didn't plan on shooting her. Stop trying to make me admit to premeditation, okay? I can't be tried twice for the same crime."

"That's where you're wrong, Lena. You can be tried a hundred different times for the same crime, if you insist on being the judge, jury and the defendant in your own trial."

"What psycho nonsense are you trying to trip me up with now?"

"You don't think about what happened?"

I scrub my hands across my face and fill my palms with my breath. "Of course I think about it."

"You replay the sequence of events over and over in your mind every day."

"Sometimes, yeah."

"You see yourself raising the gun and pulling the trigger."

"Sometimes."

"You torture yourself by watching yourself do what you did and remembering why you did it."

"I said I did, didn't I? Where are you going with this?"

"I'm going back to where we started the session," he says and shifts around in his chair. "Back to the fact that you're evasive. I'm curious to know why, if you experience all the things we just mentioned, you never bring them up in session. You talk around the elephant in the room like it's not even there."

"It's not there."

"Another lie."

"Fuck you, Kimmick. What do you want from me?"

"What do *you* want from you, Lena? You want to purge yourself of the guilt you feel?"

"I feel guilty about leaving my daughter, but that's it. Everything else was necessary."

"She's what, fifteen now? Your daughter?"

"Fourteen."

"And her name is Red?"

I crack a smile. "Beige."

"Interesting name. Why was killing a woman necessary?"

"You're killing me," I say. "Jumping from subject to subject is killing me."

"Will you answer the question?"

"Yeah. It just was."

"And will you sit down?" He chuckles. "You're starting to make me anxious. Like I have somewhere to go but I can't remember where."

I go back to the couch and fall back against the leather like I have worked a double shift and I'm exhausted. A long sigh escapes my mouth. We watch each other and say nothing. Then I say, "What do you want from me?"

"I want you to tell me about the man, Lena. I think that's a good starting place. Once we bring him into the room, we can start doing some real work here. I want you to stop looking over and around him and start looking at him."

"There is no man."

"You're a liar."

"You're telling me what my truth is?"

"I'm asking you to tell me the truth."

"This is part of the truth," I say, pushing my index finger into the cushion next to me. "This is what the truth is, Kimmick. Right now, right this very minute, you're looking at a diabolical killer. A murderer. I'm no different from anybody else as far as that goes—except for the fact that I was stupid enough to turn myself in."

"What was the alternative?"

"I could've set it up to look like a robbery gone bad. A suicide or something."

"Why didn't you?"

I shrug. "I didn't think that far ahead. Everything was down to time and place. It had to be done in that time and in that place."

"Your grandmother's house had to be the place."

"That's where it all started, and that's where it needed to end."

"Says who?"

"Says me."

He rubs his beard and scribbles something on a note-
pad. Pisses me off with his nonchalance and his absent
scribbling. He doesn't even watch himself write whatever it is he writes. He just scribbles. I sit up and lock in
on his eyes.

"Listen to me. I was the one running the show. I called
the shots, and if I say it had to be done, then it had to be
done. That's it, end of story."

"You had to be in control."

"Damn right I did. I had to do what God couldn't
seem to find the time to do. For all of the goodness and
mercy people run around talking about, He couldn't
spare even a pinch of it on me. So I had to do what I
had to do."

"Because control was the one thing you'd lost."

"I never had it."

"Control of your mind and control of your life." Kimmick digs around in a desk drawer for forever and a
day. He shuffles stuff around and makes noise as he
does it. He stops digging, has a thought, closes one
drawer and then opens another one. Keeps digging.
"Control of your body," he finally says and goes still.
"You never had control of that either, did you?"

For a second, I freeze. Then I make myself thaw out.
"You have no idea what you're talking about, Kimmick."

"Just what you tell me, which is nothing, really. Am
I wrong?"

"Let's talk about something else."

"I think we need to talk about this." Done bullshitting with the drawers, he swivels around in his chair

and laces his fingers on the highest slope of his belly. "I think we need to talk about what really happened, Lena. I think you need to talk about it, because if you don't, you'll—"

"I'll what?" I hold my breath.

"You'll explode," he says. "Again. It seems like it's easy to pick up with your life and carry on like nothing's wrong, but it's not. It takes sheer will and determination to pull it off the way you have. But something's off, something's still not right with you. Call me psychic, but I can sense it. You think you've got it all wrapped up tight, got it all under control, but I can almost promise you, you don't."

"I've had eight years to think the shit through, Kimmick, and I can almost promise you that I do."

"You'll be in the grocery store one day, buying milk and bread, and all of a sudden you'll think of something that hits you the wrong way, and—"

"And what, I'll pull out a gun and start shooting?"

"Maybe."

"You are a fucking nut job."

"Or you'll be at work and there'll be a story that triggers something in your mind and—"

"I'll pull out a gun and start shooting?"

"Maybe."

Pissed doesn't even begin to describe what I feel. He makes me sound mentally unstable. Like I'm incapable of being anything other than an animal. If I had a gun, I would seriously consider shooting him. But I don't have a gun, and if I did, I'd be in violation of my parole. It eventually occurs to me that my parole expired a while ago, and then it occurs to me that my thought process is way off to the left. Right back where it began.

It scares me to realize that he can push my buttons with his silly questions. Even scarier is the fact that he can see my thoughts. He knows my first instinct is to strike out and to hurt like I hurt, without forethought. I feel transparent, like he can see right through me, and I don't like the feeling at all.

I find my purse on the couch and throw the strap over my shoulder. "Our time is up, right?"

"Just about," he says. "But I still have one more question for you, Lena."

I am at the door, touching the knob and tasting escape. My mistake is in turning to look at him and letting him see me. Once he has my eyes, he won't let them go.

"What is your greatest fear?"

Chapter Twenty-four

"What?"

"You heard me. What is your greatest fear? I have some theories of my own, but I'd like to hear your response."

"No," I say. "Fuck my response. What's your theory?"

"I think you're afraid."

"Feeling fear and being afraid are one and the same, Kimmick. You're trying to trip me up again, and I'm not going for it. You tell me, what am I afraid of?"

He walks across the office and stops directly in front of me. We are eye to eye, staring each other down, and I can smell chocolate on his breath. He gets in my face and challenges me with his body language. Makes me take a step backward and give him some of my own body language. "My space, Kimmick," I warn him.

"I think you're afraid of letting it die, Lena. As long as you keep it locked inside you, it lives and breathes and justifies your existence. It's your excuse to kick your own ass, in case no one else feels the need to do it. If you let it out and let it die, you'll have nothing left. Then you'll have to do what everyone else does, which is live a halfway normal life and feel good about it."

"Normal is overrated."

"But you want it."

"I have it."

"Do you?"

"I had it."

"What happened to it?"

"I pulled the trigger and it went away."

"Why? Why did you pull the trigger?"

"I . . . he . . . it was . . ." I take a deep breath and slow my tongue down. "I had to do it."

"Who is he, Lena?"

"Nobody."

"Another lie," Kimmick accuses me softly. "Lying to yourself won't make him any less real."

"You know less than nothing about him. How do you even know there is a him?"

He looks at me and keeps on looking. Takes a deep breath and scratches the top of his bald head. Then he backs out of my space and retreats into his own. He sits in his chair and crosses an ankle over the opposite knee, gestures to the couch and raises his eyebrows. "I'm ready to hear about him, and I think you're ready to talk about him. Sit down, Lena."

"Why are you pushing this?" I snap. But I throw my purse across the office and it lands on the couch with a dull thud. He is right about one thing and wrong about the other. I am ready to talk, but he cannot possibly be ready to hear what I have to say.

"I'm pushing it because I care about you. Where are the men, Lena?"

"I keep telling you there are no men. They're dead."

"You said one of them, your uncle, died earlier on."

"That's right. A stroke."

"But there was another uncle. What happened to him? You don't talk about him."

"He's dead too."

"Diabetes?"

"No."

"A heart attack?"

"No."

"Another stroke?"

"No." I join my purse on the couch and cover my face with my hands. Press my fingers into my eyelids, then fold my hands under my chin. I pick one of the fifty different motorcycle posters on the walls to stare at and I keep my eyes there.

"Do you trust me, Lena? Trust that what we say here stays here and this is a safe place?"

"I know it is." I cannot give him complete trust, but I tell him what I know. In my mind, it is the same thing. "He didn't have a stroke," I say after five minutes of safe silence.

"What happened to him?" We lock eyes, and he is a mind reader. He waves a hand negligently and shakes his head. "Let me refrain. I don't give a shit about what happened to him. But I do give a shit about what happened to you. Can we explore that together?"

"Do you really want to go there with me, Kimmick?"

"If you really want to take me there with you. Do you?"

"Maybe you can't handle the trip."

"Or maybe *you* can't."

I have to smile. "You're a motherfucker, do you know that?"

He smiles back. "I'm not the only one, though, am I?"

Kimmick listens as I take him all the way back to the beginning and spin a story for him.

He gets caught up in the hows and whys, but I refuse to allow him to stall what he has started with questions that have no answers. He doesn't ask me anything that I haven't already asked myself, and if I didn't have answers then, why would I have them now? I ask him this, and then I tell him to be quiet and pay attention. What I say is important, and after I am done saying it, he will know what I know, and then he will understand.

He will know the answer to his question. He will know my greatest fear.

Halfway through my tale of doom and gloom, I notice that he is shifting around in his chair again, and I ask him if he is comfortable. He tells me not to worry about his comfort and to keep talking. He will not allow me to stall either. I wonder if he is in need of the Preparation H he buys at Target, but I don't take the time to ask. I do what I am told and keep talking.

And once I get past the first few sentences, once I see that they don't jump out of my mouth, clash with the air in the room and spontaneously combust, I lay back on the couch and fold my arms under my head.

It is not as hard as I thought it would be.

I tell him that Ellie is my mother and that Dee-Dee is my aunt, and that they were the very first sacrificial lambs. The ones who paved the way for my eventual destruction. The very first members of the sorority. Then came Vicky and me.

I remind him that my grandmother birthed four children, that one of my uncles did himself a favor and died before I could embarrass him along with everyone else. The other uncle is the one we want to focus on, I say. He's the one to watch. The star of the show. The sick bastard that I meant to kill when I pulled the trigger.

I look at Kimmick. "You remember I told you that she wouldn't move?" He nods. "Well, she wouldn't. She protected his sick ass right up until the very end. Took the bullet that was marked for him."

He butts in and tells me that I have skipped a whole block of time and asks me to backtrack a little and bring him up to speed.

"Don't you have another client waiting for you?"

"Lena . . ." He sighs.

I chuckle and take my eyes back to the ceiling. "All right, Kimmick. I'll back up a little bit and start from the beginning," I say. And then I do.

He has paranoid schizophrenia and he hears voices, talks to himself and does things that don't make sense to me. He hangs wire hangers in front of the window in his bedroom so he'll hear an intruder when he tries to come inside. Not if, but when. He walks up to me and shouts in my ear when he thinks I have said something that I really haven't said. His mind tells him that I have said something to or about him, something smart-mouthed and out of place, and he doesn't believe me when I say I haven't. He bursts into the bathroom while I am sitting on the toilet, ranting and raving about something I can't comprehend, and then he slams out of the room and leaves the door swinging behind him.

Once, when Ellie and Dee-Dee were young girls, he came home with a loaded shotgun and held everyone at gunpoint. Said the government told him his family wasn't really his family and he needed to eradicate them. He shot a hole through the dining room wall, and there is still a noticeable dent in the far wall of the kitchen to this day. He beats his mother, who is my grandmother, and he has her running around the house, doing his bidding and saying everything but "Yes, sir." A deep, booming voice and hands almost large enough to wrap all the way around a basketball, that is how I remember him. He is a big man, so wide that he seems to lean from side to side as he walks, and he is as tall as a tree. In fact, that is what we call him— Tree. Uncle Tree.

Chronologically, he is the second oldest child, the second boy, but theoretically, he is the master of his household. The oldest boy shrinks next to his power, and the girls know enough to succumb to it. His mother is his puppet, wanting to keep him calm and nonviolent at all costs, even if she sacrifices her daughters to accomplish the goal. In some twisted way, he is her favorite, her most cherished baby. She believes his mental illness is her fault, and she does everything that she can do to make up for her shortcomings as the vessel that brought forth his miserable life.

His medications are effective at managing his symptoms, and he is almost normal when he decides to take them on a regular basis. I remember times when he is stable and looking healthier, more like a human being and less like a mongrel with dark-circled eyes and shaking hands. Those times are few and far between, because what I remember most is the fiendish look on his face, the violent outbursts, and the sound of fright. I remember that I hate him and I wish him dead every day I draw breath.

"It all started with your mother and aunt?" Kimmick interrupts me to ask.

"Yes," I say. "He was always a maniac, but he wasn't diagnosed until he was around sixteen or so. By then he had raped the both of them a couple of times and beat the shit out of my grandmother at least once. I think my mother was twelve or thirteen the first time it happened to her. They were afraid of him."

"And no one ever told anyone about what was happening?" He is incredulous. "No one ever thought to call the police or Children's Services?"

"Is the possibility of a hell you know nothing about better than the one you already know how to live with?"

"Jesus," he hisses, angry but trying to suppress the emotion. "Go on."

"I think it stopped when my mother and my aunt both got part-time jobs after school and saved enough money to go half on a little studio apartment. They got the hell out of there as fast as they could."

"How old were they?"

"Somewhere around sixteen and seventeen. They lived together in that apartment for years."

Vicky is seven and I am five when we first start going to the house that smells like old mothballs and feels like a morgue. After we disobey the rules and sneak outside, we are dropped off there every weekday morning over the entire summer, and this goes on until we are fourteen and twelve, when we finally take a stand and refuse to go there again, I tell Kimmick.

"Why would your mother take you there, knowing—"

"That in all likelihood we'd be abused? Shit, Kimmick, you're the shrink, you figure it out. She says she didn't have a choice, but you just told me we always have choices, so I'm asking you, what were hers?" He says nothing, and is, for once, speechless. "The sorority, remember?"

Membership means nothing less than a slow death of the spirit and a complete annihilation of the soul. It means that Vicky and I are sacrificed to the maniac, like peace offerings, if only he will remain calm and feast in silence. We are licked and sucked, twisted and turned, touched and pawed, until we puke into our own hands from the filth of it.

"Wait a minute. You're telling me that your grandmother allowed her son to abuse you and your sister and she did nothing?"

"She baked brownies and made homemade caramel," I say. "Our favorite desserts. She let us have as much as we wanted. After." I take a deep breath and feel beads of sweat pop out on my forehead. "He liked to watch X-rated videos with us and make us do the things we saw on the screen. Most of the time he wanted us separately, but there were a few times when he had to have us at the same time. He'd—"

Kimmick shoots up from his chair, scrubbing his hands all over his face and pacing the floor jerkily. "That's enough, Lena. I think I get the gist of what you're saying."

"Are you about to throw up all those peanut butter cups you just ate?" I point to a nearby trash can. "Go ahead and feel free, if you are. I know all about puking your guts out, and I know it helps . . . a little."

Despite the fact that he says he's got the gist of what I am saying, I keep talking. I tell him about all the crying we did, all the begging and pleading, all the fighting. I tell him about the night we confessed to my mother about what was happening in my grandmother's house and about how she got this vacant look in her eyes and told us we were making things up just because we wanted to stay home by ourselves. I tell him that my vagina, unlike my mouth and my heart, was never penetrated by Tree because I wasn't old enough to have the hideous pleasure of being filled by him, but Vicky lost her virginity to him when she was fourteen. That is when we decided to revolt.

I tell him about the month Vicky missed her period. And then I tell him about the month my aunt missed hers. Tree is the father of her oldest son, the one they took away just a few minutes after he was born, at my aunt's request. Somewhere out there is another Tree, and nobody knows what he looks like or if he is a lunatic like his father.

"How do you know all this?"

"She told me."

"Who? Your mother?"

"No, my aunt Deirdre. When my mother stopped visiting me, she came. We talked."

"This is unbelievable."

"Believe it, Kimmick. This is my truth, believable or not. And it gets worse."

Beige is five and I go into the bathroom to call a halt to playtime in the tub. She likes to warm up with a little water-splashing and floor-drenching before she is ready to be bathed. I understand this, and I leave her to it, give her upwards of half an hour to do what she needs to do. Then I barge in and take control of the bath sponge and the bubble gum–scented body wash, and do what I need to do.

She knows the drill. Face, neck and arms first. Then between the fingers and on to her chest and her back. I slick the sponge down her chicken legs and ask her to squat. I soap her bottom, and then I ask her to sit so I can see about her feet. She giggles as I touch the soles of her feet and full-out laughs as I work my way around to separating her toes with the sponge. I laugh too, because listening to the sound of her laughter is like listening to angels sing.

My smile slips sideways when her laughter grows into something more. It takes on a life of its own and fills the bathroom with the sound of lovemaking. She oohs and ahhs, throws her head back and swipes her hands over her flat chest, as if she is touching breasts that are not there.

Eyes squeezed closed and mouth hanging open, she imitates pleasure that she has no concept of.

"That's when I started to suspect," I say to Kimmick. Right now, his mouth is hanging open, his eyes momentarily squeezed shut. But he is not experiencing pleasure. His is shock, and I don't blame him.

"You allowed your daughter to go to your grand-mother's house?" He wants to pimp slap me, and he is only waiting for me to say yes, I did, so he can do it and not feel one iota of remorse. And if that were my answer, I would let him.

"She caught a cold from one of those awful kids at her school, and she had to stay home for a week," I explain slowly. "I had to work, so I left her with my mother that week. Not my grandmother. My mother. I thought she'd be safe."

I don't question Beige after the bathroom incident because frankly, I am too stunned to process it completely. I push the memory away and hope that she saw something she wasn't supposed to see on television when I wasn't paying attention. It is the only explanation I can accept at the time.

Still, I know it's not the television that has her trying to kiss me on the mouth and push her tongue between my lips. It can't be the television that makes her slap her hands on her hips and prance around the kitchen naked. Like she is on a catwalk. It's not the television that has her leaning back on her bed and spreading her legs like Jenna Jameson. I have never seen her do these things before, and her five-year-old mind cannot possibly be sophisticated enough to pull them out of thin air.

She goes back to school, and her teacher is calling me at work, saying she has walked in on Beige and another child in the bathroom together. Beige is bent over at the waist, with her clothing down around her ankles, and the other child stands behind her. The teacher walks in just as Beige is saying to the other child, "Put it in." Her teacher wants to know if maybe something is going on at home that needs to be addressed. Says she might have to contact Children's Services if this sort of behavior continues or progresses. Wants to know what the *it* is that Beige is requesting from the other child, and I do too.

I start to crack. That is the only way I can describe what happens to me, to Kimmick. I start to lose my mind. Pieces of my brain separate themselves from the whole and turn colors. Pink and blue one minute, and black and red the next. A curtain falls over my eyes, and I feel myself go numb. I walk around in a daze, and I see nothing but visions of death dancing in front of my eyes.

"That motherfucker touched my child and took the game to a whole new level," I say. "Do you have kids, Kimmick?"

"Two," he says.

"Then you know."

"Yes . . . I think I do."

"Tell me what you would've done."

"Tell me what you did."

Chapter Twenty-five

"Nothing, at first," I say. "I couldn't believe it was happening all over again. Couldn't believe it was happening, period. I thought it was over and done with after me and Vicky took a stand. I guess here's the part where you can tell me I don't get paid to think."

It takes me three months to disassociate mind and matter from each other. I manage to put off doing what every cell in my body tells me to do for at least that long. Like any good mother, I spend a significant amount of time researching child therapists. I weigh the pros and cons of one over another, and come to a decision about who I will trust with my child's impressionable young mind. I never get the chance to utilize the resource I find, because there isn't time.

"Explain to me how your daughter keeps ending up at your grandmother's house."

Kimmick wants me to make sense out of something that makes no sense. His mind is clicking, trying to fit itself around a square when it is really a circle. His thoughts don't fit, but he still stretches them and tries to make them fit.

"My mother," I say, and there is finality in my tone. "The last time Beige was over to my grandmother's house, my mother had picked her up from my apartment to taken her to see one of those live shows." I frown at Kimmick and then I make a disgusted face. "You know the ones. *Big Bird on Ice* or something silly like that. Or maybe the purple dinosaur. I don't know. Anyway, that's where they were going when they left my place. She called me later on and told me she had to cut the day short right after the show, and she'd dropped Beige off at my grandmother's house. Her hairdresser had a last minute cancellation and she wanted to get in."

"Where the hell were you?"

"I had a boyfriend back then. We had gone out to lunch and then back to his place to spend some alone time together. I was supposed to be home to get Beige at six, and I was there at five-thirty, just in case."

The phone is ringing as I let myself into my apartment. I leave the keys dangling in the lock and skid across the living room to answer it before it can go to voicemail. I think it is my boyfriend, calling to inform me that I left my bra at his place, and I am ready to have a good laugh about it. Falling asleep and then jumping up, rushing around makes me forgetful.

"I know I forgot something," I say as soon as the receiver is pressed to my ear. A smile claims half of my face.

"Helena? This is your mother."

"Oh. Hey, Mama. Are you guys on your way here?"

"Not exactly," she says, and I hear the whir of a hair dryer in the background. "That's why I'm calling. Beige needs to be picked up."

"Where are you?"

"I'm at the beauty shop. You know the one over on United Drive? Betty worked me in at the last minute."

"Beige isn't bouncing off the walls, is she? Tell Miss Betty I'm sorry and I'm on my way."

"She ain't here," my mother says. "I dropped her at Mama's house. You know Betty don't allow kids in the shop unless they're being serviced."

I'm stunned speechless. When I do speak, I don't recognize my own voice. "You took her to Grandma's house, Mama?"

"I had to do something with her, didn't I? You wasn't at home and I couldn't get Vicky."

"You said you were bringing my baby home at six and it's not even that now, so, no, I wasn't home. But even so, I don't know what would possess you to take her there, of all places."

"It ain't like she hasn't been over there before, Lena. She knows Mama. She wasn't crying or anything when I dropped her off."

"When?" I bark. "When was she over there before, Mama?"

"I took her by there a few times when she was out of school a while back. Far as I know, everything was fine."

"You took my baby over there, Mama?"

"What's the problem now, Lena? I swear, let you tell it, I can't do anything right. Mama was glad to see her 'cause you never think about letting her see her great-grandbaby. She didn't mind watching her for a while so I could make some runs."

"What's a while, Mama? How long has Beige been over there? What time did you drop her off?"

"Around two, I guess," she says. "Right after the show was over, I called Betty to see if she could squeeze me in and she could, so—"

"You bitch," I say and drop the phone.

I drive like my car has rubber bumpers and wings attached to it. I almost cause two accidents, and I am sweating like a bull by the time I pull up in front of my grandmother's house. Beige is nowhere in sight, not on the porch playing and not two houses down, where there is a group of kids clustered on another porch, playing. She is not outside, like she should be on a mild and breezy spring evening, and that does not feel right to me.

I kick at the front door with one foot. Stomp on it and make it rattle on its hinges. Scare the shit out of the kids two houses down and send a few of them inside the house to alert a grown-up to my presence. She takes her time answering my demands for entrance, and the look on her face when she finally opens the door tells me everything I need to know.

"Where is my goddamn child?" This is what I say as I push past her and fly into the house. She closes the door at her back and leans against it, watching me carefully. "Did you hear me, bitch? Where is Beige?"

"I know you better watch your mouth," my grandmother says. She comes away from the door and tries to walk past me like all is right with the world, but I grab her arm and bring her up short, make her look at me. "Girl, if you don't get your hands off me, you better."

"Get my daughter and get her now."

"She ain't here. Vicky came running through here a few minutes ago and took her off somewhere."

"Took her where?"

"Do I look like I'm in her back pocket?"

I don't believe her. I find a phone and punch in Vicky's number with a finger that feels like a metal rod. I am breathing hard when she answers, and there is no time for her to speak. "Do you have my baby?"

"Yes, Leenie," Vicky croones soothingly. "She's with me. I brought her home and put her right in the tub. She was—"

I hear wind in my ears and see buzzards circling around in the air over my head. I cut Vicky off at the knees. "In the tub? Why the fuck is she in the tub? Why does she need a bath, Vicky?"

"Leenie—"

"Answer my question right now or I swear to God . . ."

"When I got there, he was . . . touching her." Vicky starts crying, and I do too. "I wanted her clean," she sobs.

I hang up the phone like I am in a trance. Walk over to where my grandmother is standing and stare at her. Then I am stomping down the hallway with a definite destination in mind. I know where I'm going, and when I arrive, the door slams back against the wall.

She is right behind me, pushing her way into the room and blocking my range of sight. He sees me come into the room and he jumps up from the bed. He yanks his pants up around his waist and bellows like I should give a fuck. Like I should be afraid of the consequences of my actions. His dick is still hard because I have interrupted a masturbation session.

An X-rated video plays on the television across the room, and the television is the first thing I shoot with the gun that I don't even realize is in my hand. When did I grab it and shove it inside my purse? How long have I been holding it? I don't know and right now, I really don't care. I am just glad that I have it.

Tree charges toward me, and then he sees the gun in my hand. He takes one, then two steps back, and stares at the gun like he doesn't know what it is. He stares at me like he doesn't know who I am.

"Now do you understand, you sick motherfucker?" I say. I catch my grandmother's eyes.

"Do you?"

"Leenie . . ." she pants. She stands directly in front of Tree with her arms out toward me, begging the way I have begged so many times before. "Put that thing away, okay? Put it away."

I pull the hammer back and the sound fills the room. "You put your filthy hands on my baby. Cocksucking motherfucker, how could you do that?" He is suddenly mute, which sends me over the edge into crystal clear rage. "Do you hear me, you bastard?"

We stand there, frozen, staring at each other, and this is when Vicky starts beating on the door. I back out of the bedroom and jerk my head toward the sound. "Both of you, bring your asses out here where I can see you." I aim the gun right between my grandmother's eyes. "Get the fucking door."

They file out, one behind the other, and I am given a preview of what the next eight years of my life will be like: Follow the leader and do what you're told. Vicky barrels into the house and approaches me from the side, moving slowly and taking small steps.

"Leenie," she whispers. "Put the gun down. They're not worth this. Here, give it to me."

A bullet shatters a lamp and my grandmother screams. I point the barrel into the black hole of her mouth and she snaps it shut. "One more sound and I'll blow your fucking head off," I tell her, and I mean it. "Where is Beige?"

"Back at my apartment," Vicky says. "Rita from downstairs is with her." She clutches her stomach and doubles over in agony. Starts up with the waterworks again and wrings her hands. "She's okay, right, Leenie? You know Rita. You remember her. It was okay to leave her with Rita, wasn't it, Leenie?" I don't answer, and she takes my silence as a bad sign. "Leenie?"

"Get out of here, Vicky. Go home and take care of my baby. Can you do that? I've got everything under control here, as you can see."

The bastard starts laughing. Tree throws his head back and howls like an animal, and my eyes get big with shock. My grandmother shushes him, slaps at his chest and tells him to be quiet. "This ain't funny, Tree. You hear? Can't you see this girl is crazy? Shut up now."

"You should listen to her, Tree," I say. "Shut the fuck up right now." He doesn't, so I send a bullet whizzing past his head.

He jumps and shuts up. He's not so crazy, after all. He mumbles under his breath the way he always does, but it is different now. I can understand what he says. He whispers to God, wants God to help him. Wants to be saved, sanctified, and filled with the Holy Ghost now, but it is way past too late.

"Go away, Vicky."

"Leenie, please. Just—"

"Go away. Now."

"You don't know what you're doing."

"Oh, I know what I'm doing all right. Know what I need you to do? I need you to go outside and get in your car and drive away. You don't want to be anywhere near this shit, believe me." Vicky doesn't move. "Do it, Vicky," I scream, and the sound of my voice is just shrill enough to send her running for the door. She has never seen me like this, not even when we were kids and living in hell. She fears what is happening to me more than she fears what I will do with the gun in my hand.

It hits me in that moment. I realize that I have always been capable of doing something like this, of aiming a gun and feeling this kind of hate. The seed was planted the first time Tree touched me, and it has sprouted into a white hot rage over the years. I was only fooling myself, thinking that I could have a normal life, the way normal people do. It was there all the time, like a defective gene and a deadly disease waiting for the right time to strike. Vicky was angry, but I was murderous.

I find my grandmother's stricken gaze and I smile. "You knew it would be me, didn't you, old woman? You knew I was your worst nightmare, didn't you?"

"You talking crazy, girl," she has the nerve to say. "You done lost your mind." She makes one last attempt to save her precious baby. "Vicky," she screams. "Victoria, come and get your crazy sister!"

Vicky takes one last look around the house, and then she takes one last look at me. She thinks about her career and everything she has to lose, and she leaves without making a sound. She does what I fail to do— think. On some level, her mind still functions properly, where mine is completely shot to hell.

Finally, it is just me and them. Them and me, and I am ready to do what has to be done.

"Move," I tell my grandmother. "Get your fat ass out of my way."

"I ain't moving, Leenie. And you ain't shooting nobody, so put the gun down."

"Move, goddammit."

"No."

"You're not even smart enough to save yourself, are you? You don't even see that this bastard needs to die for what he did, do you?"

"If anybody's gone die here today, Leenie, it's gone be you. You ain't shooting my baby."

"What about my baby? What about her, huh?"

"What about her, Leenie? She gone be all right, just like you and Vicky are. Y'all turned out all right, didn't you?"

"Vicky can't have kids," I say. "Because of this bastard and his gigantic dick. He fucked her up and now she can't have kids."

"She don't need 'em anyway," my grandmother says, and I can see that she means every word. "She wasn't doing nothing here that she wasn't gone do one day, anyway, and you know it. Tree ain't never hurt that girl and you either."

"How does your mind work?" For a moment, I am in an alternate state of reality. She blows my mind.

"My mind?" She rears back and looks at me like I am the crazy one. "You the one standing here with a gun and you asking me how my mind works?"

"How could you let him do the shit he does and not do something about it? Explain it to me."

"Put the gun down and I will."

"No. Explain it to me now."

"Explain what? You girls was stronger than he was," she says earnestly. "You know he's sick. He can't help what he does. His mind plays tricks on him and makes him do what he does. Y'all stronger."

"Do you really believe that?" It is important that I know this one crucial piece of information. "Do you really believe having him put his mouth on me was okay, because he can't help himself? Touching my baby was okay, because he can't help himself?"

"You turned out all right," she says.

"We were babies."

"Girl babies who was gone grow up to have women's pussies. Didn't hurt you to start learning what to do with 'em. You act like that little girl of yours is something special, something that can't nobody touch. Well, she ain't nothing, and you ain't either. Tree wasn't gone hurt her no more than he hurt you. Come to think of it, he probably wasn't hurting you no way. You probably liked it, just like your baby was starting to like it."

I can't listen to anymore. "Move!"

"No."

"I'm telling you for the last time, bitch. Move."

"And I'm telling you for the last time, I'm not moving. You can call me all the bitches you want to call me, Leenie, but I ain't moving. You want my baby, then you gotta go through me to get him."

"You hurt me. You hurt Vicky. And you hurt my baby. I am not in the mood to be fucked with right now, so you better move while you still can."

"You can't run me out of my own house, girl. You ain't that big and bad. Be crying like a baby in a minute, like you always did, and your tears don't mean nothing to me. They ain't never meant nothing to me, just like you ain't never meant nothing to me." She moves closer to Tree and steps in front of him like a shield.

I shoot her, because I can't listen to anymore. Her mind is warped and it needs to be put to sleep. I aim the gun at her heart and shoot her. I don't plan to kill her; it just happens. But I don't regret it. She falls to the floor and Tree loses his mind. He comes racing toward me, and I fire the gun again. I hit him in his shoulder because my hands are shaking so badly. He takes the bullet and stumbles backward, falls over an end table, and struggles his way to his feet.

In my mind, he says, "Five, four, three, two, one." He counts like he is directing a movie, telling Vicky and me when to begin kissing each other on the mouth, touching each other, and fondling each other's private parts for his sick amusement. We can begin when he says, "Action."

I count for him now. Walk toward him with the gun suspended in the air between us. He scratches and claws his way toward the door. "Five," I say. "Four, three, two, one . . ."

He is out the door and running across the porch before I can say action, but I still fire at him. It is my last bullet, and I need to make it count. I think I aim precisely, think I am about to send him straight to hell, but I don't. I end up shooting him in his ass and allowing him to get away from a death that belongs to him.

I see him fight his way into his car, parked at the corner. An old Buick Riviera that modern cars cannot touch. It is indestructible, just like he is. I watch him take off driving down the street, leaning sideways because his ass has a hole in it. I stare after his car long after it is gone.

And then I start laughing. Then and now.

"Why are you laughing?" Kimmick asks. His voice intrudes on my thoughts and startles me. I have forgotten that he is here with me, and now I look at him, clearly surprised to see him sitting up in his chair, hanging on my words.

I do not tell him about Vicky, that she did what I was cheated out of doing. I have told him that my sister is a nurse practitioner, and he is a smart man, so I say nothing. I don't even let myself think about Tree and the drugs that he overdosed on because he couldn't function without his mother to cloak his maniacal behavior. I conveniently forget about how the drugs came to be in his possession in the first place, and about who knew enough to administer a lethal injection capable of killing him—a speedball that had a deadly air bubble halfway between the beginning and the end of its impact.

The part of the story that centers around Tree driving himself to the hospital and being admitted stays with me. Vicky was working that night, but he doesn't need to know that. And he will never know that Tree was dead less than five minutes after she slipped into his room. Probably coming face to face with Satan right about the time that she slipped back out and went to find herself an alibi, in case she needed one. She never told me what she did in that hospital room to coax him into planting his own fingerprints everywhere that they needed to be planted, and I never asked.

The one time that she does visit me in jail before my trial, she mouths the words *I got him* to me through the glass separating us, and I know. I cry the first tears of joy that I have cried since the day Beige is born, and I am stupid enough to think that I can begin again and do something positive with my life.

I don't feel sorry for the body they find slumped sideways in the hospital bed the next day. They assume that he somehow stole the drugs to self-medicate, to help him cope with his grief. It is a plausible explanation, one no one cares to investigate very thoroughly, and the matter drops without so much as a slant of the eye toward Vicky, which is the way it is meant to be.

I don't attend the funeral when I am given the option. Neither one of them.

Kimmick's voice startles me, brings me back to the here and now with a jolt.

"You didn't want closure?"

"I got closure," I say and feel myself slipping back in time again. "Let me tell you the rest."

I back away from the doorway and go back to the living room, where my grandmother is waiting for me. I stare into her empty eyes, and they are black marbles inside of a shell of flesh. I marvel at what I am seeing, and I wonder how an alien being can exist among humans for so long and no one sees it except me. And Vicky. She sees it too.

I am laughing because I nail myself to the cross and I do it willingly. It has to be this way, and I accept that. I make Vicky do what she does. I leave her no choice but to play a part, and so I have to keep playing God and follow through. In the Bible it is written that God's eye is so keen and able to see everything that He can see something as small as a sparrow in flight. And if He can see the little sparrow, how can He not see the people who worship Him? Who need Him the most? I don't exactly worship Him, but if I am playing God, then Vicky is the sparrow that I have my eye on. She needed Him, and He sent her me.

"My eye is on the sparrow, Kimmick. Even if God's eye isn't on me, mine is on the sparrow and it always has been. Always. That's what's funny," I say.

"I don't get the joke," he says, looking confused.

I smile and shake my head. "It's a private joke. I guess you had to be there."

Effortlessly, I go there. The final nail that pins me to the cross plays itself out like this. . . .

I dial 911 and I wait for the police. I hear Vicky's voice in my head while I'm waiting, asking me if I will stay with her, and then I hear my own voice in a quiet house that smells like old mothballs and feels like a morgue, whispering, "Don't I always stay with you?"

I kneel down and gently close my grandmother's eyes. I am sure she is on her way to hell, but I have no idea where I am headed. I close my eyes, trying to imagine what my future holds and working out what I will say to the police when they arrive. How I will explain the fact that I have done the world a service, rather than committed a crime. I suck in a sharp breath, release it slowly, and open my eyes.

I hear sirens outside and I feel the sudden urgency in the air. They are coming for me, and I have no choice but to be ready to go with them, wherever they take me. I drop the gun on the coffee table and wipe my sweaty palms on the seat of my jeans. Then I pick it back up, step over my grandmother's body, and go to the door. I open it and step back so they can come charging inside the house.

"There was a report of a shooting here," one of the officers says. Three others push past him and swarm to the living room. They see what there is to see, and then they turn to stare at me.

"Exactly what happened here? Did you shoot this woman, ma'am?"

My eyes travel down the hallway and come to rest on Tree's bedroom door, and I open my mouth slowly. "Yes," I finally say. "I shot her." They make me feel so free, the words do. Even as handcuffs are snapped in place and my rights are read to me, I feel free. Like the world is a better place, like maybe there is such a thing as hope.

I tell myself right then and there that whatever happens cannot be any worse than what has already happened. I tell myself that I am ready for anything, that all I have to do is get off of the hampster's wheel that I've been running around on all these years. All I have to do is close my eyes and—jump.

Notes

Notes

Notes

ORDER FORM
URBAN BOOKS, LLC
78 E. Industry Ct
Deer Park, NY 11729

Name: (please print): _____

Address: _____

City/State: _____

Zip: _____

QTY	TITLES	PRICE
	The Cartel	$14.95
	The Cartel 2	$14.95
	The Dopeman's Wife	$14.95
	The Prada Plan	$14.95
	Gunz And Roses	$14.95
	Snow White	$14.95
	A Pimp's Life	$14.95
	Hush	$14.95
	Little Black Girl Lost 1	$14.95
	Little Black Girl Lost 2	$14.95
	Little Black Girl Lost 3	$14.95
	Little Black Girl Lost 4	$14.95

Shipping and handling-add $3.50 for 1st book, then $1.75 for each additional book.
Please send a check payable to:
Urban Books, LLC
Please allow 4-6 weeks for delivery

ORDER FORM
URBAN BOOKS, LLC
78 E. Industry Ct
Deer Park, NY 11729

Name: (please print): _____

Address: _____

City/State: _____

Zip: _____

QTY	TITLES	PRICE
	16 ½ On The Block	$14.95
	16 On The Block	$14.95
	Betrayal	$14.95
	Both Sides Of The Fence	$14.95
	Cheesecake And Teardrops	$14.95
	Denim Diaries	$14.95
	Happily Ever Now	$14.95
	Hell Has No Fury	$14.95
	If It Isn't love	$14.95
	Last Breath	$14.95
	Loving Dasia	$14.95
	Say It Ain't So	$14.95

Shipping and handling-add $3.50 for 1st book, then $1.75 for each additional book.

Please send a check payable to:

Urban Books, LLC

Please allow 4-6 weeks for delivery

ORDER FORM
URBAN BOOKS, LLC
78 E. Industry Ct
Deer Park, NY 11729

Name: (please print): _____

Address: _____

City/State: _____

Zip: _____

QTY	TITLES	PRICE
	A Man's Worth	$14.95
	Abundant Rain	$14.95
	Battle Of Jericho	$14.95
	By The Grace Of God	$14.95
	Dance Into Destiny	$14.95
	Divorcing The Devil	$14.95
	Forsaken	$14.95
	Grace And Mercy	$14.95
	Guilty Of Love	$14.95
	His Woman, His Wife, His Widow	$14.95
	Illusions	$14.95
	The LoveChild	$14.95

Shipping and handling-add $3.50 for 1st book, then $1.75 for each additional book.

Please send a check payable to:

Urban Books, LLC

Please allow 4-6 weeks for delivery

ORDER FORM
URBAN BOOKS, LLC
78 E. Industry Ct
Deer Park, NY 11729

Name: (please print):_____

Address: _____

City/State: _____

Zip: _____

QTY	TITLES	PRICE

Shipping and handling-add $3.50 for 1st book, then $1.75 for each additional book.

Please send a check payable to:

Urban Books, LLC

Please allow 4-6 weeks for delivery

ORDER FORM
URBAN BOOKS, LLC
78 E. Industry Ct
Deer Park, NY 11729

Name: (please print):_____

Address: _____

City/State: _____

Zip: _____

QTY	TITLES	PRICE

Shipping and handling-add $3.50 for 1st book, then $1.75 for each additional book.
Please send a check payable to:
Urban Books, LLC
Please allow 4-6 weeks for delivery